Wrath

Book One of The Event Horizon: Sins

Jasmine Johnson

BALBOA.PRESS

A DIVISION OF HAY HOUSE

Balboa Press books may be ordered through booksellers or by contacting:

Balboa Press
A Division of Hay House
1663 Liberty Drive
Bloomington, IN 47403
www.balboapress.com
1 (877) 407-4847

Because of the dynamic nature of the Internet, any web addresses or links contained in this book may have changed since publication and may no longer be valid. The views expressed in this work are solely those of the author and do not necessarily reflect the views of the publisher, and the publisher hereby disclaims any responsibility for them.

The author of this book does not dispense medical advice or prescribe the use of any technique as a form of treatment for physical, emotional, or medical problems without the advice of a physician, either directly or indirectly. The intent of the author is only to offer information of a general nature to help you in your quest for emotional and spiritual well-being. In the event you use any of the information in this book for yourself, which is your constitutional right, the author and the publisher assume no responsibility for your actions.

Any people depicted in stock imagery provided by Getty Images are models, and such images are being used for illustrative purposes only. Certain stock imagery © Getty Images.

Print information available on the last page.

Cover By Laney Fisher & Lance Smith

ISBN: 978-1-9822-4487-3 (sc)
ISBN: 978-1-9822-4489-7 (hc)
ISBN: 978-1-9822-4488-0 (e)

Library of Congress Control Number: 2020904982

Balboa Press rev. date: 04/01/2020

Prologue

It is almost impressive how someone with no eyes can make you feel as if they are staring at your soul, and seeing every secret, every thought, and every painful memory. I found out centuries ago that soul eating wasn't within Ashera's skill set; though that didn't make her less eerie. As a descendant of the great Black Annis she had the blue skin, stringy black hair, and appetite for human children. She lost her eyes in the last Great War after stealing the child of a powerful witch. Now - unable to hunt - she is a 'receptionist' for the King himself. Not bad for a Nascent.

The horrid creature hissed breaking me from my wandering thoughts, "The master will see you now." Her bony fingers gestured toward the giant hypersthene door.

I took a deep breath and cleared my mind before approaching the foreboding double doors. Unsurprisingly, the doors opened without assistance. Inside laid a grand sitting room with shiny onyx walls and a cold stone floor. Hanging from the ceiling was a massive black crystal chandelier with blue fire candles. Strategically placed around the room were pillars topped with fire basins proudly showing off the blue flames the King was known for. Short uncomfortable stools created an aisle leading to the massive obsidian throne with a tall wide back covered with an intricate snake pattern, giving the impression of a million snakes entangled together just for their master's throne. The arms of the throne were carved to resemble the Earth animal *Panthera Leo* with glowing yellow citrine gems placed as their eyes.

Sitting in the impressive throne was the King himself, Lucifer.

I always found it amusing when the humans depicted him as some horrid looking creature as if he was just another Nascent; when, in fact he was once one of Yhwh's favorite sons. Even in the darkness of this room, Lucifer's blond hair shone as if every hair was pure gold, his luminous golden wings sat relaxed on either side of his chair, and he wore a classic one shoulder toga showcasing the muscles he was so proud of. Muscles many women have swooned over for millennia, as he loves to remind me. If it wasn't for the cold black eyes and sinister smirk on his face he could easily be mistaken for one of his brothers.

"Roman! My dearest friend!" Lucifer rose with his arms spread wide. The two women who had been kneeling at his feet quickly crawled out of the way before he could walk over them, as he'd done many times before. "Andromeda and Eirian came to spend some quality time with me. They arrived moments after your arrival was announced." He laughed, watching Eirian's face turn a peculiar shade of crimson.

"I... I...," She stammered before bowing her head with a sigh. "I just wanted to see you."

Andromeda rolled her eyes, annoyed at Eirian's shyness. "I came to remind you why you should stop this Earth nonsense and come back home. Humans can only satisfy you for so long, Roman." She purred, green eyes flashing with hunger.

"I have unfinished business with Earth and I will remain there until my work is completed." I reminded her, then turned to Eirian pulling out a wooden box from my satchel. It was a simple box made from paulownia wood with a simple design of three wavy lines on top, but I knew Eirian would love it as she did all things from other worlds. She was in front of me before I could blink.

"What's that?" She asked, eyes filled with child-like wonder.

"This is just a box, but inside," I unlatched the lid to reveal three small glass vials shimmering with magic. "This liquid is called water, this solid is called ice, and this clouded one is called fog. They are all the same substance. Some say it's the purest substance on Earth. I had a witch cast a spell to keep them in their respective forms."

Eirian was softly glowing - a gift from her Sprite ancestors. "Oh

Roman, this is amazing! Thank you so much!" She carefully closed the box and sat it on one of the small stools so she could give me a hug.

"Now now, Eirian. You know how Roman feels about hugs. Andromeda, help Eirian take her gift back to her quarters. Roman and I have business to discuss." Lucifer ordered.

"Oh wait, I got you this Andromeda." I told her, pulling a small pouch from my bag, and tossed it to her. "Inside is a voodoo doll. An Earth shaman channeled feelings of hatred, anger, and jealousy into it for thirty years."

"Now *that* is impressive." She smiled, turning the bag over in her hands. "Come Eirian, let's leave the men to their work." Andromeda strutted from the room with Eirian scurrying after her clutching her box.

The door shut behind them with an audible thud. "It's not like you to pull me from the search, my liege. Has something happened?" I asked, turning my full attention to the King.

"Nothing is wrong. I received a message from Domini last night. He believes he's found one in a place called California." He replied, folding his hands in front of him.

I resisted the urge to sigh. Domini was young and a Nascent, which means he has a terrible habit of jumping into things too early in a poor attempt to prove himself. Why the King put him in charge of an entire team, I'll never understand. "When is he bringing the Sin in?" I asked through a clenched jaw. Domini also has a burning need to try and show he's better than me; even though we are a completely different race. It's always a challenge not to knock him unconscious when we're forced to be in the same room.

"He isn't. This one is too important to leave to him. Even if I did, the chances of him succeeding or even surviving are incredibly low."

This is surprising. Lucifer had always thought high of the fledgling. The hairs on the back of my neck raised as I asked, "Which Sin is it?"

"Wrath."

Skata.

Chapter One

"Enough!" Cooper declared, dropping to the ground.

"No, not enough, Coop!" I countered, throwing a couple jabs in the air.

"Our session ended an hour ago." He groaned, breathing heavy.

"And I pay you by the hour." I stood over him with my hands on my hips. Now that I'd stopped moving the weariness in my bones was making itself known. "Fine." I relented, suddenly exhausted. "Rest up before Monday, and grab an energy drink or something. You're growing soft in your old age." I snarked, then ducked out of the ring before his sweaty towel could hit me.

"I'm only three years older than you." He grumbled something else about how ungrateful I was, but I let it slide knowing I'd won the day. Cooper and I had been friends for three years now, and he's actually one of the very few people I can hold a conversation with without losing my temper.

Cherishing the empty locker room, I slipped into the farthest shower - it was considerably larger than the rest and hardly ever empty. The quiet solace of the shower gave me time to think about how off I've been lately. I'm naturally easy to agitate, I know that. I have severe anger issues that I've had my whole life. Lately, however, I've felt completely on edge like someone is following me, but when I check there's nothing there. Maybe it's time to start therapy again…

Realizing that the shower had turned ice cold, I shut off the water and grabbed towel. Dressed in capri yoga pants and an oversized sweater, I slipped on my tennis shoes and left the locker room; being sure to put the used towel in the correct basket. Coop went ballistic the last time I forgot.

"Heading home?" The man himself asked, freshly showered as well.

"I guess. My trainer wussed out on me." I teased. "I'll probably pick up some food on the way. What about you?" I grabbed my tape from beside the ring, and waved to Tony - the kid who started working here about a month ago. His face turned bright red and he gave me a small wave before rushing off with the towel basket.

"Leave him alone, Karma." Cooper laughed.

I gave him my best 'I'm innocent' look. "I'm not doing anything. All I did was wave goodbye."

He laughed, shaking his head. Swatting me with his towel as he passed by, he hollered, "Get out of here, Karma. I'll see you Monday. Don't forget about your Wednesday class." I would never. It's the best part of my week.

Once in my car, I called my favorite Japanese place. A few minutes later I was on my way home for a peaceful Saturday night. Hopefully.

火

Thirty minutes of road rage and annoying costumers who think yelling in English will make it easier for the sweet Japanese lady to understand them is enough to drive anyone crazy. The poor woman - who looked to be about seventy - looked like she was going to cry tears of joy when I ordered in Japanese. Finally, I was at home in my pajamas, eating dinner with the TV playing last weeks episode of my favorite show.

It's not long until I'm wrapped up in the drama and tuned out of the rest of the world. Sitting cross-legged in the middle of my sofa, shoveling takeout into my mouth as the villain of the week destroys yet another city. How will our heroes handle this one? Oh my go-

Three hard knocks shook me out of my trance. Cursing, I paused my show and checked the clock. *Who* is at my door at 10:40pm and *why* do they think that is okay? It can't be Cooper or Angel because they know I catch up on my shows on Saturdays. Grumbling, I got up from the couch and make sure my food is closed so Roi - my cat - doesn't steal it, and headed to the door. I peeked out the peephole to see a tall lanky guy who can't be over twenty years old. He's wearing a black short sleeved shirt and jeans which is strange considering it's October in Monterey, California, and it's dark so there's not even warmth from the sun. Poor kid is probably freezing.

Sighing, I unlocked and opened the door. "Can I help you?" I ask.

"Only if you're Karma Strickland." He replied looking oddly smug. As if he already knew my name, but wanted to prove himself right.

"I am... What do you want?" There's something off about him. He's brimming with this eagerness that I typically only see in my opponents - right before they lose.

His eyes lit up and he shifted on his feet. "Nothing much. *Just you.*»

Too many giveaways for a surprise attack, genius. When he lunged, I was prepared. He came forward with a punch letting me grab the wrist of his dominate hand and shove my elbow onto his abdomen. He gasped trying to double over. Still holding his wrist, I used my other elbow to uppercut him and used his captured arm to propel him off my porch.

"Get lost before I call the cops, kid." I started to close my door, but stopped to add. "Oh, and next time, pick a fight with someone you have a chance of beating." With that I slammed and locked my door. Lunatic.

My phone was ringing when I got back to the living room. Glancing at the caller I.D. I smiled knowing she's going to be disappointed. "Hey, Angel."

"Can you believe it?!" She yelled. She had a habit of timing the shows so she knew where I would be at a certain time. I've always found it amusing. We could just watch it together, but she can't wait and watch it when it airs. Even with commercials.

"I haven't finished the episode, so no." I laughed.

"What do you mean you haven't finished it yet? It's almost eleven. Did you start late?"

"No some kid knocked on my door and tried to attack me." I scoffed, remembering his technique. Either he's completely untrained or seriously underestimated me.

«*What?*» She yelled. "Are you okay? Did he give you a *reason*? Or is he just crazy?"

"No reason. Probably a dare. He asked if I was Karma Strickland and when I said yes he lunged at me. I'm okay, though he might want to see if he has a concussion. He hit his head pretty hard."

"Oh well, finish the episode and call me back." The line beeped a second later making me laugh. Grabbing my dinner, I settled back into the couch with my dinner and hit play.

火

"I love Sunday breakfast with my two favorite people." Angel sighed smiling over her cup of herbal tea.

Coop, Angel, and I were sitting in a booth at our favorite local diner where we meet every Sunday morning. Coop is sitting by Angel scanning the menu like he doesn't get the same thing every week. Angel looks as prim and proper as ever with her fifties inspired dress and her strawberry blonde hair in a curly chignon. Coop had stuck with his usual muscle shirt and sweat pants. Whereas I was dressed in a grey tank top, black leather leggings, and my favorite leather jacket. We were a strange group for sure.

"I love food." Cooper replied, his eyes watching the waitress walking over with our appetizer.

"Here's those muffins just like you asked; two blueberry, three banana, and one chocolate chip. Have you decided what to order?" She asked, eyes locked on Coop.

"Yes!" He rushed out before Angel and I could speak. Not that we'd ever try to order first with the starving Sasquatch at the table. We learned that lesson a long time ago. "I'll have your Texas Scramble and an extra side of bacon."

Angel looked a little green after his order - his meals typically made her nauseous. The waitress finished writing Coop's order and turned to Angel looking a lot less friendly. "Oh, I'll just have two eggs, over medium, and a side of toast, please."

With a stiff nod at Angel the woman turned to me. "I'll have the blueberry pancakes and a side of bacon." With one last dazzling smile at Coop she gathered our menus and left.

"Did I do something to upset her?" Angel asked with wide light green eyes.

"No." I replied, subtly winking at her when Cooper looked away. "It seems she's only nice to Cooper." Cooper choked on the muffin he was inhaling causing him to glare at me. Angel hurried and grabbed her chocolate chip muffin before it was caught in the vacuum that was Cooper's mouth. Following her lead, I grabbed a blueberry muffin from the center plate.

"Did the guy from last night ever come back?" Angel asked innocently, not realizing I hadn't told Coop.

I winced as Cooper's head shot up. "What guy?" My God he nearly gave himself whiplash.

"Some kid knocked on my door and tried to attack me. Jokes on him though, because I have the best trainer in Monterey." Was I sucking up in hope that he'd leave it? Maybe. Am I ashamed? Absolutely not. Coop could go full big brother mode over Angel and me.

"Don't be cheeky, Karma. Someone attacking you is a big deal. What did the cops say?" Suddenly my muffin became incredibly interesting. I wonder how many blueberries are in this one muffin. "Wait, you didn't call the cops did you?"

I sighed, dropping my muffin. "No, I didn't call the cops. He was just a kid, Coop; barely out of high school."

"He attacked you at your house!"

"Shhh! We are in public." Angel hissed, pulling him back to his seat.

"Relax. He hit his head pretty hard on the concrete, so I'm sure he'll think twice before attacking anyone again." Especially me.

Luckily, our food arrived before his face could get any redder. It was a different waitress this time, but she seemed to have the same fascination with Coop - just with more cleavage to throw around. "Texas Scramble for the hunk to keep his strength up." Did she really just say hunk? What year is this? "Pancakes and bacon for Love Handles, and two eggs and toast for Tubby."

I was out of my seat before I could think. One second I was sitting in shock, the next I was knocking the bitch on her ass. Definitely a black eye and probably a broken nose, I thought absently.

"What's going on here?!" A woman dressed in the managers' uniform ran over with our actual waitress. "We could have you charged with assault."

"I don't come to breakfast to be insulted and neither did my friend. I'm not sure what her problem is, but no one talks to us like that." I whipped around to face the girl, who was now leaning on our waitress holding her head. "And I don't know what made you think it's okay to talk to people like that, but it's not. Whether or not I have love handles is none of your business, and it doesn't matter how much someone weighs, never call someone tubby. It's immature and rude. There is nothing wrong with Angel or her weight. Am I clear?"

The girl was shaking when I finished. Good. "Yes ma'am, I understand. I'm so sorry. Agnes please put their meal on me. She's right I should've never insulted them." The girl scurried off with her head hung, her friend following behind.

"Well," The flustered manager picked up the tray and stand that our food had come on. "This has been eventful. I'm terribly sorry for Vicki's behavior. I will be taking your entire tab from her paycheck.

Please finish your meal. Sam will be your new waiter, don't hesitate to ask him for anything." She rushed out before scurrying away too.

I sat back down shaking with fury, and started eating, grumbling under my breath between bites. Sure Angel isn't supermodel thin, but she's beautiful just the way she is! And she's very insecure about her weight when she doesn't need to be. Aside from sampling her own baking creations she's one of the healthiest people I know! Some people can be so judgmental.

"Karma?" Angel asked, tentatively.

"Yeah?" Oh wow, I hadn't noticed how hot I'd become. I need to calm down. Deep breaths. Focus on Angel.

"You've been muttering in different languages for ten minutes. I just wanted to remind you of what the doctor said." *Damn doctors.*

I sighed. "Yeah, I know." Mocking the doctor's monotone voice I repeated, "'Stress and anger will do you the most harm.' I'm working on controlling it, Angel, but it isn't easy. Especially when dealing with people like that." Taking a second, I closed my eyes and tried to focus solely on my breathing. This is definitely not how I wanted to start my day...

"Hey if you're too angry to eat, I can take care of that bacon for you." When I opened my eyes Cooper had already slid the plate of bacon halfway across the table to himself.

I snatched it back with a playful frown, the anger receding to the back of my mind, but not going away. It never goes away fully. "I'll beat you up, too, Plaizer. I'm guessing you're still sore from me knocking you on your ass yesterday, judging from the way you limped to the table this morning." Angel and I doubled over laughing while he hunched over his food with a mumbled 'shut up.'

火

"You went to see her?!" I roared, resisting the urge to hit the idiot in front of me.

"I figured I could bring her in and save you the trouble." Domini replied, red eyes flashing with irritation. Well, one red eye, the other was too swollen to do anything. He had bruises covering his whole body, and though he tried not to show it, probably a broken rib or two.

Domini is a Nascent, the lowest type of demon. He was eager to be something more, which would be fine if he didn't somehow convince himself he could be a Horseman. No matter how many times it's been explained to him, he doesn't seem to grasp that being a Horseman isn't a title it's a *completely* separate race. He's too immature to listen to reason, though. In human years he is roughly three hundred which makes him an infant in demon years, and is probably why he decided to do something so incredibly foolish.

"I do not believe you did this for my benefit. I think you decided you were going to prove something to the King by capturing one of the Sins all by yourself. Did it ever cross your diminutive mind that pulling this stunt with Wrath was a terrible idea?!" I could feel my blood boiling. He had just increased the difficulty of this job by three hundred percent! He knew enough to know that Wrath is the strongest of all the Sins. Anyone dumb enough to engage Wrath in a fight will be lucky to escape with their life.

He had the sense to flinch, but kept his head high. "I admit I made the mistake of underestimating the girl. I thought her human DNA would make her weak."

"Your *mistake*," I spat the word, feeling my fury reach its peak, "was attacking in the first place!"

"If we don't attack, how are we supposed to take her to the King?" He threw his bruised hands in the air.

I sighed trying to cool my temper. "Violence is not always the answer, *child*.»

He scoffed. I need to leave before I become a walking contradiction. "That's rich coming from the Legendary Horseman of War." He mocked my title with venom. I almost laughed. It's no secret that is the exact title he craves.

"War isn't always full of bloodshed. While you're in the human world do some research on the Cold Wars starting in 1947. War is much more complicated than it seems." Leaving him fuming in the office, I grabbed the file on the sin and set out to find her. Hopefully he didn't screw up the entire mission.

火

Five hours and a dozen stores later I was finally back home. I had made the mistake of promising Angel I'd go shopping with her, and she had taken full advantage. I was now the lucky owner of five new dresses, two skirts, three shirts, four blouses - which are apparently different -, and a 'nice' pair of jeans. Theres nothing wrong with the jeans I have. They're just a little... worn. I rolled my eyes looking at the bags. For someone so eager to make me buy all of this shit, Angel sure didn't stick around to help me hang it all up. Maybe I should've picked up some hangers, too.

Before I could get to my room to start my least favorite chore ever, there were three hard knocks on the front door. Thrilled that I have an excuse to not hang these up, I dropped the bags to the floor. Unfortunately, now I have to deal with this unwanted guest. I need a sign on the front door that says 'Unless you're delivering something, leave me alone.' I flicked on the porch light and looked through the peep hole to see a very muscular chest stretching a black shirt to it's limit, but that's all. Tall people, I swear.

"Who is it?" I called. This guy was much bigger than the kid yesterday; I'm not dumb or cocky enough to just open the door. They could be some sort of team who terrorizes local women. Two unwanted visitors in two days can't be a coincidence.

"My name is Roman. I have something important to discuss with you." The deep timber of his voice vibrated through the wood.

"How do you know I'm who you're looking for?" What is up with random guys tracking me down?

"You are Karma Strickland, are you not? I know the man who

came here yesterday and I assure you I mean you no harm. I just want to talk." Talk about what?

Curiosity killed the cat, The rational part of my mind taunted.

Satisfaction brought it back, The more instinctual part of my brain replied. *We can trust him.*

For some reason, my gut was telling me to trust him. Ignoring the rational part of my brain, I unlocked the door. Opening it slightly, I peeked at the man - Roman, he had said. Standing there completely at ease was one of the most muscular men I've ever seen, and I go to an intense gym four times a week! He was almost a foot taller than me and about as wide as a bus. His dark brown eyes observed me curiously as if I were some new puzzle for him to piece together. His black hair was a tousled mess like he'd spent the past hour running his hands through it. Who is this guy?

"Hello."

"Hi." I cleared my throat and leaned on the door jamb. "What do you need to talk to me about?"

"This is not something I can say out in the open. May I come in?"

I raised an eyebrow. He's joking right? "You *do* realize that your friend attacked me, right?"

He sighed. "Domini is a fool, not a friend. He wasn't supposed to make contact with you, but he is impulsive and determined to prove himself."

Biting my lip, I weighed my options. On one hand, I could let him in and let him say what he needs to. On the other hand, I could close the door and walk away. Option one: I could be murdered in my own home. Option two: I could piss him off and be murdered anywhere. I shifted, trying to decide if my gut was right or just crazy. "Promise you aren't going to try anything?" Good one, Karma, a murderer will definitely keep his promise not to murder you.

"I give you my word."

I *really* hope I don't regret this, but my gut has never been wrong before. Stepping back, I held the door open for him. He sauntered inside taking a quick look around my living room as he went. A small statue on my end table caught his attention, and he picked it up instantly making it look much smaller.

"An angel statue?" He murmured turning it over.

"Yeah," I spoke softly, trying not to choke up. "It was my mother's."

He hesitated. "Was she nice?"

"Yeah, she was the best." I replied dropping into my favorite chair. Talking about Mom always took a lot out of me. It was nine years ago, and still hurt like it happened an hour ago.

"My adoptive mother was the same."

"Really?" I asked, surprised. I'd never met anyone who understood how it felt to be the adopted child. Sympathizing is not the same, no matter how hard Angel and the therapists tried.

"Yes, but that is not what I came to discuss." He said, abruptly. Gently placing the statue back.

"Oh yeah. Did you come to explain why your friend *attacked* me?" Whoa, too much anger too soon. I closed my eyes and pinched he bridge of my nose. This is not a good time to be so worked up. Deep breaths.

"He is not my friend, but yes, in a way, that is what I'm here to do. However, for this conversation you need to have an open mind. I will be telling you facts that do not fit within the world you've been raised to believe is real."

I couldn't help rolling my eyes. He's a little too dramatic for my taste. "Look Batman, I get it. The world is a terrible place, happiness isn't real, normal people like me are too dumb to understand everything that you do, blah blah blah. Why'd your friend attack me?" He looked angry - probably about the Batman comment. Not my fault. If he doesn't want to be compared to Batman he should loosen up. Plus, who doesn't want to be called Batman?

"This is serious." Did he just growl at me? Seriously? "The fate of the worlds depends on it."

I laughed making his jaw tighten and muscles tense. "Worlds? As in plural? Ha! Look I don't know about the whole 'life among the stars' thing, but I'm positive the last person aliens would want is me." Hell, most *humans* didn't even want me.

"I'm not an alien. However, I'm not human either." He paused, gauging my reaction.

Not human? So I have some unknown thing sitting on my couch? Great. I could kick him - it? - out and call the cops. Even if he is some mystical creature the threat of other people could scare him off long enough for me to come up with another plan... Wait, why am I even acting like this could be possible? He could just be crazy. But there it is again, the part of me saying I could trust him as if we have some type of connection. Which is also crazy, because I'd definitely remember meeting a guy like him before, let alone building a connection with him.

"I can see the conflict behind your eyes, Karma. I want to help. Surely you've realized you are different from everyone around you."

I scoffed. "Of course I'm different. Believe me, I know. Normal people don't get kicked out of *twelve* schools - including reformatory school. Normal people don't go through therapists like candy. *Normal people...*»

"Do not burn their way through furniture?" Roman interrupted. When I looked at him with confusion, he gestured to my arm.

I looked down to see that my arm had burned through the arm of my favorite wing chair. Dammit! This hasn't happened in years! Before I could even try to calm down enough to think of a solution, the arm had fully caught fire. Cursing, I hopped up from the chair ready to run into the kitchen to get water before the fire alarm went off, but was grabbed by Roman.

"Wait, Karma. Watch." Still holding onto my elbow with one large hand, he used his free hand to slowly wave over the fire. Slowly the fire dwindled and died, leaving a large black hole in my favorite chair. Dammit.

Realizing what just happened, I tried to wrestle my arm from his grip. "What is wrong with you?" He asked, not releasing his hold.

"What's wrong with me? You just put out a fire with your hand!"

He raised a brow at me, and one side of his mouth raised slightly exposing a dimple. "Need I remind you how you started that fire?" Oh great, now he's smug. "Now will you sit and listen?"

"No. No, I can't just sit down and listen, Roman! I've spent my whole life thinking that I was crazy or some kind of... Of... Demon! And trying to hide..." He laughed. The smug *bastard* laughed. "*Why* are you laughing?"

"Sorry." He didn't sound sorry. Deep chuckles were still escaping, and dammit it's making me want to punch him. I wonder if I'd break my hand... Probably, but it'd be worth it. He's an *asshole*. "I'm assuming you have questions. Ask away." He remained standing, crossing his arms. Definitely break my hand...

"Don't 'dad-frown' at me. Just, sit on the couch or something." Rolling his eyes, he sat on the arm of the couch, clasping his hands in front of him. "So, you and me, are the same?"

He tilted his head, contemplating his answer. "In a way. We are the same species, just a different class or race."

"Okay, are certain classes higher than others?"

He nodded. "Classes are based on power."

"Are you above me?" He nodded, smiling slightly. I gasped. "Is the idiot who attacked me above me?" With those skills I hope not. People - demons? - will think I'm a joke if I'm weaker than noodle arms.

"No, Domini is a the bottom of the hierarchy. The lowest class are called Nascents." Oh, good. He can stay there.

"Okay, so are you at the top?" I sat down on the couch, patting the empty cushion in between us for him to sit with me. After a slight hesitation, he slid off the arm onto the seat.

"I am not at the very top. The King is above all. My brothers and I are directly under him."

"Just you and your brothers? How many brothers do you have?" How strange that only him and his brothers make up a whole class. How much power do you have to have to be one step below the King? I could be sitting next to a nuclear bomb for all I know.

13

"There's four of us."

"Only four? That's one class?" If there can be a class with four people in it, how small can they be? "What about mine? Am I the only one?" I cleared my throat, trying to get rid of the sudden lump.

"No, actually. There is seven in your class. Counting you, of course. However, you are alone in the sense of the other six are still being located." There's six other people like me? That's a welcome change.

"So you're trying to what, gather us? Why?"

"Sort of. It would be best for all of you to meet and form some sort of bond. The seven of you are very powerful individuals. They will understand your powers and how they affect you. We believe they will also share your confusion as it seems they have all grown up in the human world. On top of that we would get you the guidance you need so no more chairs need to suffer."

I laughed. He seemed awkward making the joke, but I appreciated the effort. "Okay so what are we? You never actually said the species."

He sighed, running a hand through his hair. "To put it simply, we're demons."

The world froze.

Chapter Two

Okay, so maybe not the whole world, but at least my corner of it.

Demons.

Demons?! That's impossible! I've done everything I could to be a *good* person.

God I bet Isaac would be so happy right now. I can picture him now, arms folded, chin held high, and the world's best frown. "I knew it, Elizabeth!" *He'd* yell at my mother. "That child has been a demon all along. I should've never let you bring it home!"

I sighed. At least mother wasn't alive anymore; I could never look her in the eye knowing what I am. She'd be heartbroken. She'd be disappointed.

"Karma?" Roman murmured, wiping a tray tear from my cheek.

Furious, I wiped my face with my sleeve. "So this King? Is it Satan?"

"He prefers Lucifer."

I gave him a flat look. "Okay, so *Lucifer* is the King, and you are the class below him." He nodded his confirmation. "So, does that make you a fallen angel?"

He chuckled. "No. Fallen angels are classified as Imperators or generals as they're called on Earth. I am a Horseman."

Horseman? What is a… Wait. He has three brothers. "As in the Four Horsemen? Of the *apocalypse?!*" He nodded, eyeing me closely. Oh God. Am I even allowed to say God? Not the point. There is a *Horseman of the Apocalypse* in my goddamn living room.

What do I even know about the horsemen? Not much, mythology was never my thing, ironically. I'm pretty sure they all had one specific job to make the apocalypse happen. And they're supposed to be in some type of cage so, you know, they *don't* cause the end of the world. What did each of them do? Okay, there's one that makes you really sick, and one that... Makes you starve? Ugh I should've paid more attention when Nyssa went through that phase where she was obsessed with all of this stuff.

Why am I trying to figure this out in my head? I can just ask Roman. "Which are you? I'm not going to die of starvation or get deathly ill because I'm sitting next to you am I?" Maybe I should move back to my chair.

"No. Pestilence, or Julius, has the ability to make you sick. Maxon is Famine, which leads to starvation. You need not be afraid of my brother's or my powers affecting you. We are all in complete control of them. Maxon will eat just about anything, though, so be aware if you ever meet him." That's not so bad. Maxon just sounds like another Cooper.

"Okay, but that's only two. What are the others? And which are *you?*"

"I am War," He boasted, puffing out his chest with pride. Or was that ego? "Lastly, is the second oldest, Ace - the Horseman of Death."

"Oh. He sounds... Fun." He smirked.

"Ace is... different. He is much more serious than Julius or Maxon. Though, I'm sure being in charge of the Reapers would age anyone."

"Like the Grim Reaper?" I asked, tilting my head. "I thought there was only one."

"No," He shook his head, as if that was the most absurd idea he'd ever heard. "There are too many worlds, too many deaths for one being to cover. There are thousands of Reapers. We are getting off subject, Karma. You need to learn about yourself first."

Oh yeah. "Right. So, I'm a class right below yours. There's seven in my class - who haven't been found. I can start fires with my mind. I'm not a Horseman. There are more than seven reapers. Though I'm actually relieved I can't be one of them." I don't think I can handle taking a life.

"I am not sure you are going to be thrilled with your class." *Sounds promising.* "You are one of the Seven Indomitable Sins."

He paused, I'm guessing to let it settle in my mind. "Good dramatic pause, but I have no idea what that is." The whole 'Sin' thing didn't make me hopeful though.

Roman sighed, "The Seven Sins are seven individuals who have special abilities tied to their respective trait. They are the embodiment of the trait. You…»

I interrupted, unable to stop myself. He talked so slow. "What are the Seven Sins? Like, what are the 'respective traits?'"

"Oh," He looked surprised, though I'm not sure why considering I already told him I didn't know any of this. "The Seven Sins are Lust, Greed, Sloth, Gluttony, Envy, Pride," None of these fit me at all. Lust isn't really something I feel often, if ever. I'm not greedy or gluttonous, at least I don't think I am. I don't do well with sitting still, so Sloth is out. I'm certainly not the most envious person, not even on the small list of people I know. Maybe he should check Nyssa for that one… No definitely not. She's not that bad. Maybe pride? I don't think I'm the *embodiment* of pride though. "And Wrath."

Oh. *Oh.* Dammit. "I'm the embodiment of *Wrath.* Great. Fucking perfect!" I yelled, knocking one of my potted succulents to the floor. Staring at the shattered pieces, I groaned. "Well I guess there's no question about it now." I put my hands on my head and dropped back to the couch.

Roman gave me a small smile, looking sympathetic. "There was no question before you destroyed the plant. However, I understand how learning the truth can upset your whole world view."

I scoffed, "You *understand?* How could you possibly understand?" I realized I'd pushed the wrong button when his once understanding expression became clouded and hostile. "My mother left me in the mortal world. A happy couple was my salvation. They raised me until I was thirteen - that is when your powers start to come in. It was as if a switch had been flipped, their once loving and happy marriage began to crumble. They began arguing; arguments that escalated quickly. Lucifer was the one who found me a year later, and explained everything. If I wanted my *parents* to be happy again, I had to leave."

I felt terrible. Leaning over, I placed both of my hands over his tightly clasped ones. "Roman, I'm so sorry."

"Do not be." Came his gruff reply as he shook off my hands and rose from the couch.

"You lost your family at fourteen! That's horrible. Of course I'm sorry I brought it up. I wish you'd never gone through it at all." I stood, too, but gave him some space.

He turned to face me with a hardened expression, "It was a long time ago, and as I have said *multiple times* we are not here to discuss anything but you and your future."

I rolled my eyes. "What about it? I'm a demon. I'm the embodiment of Wrath. Life sucks. What else is new?" I'm also being a baby, but he's being as ass so we're even.

He sighed - or growled? - and started pacing. "This is a big deal, Karma. Worlds rest on your shoulders, and right now in one tantrum you could wipe out a block."

"Excuse you? I'm not a child." I moved to stand in his path causing him to stop and scowl down at me. Why does he have to be so fucking tall?! Ugh. "I've been on my own with all of this for my whole life, you douche-nugget. And I have never wiped out a whole block!" No one has ever made me quite as furious as him either, but that isn't the point.

«*What* did you call me?" Now he definitely growled, like a damn animal. I could slap him. God knows I *want* to.

"A douche-nugget. Which is exactly what you're acting like!" I shot back, folding my arms. *Stand your ground, Karma.*

He threw his hands up in exasperation, "I cannot act like something that does not exist! You are the most frustrating creature I have ever met."

«*Me?!* You're the one who is blaming me for not having control over my powers! You're the one who just showed up talking about demons, and *Lucifer,* and *magic* for God's sake! Up until an hour ago, I thought I was human!" I'm getting a headache. This is way too much at once, and The Horseman of Being a Dick wasn't making it any easier.

"You thought you were human?" He asked, incredulous. I nodded. "You set things *on fire* with your *mind.*»

Glaring at him, I debated on actually slapping him this time. I'd probably break my hand, but I'd sure feel better. "I was raised by the world's most dedicated Catholics. We weren't allowed to believe in fairies or magic, and the last thing I wanted to be was a demon! I tried my hardest not to do anything that could be considered satanic. Not everyone's parents were as loving as yours!" Angrily, I wiped some tears from my cheek. "Can you just leave, please?" I slumped down onto the couch. Who in Hell decided Wrath and War were a good mix, anyway?

"I will be here tomorrow night at six."

"Don't come back." Seriously, go away. I can't handle any more demon talk.

"I will be here tomorrow to begin your training. Whether you like it or not, your life is about to change significantly. Eat before I arrive, you will need the energy." With that he turned and, thankfully, left my home.

Roi -coming from the shadows as usual- slowly climbed onto my lap. Resting my head on the back of the couch, I buried my fingers in his thick black fur. "Yoga. I need yoga. And vodka. Thank god I have some."

Chapter Three

I debated for an hour before deciding Roman didn't control me. So when six o'clock rolled around, I wasn't sitting at home waiting. Instead, I was at Cooper's gym running through drills like I was every Monday night for the past three years.

"Hey Karma, do whatever exercise you want; I have to handle some things. I'll be out in a minute." I sent Coop a quick smile and wave so he knew I heard him, and starting wrapping my hands.

For the next half hour I worked out my stress and frustration with Roman on the heavy bag. I spent most of today trying to figure out if I believed everything he said. There were some things I couldn't ignore - igniting my couch - but at the same time logic and *demons* don't mix. I will admit that a large part of me *wanted* to believe him. In a weird twisted way, he was giving me everything I'd always wanted, a place to belong, people who understood me, a reason I was so different, the reason none of the meds or psychiatrists worked, the list goes on.

What does this mean for the life I have here? If I agree to this training and destiny shit and jump into this world with angels and demons, what happens to my house? My cat? Will I be able to talk to Angel anymore? Or have training sessions with Cooper? What if Nyssa needs me? We may not be biological sisters, but she's still my little sister in every way that counts.

You could've asked Roman, The little voice in the back of my mind whispered, *If you hadn't stood him up.*

If he would've asked me for a time I was free instead of ordering me around, I wouldn't have stood him up. I don't know how it works in Hell, or wherever he lives but just because he's some *'legendary' Horseman of the Apocalypse* doesn't mean I'm at his beck and call.

"You ready for this, K?" Coop taunted, jogging up to me.

Laughing, I caught the heavy bag and took in his determined stance. Mocking him, I placed my hands on my hips and puffed out my chest. "You think you can take me, Plaizer?"

He laughed, "You know I still remember the first day you waltzed in here."

I snorted. I remember that day too; I got my ass handed to me in the ring before we started real training. "Yeah I remember too, you got off on taking advantage of a beginner." We climbed onto the raised mat together, and I used the opportunity to jab him with my elbow.

"I wasn't taking advantage. You were too cocky, too hyped. If we wanted to get anywhere you needed to be knocked down a few pegs. You're welcome."

Bullshit. I snorted, but didn't reply. Facing each other we got into our stance. Smirking at my over confident teacher I started the count down. "Three, two...»

"Karma!" I jumped, looking to see a pissed off Roman. *Great.*

"Who the hell is that?" Cooper asked, standing tall.

"Roman," I sighed, hopping from the mat. Approaching the beast, I crossed my arms, "Why am I not surprised you found me?"

I'm sure we looked comical standing toe to toe. Considering I'm only five, seven and he has to be over six feet tall, we were both frowning with our arms crossed, glaring holes into each other. He looked like a giant who could step on me at any moment, with the ego to match.

"Karma, we do not have time for you to be a child. This is serious." He all but growled at me.

"Look, Batman. I have a life. Did you honestly expect me to ask 'how high' when you say 'jump?' I don't answer to you. If you want some of *my* time, try asking. You picked six o'clock without asking me. Had you asked, I could've told you I had plans." I unfolded my arms, hoping to ease some of the tension. I'm not sure the gym would survive both of us pissed off.

"Goofing off with your boyfriend does not take precedence over this." His shoulders lowered slightly, letting me know he was working on staying calm too. Considering how easily he makes me angry enough to start fires, and the probability of everything around us being highly flammable, it was a small blessing.

"Cooper isn't my boyfriend, and we're not "goofing off" we're training. Working out is a great stress reliever, something I'm sure you know." Considering you're built like a fucking truck.

"So this is how you have been managing it?" He asked, relaxing noticeably and taking a quick look around. I nodded, bracing for whatever comes next. "We will start here."

«*What?*" Surely he's joking. "You want to spar?"

"Yes. You do Muay Thai, correct?" He slipped off the pullover he wore to display another tight black t-shirt.

"Yeah. Do you own any loose shirts?" Oh God, I hadn't meant to say that out loud. Well now you have to own it, Karma.

His lips twitched, amusement filtering over his face. "At home I do. Here though, I have to buy them, and so far this is the biggest I could find. Ladies first." He gestured for me to get back on the mat where Coop still stood, glaring.

"Karma are you really going to spar with this guy? He's almost near a foot taller than you, and wider than a goddamn train." Good old Cooper, always worrying about little me. One day he'll realize that I can look after myself.

"He's not going to kill me, Coop. Roman's not a monster, he's just arrogant. Think of him like a tutor." Cooper still didn't look convinced, but he hopped off the mat. The heavy bag had been good, but this going to be fantastic. I'll be happy with one solid hit to his face. "Okay," I said, turning to Roman. "Count us down, Coop."

火

I wished he'd killed me, I thought, slipping into my epson salt bath, *At least I got my hit to his face.*

To his credit, Roman held back quite a bit. He also tried to make me stop at round three, claiming I'd be sore tomorrow. That didn't stop me from making us go *eight* more rounds. Him and his demon not-friend been a big boost to my stress this last week and it felt *so* good to get a few hits on him. I just hadn't taken the adrenaline into account when I kept egging him on.

Now it's two days later and I'm still suffering. One of my professors had asked if I needed to go to the hospital when he saw me. Cooper had someone fill in for my class at the gym. Words cannot express how happy I am that I only have training with Cooper today. He already knows I'm not coming. No showing to a college class is never a good idea. No matter how much pain you're in.

"Karma?" You have *got* to be kidding me. How did he get in?!

"Roman, breaking and entering is a crime. Get out." I groaned, rubbing my head where I'd slammed it into my tub when he scared the shit out of me.

Since my eyes are closed I felt Roman's presence - instead of seeing him - when he entered the bathroom. "There you are."

Keeping my eyes closed so I wouldn't blush with embarrassment, I addressed the intruder, "I don't know how it works in Hell - or wherever you're from - but on Earth it's considered rude to walk in on someone in a bath."

He was quiet for a moment. So quiet I had to open my eyes to see if he was still here. He was, but I could tell that I had confused him.

"You didn't know that?" I asked, turning to hide most of my nudity as I looked at him.

"Actually, I did not. Most of my time here was spent with my own kind, or humans that specialize in the mystic arts. When I had first arrived I had been curious about the motion picture shows and went to see one. The man in the screen stepped into a woman's bath so easily, and she did not mind. I had just assumed it was normal to do that here." He explained.

"Well, lesson number one, movies aren't real. Don't believe the stuff you see, it's all fiction. Two, *what movie* did you see?"

"The man selling the tickets thought I would enjoy it. It was called Man of Iron or Steel. Some earthly metal."

What? Those are two completely different movies! Ugh, now I have to know what it is. Why couldn't he just say he forgot? What do guys pay attention to in movies? "Oh! Did the superhero have any facial hair?"

«No.»

I nodded, "It was Man of Steel. It's about Superman. You probably wouldn't like Iron Man; too much humor. For future reference, don't step in people's baths."

He rolled his eyes, "What is that smell?"

"What smell?" Should I be offended?

"If I knew what it was, I would not have asked. I would think it was flowers, but there does not seem to be any in here."

"It's lavender and it's in my bath." He nodded, eyes glancing at the water before looking away. "So are you going to just stay and talk about what you want, leave like a gentleman, or - hey! - *why not just jump in here with me*?"

His eyebrows rose, "I thought that was inappropriate?"

Oh my God! «*It is*, but standing there is creepy! You'd be the *perfect* Batman!" I scoffed, wanting to drown my self in my once calming bath.

"Stop calling me that. We need to discuss your *schedule*. This has to have priority over everything else."

"Okay," I sighed, running a hand through my hair. "So when do you want to start?"

"After you are done bathing." His eyes flicked to the water.

He was frowning again with his nose scrunched. There's nothing wrong with lavender. Wait, I can barely move because of him, and not in the fun way. No training until I can breathe without nearly collapsing in pain.

"Do you know how bad my body hurts right now? No. There's no way I'm sparring with you any time soon, and I'm definitely not doing it with *magic*." I thought Cooper liked to pick on newbies. Roman must be out of his mind.

"Well there are ways to practice without fighting. There is a special massage that helps move your Chi to help you control your magic."

I froze, "Did you just offer me a massage?"

"A Chi Massage, yes. For training purposes."

"Sure, whatever. I'm so in. Now, please *get out*.»

With an odd, devious smile he turned to leave, "I'm going to make tea."

Sweet tea, *and* a massage? Maybe there is hope for us.

Chapter Four

"How on Earth did you possibly make me hate massages?" That was the worst experience of my life. Apparently, Chi is tough to move normally and mine was blocked - which is also painful.

"I never said…»

"And who drinks hot tea?! You animal! That was more awful than the massage!"

"Hot tea is the way it has been made for centuries. How else would I make it?" He replied, crossing his arms.

"You could make sweet tea which is why I bought it."

"It is sweet."

"But it's hot. I don't like hot tea."

"Cold tea?"

Oh dear God. "You're in America. We don't drink hot tea."

He scoffed, "Plenty of Americans drink hot tea." Rolling my eyes I turned in my chair so I was facing away from him. He sighed from his spot on the couch.

"Look, I never said the Chi massage was pleasant, and I had never heard of *cold tea*." He spat the words like he was tasting 'awful cold tea.'

To be completely honest, the tea was pretty good, but after having your bones broken and expecting a completely different drink than you were given is awful.

Turning back to him I declared, "When I am able to move again, I'm going to make you sweet tea."

"That is not necessary."

"Is too, and you're going to drink it. So besides beating me up again, was there any other reason you're here?"

"I came so we could train, but that does not seem like it is going to happen today. So I will be taking my leave." He rose from the couch, but I called out to stop him.

Even though he has a special talent for pissing me off, he's also my only source for answers. "Wait, Roman," He stopped, turning back to me. "Can you answer some questions?" They'd been piling up over the last two days, and the internet was no help.

"Of course," He replied, taking his seat again. "Ask away. I will answer to the best of my ability."

Taking a deep breath, I reminded myself to try and stay calm no matter what his answers are. "Okay, so if we go through with all of this, and I learn to control my powers, you take me to see Lucifer, and we track down the others, will that become my life? Do I have to say goodbye to the people I love?" There wasn't many of them, but I need them. Especially if I'm going to be spending so much time with Mr. Dark and Brooding. "And what about school? I'm too close to my degree to give up now." This is my last year at MIIS, mom would be devastated if I dropped out.

"Keeping in touch with the people you care about should not be an issue. Humanity has improved greatly in the years I have been gone. However, you will not be seeing them in person as much. Your schooling will be more complicated. What is your degree in, again?"

"Translation," I replied, "Hey! What if we say I'm studying abroad? If I can't stay here until June, I can still get my credits for studying abroad and still graduate. To do that, though, we need them to approve it, and I'll need an actual place to study over there too." Damn, that won't work.

"Do not worry about getting it approved, I will get it covered. That will also pacify your friends when they ask why you are leaving." He nodded, looking incredibly pleased. "Anything else?"

"Yeah, do you have cable in Hell?" I almost laughed at the face he made, poor guy. Can you blame me, though? I'm a proud twenty-first century girl.

"No. The Underworld has magic, making your electronics obsolete," My disbelief must've been written on my face, because he sighed continuing, "For example, why would I use a device that shows me a blurred moving image of you with terrible sound quality when I could do this." He waved his hand in a circle creating of fog. The middle of the fog cleared to show a beautiful man.

The man was standing on a balcony staring out at something I couldn't see. What I could see, however, were the large golden wings coming from between his shoulder blades. The man turned to us letting me see his blond hair, chiseled features, and black eyes. Truly black eyes, the kind that could swallow souls and only feel joy.

"Roman!" He greeted extra cheerfully, throwing his hands up. "How is my oldest friend?" Roman has friends?

"I am well." He replied, almost sounding nice. What is happening? Where's the Roman I've been stuck with?

"You have friends?" When he glared at me, I realized that was probably rude, but can you blame me?

"Why is that shocking?"

"I thought you hated everything," I shrugged.

The man in the circle-portal-thing laughed. His laugh almost sounded like music, which was more eerie than soothing. "Who is that?" His head tilted slightly, obsidian eyes studying me.

"This is Karma Strickland."

"The Sin! Hello, dear." His eyes sparkled. Okay, so this guy knows me, but I didn't know anything about him. I looked toward Roman for help. He cleared his throat before finishing the introductions, "Karma, this is Lucifer. King of Hell."

I felt the blood drain from my face. I had realized that I'd meet him eventually, but I didn't think it would be so soon. He also doesn't look anything like I'd imagined. I pictured either the red beast with horns or some gray skinned, red eyed gargoyle-type creature. This man was beautiful. Then again, there was a demon next to me who could put the Hemsworths to shame. Not that I'd ever tell him that.

"Sorry," I said, shaking myself from my totally inappropriate day dreaming. "Hi. I don't have to say 'your majesty' when I address you, do I? Because I'm not really comfortable doing that."

Lucifer frowned at me. Well, fuck. "Roman, how is she doing that?" Doing what? "Did you put some type of ward on her?" He better *not* have.

I turned to Roman - intending to let him know exactly how I felt about him putting anything on me, but stopped short. He was smiling. Roman, the grumpiest man I've ever met, was smiling. A real, actual smile. It was like he was a different person entirely. My fingers twitched, itching for my camera.

"No wards, Lucifer. Guess she's just immune."

Lucifer pouted, looking like petulant child. "Impossible." He snapped, "Karma." I looked back at him, trying not to frown. He is technically my King, or is boss more accurate? Side note: Roman would make a wonderful model to photograph. I wonder if he'd pose for me... Probably not. "Tell me about yourself. What do you like? Personally, I love walks in my gardens, and picnics." Weird. Before I could answer he continued, "What do you think best represents beauty? A beautiful woman wearing the most exquisite jewels, is it for me."

"He has a lot of exquisite jewels," Roman added, seeming amused. "A whole castle full." Lucifer nodded eagerly in agreement.

"Er... Well, I like photography, or tv, and I would have to say the spot where the ocean meets the mountains on the pacific coast is the most beautiful thing to me. Though a field covered in undisturbed fresh snow is a close second." This has to be the world's weirdest interview. If I don't like picnics do I get my powers taken away? That might not be so bad actually...

"You don't like jewels or picnics?" He almost demanded.

"No, not really." Was my cautious answer. Roman was nearly pissing himself at this point. He wasn't doubled over laughing - don't think he's capable of that - but his utter joy at this situation was palpable. Lucifer, on the other hand, just seemed to be getting more upset with me.

"Just finish training her, Roman." He growled, yelling off to the door behind him, "Get Varena!" With a wave of his hand, the circle of fog dissipated.

"That was amazing," Roman snickered, looking like a kid on Christmas morning.

"What just happened? Did I just piss off Satan?"

Roman stopped his unnatural laughing, and refocused on me, "No you did not. Well a little, but not enough to need to worry abut it. Lucifer is not used to women not falling at his feet."

"He was flirting with me?" I hope not. If so, we aren't going to get along very well.

"I think enticing would be a better word. He was not happy with your lack of amazement over him."

Amazement? Sure, the wings are cool, but I'm not going to fangirl over him. "So what, demon girls just fall at his feet?" Roman nodded, watching me curiously. I scoffed, "Fuck that."

Roman shifted, folding his hands in his lap. He was back in 'mentor mode' now, so no more laughing. "Any more questions?"

"Just one. Are all of your friends creepy and weird?" He glowered at me instead of answering. I tried to laugh, but my body quickly reminded me how much pain I was in. "Oh God that hurts…" I groaned, curling in on myself.

Roman made an oddly triumphant noise. I knew that massage was a cover up for him to kick my ass some more. When - if - my body heals, I'm going to set him on fire.

"Wait, I do have a question. An actual question." He looked at me, eyes searing into my soul to see if I was joking. I rolled my eyes, "I'm serious, I swear."

"Okay."

"What about God? If Lucifer is real, I assume God is too, right? Are we even allowed to say God since we're demons?" Shouldn't I be choking on his name or something? I have an angel statue in my living room and have been around more crosses than people, aren't they supposed to burn me? Are they going to start burning me?

Roman nodded like he was expecting this, "God is a name created by man. We know him as Yhwh. You can call him by any name you choose."

"So, is he involved with the whole apocalypse thing?" It just doesn't add up. Everything I'd ever been told about him, pointed out how loving and protective of his creations he was. If all that is true, how can he sit idle while the world is ending? Is Heaven threatened in this too? I would think that counts as a world.

"He is definitely involved. After all, this is his war as well."

"It is? Then why isn't he stopping it? He's supposed to be all powerful! Can't he just snap his fingers and fix everything?"

Roman scoffed, "He is not all powerful, and this is not something he can stop. The Graeae said only the seven could ward off the Grand Extinction. They are never wrong."

"The Graeae?" Is that a person or a demon?

"Yes, though I am not sure what name they are called on Earth. They see people's future, timelines of lives long passed and not yet begun." Sounds dramatic. "Their prophecies are never wrong."

"Okay," I think that made some form of sense. "So does that mean God, or Yhwh, is hunting me down, too?"

Roman sighed, becoming frustrated. Maybe this was too many questions at one time. "We do not know what he is doing." He grumbled, running a hand through his hair. "We do need to be ready in case he does try to contact you, though."

"Be ready for what?" God is benevolent to his creatures. Right?

"You said you were raised by Catholics. Right?" Technically, I said the world's most dedicated catholics, but whatever. I nodded, unsure where he was going. "So you worshiped him. Which means you look at Yhwh as good and Lucifer as bad."

Well duh. God and his his angels are supposed to be caretakers who love and protect all life. Lucifer and his demons were the beings of all evil - of Sin. So where does that leave me? I'm not evil. The worst thing I've ever done was stealing a candy bar on accident when I was eight, and mom took me back to pay for it. But I'm the embodiment of Wrath, one of the Seven Indomitable Sins. That isn't something to be proud of.

"Nothing is black and white, Karma. Lucifer is not completely evil, just as Yhwh is not completely good. Neither qualify as good, honestly. Yhwh is a trickster. He loves toying with people, playing on their emotions. If he comes to you, do not follow him blindly. You have not quietly sat there and believed every word I have said, so do not do the same for him simply because of a book."

"Okay, I'll be careful." Now I'm worried about *God* trying to track me down. Is there anyone I can trust? I sighed, feeling incredibly overwhelmed.

"I will get started on your schooling. Tomorrow, you can talk to your friends. For now, sleep would be best. You need to recover so we may continue your training." *Oh joy.*

He was right about the sleep thing, though I wanted to disagree to prove I don't follow his orders. Right now, though, is not the time. I'm exhausted from the information and still in an immeasurable amount of pain from the past few days. I pushed myself up, read to walk him out and lock the door. That's when it hit me, I never found out how he *got in.*

"Roman?" He glanced at me, tense because of my tone. "How did you get in my house earlier?"

"I used atheric. It is a spell that places you where you wish to be. It works best if you have already been there before."

"That sounds badass! You can teleport!" Can I? God, I hope so. He should've started with that.

"I suppose? Is that a common human term?"

"Yeah. It's when a person travels to a place with magic instead of a vehicle or legs." That was a terrible definition, but he seemed to understand.

"Then, yes. Though, it is called atheric not teleport. You will learn it later in your training. *Much* later. First you will need to be much more in control of your magic. If there is a time where we need atheric, you will travel with me." Ugh. So I have to learn lame magic first? I *can't wait.*

We reached my front door, and gladly held it open for him. "This is how humans leave a place." Roman just frowned at me. "I left this way on our first meeting, because you were uncomfortable with the existence of magic. It would be best if I used magic where humans could not stumble upon me."

I gasped, "You're going to show me your totally awesome magic that only masters can do? What did I do to deserve this honor?"

Somehow his frown got deeper, "Are you being sarcastic?" He knows what sarcasm is? Giving him a blank look, I leaned on the now closed door and crossed my arms. Growling at me, he clasped his hands in front of him, took a steady breath, and spoke softly, "*Kinisi.*" Shadows appeared on the floor, swirling around his feet. A black smoke rose from the shadows until it swirled around his entire body. Once he was completely encased in the smoke, it disappeared into the air taking Roman with it.

Dammit, that was cool, but he's not going to teach it to me until I'm a million years old like he is. Maybe I can find another demon that will teach me. He does have three brothers after all. Feeling my muscles start to cramp, I cursed Roman for not teaching me the spell. He could've at least atheric-ed me to bed.

火

A knock came at the door - luckily - before I could stumble too far. What now? I swear if it's that idiot Domini from before, I'm going to put this magic thing to the test by turning him into a bonfire. Opening the door, I found Angel and Cooper waiting on the other side. Some of my irritation melted away at the sight of Angel holding a small Tupperware.

"You look like shit," Cooper so elegantly stated, earning a tired glare from me and an elbow from Angel. An elbow jab from Angel wouldn't do much - or any - damage to a brick wall like Cooper, but I still appreciate it.

"Be nice, Cooper, or I'm sending you home." Once Cooper looked properly chastised, she turned back to me. "Cooper told me some random guy showed up at the gym the other day and beat you up. I worked doubles yesterday and the day before, so I brought some brownies to make up for it."

"Forgiven," Angel was one of the best bakers in Monterey. "But he didn't 'beat me up' he barely won."

"Karma, don't lie. That man could've been in the ring with the pros. No matter how skilled you are, I wouldn't put you in the ring with a champion twice your size! And there's no way in Hell I'd let you go *eleven fucking rounds* with him! What were you thinking?" Oh great, so now even *Cooper* thought Roman was amazing.

"Cooper!" Angel scolded, "We are not here to make her feel worse! Knock it off." Angel huffed, dropping herself into my beanbag chair. "I'm so confused. Can we just talk for a second, and *not* attack our best friend?"

"I'm okay, Angel. Though, fair warning, I'm in a shitload of pain, so I might not last long."

"Still?" Cooper asked, taking a seat on the couch.

"Yeah," I lowered myself carefully into my favorite chair. "It got worse after Roman's failed massage tonight."

"Wait, the dick is here?"

For some reason, Cooper calling Roman a dick irritated me. He was one, but Cooper didn't know that. He hadn't even spoke to him. "He's not a dick, Cooper, and he already left." Thank God - or Lucifer? - that they didn't arrive a few minutes earlier.

"So, who is this Roman, anyway? You haven't mentioned him before." Angel asked, letting Roi hop into her lap. He purred obnoxiously as she scratched behind his ears.

"Ah, well," How do I explain him without mentioning magic or Hell?

34

"What happened to your chair?" Cooper asked, spreading out over the whole couch. He gestured to the burnt arm. *Fuck.*

"An accident." *Don't ask anymore questions please.*

Cooper opened his mouth to ask more questions I can't give him answers to, but was cut off by Angel. She was living up to her name tonight. "Who cares about the chair? Throw a blanket over it. Who's Roman?"

"He's a guy that I met…" Where would I possibly meet him? They know it wasn't at the gym. I can't say a different gym, Cooper would never speak to me again. "School. He's a guy I met at school." That could work. He is supposed to be a teacher to me.

"He's still in college?" Cooper asked, incredulous.

Okay. I can do this. Lying to my best friend's faces shouldn't be too hard. Right? "No. He's already graduated, but MIIS brought him in to talk about studying abroad, and how it benefits language based majors." That actually made sense. If I knew lying came so easy, school could've gone much smoother.

"Studying abroad? Is that something you're considering?" Angel didn't appear upset - like I thought she would - just simply curious.

"Surely not." Cooper denied adamantly, shaking his head.

"Yeah, I am actually."

"You *can't* be serious." Well Cooper was upset. Funny, I had thought it would be the complete opposite.

"Sure I can. My degree is in translation, why wouldn't I want to go to a country to learn more about one of the languages I'm studying?"

"You're talking about leaving everything. What about the cat?"

"Roi," I corrected, absently. Honestly, I hadn't thought about him. Knowing him, he'd probably love Hell. I wonder if Lucifer likes cats. "I'll ask Roman if I can bring him."

«*Right* call the guy you barely know. *Great idea!*" I sighed - though it sounded oddly close to a growl at this point. I already didn't feel good, and Cooper was grinding my nerves.

"How are we supposed to cheer her up, when you can't stop

being a… a… A donkey!" Oh shit. That's the closest Angel has got to actually swearing in the five years I've known her.

"Angel! I have to tell her the truth. She's being stupid."

"That's it. Get out." Did she just kick Cooper out of my house? I don't mind. I probably would have if my body didn't feel like it was crumbling.

"What?"

"Get out. We need girl time and your honorary status as one of us is revoked. Shoo!"

"Fine. Be stupid with Karma." With that, Cooper stormed out of my house. Honestly, I'm thankful. I love Cooper, he's the brother I never had, but he can be so aggressive when he believes he's right. It's exhausting. He'll cool down, though, and reach out to us.

"Okay," Angel beamed at me, curling up with Roi again. "So who *is* Roman? What does he look like? What does he like? Do you like him? Can I meet him?"

What did Cooper tell her? The chances of me *liking* somebody are about the same as rain in Egypt. "He's an attractive man, but I'm not interested in him. Not like how you're implying, at least. There's a lot he can teach me, but he's like a billion years old." Which probably isn't much of an exaggeration.

"Darn." I laughed. Angel was always hoping I'd find someone I liked. If she paid as much attention to her own love life that she did to mine, she'd be married by now. "When can I meet him? Does he like cookies? I can make him some!" Even if he doesn't, I'm going to say yes. The box of brownies she brought tonight are already gone, and I don't remember eating half of them.

"I don't know if he's ever had cookies, but yes you should bring some."

Her jaw came unhinged, "How can he have never eaten cookies? Is he ever happy?"

I snorted, "No." The only time I've seen him happy was when we were talking to Lucifer. Angel isn't religious, but I don't think she'd react positively to that little fact. Well, it's Angel; she's the most positive person I've met. I'd pay to see him have to sit through a conversation with Angel. "How about, before I leave all of you come have dinner here? You, Cooper, Roman, and me. That way you can ask whatever you want, and Cooper can be put at ease."

"That sounds perfect! Just one small change," I knew this was coming. "Can I cook?"

Of course she can cook. I can barely make eggs. "Of course. One condition: you have to make your chocolate lasagna masterpiece." A few years ago, Angel came up with this chocolate heaven layered the way a lasagna is. It's about a million calories, but it's amazing. Cooper - who refuses to try it - has a blast kicking my ass the day after I eat it, but I won't be here the day after this time.

"Cooper yelled at me last time I made it." I could see the debate going on in her head as she tried to figure out who to make happy. "Whatever. He made me mad today." *Yes.* Thanks Coop! "You need some good comfort food before you leave. Especially since you don't like a lot of European cuisine, and if they're sending you somewhere based on your studies that lands you either in Spain or France. I guess they could send you to Russia or Japan, too. Have you ever had Russian cuisine? I haven't. You like Japanese food though. I'll make tater-tot skewers, bacon wrapped meatloaf, and chocolate lasagna. A full American feast with no avocado! Maybe Cooper will be too distracted by the bacon wrapped meatloaf to be too upset about the chocolate lasagna." She was totally rambling at this point, but I let her go. It's not like she actually expected me to answer any of those questions.

"That sounds amazing." Roman better come. "I'll make sweet tea." *And force feed it to him.*

"Let's do Saturday at three. This is going to be so much fun!" At her increased excitement, Roi grumbled and sulked down the hallway toward our room. "Aw, I woke him up."

"I think he's got the right idea, Angel. Are you staying over?" This day had drained the pathetic amount of energy I had leaving me feeling like jelly.

It wasn't weird for Angel and I to have impromptu sleep overs. Mostly due to the fact that when we met my favorite pastime was drinking, and Angel - who refuses alcohol - was a DD that was always available. We built a friendship on way too may drunk confessions, and the sixty or so times I drunkenly proposed. Even when I stopped binge drinking, we still crashed at each other's homes. Typically, she helps me study before a big test, and we crash around two in the morning surrounded by books. We'd set up a semblance of a morning routine, where she'd wake up with me around six and cook breakfast while I went for my run. I can make breakfast, but I would never ask her not to. It started when we were roommates, and I know she worried if she thought I wasn't eating. It was basically a way for us to lean on each other under the guise of 'girl time.' That's exactly why I offered tonight, I need to talk to her about this whole demon thing, without mentioning demons, and I'm too exhausted to censor myself tonight.

I pulled Angel up from the bean bag, and was immediately wrapped into a hug, "Everything is going to be okay." She whispered. I relaxed into the embrace blinking back the relieved tears. She had no idea why I needed those words, but she still knew to say them. I wish she could come with me. How am I supposed to leave the support I've relied on for five years?

Chapter Five

"Okay, so Roman's study abroad plan has completely shaken up your life?"

The 'study abroad' story was hard to stick to when trying to convey how much Roman was uprooting my life, but Angel was trying to understand. There was no mention of last night as we started the day, something I was especially grateful of. I was still too sore to actually make it outside for my run, so I'm sitting on a barstool while Angel cooks. It was oddly peaceful after the past few days.

"In a way. Going with him could do a lot of good," Like saving worlds, and lives. "But what if I fail?" Then all those lost lives are on me.

"Failing isn't the end of the world. If you try, you have a chance of succeeding. If you back out now, you automatically fail." I'll never understand how she always says the right thing, but I love her for it. Minus the fact that failing *is* the end of the world, but I'm ignoring that part for now. "Plus," She added, "If the world of translation decides to hate Karma, you can always be Danielle!" She laughed at my groan.

"Oh God," When I went out almost every night, there would always be at least one person who swore we had 'a connection' and that that 'connection' made it possible for me to feel sexually attracted to them, because that's how it works apparently. So I told them my name was Danielle, so they couldn't track me down. Angel came to rescue my drunk ass from a bar, and the idiot that wouldn't leave me alone asked if she was a friend of mine, using my fake name. Angel cheerfully asked me the next morning which name I preferred as she handed me a bottle of aspirin. She's never let it go, and reserves it for special moments.

"Do you think I'm over thinking this?" I asked, switching back to the important topic.

Angel set the bacon to the side and started making eggs. She kept the bacon in her line of sight though, so I couldn't steal some. Not that I'd dare after she smacked me with a spatula last time. "Can you make toast? Remember we don't want it charred, just lightly toasted." She rolled her eyes when I stuck my tongue out at her. I'd only burnt it once. Twice. Several times. Whatever. "And yes, I think you are. You've always been an over-thinker, Karma. I think this could be good for you."

I moved around the kitchen - keeping my distance from the plate of bacon - and tried to avoid the furry fatass stretched out behind Angel. Roi has this amazing talent of stretching himself out like taffy in the most inconvenient places. "If I can't bring Roi with me, will you take care of him?" I wouldn't even trust Nyssa with Roi, but if I had to leave him Angel was the best bet.

"Of course! You know, I love him. He'll miss you though." She pouted looking down at the furball. She dropped him a small piece of bacon, making him purr loudly. "When will you ask Roman?"

I shrugged, "Whenever I see him. Which will probably be some time today." Shit, he's going to use his magic to get in. Magic that Angel can't see. Shit.

"What's wrong? You went from sleepy grumpy to actually grumpy."

"He probably *will* be here soon..." I grumbled. Can I really kick out my best friend *for a guy*? It's not just any guy though, it's Roman. Roman who practically breathes magic. If she stays, she could find out about magic, and me being a demon; which is *dangerous*. If I do, I have to be rude to the person who sat with me last night, and through every other night like that one.

"Don't worry about me. I'm taking one of your Tupperware," Considering I've never bought Tupperware, it's most likely hers, but I'm not telling her that. She set my food on a plate and packed hers up. "This just makes me more anxious for Saturday." Taking one of my forks, and a piece of - lightly toasted - toast, and kissed my cheek, "I'll see you later." I yelled a quick goodbye as she flounced from my house.

火

I sat down with my breakfast, and nearly shoved my fork through my cheek when a voice came from *right behind me*, "Karma."

"Jesus fucking Christ, Roman!" I spun around to glare at him. He scowled back, "What about him?"

"What... What about who? Jesus? Do you *know* Jesus?" This has to be some lame attempt at a joke. He can't be old enough to know Jesus.

"I did. The humans embellished him drastically. *Poutsos.*" He growled the last word, so I'm assuming it's something of insult.

"So not only have you met Jesus, but you don't like him?" Of course he didn't. He doesn't like anybody. How do you hate Jesus?

"Truth be told, I don't like humans as a whole." *Ouch.* «*Jesus,*» He spat the name. "Ranks lower than others, though. He truly is Yhwh's son. The only one worse than him was Adam." I hope he doesn't ever come across any one religious, or at least doesn't speak to them. He'll probably be tortured or stoned.

"Never mind," I shook my head vigorously, "No more talk about Jesus, *or. Adam.*" It's too early for this weird ass conversation. How old do you have to be to know Jesus and Adam? I turned back to my plate, ignoring the frustrating horseman behind me. Roman took a seat beside me, though I'm not sure my stool will last long under his weight.

"You brought him up."

"Not intentionally. I didn't think he was real after I met you. Anyway," I sighed, running a hand through my hair. "What's the plan for today? I'm feeling much better."

"That is good to hear. I was planning on base magic."

Wait, really? "I thought I wasn't allowed to do magic? You said I was too *inexperienced.*" Which I still think is bullshit.

He rolled his eyes, and stole a piece of my bacon. He corrected, "Base magic. You are too inexperienced for atheric. However, controlling the flames that appear when you lose your... This is delicious."

"I didn't make it, but I'll tell Angel you said so."

"Who is this Angel you keep mentioning?" His eyes stared intently at my plate, practically salivating, despite the face that I was still eating from it. I sighed, taking a last piece of bacon and pushed the plate toward him. He dug in like an animal. He's happy though, so I'm not complaining.

"She's my best friend. Hey, do you have plans on Saturday at three?"

"We are just going to ignore the irony of your best friend being named Angel?" I pointedly looked away. He scoffed, "Why did you ask about Saturday?"

"Angel wants to meet you," He frowned, "And she's going to cook." Mentioning Cooper would probably make him say no, so I'll keep that to myself. "Like a dinner party with only a few people."

"We do not have time for parties, Karma." He growled.

"Look, I know that the world is ending and all, but we have to do this right. I told them that you're a guy that the college called in to encourage students to study abroad. They think I'm leaving the country with a stranger. You have to remember, they are my family. I can't just disappear."

He made that noise that's somewhere between a growl and a sigh while rubbing his chin. "Fine. I will be there. I have a meeting with the king of your college to organize your absence. I will use your study abroad story."

I couldn't help the small laugh at the word king. Sliding off my stool, I headed into the living room with Roman following. From my brief experience with magic it's destructive, and I really don't want to destroy my house. He better have somewhere else for us to practice. I don't even have a backyard to use.

"Are you ready for your first lesson?" He remained standing, avoiding the furniture.

"Do we have to practice here?" What happens if Roi gets in the way? No. I'm not taking that chance.

"No," He shook his head, looking distastefully around the living room. "We have a base nearby, it is a secure place we can train. Are you ready to go now?"

"No, I'm in pajamas. Give me a minute." I ran back to my room to change out of my pajamas. I wouldn't admit it out loud, but I'm actually excited to start learning actual magic. I slipped on the clothes that I trained in with Cooper and my tennis shoes, and met Roman back in the living room. He hadn't moved, he just stood there with his arms crossed. "Okay, now I'm ready. Let me grab my keys."

"Keys? What for?" He asked, watching me search. Chivalry is dead. Can't say I'm surprised.

"So we can lock my door and use my car." What other reason would I need keys for? I swear, he's a genius with mystical stuff, but the second I mention anything from this world it's like he's a child.

He scoffed pretentiously, "We do not need your metal box. We can use atheric." Before I can snark him - after all, I'm too *inexperienced* - he held up one of his hulk sized hands. "*My* atheric. You are not ready."

Of course I'm not. Still, this is going to be me in the middle of *controlled* magic. Despite Roman's ability to be a notorious dick, he is the most experienced magic user I know. Technically he's the only magic user I know, but still. This is going to be awesome.

"Alright," I said, shaking out my worries. "Let's do this. *How* do we do this, exactly?"

"Come here, Karma." I wonder if he does that rolling on the 'K' on my name on purpose. Maybe it's normal for his altered accent. He pulled me into his side, encasing me with one of his overly large arms. "Remember to breathe." Should be easy enough with his bike tire bicep in my face. "Holding your breath could stop your heart." Well, that's *fantastic*. "Oh, and try to stay relaxed. Keeping your muscles relaxed is important. If they are too tense, they could freeze that way."

"Magic sounds *fun.*"

"It's a lot more fun when you are not human and breakable." He's so wonderfully condescending. I wonder how he'd react if I bit him.

"So I could possibly die. Great. *Why* can't we take my car?"

"Whining. So mature."

Before I could show him how many *mature* words I know, black smoke was rising from the floor. I kept my breathing steady and my body relaxed. Something that is a lot harder when someone *stresses me out.* The smoke swirled around our feet - jeez, his had to be about twice the size of mine. As the smoke got taller, I pressed myself into Roman's side. I'm not sure what would happen if my foot or arm stuck out, and I really don't want to find out. Roman held me tightly to his side, allowing me to focus on his steady breathing, and use it to relax my own. If only I'd actually listened in those anger management classes. I felt the ground fall out from under my feet, but I didn't fall with it. All I could feel was Roman's solid weight beside me. There was no smell, or sound, or light. Just Roman and me, floating aimlessly. It was oddly calming; like I could spend an eternity here.

Before I could analyze it anymore, I felt solid ground again. I opened my eyes to see some sort of warehouse. It was a large open room without windows and concrete walls. There were several desks with computers that a dozen people - demons? - were moving between. Behind the desks there was a half wall, that separated the working stations from the training matts in the back. The far back wall was covered in medieval type weapons - swords, staffs, maces, daggers, axes, you name it, it was displayed on that wall.

Roman led me to the back half of the room quietly, simply nodded at a few people who glanced at us. I couldn't tell if it was fear or respect in their eyes as they looked at him. Maybe it was some strange mixture of the two. Luckily, all of the faces were unfamiliar. I could think of one I don't want to see today. Or ever.

Once we had passed the tables, I could see the full training area. On my left they had set up a place to practice archery, complete with several different types of bows and arrows on a stand nearby. I watched as a woman hit the bullseye every time, splitting the arrow she had sent before she'd fired again.

"You are going to give her a tour? That is how you decided to handle this?" *God fucking dammit.* That asshole from before - the first demon I met that I know of - marched over to us, glaring up at Roman. He looked as cocky and annoying as the last time I saw him as he glared up at a - now tense and softly growling - Roman. I take it Roman wasn't a fan of him either. Good.

"Karma, this is Domini. Your first impression of him was probably correct."

I bit back a smile when Domini's frown got even deeper. Turns out Roman and I do have something in common. Given our magics, extreme dislike shouldn't be shocking. It was also hard to not laugh at the healing black eye he was still sporting - courtesy of me.

"Is there a reason you are treating *her* like some sort of guest, Roman?" My brows rose at his tone. I was under the impression that Domini was several classes lower than Roman, and even me. Can he talk to him like that without dying?

"She is a guest. Would you rather I attack her? Like you did?" Where is this Roman all the time? Bitchy sarcastic Roman and I could be friends.

45

"Afraid she will kick your ass, Horseman?" Did he just admit I kicked his ass?

No. Wait. I don't want to fight Roman, ever again. *Ever.* Unless the magic lessons turn me into some sort of ultra badass, I'm not sparring with him again. *Fuck that.* I like my body in one piece. "I'm not getting in front of your fist again. However, Domini I will happily kick your ass if you want. Again." I smiled at his glower, itching for him to take the bait.

"Not today," Roman cut in. "As fun as that would be. We are beginning your magic training today." Damn.

"Okay. Let's get started." I'm sure I'll find another opportunity. I'm ready to try and control this magic.

"You are going to *train* her? Why?"

Now, Roman was full on growling. "What did you think the plan was once we found them?"

"Throw them in a secure cage?" What? "Have you forgotten that the Sins play a key part in the end of every world?" Of course he hasn't, but isn't the point of the Sins to *stop* the apocalypse? They need us.

Roman simply rolled his eyes, grabbed my elbow, and led me away from Domini. Thank God. I'm going to need years of magic training to handle him without some sort of explosion. Roman led me to the right side of the training room where there were several types of weights along the wall with a pile of mats beside them.

Roman turned to me with his arms crossed, "I know you study Muay Thai, but have you ever tried Tai Chi?"

"Actually, yes. When I first stared therapy, my doctor thought it would help."

"You do not study it now. What made you switch?"

I laughed dryly, "The instructor grabbed my ass, so I threw him through a window. They banned me after that." I shrugged. It didn't really bother me. "I did Tai Chi at home until I met Coop."

Roman frowned, but moved on. "Let us get started then. The key is to focus your energy. I am not referencing your energy that you typically use to practice. I am talking about your magic energy. The one that controls your power. We want the power to come on your command, not just from your anger."

I smirked, "Batman and The Hulk? I'm okay with that." Anger strength? Sounds easy enough.

"Stop calling me Batman." He grumbled, making me laugh harder. There is no way that nickname is going away any time soon, it's too perfect.

For the next hour Roman had me copy his movements while trying to find the center of my magic. According to Roman, it was located somewhere inside me. This was not as easy as I'd originally thought, and Roman's monk-like words weren't helping. It took a while, but I soon began feeling a new kind of energy move through my veins. It wasn't the white hot fury I felt whenever my magic had activated before. Now it felt more like a soothing warmth. Instead of burning through my veins, it moved with me making me feel stronger.

"You feel it," My eyes snapped to Roman, who was watching me carefully. "Your magic is not meant to be painful. It is an energy inside you that you can bend at will. Now, like this," We moved to the 'hold the ball' position, "Feel the energy. Focus your magic into the space between your hands. Will it to form a ball. Remember to breathe."

Okay. I took an even breath, and focused on the space between my palms. I pressed on the magic energy, willing it to form in my hands. Red sparks appeared, but didn't turn into anything significant. I've never had a problem with lighting fires before.

"Remember, Karma, you are meant to *bend* your magic, not force it. Flow with the magic. It is a part of you." A black flame swirled in between Roman's hands. It swirled, and weaved through itself with ease. His flame was contained, but could obviously do some damage if he were to lose control, or let it out. Roman himself seemed perfectly at ease holding his flame. Show off.

Relaxing into my stance, I tried to flow with the new energy instead of willing it to do what I want. Slowly, a small dark red flame began to form. It wasn't as intricate as Roman's, but it's something. Roman nodded, "Very good, Karma." Despite myself, I swelled with pride at his praise. I refocused on my tiny flame. Maybe I can make it bigger if I just try. Sweat dripped down my face, as my limbs began trembling. I ignored the fatigue settling into my body, and breathed into my flame. Come on, surely making it a little bigger should be a little easier.

"Karma, stop." Suddenly, Roman was beside me. "You need a break. *Stop.*" Dropping my arms, I went to stand straight again, but my limbs wouldn't cooperate. I wavered on my wobbling legs, trying to catch my footing. Roman caught me as my knees gave out. I slumped over his arm, breathing heavily. "That is enough for today. It is time for you to return home." Roman slipped his other arm under my knees, lifting me into his arms. "*Kinisi.*" This time I couldn't focus on how anything looked or felt. The strong magic still flowed through my veins, making my skin throb. I whimpered into Roman's chest. Magic sucks.

Chapter Six

I *really* have to stop spending time with Roman.

I'm supposed to be packing for my whole 'study abroad' thing, but leaving my bed seemed to be the hardest thing right now. Roi didn't seem to mind, though. The overly fluffy cat was curled up on my pillow next to me, purring loudly. Spoiled brat. Maybe another hour wouldn't hurt…

"Wake up, sleepyhead!" Angel cheered, busting into my room. "You're *supposed* to be packing!" She sang, jumping onto my bed making Roi and I bounce.

"Go away, Angel," I groaned. Roi meowed loudly, voicing his discomfort as well. He moved to curl up on my chest, hiding his face. "We're sleeping." Who decided on having a morning person as a best friend?

"No ma'am! You need to pack. You have to leave soon, or do you plan on just taking the clothes on your back? Friendly reminder, you sleep in a tank top and silk shorts. Plus, Roi needs a bag, too." She pulled Roi from my arms - gently, of course - and cuddled him to her chest. "There's breakfast downstairs…»

Dammit. I should've never revealed my weakness for her cooking to her. Groaning, I pushed up from my blanket cocoon, and gave Angel my best glare. She simply laughed in response. Best friends are the worst. "I have to brush my teeth. I'll meet you in the kitchen." I grumbled, shuffling to the bathroom.

Fifteen minutes later, I was feeling much more awake, and less grumpy. Angel was downstairs mixing Roi's food with what I'm assuming was cooked salmon. Angel tried to make him special foods at least once a month. Apparently, normal cat treats aren't good enough for a King like Roi. He is going to miss her.

"He loves his treats. Just like his mother." She shook her head, watching me devour the blueberry muffins she'd brought. "Tell you what, since you're in zombie mode I will pack Roi's stuff. So all you have to do is pack your own stuff. Sound good?"

"Yeargh," I nodded. Her face scrunched up, and she mumbled something about 'ladylike' and 'talking with my mouth full' while she retrieved the large suitcase I'd brought for Roi's stuff.

"I love this suitcase, by the way." I agreed, looking at the large black case covered in small multi-colored crowns and scepters. It reminded me of Roi the second I saw it. "What do yours look like? I'm assuming you bought new ones since I convinced you to throw away the ones you came to Monterey with."

I frowned remembering the two old suitcases I'd stolen from Isaac. They were brown and broken with missing wheels and latches. A lot like the house they'd come from. The new cases weren't anything special, just simple black cases that were hard to damage, but they're mine. To Angel, I just I shrugged, "Nothing special. I guess I'll go start packing. So fun." I didn't have to look to know she rolled her eyes. I threw my plate in the sink, and left Angel in the kitchen with the fat and happy cat that was still feasting on his salmon. He didn't even look up at me.

I had to get this over with quickly. I'd promised Angel I would help her move the last of her boxes over before I left. She had volunteered to watch over the house and rebuild the garden while I was gone, knowing I was stressed about leaving it, but last time I was at her apartment I got to meet her new neighbors - an aspiring rock band that believed the only way to make "pure music" was to hotbox with the moon light shining through the window. After that, I basically demanded she move in. There's no way I could leave her living next to people who believed the Moon Goddess was angry at humanity for pop music. Angel was thrilled, and completely packed or sold her stuff within the week.

I set my suitcases up on my bed, and began pulling my favorite clothes from my closet and drawers. I folded them as neatly as I could manage, and pressed them into the case. This is going to take forever.

"Are you almost ready?" Before I could stop myself, I was swinging at the person behind me. Not person, demon. Roman caught my wrist effortlessly, already scowling at me.

"Jesus, Roman! Stop doing that!" My chest heaved, trying to slow my heart rate back down. Roman moved to peek in my suitcase. His scowl got impossibly deeper as he saw two meager shirts folded inside.

"Why do you insist on mentioning him?"

"I say it when I'm startled. Why do you get so mad when I say his name, anyway? Don't tell me you have a grudge against Jesus; that's just crazy." A thump came from the front of the house reminding me that we were not alone. Angel is just down the hall. Dropping my voice to a whisper, I leaned toward Roman, "You can't be here right now. My very *human* best friend is right down the hall. You can't just suddenly be in my room."

"Your friend that cooks? I shall go then." That was easy. Black smoke began swirling around his feet right as Angel poked her head in the door. I threw my unfolded pile of clothes on the smoke, effectively putting it out.

She didn't seem to notice, "Hey, do you... Oh! Hello." Pink tinted Angel's cheeks as she noticed Roman standing in front of me. "Where did you come from?" Good question.

"The window," Roman gestured to my - now open - window. Now that is cool magic. When is he going to teach me useful stuff?

"It's just me up front," She laughed, "You didn't have to sneak. I *knew* there was something more to this." Angel knew me well enough to know nothing, ah, *explicit* had happened, but judging from her wink as she shut the door she definitely thinks that's where were headed. I dropped my head into my hands feeling my cheeks warm. There's no way Roman was just going to let that go. Hopefully Angel doesn't share her assumptions with Cooper, he'd lose his shit and I don't think I could handle that on top of this embarrassment.

"I do not understand." Here we go. "Why did she close one eye at you?" I wanted to laugh at the innocence in his question, but refrained knowing it would only piss him off.

"It's a best friend thing. Don't worry about it." And don't ask me to explain further.

"Although I am naïve when it comes to human traditions and mannerisms, I can tell when someone is lying. Why did she do that?" I'd slam my head into a wall if I didn't think Angel would tease me about her misguided thoughts.

"It's called winking. She did it because she thinks we're sneaking around." That only confused him more. "I told them that you are from my school, which means if we were together, we'd have to keep it a secret. For ethics or whatever."

"Then *why* did you tell them that? We are supposed to be together."

I sighed, the wall isn't looking so bad. "*No,*" Great now I'm growling like Roman. "I mean, you know, a *sexual,* relationship."

He seemed to think for a moment before realization dawned. I could practically see the light bulb above his head. He scowled, or rather, continued to scowl, "I forgot that humans think sex alone forms a bond. It did not appear that Angel disapproved, however."

"Yeah," I rolled my eyes, "But that's Angel." Plus she's been trying to find someone for me since we met. I'm sure she's dancing at the mere prospect of this going how she hopes.

"I will never understand humans." He shook his head, moving to sit on my bed. I forgot I threw all my clean clothes on the floor. Great. "They are remarkably skilled at comfort, however." Roman looked even larger on my queen sized bed, it was almost laughable. His legs couldn't fit with his torso and my suitcases, so they simply dangled off the side like a child's.

"You're lucky that you seem to be as clean-obsessed as I am, or I'd shove you off my bed." Deciding to ignore him, I resumed packing my bags. I laid my heap of clothes over Roman's lap, and resumed folding.

Roman scoffed, "If you love being clean so much, why is there all of this short black hair everywhere? Your hair is much longer than this."

"That's Roi's. He's clean, too."

"Roi? French for 'King', yes?" I nodded, slightly surprised. Roman sat up, and began folding the clothes I'd laid over his lap. "Who is that? Another friend?"

"He's my cat. He's coming with us no matter what you say."

"I have been here multiple times, and have never seen an animal." Honestly, that's not surprising. Roi hates most people, especially new people. Cooper didn't know I had a cat until he stepped on Roi's tail and got a nasty scar on his ankle for it. Plus, my house isn't typically well lit, and Roi is black and gray, so hiding isn't really that difficult for him. He really only comes out to search for Angel.

"He's weird around most people. Right now, he's probably following Angel around. He loves her."

He seemed to accept that answer, and helped me continue to pack. Roman was actually a big help to my complete surprise. He also re-organized my suitcases so everything fit better. Angel called out to us about two hours later, announcing food. I smirked at Roman, "Have you ever had any Earth food other than my breakfast you ate the other day?"

"No," He scoffed, obnoxiously, "I try to avoid it as much as possible. That seems to be impossible with you, though. It is no mystery why humans are so round, they eat too much." One day I'm going to slap him.

"I eat a lot, because I work out a lot. So fuck off and come eat."

He kept himself firmly planted on my bed with his arms crossed and scowled at me. He'd actually stopped frowning for an hour, but I suppose that's over now. My eyes nearly rolled from my head; Roman may be 'against humans' or whatever, but he's just as stubborn as any other man. Oh, I know how to get him to come eat. Hold in the laugh, Karma, you can do it. "Staying in the room instead of socializing? Total Batman move." I closed the door behind me, and bolted down the hall before I started laughing.

"What's so funny?" Angel asked, setting the plates down on my kitchen table. I'd calmed down to a wide smile by the time Roman stomped into the kitchen. Angel giggled, "You look like a bear."

I bit my lip, as his face turned dark red. "Is it normal to compare people to animals? Karma calls me a bat, and now you have called me a bear. I *do not* understand." Seeing his deep frown in the same room as Angel just became my favorite thing. Her bright smile clashed with his furrowed brows hilariously.

"Wait," Angel turned to me with her head tilted slightly. She looked like a mom who was amused, but fully prepared to give a two hour lecture if I didn't behave. "Why do you call him a bat?"

"I call him Batman, not just a bat."

She nodded, moving to my liquor cabinet. I don't drink much, but I like having my favorites on hand. "I don't think you can blame her for that, Roman. From what I've seen, it's pretty spot on. Plus I'm sure you're a wonderful bear when *you're alone*." She sang, pointedly ignoring my sigh. The insinuation went right over Roman's head, as expected. "None of these are wine, are they?" I didn't have to answer that. She knows damn well I don't drink wine. Instead she plucked my favorite bottle of bourbon. "What's this? Is it good?"

"Bourbon, and it's expensive. Please be careful."

"Oh, gross. Roman, do you like bourbon? Come sit with us, the table doesn't bite. The food is going to get cold." Roman hovered on the wall, still looking uncertain about the whole ordeal. I happily took the seat with the biggest plate while he debated. Angel frowned lightly at me before switching the plate in front of me with one with a slightly smaller portion, but still not as small as hers. She had a habit of saying I had a 'garbage disposal' as a stomach.

"What is this?" Roman finally joined us at the table. He dwarfed my chair, making me worry about the integrity of its legs.

"Those are cashew chicken lettuce wraps. I would've made something better, but Karma can't grocery shop to save her life. Why do you have *four bags* of beef jerky?"

What kind of question is that? "Because they might not have it in... Erm...,"

"Nantes." Roman supplied.

"Yeah, that. What if they don't have my favorite brand? This is *amazing*." I will never understand how she can make delicious food from the limited ingredients in my home. Maybe she's a fairy or something. Do those exist as well?

"You're addicted." Angel shook her head in mock disappointment. Ignoring both of them, I dug into my lunch. "Anyway, I promise the food will be much more exciting on Saturday, and thank you for agreeing to come."

"It is no trouble. I think it is nice that you want to see her off and get to know the person she is going away with." What? So he can be nice to everyone but me? Maybe he just likes strawberry blondes...

Angel cast me a sideways glance that clearly said, 'good job!' Now there's no way I'm ever going to convince her we're not sneaking around. *Great.* Reaching to the middle of the table, I grabbed the bourbon and poured myself a generous glass. "Karma, behave. You're being awkward." She took the bottle from me.

"I certainly do not mind," Roman smirked. "A quiet Karma feels like a gift."

Asshole. "You're hilarious, and I'm not being awkward. I'm just tired." I finished my food, but saved a piece of chicken, and called Roi. I tsked to get him to come to me. I heard a soft thump as he hopped off the couch in the living room, and headed toward me completely unhurried. Roman frowned, turning to see him stalk toward us.

"What is that?"

"My cat." I reiterated. Roi hopped into my lap and sat, knowing I had food for him somewhere.

"This is the thing you are bringing with us?"

"Yes." I gave Roi the chicken, and smiled at Roman. After he took the chicken I buried my fingers into his thick fur. "How are you still frowning? He's adorable."

"He looks like the Beast of Bodmin."

I don't know what that is, but judging from his deep frown, it wasn't good. "So you don't like people or animals?" I'm beginning to think he's lying to make himself seem more dark and brooding.

"I like real animals." He scoffed.

Excuse me? "Cats are real." As proven by the cat in my lap.

"A real animal has a purpose. Horses are real. That *thing* has no use. What are you going to do with that?"

"He's a cat. You're supposed to cuddle him, take pictures, and stuff. He calms me down. You have a horse?" I guess that would be where he got his title…

"Yes." He actually seemed proud of his horse. Then again, if I had a demon horse, I'd be pretty damn proud too. I already treat Roi like he hung the moon.

"What's his name?" Angel asked, shocking us both. I guess I'm not the only one who forgot she was here. Oops. I'm glad I didn't say anything demon related out loud.

"Ruin," He boasted.

"Aww," She cooed. "Roman, Ruin, and Roi. Karma change your name." I couldn't hold back the laugh at Roman's utter confusion. Now he's scowling at me.

"Are you *laughing* at me? You named that cretin 'King.'"

I scoffed, "You named your horse 'Ruin!' That's terrible. I named him King because I want to treat him like one."

"Judging from the hair everywhere, you succeeded.»

He was getting to me. I growled, "At least I didn't name him after a disaster! Who does that?" He gave me a flat look, eyes burning with anger.

"Well," Angel cheerfully interjected. "You two are the life of the party, aren't you? Oh, K, I'm almost finished packing Roi's bags. Everything is organized and I packed the stuff that I totally did not buy him and sneak into his suitcase." I knew it. Her purse was overly large this morning. At least it gave me something to look forward to on this hellscape of a trip.

火

My house smelt amazing. Angel had been here since nine this morning; it's almost three in the afternoon now, and I'm starving. Angel banned me from the kitchen around noon when she caught me stealing tater tots. Now I'm on the couch being miserable. Even Roi was allowed in the kitchen. It's not fair. A loud knock came from from the front door, nearly scaring my soul out of my body. Thank Not-God for something to distract me from my stomach.

Roman stood on the other side of the door, looking incredibly uncomfortable. His brows nearly rose into his hairline when he saw me, "You look nice, Karma." Oh. I wasn't expecting that at all.

"T-Thank you, Roman. You look nice, too." I don't think I dressed up that much. I hadn't intended to. I was just in high-waisted leather shorts, and a white cami with a cage bralette with black combat boots… That perfectly matched Roman's black pants and white v-neck. Goddammit. Angel was going to have a field day with this. *Dammit.*

"Is there a black and white dress code?" *God-fucking-dammit.*

"Hey, Coop. You're right on time for once. And, no, this was an accident. Angel is in a dress covered with rainbow dinosaurs." That she loved, and kept twirling in. I stepped back to allow the men into my house. They didn't waste anytime putting space in between the two of them. Roman entered first - something that seemed to upset Cooper. We're off to a great start. We all settled into the living room; me in my favorite chair, and the guys on opposite ends of the couch.

Roi came from the kitchen, and hopped into Roman's lap. Roman scowled down at the black furball, "What is it doing?"

"Honestly, I don't know." Roman wasn't exactly nice to him the other day. "He really only likes Angel, and me."

"You don't really socialize with that many people. Who else is he supposed to like?" Cooper snarked. He's just upset because he still has the scar Roi gave him when they met.

«*Oh, Cooper*,» Angel sang, poking her head out of the kitchen with a large plastic smile, "I need your help with something."

"In the kitchen?" Cooper was worse in the kitchen than I was. At least I had the ability to improve. Cooper has set microwave popcorn on fire. Twice!

«*Now*.» She demanded.

Oh, now I get it. She was saving me from Cooper's mood. Once he was in the kitchen, I moved to the cushion beside Roman. Looking slightly confused, he shifted toward me with his hands folded over Roi's back, prepared for whatever I was about to talk about. "You worked out everything with my school, right?" School was my main priority. I had made a promise to Mom that I would get my degree. It was the last promise I made her, I can't break it. Well, one of the last.

"Yes," He nodded, keeping his voice quiet. If I had wanted Coop or Angel to overhear I wouldn't have moved. "The *dean* was quite easy to convince." My face must have shown my disbelief, because he leaned closer to whisper, "Lucifer may have done most of the convincing, but I promise he is completely unharmed." To be completely honest, I didn't really care if he was harmed or not. Everyone knew Dean Whalen was a terrible person, but maybe setting *Lucifer* on him was a little harsh. Too late now, I guess. "As far as your school is concerned, you will be spending the rest of the school year studying in Nantes, France with me. You do have to come back in June to take your last tests and get your bachelor."

Sounds easy enough. I nodded, "Where will I actually be?"

"Where we were the other day. We will stay at the West American

Headquarters until we locate another Sin. It is a good place to continue your training."

"How long do you think training will take? Spending too long with that Domini guy doesn't sound like it's good for my sanity." Or Roman's, for that matter. Though, maybe having someone around that can make me angry would help with my magic.

He huffed, wringing his hands. "I am not thrilled about it either, but Lucifer gave the order for us to train there until we find the next Sin. Judging from the way he has been talking, I believe his plan is to have the two of us bring the next Sin in, and train them." That would be interesting. I can't really remember what the other Sins were, but I'm not too positive about having all of us in the same room. We don't exactly sound like a party. More like someone's worst nightmare.

"Sounds like a good plan. Though, I still don't think you and me in the same room with *Pride* is a good idea. Unless he's trying to build a bomb." Roman actually laughed with me, as I let my head rest on his shoulder.

He shook his head, still chuckling, "This is going to be Hell, and not the good one where everyone is afraid of me." It's so easy to forget that he's one of the top demons in Hell. It's so easy to just label him as some regular asshole.

Right on time to disturb the peace, Cooper marched back into the room with Angel on his heels. Seeing Angel's brows start to raise, I picked my head up from Roman's shoulder. Too late. Her smile grew to cheshire size. "You asked her to make that heart attack for dessert?" Oh, I expected this.

I rolled my eyes so hard my head throbbed, "You don't even eat dessert, Coop."

He crossed his arms tightly across his chest, making his muscles bulge, and is he puffing out his chest? I'm assuming that is for Roman's sake, not mine. Men are so strange. "So that's the plan then? You leave and gain two hundred pounds?"

Angel frowned, slapping his arm, "Really, Cooper?"

"Do not worry," Roman interjected. "I will make sure Karma does not become a potato."

I smiled, cutting into the conversation before either of them could make him feel bad for his attempt at slang. "See? I'm not going to be a couch potato, Coop. Roman will make sure of it." If there's anything I've learned from our training sessions, it's how much he enjoys kicking my ass.

"I bet," Angel giggled under her breath.

"Anyway," I glared at my best friend, but only succeeded in making her giggle more. "If Cooper is complaining about dessert, does that mean dinner is ready?"

"It took you much longer to mention food this time." Roman teased, earning an elbow in his stomach.

"Yes!" Angel answered. "Cooper, go set the table with Karma. Roman, you can come sit with me. We don't have to help, because I cooked and you're the guest." Roman shot me a panicked look as she led him away.

"Behave, Angel."

"So only *you* can be naughty with him?" She laughed, earning glares from Cooper and me. "I'm kidding! So Roman, I noticed your accent, where are you from?"

"Greece." He left out the city, intentionally I'm sure. There's no telling how old he is. The city he grew up in is probably ruins by now. Ooh, I wonder if we could visit sometime. I've never seen ruins before.

"Oh wow! I bet it's beautiful!" Roman seemed more relaxed now, so I didn't feel like I was abandoning him by following Cooper. Angel was mostly harmless anyway.

"I still don't like this Karma." Cooper sighed, bracing himself on the counter. "He's a stranger, and you plan on just running off with him? Do you even know where you're going?" He got the plates down carefully.

"Nantes, France." It's a good thing I'd asked Roman some questions earlier. I've been so distracted lately, I didn't even plan on the questions they were going to ask. "I'm not just running off, Cooper." I expected Angel to be the one to think I was running, considering she knew how I got to Monterey in the first place. I'd never told Cooper the real reason; I'd always said that MIIS was the best place for my degree. I'm actually kind of grateful I never told him. With the way he's been acting lately, I don't think I trust him not to bring the past up in an effort to make me stay. "I'm taking my phone with me, so you can still check up on me. Let's just get the food and go out there. Try to remember that tonight is supposed to be friendly and fun."

"Fine." He snapped, picking up the tray of loaded potato skewers, and a bowl of garlic roasted carrots. "I'll be nice to the Spanish guy."

"He's not Spanish." I grumbled, grabbing the bacon wrapped meatloaf and jug of sweet tea.

Angel was standing and giving Cooper placement orders, because the food *had* to be in specific places on the table. "Karma, the meatloaf goes in the middle. Roman, would you like some water?"

"No." I answered. "You have to have sweet tea before anything else." I poured him a large glass that he scowled at.

His scowl moved to my face, "I am not drinking cold tea, Karma."

"Drink it."

"No. It is an abomination."

"Dammit, Roman!"

"Karma," Angel soothed, prying the pitcher of tea from my hands. "It's just tea."

"No, it isn't. Look, I know you don't understand what's going on, but this is important. *Drink it*, Roman."

He growled, and took a small sip. Grinding my teeth, I took the seat next to him, and pushed the glass back toward him. He was full on glaring at me now. Still glaring at me, he took an actual drink of the tea. Surprise overtook his face making me grin, "It is not bad. Stop smiling."

"I *told* you it was good."

My smugness only made him more mad, "Boasting is childish."

"Anyway," Angel butted in, slicing the meatloaf. She knew my weakness too well. "Hold up your plates."

Roman mimicked my movement, and Angel filled our plates. He got more food than me. Again. So did Cooper! How unfair. Well, I guess he is three times my size, so it makes sense... No it's still not fair. I stole two of his skewers.

"Karma, you are not five years old. Don't steal." Angel scolded. "So Roman, have you been to Nantes, or is this going to be your first time there, too?"

"I have been once. It was some time ago, so I am sure there are some changes." Some time must translate to thousands of years.

"So you just went to France by yourself?" Cooper asked, as judgmental as always.

"No," Roman shifted in his seat, making my chair squeak. He was thinking hard about his answer. "I went with my, *ahem*, best friend." He glanced at me secretly asking if that was the correct term.

"Oh, that's right. You went with your friend *Luke*, right?" Maybe I should've briefed him on words that he shouldn't say...

I could see some confusion in his eyes, but he hid it well enough for Angel and Coop to not see it. He nodded along, "Yes. We went to Nantes Cathedral." He turned back to me with a small smile, "It is actually where we met Ace."

Ace was Roman's brother, and the Horseman of Death. From what I remember, I think he's the first one Roman met. Making him the second oldest horseman. "In a gothic church? Sounds about right." Unable to help myself, I used my thumb to wipe the cheese off his cheek. I don't understand how it hasn't bothered him. It was there for a while.

"Oh, thank you. This yellow stuff is messy." Realizing the distaste was clear in his voice, he quickly turned to Angel. "It is delicious, though."

"Thank you!" She beamed. "I don't think Coop and Karma tasted any of it."

"I tasted it!" Cooper replied, helping himself to another slice. I kept quiet. I had tasted it, but I hadn't savored it the way Roman was. It's her fault though. If she wanted me to savor it, she shouldn't have starved me for so long. "Bacon wrapped meatloaf is the best idea you've ever had."

"I must agree," Roman said, dabbing his face with a napkin. He was being much more careful now. I hadn't meant to embarrass him or anything. "I typically stick to… Greek food-" Meaning food from Hell. What does Hell food even taste like? "When I am in California, but I truly enjoy this."

"I don't think I've ever had Greek food. Though, I've always wanted to try moussaka, if I'm pronouncing that right?" Angel twisted her hands, glancing at me. She didn't want to offend his culture, and was used to me telling her if she'd got a pronunciation correct, but I've never studied Greek.

Roman didn't seem to mind. He actually seemed happy when he was talking about his home. I wonder if he misses it… "That is very close. It is very good, if prepared correctly. My mother would make it on my birthday every year."

Angel practically melted, "Well you'll have to come back with Karma, so I can make it for you." She was such a sucker for mom stories. Hell, that's probably the whole reason she put up with me in the beginning.

"That sounds like fun." My jaw hurt from how hard it dropped. Since when does Roman know the word fun? Angel has to be some sort of fairy. There is no way she's not using magic.

"What is moushsalka?" Cooper asked, butchering the word.

"No. It is pronounced *moussaka*." Roman corrected, not noticing Cooper's shoulders shake with agitation. Even if he did notice, he probably wouldn't care. Cooper is just some human to him. Angel noticed though, and was quick to explain what moussaka was. I listened until I realized there wasn't actually any mousse in it, and finished off my food before heading to the kitchen to get something I know has mousse in it.

"Angel," I called, "Where is it?" If Cooper has thrown it away, I was going to kill him. They can't blame me for burning him alive if I could do it from a distance.

"Freezer."

Yes! Cooper can sleep easy tonight. I brought the chocolate lasagna into the dining room, and sat it in between Roman's seat and mine. Roman's brows furrowed as he looked it over, "What is that?"

To everyone's shock, Cooper answered, "Chocolate lasagna. It's layers of crushed Oreos, chocolate mousse, and whipped cream. So basically food Hell."

Little does he know Roman prefers Hell. "Don't listen to Coop. Never trust people who work at a gym about food. It's amazing. Want a piece?" I was going to give him one anyway, but if he says 'no' I'll make it small.

"No, I do not think so." He was still frowning at it while I cut into it. "It does not seem like a good idea." He wasn't surprised when I placed a tiny piece on his plate - just in case.

I gave myself a generous piece, and was sure to look Cooper in the eye as I shoved the biggest bite I could manage into my mouth. Angel giggled into her hand, and handed me a napkin, "Did you get any in your mouth?"

"You're disgusting," Cooper shook his head, but couldn't stop a few chuckles from escaping. He must live such a sad existence without chocolate. He cast me another disapproving look, before focusing on Roman, "So Roman, will Karma *actually* be keeping up with her training, or will it just be you pummeling her into the ground again?"

"Hey!" I wasn't *that* bad! If I was it's his fault. He's supposed to be my trainer.

"He kicked your ass, Karma. How long did it hurt to breathe?" Like I'd tell him. Fucking traitor.

"I held back quite a bit when Karma and I sparred…" Roman

didn't mean it maliciously, of course. However, the only person at the table that knew he could kill me with minimal effort was me. I could see Angel wince out of the corner of my eye.

"If that was you *holding back*, you should go pro. Karma is one of the best fighters I've ever seen, and you treated her like nothing more than a fly." If he keeps this up, I'm going to kick him.

Roman frowned, now fully confused, "I did not mean to treat you as if you were an insignificant creature. I believe you fought valiantly." Angel squeaked quietly. "In fact, I believe you could win against Julius." Holy shit. I could see the sincerity in his eyes, he wasn't joking. Unable to graciously accept a compliment of that magnitude, I stuttered out a quiet 'thank you'. Fighting one of Roman's brothers - let alone *winning* - didn't sound like a small feat. Hell, he even looked excited about me fighting Julius. Maybe he doesn't hate me as much as I'd thought. At the very least, he seems to like me more than one of his brothers.

After Angel and I finished our desserts we gathered the dishes and took them back to the kitchen. The guys were quiet, but didn't seem to be agitated. Maybe they could be mature for five minutes. "So that Julius guy must be something special. I don't think I've ever seen you react to a compliment like that."

"He's Roman's younger brother. I was under the impression he was just as strong as Roman. It just took me off guard." As Angel put the leftovers away, I rinsed out the dishes and left them in the sink. "I'll wash these before I go." She did cook, after all.

"So he wants you to meet his family?" She teased, "Don't worry about those. You're letting me stay here while you're gone, the least I can do is clean up."

I sighed. We'd been over this. "Angel, even if you hadn't needed a place to stay, I would've begged you to stay here. I can't just sell my Mom's house, or rent it to some random that wouldn't care for it properly. It's not like my grandma is going to come down here and check up on it, and I'll be gone for months. You're the only person

I trust with this place. If you're so hellbent of thinking of this as a favor, just think of it as me paying you back for all these years."

Unshed tears shined in her eyes, "You don't have to pay me back, K. We're best friends. Can I hug you?"

"Bear hug?"

"Bear hug!" Angel's version of a bear hug was squeezing my waist as hard as she could until suffocation became an actual possibility. In respect for my dislike of touching, she kept them to a rare minimum, and always asked before hand. Even with limited air in my lungs, I tried to give her the best bear hug I could manage. I wish I could take her with us. I can't risk her safety like that, though. I'm barely on board with risking my own safety. "I'm going to miss you, K. Bring me back something from France, yeah? Something cool, like an authentic french cookbook."

"I'll get you the best one I can find." I don't know how, but I'll figure it out. Maybe Roman can use atheric to take me for like a day. Actually, maybe like a week. I would love to take pictures in France.

We walked back into the living room to find the guys on opposite ends of the living room. Cooper sat on the far end of the couch while Roman sat on my favorite chair. I'm half surprised it wasn't snowing in here. Cooper stood when we entered, "So you leave today, right?"

"Yup! We just have to pack up the car and capture Roi."

"The kids were bummed when Nikki took over. I promised I'd ask if you had time to stop back by."

I sagged thinking about my students, "I'll come see them the second I get back. I'll even try to come back for Christmas or something."

"Found him!" Angel bounded back down the hall with my favorite black fluff curled up in her arms. She stopped beside Roman, allowing Roman to play with his thick tail. "I thought you didn't like cats, Roman?"

"I still do not see his purpose, but I do not mind him coming with us. He actually reminds me of Ruin." Roman held Roi while Angel secured the collar he only wore when he left the house.

"Ruin is your horse, right?"

"Yes," He smiled the smile of a proud pet parent. "They are similar in temperament. Cats are not common where I live, at least not small, domesticated ones like him." Roi is actually a large breed of cat, and bigger than most full grown cats I've met. Then again, Roman might not even see an animal if it's too small.

"Cats aren't popular in Spain?"

"He's not Spanish, Cooper! He's Greek, he said that earlier. Behave." Angel sighed, lifting Roi from Roman's lap. "I'm going to miss you, your majesty. I snuck some treats into your bag so you won't miss me too much."

"You're going to make him fat. Cooper is worried about the wrong person you're stuffing with food." I opened the carrier, and fluffed the bed inside. Roman was going to be pissy about driving to headquarters, but he's going to have to suck it up. Magic won't be touching Roi for as long as I can help it. "Bring him over. If we don't get to the airport on time, Roman will be hell to deal with." Reluctantly, she brought him over to his carrier. I hated locking him in here, even if it was one of the coziest carriers I'd ever seen. It was a carrier fit for a king, Angel made sure. She must of also put in a strange green ring and a large piece of... Jerky? Before I could ask, Angel spoke up,

"Ooh! I got those for him." Well, jerky is much better than the dead squirrels Roi tends to bring home. "That's a catnip ring that also cleans his teeth, and that's salmon jerky. I put more in his suitcase." Angel placed the treats around Roi once he'd laid down, and scratched his head.

"As if that case wasn't heavy enough..." Roi had a fuck ton of shit he needed on a daily basis. His suitcase was twice the size of mine.

"Is it this one?" Cooper asked, lifting up the colorful suitcase. "What did you put in here? Bricks?"

"Cat food, toys, a blanket, kitty litter, and a litter box. Oh, and whatever Angel snuck in there."

"Oh hush. It's not like I didn't sneak stuff into yours too." What? "Never mind." She carried Roi's carrier out the door before I could interrogate her further. I rolled my eyes, I'll find whatever she snuck in there eventually. Roman grabbed my other case and followed me outside. We found Angel and Cooper beside my Range Rover. "See, Cooper? There's two more. Turn it."

"Fine," He grumbled, turning the suitcase how she wanted it. "You know, I still don't think it's fair that you get a new Range Rover every year, Karma."

I laughed dryly. "Perks of being daddy's favorite." Recognition flashed over Angel's face followed by sadness. "I'm fine," I murmured to Angel as I pushed the suitcase into the trunk. "Where's my boy?"

"Back seat. I folded out all of the sides of the carrier so he can stretch out, too." Oh, yeah. I forgot it had fold out compartments similar to an RV. If she had completely unfolded it, it was taking up the whole back row of seats. "Your carry on - complete with snacks - is in the back floorboards with Roman's backpack. At least, I think it's his?"

"It is." He nodded. How did he get into my car? Never mind. I know how. Seriously is there anything he *can't* do with magic?

"Good. Karma did you get your passport?" I nodded, closing the trunk. I don't think I actually need it, but appearances need to be kept. "I packed all of your snacks and made sure your liquids were under three and a half ounces."

"Anything else, helicopter mom?"

"I'm sorry. I know." She wrung out her hands, eyes misting. "I'm just going to miss you. Plus, Cooper will be a donkey butt any time I try to mother him."

"Because I'm a grown ass man." He placed a hand on my shoulder, "Keep training, but don't kill yourself." How heartfelt.

"I'll do my best," I laughed. I won't kill myself, but I might not get a choice on living through whatever is going to happen.

Cooper focused on Roman begrudgingly, "Take care of our

girl." They shook hands - hopefully Roman didn't squeeze too hard. Cooper rubbed his hand, trying to hide his wince.

"Roman, do you like hugs?" His frown was answer enough. "Can I give you a tiny one?" She smiled hopefully as he smirked at her.

"Isn't everything you do tiny?"

She laughed, and ducked under his large arm for a tiny hug, "Take care of yourself, too."

Roman actually returned her hug with one arm, "Thank you. I will make sure Karma is alright, as well. Especially if there will be moussaka when we return."

"I will make it perfectly!"

Cooper hugged Angel goodbye and headed to the gym, Angel headed back into the house promising to take care of the house, and Roman and I stood outside arguing for *ten minutes*. Finally, I won and Roman climbed into the passenger seat grumbling in Greek. He's lucky I don't speak Greek. Roman wasn't too fond of me driving, but it's my car so he can get over it.

"Alright, I'm going to need an address. Where is HQ?"

"Address?" He balked, looking around the car. "Are we taking this *metal box* the whole way?"

"Yes," I held up a hand, "Don't start. There is no way I'm letting magic touch Roi. It makes me uncomfortable. So figure out a way to get the address." He growled but spun his magic FaceTime. That bastard - Domini - answered looking like an angsty teenager.

"What is the address to headquarters?" Roman demanded. Domini smirked, ready to say something annoying, I'm sure.

"What, the great Horseman needs my...»

"Listen," I snapped. Roman and I were going to be in the car together for an unspecified time, the last thing we need is this asshole putting us in a bad mood. "We need the address, *now*. If you don't cough it up we're both going to take our frustration out on you when we *do* get there. *Or* Roman can atheric there now and start kicking your ass, and I'll finish you off when I get there. What do you think, Roman?" Malice shone in his eyes, mine probably mirroring his exactly.

"Fine. One moment." Domini grumbled, "Socrates, what is the address of this place?" A mumbled answer came from somewhere off to the side, and Domini angrily repeated it to me.

"Wait…" This can't be right. "This is saying they're in Telluride, Colorado?"

"Yes. That is correct."

«*What*? We were in Colorado the other day?" Roman nodded, "That's a *sixteen hour* drive!"

Roman waved Domini's face away, "Then let us begin our journey."

"How long have you spent in a car? Total time." I'm already dreading his answer.

"Never. I have no use for human's metal boxes."

Wonderful. We're going to die in here.

火

Five hours into the trip, and I was about to shove Roman into oncoming traffic. If it weren't for the lives of the other drivers, I certainly would. He wasn't complaining, but as time went on he grew more and more restless, and if he tried to turn off my radio *one more time* I'm going to shove an entire bottle of sleeping pills down his throat.

"Stop doing that!"

"Silence is better than this screeching nonsense. Turn the music box off."

I'll show him screeching music. "No. Be nice or I'll make it worse." He looked traumatized at the mere thought of it. I laughed at his horrified expression, making it turn into his signature scowl. "We're about to stop for gas anyway. So you can get out, and stretch your legs." And I can go to the bathroom, and go more than three seconds without hearing Roman huffing and puffing.

"Gas?" When I pulled up to the pump, recognition flashed in his eyes. "Ah, fuel for the box. It is almost impressive this world has survived this long." Honestly, me too.

"Oh, and Hell is better?" Yeah humans have knack for killing the environment, but demons can't be much better at planet conservation.

"Demons are a lot of things, but we never destroyed our home. Where are you going? The cat is still in the box." He followed me out of the car, causing the woman at the pump in front of us to miss her gas tank, and spill gas on the ground. Smooth. He wasn't all that great.

"Well, first I'm going to go inside and use the bathroom. Then, I'm going to pay for the gas, and come outside to pump the gas. If going to the bathroom is something you do, take care of that now. If not, try to stretch your legs a bit. We still have eleven hours to go. And I left the air conditioning running for Roi, but it's locked. He's okay." I can't believe he cared enough to ask about my 'useless' animal. Roman followed me inside, eyeing the woman carefully.

I had to pause outside the bathroom when I realized Roman intended to follow me inside, "You can't follow me in here. That's the men's room." He frowned, crossing his arms. "Fine. Just wait here." Hopefully he doesn't run into any children. He might scar them for life. Too soon, I had to go back to meet Roman outside the bathroom. At least that's where I thought he'd be. Where did he go?

I found him three aisles over with two middle aged women talking to him animatedly. Roman looked completely out of his comfort zone as they cornered him, but was still being polite. Apparently, he really is nice to everyone except me. Then again, the women looked like cougars who wanted to sink their claws into Roman. Can they be cougars if Roman was a billion years old? "Are you playing for the Chargers?" One of the ladies cooed, placing a hand on his bicep.

"No no, he plays for the Cardinals! You're a linebacker, right?" The other lady leaned into his side. So I was right, they were cougars that were also gold diggers. Can you be both? They're going to be so bummed when they find out he's broke. Is he broke? Do demons have currency? If so, he's probably loaded. I wonder what the exchange rate is. Do I get paid for being a Sin? That'd be nice.

"Karma!" Shit he spotted me. The women looked up as I came closer. They immediately pulled their claws out, making me laugh. That only seemed to agitate them more.

"Hey, babe!" What? Did he honestly not expect me to pass up the opportunity to make Roman uncomfortable, and piss off a couple of cougars? This is great. Plus, his eyes are begging for my help, so I'm helping. I slipped my hand into his, effectively pushing the one with her hand on his arm away. Plastering on my best smile, I leaned into him, "Are you ready to go?"

"Oh honey," One of the women purred, casting me a dark look. "Wouldn't you rather have someone more mature?"

"Or at least easier on the eyes." The other woman shook her head at me, "Women are supposed to be thin and delicate. You're much too… Too…»

She just kept waving at my arms. "Muscular?" I filled in, trying not to roll my eyes. If I don't get that under control I'm going to give myself a migraine.

"Yes," She sneered.

Roman took his hand from mine, and slung his arm over my shoulders. He was a lot less tense now. "I am happy with Karma." I leaned into his side, my smile widening. This is much more fun with him playing along.

"We have to go if we want to make our reservation." Roman actually looked excited. Who knew he was such a good actor? I didn't want to forget our new friends, though, and smiled at them, "Oh, and there's no way you two could keep up with this animal in the sheets. Wouldn't want you to break a hip or something. Stick to knitting." I winked, reveling in their red faces. Roman kept his arm around me while I paid for gas, and the entire trip back to the pump.

He didn't climb back in the car, instead he leaned on the

side and watched me with rapt attention. "Although they destroy everything they touch, their ability to build whatever they dream up is... admirable."

"Thanks. I think." Though I don't think he thinks of me as human, I think of myself as one. It's too hard to call me a demon after everything that's happened. I put the nozzle back, and turned to Roman. "I have to take care of Roi before we go. It'll only be a second. You can stay in the car, so no one else tries to jump your bones." Roman frowned at the term, but stayed in the car. Five minutes later we were on the road again.

Roman stayed quiet, and we made it a whole hour without him complaining about my music. Then he turned off my damn radio. "What did you mean when you said someone would try to jump my bones?"

"It's a slang term for sex. Those women in the gas station wanted to jump your bones."

"Ah," He nodded. "That was fun. They looked like furies." Not sure what those are, but they don't sound fun. "And who knew you could actually be considered attractive when you are not being petulant."

I scoffed, "Who knew you could laugh and smile instead of frowning and being grumpy one hundred percent of the time."

"So there is something worse than your screeching music; your pathetic comebacks." He laughed, turning the radio back on. Despite his best efforts, I caught him nodding along to The Chainsmokers on a few occasions for the next eleven hours.

Chapter Seven

We pulled up to a beautiful two story log cabin just as the snow flurries began to fall. I glared at the tiny snowflakes, pushing down the nausea and bitter memories that were threatening to bubble to the surface. The past is the last thing I need right now. Roman directed me to the "large door" a.k.a. the garage, and told me to park there. Once we were stopped, Roman hopped out to pull up the garage door.

"Follow me. I will send someone to get your cases." Rolling my eyes, I moved to the back seat to fold up Roi's crate to take him inside. "Oh right. The cat." He grabbed Roi's case from the back, and carried it inside. He frowned down at it, "This is not as heavy as your friend made it out to be. We will set up his things before I show you headquarters."

Roi pushed his head into the mesh on his bag, his big eyes staring at the snowy cabin. "Beautiful, huh, bud?" He mewled in response, pressing a paw into the mesh. "Speaking of which, last time we were here, everything was concrete. This is a log cabin. Right?" For all I know it could be magic making it look like that.

It wasn't. The inside of the cabin was just as beautiful as the outside. The door from the garage brought us into the kitchen that was filled with state of the art appliances. I placed Roi's carrier on the ground, and let him out. He went straight into the living room, following Roman. Roman already had the suitcase open on the floor when I got in there. Roi was sitting beside it, waiting for me to set up his litter box. Meanwhile, Roman got to work setting up Roi's elaborate bed by the back wall - wall that was completely made from windows - and was now filling his water bowl.

"I put the cat food in this tiny closet, do I need to fill his food bowl, as well?" Roman the cat-dad? How adorable. Roi rubbed Roman's legs as he passed him, confusing the brute of a man.

"No, we fed him a few hours ago when we stopped." I put Roi's suitcase in the closet with the cat food then turned back to Roman who was petting the lazy cat that was curled up into the plush cat bed. "All done. What next?" With a final pat on Roi's head he stood back up.

"Follow me." Roman led the way to a door on the opposite wall from the windows, and far from the front door. When we entered, I'd assumed it was a hall closet like the one we put Roi's stuff in, but inside was a long staircase with only one light bulb. Dear God, I'm in a horror movie. If a nail on this wall takes off any of my clothes, I'm going to kill Roman. I followed him down the stairs after closing the door so Roi wouldn't come down here. The last thing we need is a cat in this b-movie. At the bottom of the stairs was another door, except this one is made of a strange metal instead of wood like the one upstairs. It hummed under Roman's hand, then slowly swung open revealing the concrete room we were in last time. The room Domini was undoubtedly waiting in.

I sighed, "Can't I just go wonder around the cabin? I don't want to be down here."

Roman growled quietly, "Unfortunately, until we stop the end of worlds or a Sin is found on the other side of this rock, we are stuck here." On the bright side, Roman doesn't want to be around him either. We can be miserable together.

Domini spotted us immediately storming across the room with his chin held too high, "You said sixteen hours! It has been eighteen hours. Did you two stop to houghmagandy on the way?"

"To *what*?" I laughed. Maybe a little too loud, judging from Roman's face. Domini's tiny hands clinched at his sides as I laughed at him. "If you don't want to be laughed at, don't use words like hou... Hugh... How did he pronounce it?"

"Hough magandy," Roman supplied. He hid his amusement well, but I heard it. "He is asking if we jumped each other's bones." Good job, Roman. Look at him learning current phrases.

"Oh, ew." My spine hurt from curling in on myself so much. "No we didn't. Humans and cats need bathroom breaks. Plus, Roman kept getting claustrophobic."

"Well *humans* need to keep their flesh desires to themselves." Yeah, okay. That won't be a problem.

Roman led me past the grumpy brat toward the computers. A man sat in the desk Roman was headed toward, and quickly got up from his chair, and rolled another over for me. Roman nodded at him, "Thank you, Socrates."

The man - demon - bowed his head, "My pleasure, Sir Roman. Is there anything else I may assist you with?"

"That is all." Socrates bowed respectfully, and went to talk to someone at a different desk.

I collapsed into the chair he provided, watching Roman actually work a computer, "So, what class is he?"

Roman's eyes flicked to my face before refocusing on the screen in front of him, "He is a Nascent. That is how they are *supposed* to act when speaking to their superiors. Lucifer spoiled Domini, and ruined him." Is Lucifer capable of spoiling someone? He doesn't seem like the fatherly type.

"Okay," He didn't seem keen on explaining more, so I scooted up to the screen that he was so invested in. "So what are you looking at?" All I could see on the screen was a world map. There was a blinking red dot on the edge of California, which I'm assuming is me. Why is it red? Scattered over the rest of the map were a series of solid grey dots, and blinking blue dots.

"The red dot is where we discovered you," I prefer the term stalked then assaulted, but okay. "Grey dots are where we thought a Sin was located, but did not find one. The blue dots are locations of possible Sins. I prefer to check in periodically to see if there have been any updates from other diversions. Nothing so far." He ran a hand through his hair, "Are you in the correct attire to continue working on your magic energy?"

"Yeah." I wear the same thing no matter what I'm doing. Leggings are wonderfully versatile that way. Plus, sitting down for so long was hell on my circulation. Some exercise before bed sounds like a great idea.

火

Oh my god. I collapsed on the mat, sweat covering every inch of my skin. "Karma, are you alright?" Roman knelt in front of me, brushing escaped wisps of hair out of my eyes.

He'd had me doing the same exercise, but something had gone wrong. My magic was hotter this time. It didn't flow this time, it burned it's way through my veins. Black spots danced across my vision, partially obscuring Roman's concerned dark brown eyes. "I can't feel my legs. Well, I can, but I really wish I couldn't." I wish I couldn't feel any part of my body right now.

Roman slipped his arm under my knees, and one behind my back and lifted me from the ground. I groaned, letting my head rest on his shoulder. Roman carried me through the magic door, up the creepy stairs, and up another set of stairs to the second floor. He carried me into a beautiful rustic bedroom that was about the same size as my living room back home. There was a king sized bed in front of a large window that showed the mountains, and snowy drizzle. One of the other Nascents, who I discovered was named Lonan, had brought up my luggage while we were training. The kind demon had offered his assistance with anything else I may need as well. Roman laid me down on the bed carefully, and after checking if I needed anything else, he left me alone in the room.

About thirty minutes later when the pain subsided enough, I dragged myself out of bed to my suitcase. I pulled out my favorite pair of sweats, oversized sweater, and everything else I needed for a shower. I shuffled to the en-suite bathroom, and nearly dropped everything I was holding. There was a fireplace next to the bathtub. A fireplace! Two large windows were on either side of the fireplace, though frost covered most of the view. There's no way I'm leaving without taking a bath, but I'm too hungry right now. Shower first, then food, then maybe a bath. The shower didn't have any walls, just a small curb to keep the water from escaping, and a rain shower head in the ceiling. Maybe Roman *is* loaded…

I sat my clothes down on the counter, and pulled out one of the white fluffy towels and hung it on the shower rail. When I get home, I need to invest in some nice towels. The soap in the shower smelt like hand sanitizer, though. Even the two-in-one shampoo conditioner. Ugh. Roman is going to have to give me a day to run into town soon. I'm not okay with smelling like a hospital. Plus, I want to look around town, I only got a glimpse of the cute little town on the way in. I can even take my camera…

"Karma…»

I whipped around to see Roman standing in the doorway, and tried to cover myself best as I could. Why did I leave the towel so far away? His eyebrows rose to his hairline as he flicked his eyes over my nude figure. He focused his eyes on a tile behind me. "Thanks for not staring. Can you hand me my towel?" He kept his eyes focused on anything that wasn't me, but some how managed to hand the towel to me perfectly. I wrapped it around me tightly, "You can look at me now. So, why did you come in here?"

Roman's eyes focused solely on mine, "We need to head into town for food. I wanted to see if you were ready to go now. Well… Soon, at least."

"Yeah," I laughed, "Give me a few minutes. I'll meet you downstairs."

Twenty minutes later, I found Roman downstairs on the couch with Roi curled up in his lap. He stood when I entered the room, and carefully placed Roi on a different cushion. "Ready?" He frowned at me, tilting his head. "Your hair is dry?"

"Blow dryer. It's a human thing. I'm ready to go." Miraculously, Roman got into the car without any complaints after opening the garage door. "I have to ask; why aren't you insisting on using aethric to head to town? I thought you hated my car." Especially after eighteen hours in it. Even I kinda hated it at this point.

"I do. However, the cabinets are barren, and you eat much too often for the house to not have food." On cue my stomach growled angrily. Roman just sighed. "Do you need an address for town?"

"No we passed it on the way here." Roman relaxed into his seat, listening to the special playlist I made after my shower - a collection of every Chainsmokers song I have at my disposal. We sat quietly, and listened to the music on the way into town. All of the street lights were on when we arrived, making it look like someone took a town from a storybook and plopped it in Colorado.

"Why are you going so slow? Park the box somewhere, so we can get this over with."

Of course he's immune to the beauty of this place. I pulled into a spot in front of the only grocery store in town which happened to be beside a small general goods store. "Hey, you go to the grocery store; I have to run into this place real fast."

"How will you find me inside?" I forgot he doesn't believe in phones. His preferred method of talking to someone isn't exactly inconspicuous either. "In fifteen minutes, meet me in the fruit section." He agreed, and headed toward the grocery store. Hopefully he'll be okay for a minute.

The general goods store was tiny, but had everything I needed. I grabbed a box of epson salts, and non-shitty brands of shaving cream, shampoo, and conditioner. They weren't perfect, but they didn't smell like antiseptic. I only saw one person working in the whole store, and she was rushing through stocking candy bars.

When she noticed me headed for the counter, she jogged over to meet me, her blonde hair partially falling out its ponytail.

"Hi! Did you find everything okay?" She beamed, her bright green eyes looking a little witch-like. Can eyes *be* that color?

"Yeah, thank you." My eyes were drawn to her name tag, and I couldn't help asking, "Is your name really Medusa? I don't mean any offense. I'm just curious."

Her smile fell a little for a minute, but was back in full force in a few seconds. "Yeah," She laughed, brushing a lock of hair out of her eyes. "I like it though, it's unique."

That's bullshit. I scoffed, "My name is Karma, so I feel your pain."

"Karma? That's pretty!" I gave her a flat look. "I'm serious! I like it."

Oh. "Oh. Well, thank you. Sorry I'm a little too used to people immediately mocking it. For the record, I think Medusa is pretty badass." It takes some balls to walk around with that name.

She laughed, "Thank you. I'm not feeling like much of one lately."

I know that feeling. "Yeah, me either. Maybe I just need a different teacher." At least life isn't just kicking me. The only thing I've learned from these magic lessons is that I can't handle my magic. I'd like to blame Roman's teachings, but it's my fault. I'm not strong enough.

Medusa smiled, patting my hand, "I don't know what kind of teacher you have, but trust me, he can't be worse than mine." Then she froze, "I don't mean to be rude. He's helping me a lot, but he's so mean some times. I don't understand how someone can be so grumpy all of the time. It's crazy. I don't think I've ever been angry for more than an hour at most." *Jesus Christ. Really?*

"So I'm not the only one with a stoic, infuriating man that I have to spend time with?"

"Absolutely not! Do you want your receipt?" I declined, receipts are so weird. I was just going to throw it away, so why print it? "I'm actually known for being patient, really *really patient*, but it's like God put him on this Earth just to get rid of every ounce of my patience. He's like a general. All. The. Time." She groaned, handing me my bag. She wants a general? I should've made Roman come in here with me. Might lessen her hatred of the jackass she's stuck with. "Hey, how long are you in town?"

"I actually don't know. We're staying in a cabin a few miles outside of town, so about an hour, I guess?"

"Well, do you want to meet up sometime next week? I'm off Tuesday. We can do lunch? Get away from our overbearing men? Sorry if I seem a little over excited...»

I laughed, "That sounds great. How about one o'clock on Tuesday?" For some reason, I actually like Medusa. I don't know what it is about her, but I like her. Maybe we're kindred spirits or something. Especially since our parents got our names from the same 'What To Not Name Your Baby Girl' list.

"That sounds great. We can go to *Steamie's*. It's the best place in town. They serve burgers, by the way. Are you a vegetarian? They have veggie burgers too. Sorry I forget you're new in town. I feel like I've known you forever." Before I could tell her I felt the same, a large man walked through the door, making Medusa deflate. Physically, he looked completely different from Roman with blond hair and ice blue eyes, but he reminded me of my impatient companion... The one that was waiting on me right now. Shit.

"Medusa," He barked, "There you are." He stalked over to the counter, but stopped to scowl at me. This guy is the textbook definition of 'holier-than-thou'; she might actually have a worse companion than I do. That sucks. She seems way too sweet to have to deal with this guy. "Who are you?"

"Michael, stop. Karma you should probably leave before he starts talking."

Taking my new friend's advice, I grabbed my bag and went to leave. I was pulled to a stop by Michael's gorilla hand on my elbow. When I turned to ask what the fuck his problem was, I found him trying to stare into my soul. My teeth dug into my cheek as I tried to calm myself down. I really *hate* being grabbed. "Can I *help* you?" I snapped, feeling a dull burning in my throat. Heat rushed through my arms, warning me to calm down. Maybe Roman has taught me something.

Suddenly, the large gorilla hand on my arm got colder. *A lot colder.* It felt like I had dunked my elbow in a bucket of dry ice. Cold smoke unfurled from his fingertips as his grip tightened on my elbow. "Ow! Get your hand off of me!" I growled, tugging on my arm. The coolness turned to white burning pain.

"Michael!" Medusa - now on our side of the counter - threw herself into his arm, successful breaking us apart. I cradled my arm to my stomach still feeling the chill. "What is the matter with you?"

"Medusa. Move."

"No! You can't do that! Go, it's okay. I've got him." She smiled reassuringly, and waved me away.

I darted from the store, and rushed into the grocery store where Roman was waiting for me. I found him easily due to him being a goddamn giant. After making sure my sleeve hid my bright red elbow, I joined him by the strawberries. He frowned as he saw me approach, "That was not fifteen minutes." He grumbled, placing a large thing of strawberries in his basket. "What is in the bag?"

"Human stuff. Sorry it took so long, I couldn't find what I was looking for." Habanero soaked needles pricked all over my elbow burning their way over my skin. I took control of the basket from Roman, and practically ran through the store so we could get home faster. The last thing I want is that Michael bastard to come looking in here for me. I'd be perfectly happy if I never saw that asshole again.

"This is the fastest I have ever seen you move. What is the hurry?" Roman kept pace with me easily despite the comment.

"To get actual food. I can't live off fruit." With a slightly confused Roman in tow, I went through the grocery store, and grabbed anything I wanted and could eat with one arm. Every so often, Roman would pick something out of the basket to inspect it curiously. Which he did with potatoes, Oreos, chips, and broccoli.

"Humans are strange."

For someone who didn't speak more than twelve sentences on our eighteen hour drive, he sure has a lot to say about damn groceries. He grumbled about laziness when we got to the chicken and hamburger meat; quietly bitching about the honor of hunting. He asked why there were so many kinds of rice, and called me ignorant when I didn't have an answer. When we got to spices, and he asked what they were I realized I was essentially shopping with a toddler.

"Why do you need so many of these?" Has the man never seen salt before?!

"They make food taste better." He made a disbelieving noise, but stopped talking. For about half a minute. "Why did you stop?"

He was frowning at a small jar he was holding, "*Horse radish?* Is it made from actual horses?"

"Calm down. It's not made from horses. I don't think…" I don't know where it comes from.

"Then why…»

"I don't know. Do you want anything, or can we go?" He said he doesn't eat human food, but still put the horse radish in the basket. I didn't ask. Roman's gentleman side came out once we reached the register, and he paid for the groceries with… Something? Where did he even get money? We bitched at each other the whole time we loaded the groceries, because Roman insisted I was doing it wrong. He continued his complaining as he struggled with the seatbelt. Mid eye-roll I saw Michael leaving the general goods store. I was peeling out of the parking lot before Roman finished closing his door.

Roman's head whipped toward me, "Karma! The metal boxes are bad enough *without* the doors open! Have you gone mad?" Roman's jaw was clenched so hard I was actually worried about him.

"Sorry, it's just," Eh, I can't tell him about that Michael guy. Roman is an ass, but he won't handle the news of some other magical person in the area well. "We have cold stuff. Yeah stuff that has to go in the fridge, or it'll go bad." He huffed obnoxiously, and started grumbling in another language. Honestly I'm not even sure it was Greek. When I turned left I had to pull my arm back to my chest from the intense burning pain. Hopefully Roman was too distracted with his cursing to notice what was going on with my arm.

"Are you alright?" God dammit. Roman reached for my arm in the closest thing I've seen to concern.

"I'm fine." I jerked my arm out of his reach, and held in my hiss of pain. I have never been so happy to see that unmarked road. Roman hopped out to open the garage, not saying anything else about my arm or how I'd reacted. I left Roman in the garage to get the groceries, and went inside to find help.

Opening the door to the basement, I yelled, "Domini, bring your ass!" That should get him angry enough to come up here. Sure enough, I heard a crash, followed by cursing, and then Domini stomping up the stairs.

He slammed the door open a few moments later, "*What* do you want?"

"Hold on," I shoved him out of the way, and poked my head through the door again. "Socrates, can you come up here, please?"

Domini's face grew red as Socrates bounded up the stairs, "Yes, ma'am?"

"I need you two to help Roman with the groceries." I fixed Domini with a glare, "That includes putting them up as well."

«*Absolutely not.*»

"You don't have a choice, asshat. Something tells me Lucifer would care much more about my happiness than yours." Socrates - wonderful being he is - already went to the garage, letting Roman in on his way out. I turned to Roman, "Okay, these two are going to help you. I have to run upstairs. Be right back." I darted up the stairs without waiting for his reply. I slammed my bedroom door, locked it, ran into the en-suite bathroom, and locked this door too. The burning in my arm got worse as I struggled out of my sweater.

Holy shit. My elbow was now bright red and throbbing. The imprint of that bastard's hand was glowing blue in the sea of red. Magic is such *bullshit.*

"Karma?" Roman called from the other side of the door. Hiding my arm on my side of the door, I peaked my head out the bathroom door. Roman was standing in my room holding a box of strawberries, a package of hamburger meat, and a bag of chips. "There you are. Where do these go? In the refrigerator box, or the closet with the shelves?"

He didn't look suspicious of me. That's good. "The bag goes in the pantry - the closet with the shelves - and the other two go in the fridge."

He was scowling at me now, "This would be much easier with the help from the one who understands what all of these things are."

"I'll be down in a minute. I just had to do... Human stuff. Just give me a minute." Roman huffed, but left my room. Locking the door again, I leaned against it as I slumped to the floor. I need this pain to stop before I go down there. Maybe... She better answer.

Three rings. Come on... "Hey, K! How's France?"

"It's great. I need some medical advice. Do you have a second?"

"Of course!" Angel chirped. I could picture her sitting cross-legged on the plush rug in the living room with a cup of tea, and a notebook ready to write down my symptoms. Is it bad that I miss her already? "What's going on?"

"Okay, so my arm is really red and it burns. There's also a strange tingling where it's red. How do I fix it?"

"How'd you hurt it? Why are you talking so quiet?"

Some creepy guy did magic voodoo to me, and I'm being quiet because I can't tell my over powered mentor in fear of him hunting the guy down. Not that I'd mind, but that could put Medusa in danger. Yeah, I'm not going to tell her that. "I don't know how I hurt it. And Roman is sleeping so I have to be quiet. He's an ass when someone wakes him up." I'm not sure if Roman sleeps honestly. Angel doesn't need to know that, though.

"Maybe you should go see a doctor…" She continued before I could let her know how I felt about that terrible idea. "Never mind. I know how you feel about doctors, doctor's offices, and hospitals. Aloe vera is supposed to help with burns and take ibuprofen to help with pain. If it gets worse, you have to get it checked out. I can *hear* you rolling your eyes."

"That's impossible," She was right, I had rolled my eyes, but it's still impossible. "I'll keep an eye on it, and if it's not better in a few days I'll get help." Definitely not from a doctor, but help nonetheless.

"Nothing is impossible when you're best friends. Take care of yourself. Give Roi his daily six treats, okay?" Absolutely not. We said our goodbyes - Angel making me promise to not study too much. I wrestled my sweater back on, something that took a lot longer than it did this morning due to how many times I had to pause from the pain. Finally getting the damn thing on, I took a steadying breath and straightened my arm as much as I could manage before heading to meet Roman and the others. I could already tell hiding this was going to be a bitch.

Chapter Eight

Well, last night was miserable. Every time I rolled onto my hurt arm in my sleep, I'd wake up in immeasurable pain. So, it's safe to say I didn't get much sleep. I drug myself out of bed and into the bathroom to prepare myself for my morning training with Roman - something he had kindly informed me about last night during dinner. Apparently we are going to train in the morning, break for 'sustenance', check the reports on any other Sins, and train again before dinner. *Yay.*

I checked my elbow in the mirror, noticing it had become a deep red instead of that pulsing red from last night. I don't know if that's a good sign, but I doubt it. Angel had suggested every remedy she knew and could find on the internet, but none had worked. When I see Medusa again, I'll have to ask her what the hell that guy did to me. I wonder if he was some type of demon... Certainly I didn't accidentally run into one of Roman's brothers, and I hadn't seen that guy around here at HQ. After making myself slightly less zombie-like, I slipped on a long sleeved shirt and some shorts, and headed downstairs. I pulled my hair into a low ponytail - not by preference, but because my arm couldn't go that high.

I found the grumpy Greek on the couch with Roi curled up in his lap. He looked up when I entered, "Are you ready to begin training?" Then, he paused looking over at Roi's half empty food bowl. "Do you require sustenance in the morning as well? I noticed King eat this morning."

"I can eat something small before we start." He nodded, staying firmly planted on the couch with the fluffy snoring cat comfortably in his lap. I brought my boiled eggs to the couch, and turned on Netflix. I'd set it up last night when Roman went downstairs to talk to the demons about… Whatever they do. Roman looked curiously at my eggs as he settled into the couch, but adamantly denied one when I offered. He's so weird.

He watched me navigate the shows for a while before asking, "What are you doing? We have training to do." I waved him off. He could say that till he was blue in the face, but he was still relaxed. I think we deserve a small break after yesterday. Plus, Roi was comfy, and the first rule of pet parenting is not getting up while your pet is asleep. "What are you doing?"

I sighed, "Watching…»

"No, I got that." He waved my statement away. My hand itched to slap his. "Why are you starting at season three? That is not how you count. Begin at one."

"No." It's my show. I'll start when and where I want. He doesn't even like "human things", he claims they're time consuming and wasteful.

"Why not?"

"Two words," He raised his brows at me, so sure that my reason wasn't good enough. "*Ben Wyatt.* Now shut up." Roman frowned as I pressed play. We were barely five minutes in the first episode when Roman chose his favorite character. He even deemed him a "smart human" which I think is a compliment. With a smug smile, I turned to my grumpy mentor, "So, you like the show?"

"The happy blonde is annoying. So is that one. I like that one, and her dad."

"Ron isn't her dad, but I'm not surprised they're your favorites." Maybe Roman just needs an optimistic goofball to make him loosen up. That would be a sight.

"Penguins?" I laughed, and nodded.

火

All good things have to come to an end. Roman had added a new thing to our schedule - Netflix and breakfast - but as soon as one episode was over, it was time for training. These past two days have been hell. Not only is training with this damn elbow a nightmare, but any sort of physical exertion in a long sleeved shirt is it's own brand of torture. I don't know how many is too many when it comes to pain relievers, but I'm sure I'm dancing close to the edge of overdosing. The mark had moved to cover most of my upper arm, and was now transitioning to a deep purple. It wasn't hurting as much, but was slowly becoming numb. I'm not delusional enough to think I can ignore it for much longer. It's getting worse, much worse a lot faster than I'm comfortable with.

Currently, I was sat beside Roman at Socrates' desk. Yesterday when we checked the map, there had been a series of blue and grey dots that gave Roman some form of hope. Today though, all the blue dots were grey, and there weren't any new blue dots to be seen. Roman's shoulders sagged slightly, "*Skata.*" He ran his hand over his face, sighing tiredly. "*O Loútsier mas sósei.*»

I huffed as Roman continued to speak in Greek. I cannot believe irony of the situation I'm in. How is it that I've been studying languages, am getting a degree in translation, speak *five goddamn languages* - fluently! - and I get the mentor that speaks Greek. Ugh. "Well," I interrupted his ranting. "I don't know what you've been saying, but I'm guessing the lack of blue dots is worse than I thought? Won't more show up sometime? It's a big world." I didn't think Roman could look so hopeless. Especially after that rant that I'm pretty sure was mostly cursing.

His eyes focused on me for the first time since we sat down, "It will take time for them to find more possible suspects. Do you believe you would be able to recognize another Sin on sight?"

"I…" Michael's face flashed in my memory. Could he be another Sin? If that's how we're supposed to greet each other, I don't want to meet more. "I don't *think* I can. I haven't really had a chance to test it."

He quirked a brow at me, his inner asshole peaking through, "Was the long pause necessary?"

"I was thinking."

"It takes that much effort?" Was he smirking at me?

Growling at him, I pushed out of my chair, "I'm heading to bed, you ass. I'm too tired to deal with how much of a dick you are when you're stressed. *Goodnight.* Sleep well - if that's something you do." He rolled his eyes, but otherwise ignored me as I left. I tried to dodge Domini as I left; if I'm too tired to deal with Roman I'm definitely too tired to deal whatever Domini found to complain about. I'd probably hit him the second he opened his mouth.

"Wrath, I need to speak with you." My jaw immediately ached from grinding my teeth. It's not like he doesn't now my name. Yet he insists on using my Sin like it's my name. I kept my back to him, continuing on my way.

"I'd advise against that." Roman added dryly. Without looking at him, I knew he was watching Domini do whatever idiotic thing he was thinking of doing. For his sake, I hope he heeds the warning. I'm not in the mood.

Pain flared up my arm as his hand wrapped around my elbow. Black spots danced across my vision. All the nerves in my body were in agony. Before I could process my movements, I was facing Domini and he was on his back, unconscious. At least I think he was. I hope I didn't accidentally kill him. According to Roman, I had come close at our first meeting. My arm dangled limply at my side, randomly flaring with pain every minute or so. Roman chuckled, "Giacinta, put him somewhere out of the way."

A girl with long pale blonde hair, and ice blue eyes who looked to be about thirteen rose from her own computer. With one arm, she grabbed Domini's leg and dragged him to the other side of the room.

She turned to Roman with a shrug, "Does that work, Sir Roman?" Roman nodded, seeming unaffected by this abnormally strong child. She smiled happily at me, "Thank you, by the way. Hopefully he will be out for a few hours, so we can all get some work done. With Tehila gone we haven't had a way to shut him up."

"If you ever need me to hit him again, just ask. I'll be more than happy to." Thrilled, actually.

A snicker came from behind a screen somewhere, "I bet it's nice to win after getting your ass kicked by Roman for these past few days." His words were punctuated with a loud scream. Ha! Smoke came from the - now dancing - demon's ass, but not from anything else.

Roman nodded his approval, "Controlled fire to a specific area. Very impressive, Karma. You did not even melt the chair."

"Hell yeah. Can I get a high five for that? Just this once?" Despite looking agitated at the whole ordeal, Roman reached up to give me an unenthusiastic high five. A small scream escaped my lips as our hands connected. Wrong arm! I cradled my arm to my chest. *Why* did I do that?

"Are you alright?"

"Yup. Yup. I'm fine. Goodnight." I darted from the basement. Roman called after me with urgency. I ignored him, and locked my door. If Roman comes up here and finds my door locked, the old chivalrous gentlemen wouldn't barge in. With as much as I could manage, I slipped out of my long sleeved shirt and climbed into my bed. I could see my arm and the growing dark purple that was slowly growing from the corner of my eye. I'll find some way to deal with it tomorrow. I might just have to come clean to Roman... But what will he do then? Roman is in charge of keeping me alive, so what happens when he finds out someone tried to kill me? What would he do to that Michael guy? Would he leave Medusa out of it?

I rolled over, blinking repeatedly. My room smelt… Wrong. Was someone singing? Do demons sing? Maybe it's Giacinta? I pushed myself up with one arm, keeping the other tight to my chest. I wasn't in the cabin anymore. In fact, I'm not in Colorado at all. I'm in Michigan. I'm home. My duvet was still the deep maroon it was when I picked it out with Mom when I was fourteen, and wanted my room to look more mature. Though the large stuffed panther I kept by my bookshelf took some of the ambiance away. All of my furniture was still a deep cherry wood, too. A small sculpture on the dresser caught my attention, setting off warning bells in my head. I crawled out of the bed, and went to the dresser to pick up the small glass sculpture. The sculpture was of a mother and daughter in third arabesque, the daughters hand clutching her mother's. Mom had bought it for me after my first recital. I cherished it. After her death, *he* threw it out of my second story window, effectively destroying it.

This isn't my home.

I turned for the door, ready to hunt down whoever was singing and demand answers. Every muscle in my body tensed as I noticed the man blocking the door. Chills danced over my skin, as every hair on my body stood on end. The man stood with his back impossibly straight, with his hands folded in front of him, and his eyes closed. He managed to look relaxed and prepared for attack all at the same time. With the light from the window shining on him, his light blonde hair resembled a white shimmering curtain around his face. He was dressed in crisp slacks, a formal button up, and a long trench coat - all a blinding shade of white. He looked like an angel.

He looked like an angel.

Oh *fuck*.

His eyes opened, revealing flat and cold golden irises. They looked like Lucifer's. He looked over my defensive stance with a smile, "Hello, Karma." He had a deep timber in his voice, one that could easily be mistaken for soothing. To me, it sounded more menacing - like a python attempting to calm a rabbit before swallowing it whole.

I scowled, "Who the *fuck* are you?" I'm not a rabbit, and I am not too fond of the holier-than-thou mythical creatures right now. Or ever, for that matter.

"My name is Yhwh, or God if you prefer." Double fuck. I groaned internally, Roman is going to kill me. "I see Michael did quite a bit of damage on your arm." He nodded to my mostly purple arm that was slowly turning a strange shade of black. I don't have enough curses in my arsenal to accurately react to this shit storm. "I am willing to fix it for you."

That's some bullshit. I scoffed, trying to hide my unease, "For what price?"

His smile widened, "I just want to talk." Oh that sounds fun. God and a demon have a chat, demon dies. Seems pretty simple to me. I can't believe I'm actually missing Roman right now.

"About what?" I had to be dreaming, which means all I have to do is keep him talking until I wake up. Hopefully. If it turns out that he can keep me asleep, then surely Roman will find a way to wake me up. He won't let me sleep past breakfast or morning training. Right?

"Saving worlds, of course. Until you crossed paths with Michael, the thought of the Sins awakening as well had not crossed my mind. However, if you truly wish to save humanity, you are on the wrong team, my dear. Lucifer does not care about the human race. He plans on using you and your six counterparts to wipe humanity from creation, so that demons can rule Earth."

"How do I know that's not what you're planning to do with the angels?" I clinched my hands into fists to hide the trembles I couldn't hold back. Something about him was deeply unnerving. I'd like to wake up now.

God laughed, a deep threatening sound. It was almost identical to the sound *he* used to make before his control snapped. That *sound* in *this room*… "I created humanity. Why would I wipe out my own creation?" Is this a bad time to bring up Noah and the ark? Probably. Before I could bring it up anyway, he continued, "You are wary of me. Probably courtesy of your mentor. Who is in charge of The

Indomitable Sin of Wrath anyhow?" When I clinched my jaw and glared at him, he laughed and shrugged, "That's alright. Follow me, I have someone you will want to see."

Begrudgingly, I followed him down the hall of my childhood home, well the corpse of it at least. My eyes roamed over the many pictures on the wall, that were no longer hanging in the real world. I paused at one of my favorite photos, frowning slightly. It had been taken on Easter by one of the neighbors when I was fourteen - right before mom had gotten sick. Mom was standing in front of the large oak tree in the front yard. *He* had his arm over her shoulders, and was smiling down at her. One of her hands was resting on my shoulder as I beamed at the camera in the dress the "Easter Bunny" had brought me that morning. Mom had even curled my hair that morning. Her other hand was supposed to be resting on Nyssa's shoulder while Nyssa held my hand as she did all day that day. She had been so excited that our hair and dresses had matched, and honestly, I had too. She was supposed to have beautiful ringlet curls that reached her knees, gleaming brown eyes, and the world's brightest smile, but she didn't. Nyssa wasn't in the photo at all.

I looked over the rest of the photos lining the walls. Christmas morning when she was five? No. Family photo after I won top overall in my first national championship? No Nyssa. When she won her first spelling bee? Poetry competition? Debate? All empty. Nyssa wasn't in any of them. So many blank spaces. How could an entire person not be here?

"Karma? Are you coming?"

"What?" I jumped, whirling back around to face him. He seemed to be studying me, trying to find out what had distracted me so much. "Yeah, yeah. I'm coming. The... Memories sucked me in." If my subconscious was hiding Nyssa from him, I was going to trust it. I haven't even mentioned her to Roman, and I trust him much more than God.

As we approached the door of the kitchen at the bottom of the stairs, the singing was clearer. I recognized the song of my childhood. The specific sounds that soothed me to sleep, and stopped my tears. The voice that would hum my songs while I rehearsed at home. I knew who it was before I walked through the door, *Mom.*

She was dancing around the kitchen looking every bit as graceful as I remembered. Her golden blonde hair swayed with her, the curls never losing their volume. The long sundress she was wearing flared out as she danced around. My throat burned as I held back tears.

"Elizabeth," My lips pursed at the sound of his voice. I had almost forgotten he was here. "You have a visitor."

Mom startled, her singing abruptly cut off, "Oh! I'm terribly sorry... Karma?"

"Mom." Every fiber of my being told me to hide all weaknesses from him, but...

"Oh, honey!" Still as graceful as only a ballerina could be, she crossed the kitchen to envelope me in a tight hug. Lavender and vanilla surrounded me, instantly lowering all my defenses. It's *her.* Has she always been this tiny? I could feel my tears soaking her hair, but couldn't make them stop. She ran her hand through my hair soothingly, just like she used to do. I never thought I'd get to hug her again. How can I possibly let her go? Mom was the first to pull away, "Let me look at you." She smiled, eyes scanning over me until coming to a stop at my arm. She didn't touch the mainly black spot on my arm, instead she used my wrist to turn my arm so she could see better. "What happened?"

I laughed, "Would you believe me if I said magic? It's not a big deal." I didn't want to talk about magic, or me being a demon. I just want to keep hugging her. "I've missed you."

"I've missed you, too. *So much.* You're not supposed to be here, though. You're so young."

"I'm not dead, Mom. I'm just visiting like he said, honestly."

She frowned at Yhwh, "You brought her to see me?"

He nodded, still smiling, "I wished to speak to her. I thought she would like to see you again." He was trying to charm her into believing him. Judging from how tense her arms were, I'd say she wasn't buying it either.

Suddenly, a man was standing next to Yhwh, "Father, Gabriel wishes to speak with you. He said it is of upmost importance."

Yhwh looked agitated at the interruption, but nodded nonetheless, "I will return shortly." Gripping the Angel's shoulder tight enough to make him wince, they disappeared as quickly and quietly he'd appeared.

"Karma, do not trust him." I'm surprised my jaw didn't completely unhinge at her words. Mom had always believed in the grace of God when she was alive. Her eyes were serious though. Something was making her worry. "I don't know what is going on with Earth or with you, but I don't trust him. I don't trust any of them. None of the angels paid much attention to me until a few days ago. At least, a few days here. I don't now if time is different on Earth. Anyway, a few days ago some angels started "visiting" me to ask questions about you. Once that began, you showed up in the pictures. It was only Isaac and me. For some reason you were hidden from them. It was like you didn't exist." She wasn't saying it, but I understood. She didn't want me to mention Nyssa. Good. That means she won't tell them about her either.

I sighed. Every part of me wanted to hide the truth from her. Hide the fact that *he* was right. But she's my mom. The one person I could never keep a secret from, "I'm a demon, Mom. One of the Seven Indomitable Sins. That's probably why I wasn't there. I'm not human. I never was." Nyssa and I were always close, so maybe I inadvertently hid her too. At least that's one good thing to come from this.

Mom was silent as she processed her shame, "Does that mean you have one of the Seven Sins as your main personality trait?"

"Yeah, basically."

"Is it Wrath?" My head snapped up. How did she know? She laughed lightly, making me feel a little better. I missed that sound. "You've always had a temper, honey. Like when you broke Robert

Summer's nose in the fourth grade because he tried to kiss you." He deserved that. The principal didn't agree though. I was in in-house suspension for two weeks. Mom laughed at the memory, and pulled me back into a hug, "You didn't let your anger control you though, and I want you to use that same determination with this. I do not care what they threaten, Karma. You don't have to trust or listen to him just because he's God. *You* chose who to trust. I have absolute faith in your judge of character. You have never let anyone or anything control you. You are one of the strongest people I have ever known - even at fourteen. Demon or not, you are my daughter, and you make your own path. "She pulled away, tears running silently down her cheeks. Her hands held my head up, making me look her in the eye," There is so much I want to say, but I don't think we have the time. I'm so thankful that I had you in my life, and got to watch you grow. When I got sick you never strayed from my side. Even when Isaac could hardly look at me, it was you that made me smile.

"I don't care if they called you a demon and gave you some title. *You* are Karma Strickland, and you are my daughter. You don't follow people blindly. If they try to make you do something you don't want to, you truly embody Wrath and *watch them burn.*" She placed a firm kiss on my forehead, "I love you. Always."

"I love you too, Mom."

"I am back," A loud rumbling -that seemed to come from the sky - interrupted Yhwh rattling all of the white ceramic dishes, and making Mom and Yhwh frown. "It seems we will have to post-pone our conversation, Karma. Time to wake up." Yhwh disappeared looking incredibly annoyed.

"Karma. Wake up." *Roman.* It's a good thing Yhwh left when he did.

Mom looked at me with raised brows, "He sounds cute."

"Mom!"

"Karma!"

Mom laughed, ruffling my hair, "I love you. Now wake up. That voice sounds much better than any dream."

火

I groaned, sitting up in my bed with teary eyes. Roman called my name again, "Relax, Roman. I'm awake."

"Meet me downstairs, and hurry up." I could hear him grumbling in Greek as he walked away.

Exhaustion weighed heavily on my bones as I made my way to the bathroom. In my sleep my arm had turned to a dark black and now covered every inch of my arm from my wrist to my shoulder. *Fuck.* I slipped on a shirt and some sweats. Mom was right. I decide who I trust. The jury is still out on Lucifer and Yhwh, but the results were in for Roman. I wouldn't tell him about Nyssa - no demon needs to know about her. He'll just have to promise to not seek out this Michael guy, especially if he's tied to Yhwh. Hopefully he can undo whatever has been eating my arm.

Roman was standing in the living room waiting on me when I got downstairs. "That was actually…" He froze mid-compliment as he saw my arm for the first time. "What happened?" With a gentleness I didn't know he possessed, Roman lifted my arm to inspect it. I told him everything that had happened in the general goods store, repeatedly insisting that Medusa was not part of the aggression. Roman inspected my arm with glowing red hands while I spoke. He wasn't explaining what magical voodoo he was doing, but it didn't hurt so I wasn't complaining. After about five minutes after my story ended, Roman growled, "You should have come to me immediately."

"This isn't something I want Lucifer to know about. If Medusa is caught up in this too, we need to know. She might not be fully aware of what's going on. If she isn't a part of this, we need to get her away from that Michael guy. He's dangerous."

Roman nodded, "Follow me. This is too open." Roman led me back up the stairs, but into the room next to mine.

"This isn't..."»

"I know."

Oh. *Oh.* There was a pile of meticulously folded clothes in the corner, an open notebook with a fountain pen on the desk, and the slightly wrinkled - but perfectly made - bed made me realize who's room we were in. This is Roman's room. I guess he does sleep. *Karma, you are an adult,* being in his room is not that big of a deal. Except that it is. Roman is one of the most secretive and invulnerable people I've ever met. For all I know he was some spell around his room that makes unwanted visitors spontaneous combust when they enter.

In an attempt to ease how awkward I felt, I wandered to the desk and picked up his fountain pen. "I've never actually seen one of these in person. It's a dead giveaway that you're super old. You might want to hide it before you bring any pretty girls in here." I teased.

Roman was frowning down at his suitcase, but absentmindedly replied, "It is a little too late for that considering you are in here holding the pen. Found it. Put that down - *gently* - and come sit here." He looked up a moment later when I hadn't moved. "We need to fix that arm *fast*. Unless you have suddenly become paralyzed, *come sit.*" Feeling slightly robotic, I moved to sit on the bed. I had to beg for a high five, but a compliment just rolls off the tongue? He's so strange. Roman held up my arm to cover it in a creepy blue lotion-like substance that he'd pulled from his suitcase. "This is going to hurt."

Great. "I'll be fine, just... Holy *fuck*!" An intense burning sensation consumed my arm. My first instinct was to run, but Roman forced me to sit back on the bed. I couldn't hold back my screams as the burning seemed to rise a thousand degrees. I have never felt pain like this. Black spots danced across Roman's face threatening to overtake me. Cutting it off would've been easier.

"Almost done." Roman grunted, still pining me down, watching my arm. My nails dug into his arm, sending small lines of black blood running down his arms. After what felt like three years, but was probably about a minute, Roman released me. He carefully wiped the blue goo off my arm, ignoring the rivers of blood down his arm. "There you go." He murmured, looking over my arm. It had returned to its normal color, and I could feel all the way to each finger again.

Brushing as many of the tears away as I could, I smiled weakly at Roman, "Thank you. Sorry about your arm." He waved me off as he casually inspected the tiny wounds. I could feel the sweat traveling down my face and neck to soak my tank top, and noticed Roman was actually sweating quite a bit too. I didn't think I was that strong. "I'm going to shower, you should too. If the guys downstairs find out you can sweat *and* bleed they might try to take you down."

Now he looked at me. He was frowning, per usual, but it was more jokingly insulted rather than angry, "They could try. If you are trying to decide how to thank me for saving your arm, making that breakfast Angel made would suffice. Not the weird thing you typically make."

I snorted, "They're still the same food, you know." He wasn't convinced. There is nothing wrong with hard boiled eggs. One day I'll expose him to the monstrosity that is deviled eggs, and he'll never complain again. He did save me from possible amputation though, so I won't be difficult, "Give me twenty minutes, and I'll get started."

火

I don't know if Roman knows how easy it is to make bacon and scrambled eggs, or that he could master it in about an hour, but I still made them. I'd also fried some potatoes, and was heating up some jumbo flour tortillas. Cooper would be pissed, but he wasn't here. After the weekend from Hell that I had, I deserve some extra carbs.

"I knew you couldn't resist," I jumped at the sound of Domini's voice. Where did he *come* from? I was alone like half a second ago.

The little troll stood with his arms crossed, glaring at me accusingly. Of what? I don't know or care, really.

I rolled my eyes, refocusing on the tortillas, "I don't know what you're talking about. How's your head?"

Unsurprisingly, he ignored my question in favor of focusing on whatever had riled him up in the first place. He looked like a giddy little kid, the only difference being that kids are cute. "I am talking about your flesh desires. I knew you and The Horseman would be too weak to resist them."

"What?" I took the food off the stove, and gave the smug moron my full attention. "What the hell makes you think we did anything like that?" Last time Domini was in the same room with Roman and I we were on the monitors, and training. Not to mention, I think Roman and I would be too busy vomiting at the mere thought of being sexual with each other to actually do anything.

The twerp turned his nose up at me, "I came to retrieve him this morning, and heard the two of you His primal grunts and your *whorish* screams. Ugh."

Roman gets primal, but I get whorish? Is he jealous? I wanted to laugh at his entirely false conclusion, but was distracted by The Horseman - as his fanboy called him - coming down the stairs with his shirt in his hand. With a smirk, I called over to him, "Breakfast is almost ready. Keep the shirt off." Then I winked.

Roman wasn't confused for long. Domini's anger got the best of him almost immediately, "You are repugnant! Both of you!"

"Do you have a problem with Karma, Domini?" Roman stood protectively in front of me, effectively blocking Domini from me. I had the strongest urge to poke his bicep, but resisted knowing it would mess up our skit. I did, however, trail my fingers up and down his forearm where my nails had left little crescent marks.

Domini's eyes locked on the marks, "I have a problem with both of you, and your utter *lack of professionalism.* What would the King think of your fraternizing?"

I ducked under Roman's arm, and wrapped my arms around

him. "He's in full support! He thinks we should name our baby Vulcan after the fire god." For the sole purpose of seeing his reaction, I reached up and kissed Roman's cheek. Roman tensed slightly, but it was worth it when Domini's face turned bright red.

Roman - being an excellent partner in crime - held me closer and whispered, "I thought that was a secret."

Can demons explode? Domini is scary close. "You... You..." Whatever Domini was planning on yelling at us was cut off by a scream. If my scream of pain was "whorish" then his was certainly babyish. He continued to scream while jumping ten feet in the air screaming in some version of Gaelic about a *molach deomhan* - whatever that was. Then, in a whirlwind of childish rage, he went back into the basement like a good little troll.

Once the door closed, Roman and I doubled over with laughter. I looked up to see Roi come around the counter looking oddly pleased. Roman lifted Roi into his arms, petting his ears. "*Molach deomhan* means 'furry demon', though I think *kalo agori* is more fitting." He cooed the words in his native tongue at the purring ball of fur.

"Being a demon isn't so bad," I kissed the cat's tiny pink nose. Roman was watching me like I was a puzzle he was trying to solve, but my stomach growled before I could ask why. "Breakfast is done. Hungry?"

"I do not get hungry, but I am ready to eat." Knowing he was watching me, I made my plate first. Sure enough, he was intrigued by the whole burrito idea, and asked me to make his like that too, but with more bacon. I made his bigger than mine, much to his delight. He was eating before he made it to the table, and only paused to compliment my cooking. He looked up a few moments later, "You are not finished yet?" I rolled my eyes at him, deliberately taking a small bite. "You seem happier today."

"Yeah," I sighed, remembering my mother's singing. "Remember the dream with Yhwh?" He nodded. "My mother was there. It was really her, and I know it sounds strange or sappy but...»

Roman shook his head, "It is not strange. You love your mother and you miss her. Letting you see her was a smart strategic move. What else happened in your dream? You did not explain further earlier."

"Yhwh kept telling me that I was on the wrong side. He asked who was mentoring me, but I refused to tell him. I should've said Domini, the longer we stay here, the more annoying he gets." Roman allowed a small chuckle before motioning for me to continue. "There's not much else honestly. After he took me to my mom someone else showed up and told him that 'Gabriel' needed to talk to him. He tried to come back, but you woke me up."

He mulled over that for a moment while I finished my burrito. Taking our plates, I washed them off before placing them in the dishwasher. Roman didn't speak again until I was finished cleaning up the entire mess from breakfast. "Karma." He had come to lean against the counter beside me, twisting his shirt between his hands as he thought. "Did Yhwh mention anything about Virtues?"

"Virtues? I don't think so. What are they?"

"Virtues would be your angel counterpart - if they exist. There are seven of them as well." Angel counterpart? Does that mean Roman has an angel counterpart, too? Talk about someone I definitely don't want to meet.

"Wait, he did say something I thought was strange. He said before Michael met me the thought of the Sins awakening *as well* had never crossed his mind. If Michael is hanging around Medusa, do you think she could be a Virtue?"

"It is highly probable. Michael is the leader of Yhwh's army, he would not waste his time on an ordinary human. We need to go find this Medusa, and see how much she knows."

"Without telling Lucifer about her. Actually," Roman paused his march to the door, slipping his shirt over his head. "We have lunch plans today."

"Good," He nodded. "I will join you."

"You can't. We made these plans when we were complaining about you and Michael being assholes."

"And here I thought we were getting along."

"We are *now*. I had just spent eighteen hours in the car with you, and you were being an ass. Anyway, it's a girls lunch. No boys."

"Inside."

"What?"

"I can't come *inside*. I will wait at a nearby location. Michael is smart, he won't let her go alone knowing what you are. I will remain close by." Judging from the hardness in his eyes and the set of his jaw, he wasn't going to budge on this. Plus, Michael is an Archangel, the leader of God's army. If things go south, I'd lose alone, but Roman? They might take Telluride off the map, but he'd survive. I relented with a small 'okay' suddenly feeling how small on the scale I am compared to my mentor. I may only be one class below him, but my magic was a raindrop compared to his ocean. I can only imagine what Michael is capable of when provoked. I've already seen what he can do.

"Hey, Roman? Have you ever met him? Michael, I mean."

"Yes. I was there for the multiple wars with Heaven. Michael and I have met many times."

I nodded, "Have you ever met, I dunno, *not* with swords?"

Looking incredibly offended, he scoffed, "I am a seasoned warrior, and leader of Lucifer's army. I am the Horseman of War. I have won countless battles, and many enemies have fallen before me. *I do not use a sword.*"

The sword is offensive? *Okay.* "Sorry, I guess. I didn't realize swords weren't badass. What do you fight with, so I can avoid offending you next time."

"Double edged battle axe." He boasted. Though, he's being a pompous ass about weapon choices, a battle axe does sound awesome. I wonder if it's here... "You cannot see it."

"Why not? Roman that sound *so* cool! What does Michael fight with?"

Roman's expression said it before he ever opened his mouth, "A zweihänder, an ugly weak sword." I snorted, which turned to full on laughter much to his annoyance. He doesn't like swords because his frenemy has one. "I need to speak to Lucifer, and not be around you. Word of advice, change before lunch." I gasped, flipping him off as he disappeared into the basement.

Chapter Nine

I made it to *Steamie's* on time even after having to drop Roman off on the corner. *Steamie's* was a small burger bar with a nice homely feeling. I like it already. I found Medusa easily, at a table toward the back of the restaurant. She got up with a wide smile, "Hey! How's your arm? I know Michael grabbed you a little hard. I'm so sorry about him." She gave me a light hug, after I gave the okay, that I returned happily. "I haven't ordered anything, yet. I wasn't sure what you'd want."

"My arm is much better, thank you. Any ideas what I should order?" Probably shouldn't tell her that I almost lost arm thanks to that bastard. I still don't know how much she knows.

"I prefer the steamie, but if you like barbecue sauce I suggest the yeti." Yeti, it is. "However, I will cut you part of mine to try for next time. They make their own sauce, and it's *amazing*. Best burgers in town hands down. Oh, and you have you get a milkshake. It'll change your life." How could I say no to that?

"You might be my new favorite person. Don't tell my best friend who's taking care of my house." She laughed, drawing an X over her heart. "So how is Michael, and his sunshiny optimism?"

She rolled her eyes good-naturedly, "I don't know. Well, I do know he's never happy. He's been having some… Ah… Issues. With his dad."

"Medusa, I need to be honest with you…»

"Hi, welcome to *Steamie's*! Are you ready to order?" We politely gave our orders, though I was still brimming with irritation at being interrupted mid-sentence. Our waitress flounced away, promising to be back soon. For once, I hope she's wrong.

"Um, Karma?" Medusa asked, placing a hand on mine. "Are you okay?"

"What?" Looking down, I realized I had my silverware in a death grip. I dropped the utensils that were now partially melted. "Oh god, I'm so sorry."

Her eyes widened, looking at the silverware, "You're one of them, aren't you? Look, I'm cooperating with with Michael, do I really need two angels hanging around?" She moved to stand.

"Oh no, I'm not an angel. Honestly." She lowered herself back into her chair, though she still looked nervous.

"You're not?"

"Well, no. I am a demon, though." I laughed awkwardly.

Medusa froze, "A what? Do demons eat people? I thought this was a soon-to-be friendship…" That is a really good question. I don't think Roman eats people…

"It is. At least, I would like it to be. I'm not evil. I'm a normal person. I was raised by humans - like you - but when an asshole showed up on *my* front door, he told me I was a demon instead of an angel."

She shifted in her seat, chewing on her bottom lip, "So, yours is a jerk too?"

"Oh definitely." I laughed. Don't get me wrong, I'm an asshole too. It's part of the reason we get along so well. Back to the actual subject, "Are you really a Virtue? That's our theory, at least."

"Our? Does your mentor actually talk to you about all this Heaven and Hell stuff? Michael doesn't think my *tiny human mind* could handle it. All he told me was that there's an apocalypse coming, and that I have a roll to play in stopping it." Maybe Roman is right. This Michael guy seems like a righteous bastard. Guess my first impression was right.

"Really? Roman is pretty open with this stuff. Oh shit. Don't mention his name to Michael, please. Apparently, they know each other."

"They do? Are they friends?" She was much more interested now. Her glossy pink lips pouted as she thought, "Do Archangels and whatever yours is have friends?"

"According to Roman, they aren't friends. Imagine a fourteen year old boy talking about the kid that stole his first girlfriend." Roman had looked like a petulant child when he spoke about Michael. Medusa laughed.

"I won't mention his name." Her eyes focused just behind me, "I can see our food coming, but after we eat can we go somewhere without human ears and you can get me a little more up to speed? Would that be okay?"

"Yeah! I'll do my best. Being in the dark about all of this can't be fun."

火

"That was one of the best burgers I have ever had." I rubbed my stomach making Medusa laugh. Cooper would've even liked that place. Well, if he didn't know I ordered a milkshake. I'd never even heard of steamed burgers, but they were pleasantly surprising.

"I could tell." She laughed again. "You ate all of yours and half of mine."

"You gave me permission," I reminded her, bumping her shoulder with mine. "If you're ever in Monterey, I'll take you to *The Monument*. It's my favorite burger place back home."

Medusa led the way after leaning the restaurant. She'd mentioned a park that didn't get too busy around this time of day. I'm not sure where Roman was, but I doubt he'll have trouble tracking us to a park. There was a slight chill in the air as we walked through town. We came to a stop in front of the park, my fingers instantly twitch for my camera. I'm so happy that I thought to bring it. This whole town is a perfect picturesque landscape and this park was no different. The trees rustled in the breeze, the bright green leaves perfectly in place. The grass was all the same height, not one blade out of place. Flowers of every color decorated the park. We made it to a bench in the center of the park just as one of the many little birds landed on the back.

"Wait," I murmured, grasping Medusa's arm. She stopped beside me, looking at me curiously. I pulled my camera from my bag as quietly as I could manage. Medusa stayed quiet while I took a few pictures of the adorable bird. Lucky for me, it waited until I put my camera away before flying away. I took a few more as it went. "Beautiful."

"You're a photographer?" Her ponytail blew in the wind as she tilted her head at me.

"Not a professional." I shrugged. "It's just a hobby. This park is every photographer's dream. This whole place, actually." Its so still and beautiful here. I love Monterey, but it's hard not to fall in love with this quiet peaceful town.

She looked around seemingly unimpressed. Medusa shrugged, taking a seat on the bench. "I grew up here, so it's a little hard to appreciate it the same way a tourist would. I've never been anywhere else. What about you? Did you grow up in Monterey?"

I sat on the bench beside her, laying my arm over the back of the bench. I sighed deeply, "No. I moved to California when I was seventeen to finish high school at my grandmother's house. Then when I graduated my grandmother signed over my mom's old house in Monterey to me so I could go to college there. I don't know where I was born exactly, but I was raised in Michigan. I guess I'm technically from Hell? I don't know if I was born there, though."

Medusa was invested now. She shifted, turning to face me fully. "Do you miss it? Michigan?"

I let out a short dry laugh at the mere thought of missing that hellhole. The other kids who would either bully me or were too afraid to even look my way. The amount of times I was told just how unwanted or evil I was. That damn house. That fucking street.

Mrs. Downey who lived on the end of the street and would always mention how "sorry" she felt for my parents. Not because of my mother's sickness, but because they couldn't return me after Nyssa was born. *Nyssa*. That's the one thing I miss. The *only* thing. Maybe when she's eighteen and this apocalypse stuff is settled, she can come stay with me for a bit. I don't think I could set foot in that city. Let alone that neighborhood, or that house. I do miss her though…

"Karma?" I snapped back to the present. Medusa was watching me with the most concern I'd seen in quite some time. In fact, the last time I saw that expression it was on Nyssa's face. Years ago. "Hey," She placed a hand on mine with caution. "It's okay. I'm glad you got away from whatever was in Michigan." With a bright smile, she moved on. "So, I have a few questions. If that's alright."

"Of course. I'll do my best to answer them." I don't have all of the answers, but I seem to know a bit more than she does. If there's anything I can't answer, I'll just remember them so I can ask Roman later.

Medusa wrung her hands in front of her. She took a deep breath, her eyes locking on mine. "You're a demon, but you didn't know before you met your mentor?"

I nodded, "Yeah. I'm one of the Seven Sins, but thought I was human - and was raised as one - until Roman showed up."

"One of the Seven Sins?" I didn't respond. She didn't really seem to be talking to me, but rather talking out loud to herself. "I'm one of the Seven Virtues. Do the Sins have specific qualities, too? For instance, I'm the Virtue of Patience."

I balked, "Are you fucking serious?" She raised her brows at me in shock. "Sorry. I'm the Sin of Wrath. I'm almost positive we're each other's opposite. We're probably not meant to be friends." I laughed. That explains a lot about her though.

"We seem to be doing okay." She giggled, "Is it just us? I haven't been told if there's any other Virtues, but I don't think Michael would tell me. We're on a pretty need to know basis. Not by my choice."

"Doesn't the lack of answers drive you crazy?" I could never handle being in the dark like that. I'd strangle Roman if he tried to keep something from me. Well, I'd attempt to.

"Not really." She shrugged. "I'm sure to a great celestial being, I do seem too small to understand things like this. He doesn't seem to spend much time around humans in general."

"You are patient." It's almost nauseating. I would put Roman through absolute hell if he ever tried to pull that 'You're Too Stupid to Understand' bullshit. "We haven't found any other Sins. Yet. We're looking, though."

"Do you know what the other... Ah... Sins are? Michael said the other Virtues are Chastity, Temperance, Generosity, Diligence, Kindness, and Humility." It sounds like a church group. Medusa laughed, shaking her head. "We sound like a church group. The kind that goes *caroling* on Christmas morning."

"They do sound like a...um... *fun* bunch." She gave me a flat look, but couldn't hold it for long and started laughing. Thanks to Roman's intensive repeated review/quiz on the way here, I could actually list my counterparts. Not that I'll ever thank him or anything. "According to Roman, the other Sins are Lust, Gluttony, Greed, Sloth, Envy, and Pride."

«So... A bar fight? Are you sure you want to find the rest? One bad argument could get bad alarmingly fast."

I'd been thinking of that a lot lately. I sighed, running a hand through my hair, "I think so. I mean, yours sound like an absolute bore, and mine sound like tequila personified." She snorted, nodding in agreement. "At the same time, they are the few people who will understand what it's like to be us. Plus, we can't save the world without them."

"Right," Her shoulders sagged. "I don't know how I forgot that. It's all Michael and Yhwh seem to talk about."

"So you've met him, too? I've recently met Yhwh. He's... Not what I expected." He is annoying though. More annoying than Lucifer, honestly.

111

"You mean terrifying?" She shuddered. "He's so *cold*. I never thought God would be so scary. When Michael said I was going to meet him, I was so excited. I'd thought Michael was just stressed - being in charge of God's army can't be easy, right?"

"In reality, he's just like his father?" Seemed that way to me. They're both assholes.

"Yeah. Though, I don't suppose I can complain...»

"Why not? Some *jackass* shows up on your front door, drops a crazy amount of responsibility on your shoulders, won't tell you a damn thing, introduces you to one of the scariest beings in the universe, and a truck load of other shit. You have every right to complain." Lord knows I want to, but Domini would get all smug about how I can't handle it, and bring up his idea to lock me in some cage.

"Well yes, but you have Lucifer. Surely he's worse, and a lot scarier."

I shrugged, watching a squirrel dart across the ground. "I've only spoke to him once, but he wasn't like Yhwh. Yeah sure, he was scary and I couldn't really see any compassion in his eyes, but he was honest. With Yhwh, he looked at me like a pawn. Like some*thing* he could maneuver the way he wants and dispose of after. Lucifer didn't want to play games, though. He doesn't want the world to end. He doesn't seem to care if I'm on his side or not as long as everyone survives. I don't really know *why* he wants the world to survive, but he obviously does."

"Lucifer is better than God? That's fantastic." She gnawed on her bottom lip, "This whole thing is crazy."

"Definitely, and I don't think our "mentors" understand how much of a shock this can be to a person." Seriously. They just shrugged at all of this.

Medusa stiffened suddenly. Her eyes focused behind me, "Is that Roman? He doesn't look like an actual human male."

Oh *hell*. I turned to see Roman stalking into the park, disrupting the calm atmosphere. All the squirrels had disappeared from the area, and the birds had gone quiet. I told Medusa to hang on, and went to meet him. He stopped, crossing his arms. I jogged to meet him, leaving Medusa a few feet behind us. "I thought you were staying back," I snapped.

"*I* thought you were going to stay at the restaurant. Why did you wander?" He scowled down at me. Sometimes I really hate how *fucking* tall he is.

"We were talking about stuff humans shouldn't overhear. What did you want me to do? Look," I sighed, stuffing my hands in my back pockets. "You can't just show up. We're trying to keep you away from Michael, remember? So go back to where you were hidden, and *stay.*"

"Karma, need I remind you that I am not your pet. You cannot...»

"Karma?" Medusa came up behind me, holding my camera. She glanced at Roman before squaring her shoulders to me. She handed me my camera, eyes darting between Roman and me. "I should go. Michael gets angry if I disappear for too long."

Roman scoffed, "That is because he is a... What do humans say? Control freak," He nodded. "And an asshole."

Medusa snickered into her hand, "So you were right about that, huh?" Roman was getting pissed, so I held in my own laughter and avoided his eyes.

"So when you said 'discussing sensitive information' you meant talking ill about me? How mature of you, Karma." Seeing that I was still silently laughing, he turned his attention to Medusa. "Hello. Medusa, correct?"

"Yeah," She giggled. "Hello. Is there a formal introduction I'm supposed to do? Medusa Sinclair, Virtue of Patience. It's nice to meet you." She smiled politely at him, keeping her hands clasped in front of her.

"That was exemplary. Karma could never be that polite." Now Roman was the smug ass in the group. Smirking down at me he continued, "How are you getting along with the Virtue of Patience?

I would have thought simply being around her would put you on edge. Is that not the case?"

"No, actually. She's pretty calming." I shrugged. Medusa smiled at me, her pink dress blowing in the breeze. I could only imagine how mismatched the three of us look. Roman and I were dressed in black and grey with pants and combat boots while Medusa wore an A-line style dress with bell sleeves and flats. She's wearing pink for God's sake. "Oddly enough, we get along great. Maybe it's a yin yang thing." It makes sense. I feel much calmer around her. Though, I'm not sure why exactly.

"Opposites attract." Medusa supplied. "Not all of the time, though. Michael doesn't seem to like me all that much. The two of you get along much better than we ever could." We frowned, exchanging a look. Roman and I barely get along. Medusa laughed looking between the two of us. "You have no idea how the two of you look right now. Arms all crossed, standing with your feet equally apart, frowning down at me." I shifted, dropping my arms. Roman's just tensed more. I could even see a black vein bulging along his arm. "You're adorable. Do you have something I can write my number on? So we don't lose contact."

"Yeah. Good luck with Michael." I handed her a random receipt from my bag and a pen. Once she was done, she laughed and kissed Roman's cheek before heading back toward *Steamie's*.

Roman scowled at her retreating figure, "I did not like that."

"I'm sure she wouldn't have done it if she knew. I'll let her know how you feel about that when I tell her how I feel about being called adorable. Let's go back to the cabin. Did you bring the car down here?" He gave me a flat look. Of course not. Damn him. "Well, now we have to hang back and wait. The car is on the other side of *Steamie's*. The last thing we need is you and Michael taking Telluride off the map."

For the next twenty minutes, I took pictures of the park, and even managed to sneak a few of Roman as he followed me around. I wish I could go take photos in the mountains, but that doesn't seem likely to happen. Roman and I walked to the car in silence once we were sure it was safe. I don't know what kept Roman quiet as we made our way back, but it fully allowed me to enjoy the general aura of Telluride. Who knows, maybe even he's affected by the soothing nature of this place.

火

"Karma, may I talk to you for a moment?" We'd barely taken two steps into the cabin when Roman broke his silence.

I stopped, leaning on the kitchen counter, "What's up?"

"You said you dreamed of Yhwh?" I nodded, slightly concerned where he was headed with this. He leaned on the counter beside me, "Just in case, if you see Yhwh again, be cautious. He can be underhanded. He is a mater strategist, and will manipulative you the second he gets the chance."

I nodded, again. From our brief meeting, I could tell he wasn't the benevolent God everyone loved so much. "Yeah, I don't trust him. To be completely honest, I never have. Not even before I knew he was real." Church was always suspicious.

Roman raised a brow at me, "You keep an *angel statue* in your living room. Excuse me if I don't believe you."

"That belonged to my mother. It's one of the only things of hers I have left. After she passed...» *Count your punishments.* I squeezed my eyes shut, trying to block out the decade old echos. *I can't hear you counting.* I bit my lip, looking at Roman. He just sat there quietly, completely unbothered by my inner freak out. I took a deep breath, following his outrageously steady breathing. "I lost any faith I had in any God a long time ago. As a young adult, I figured that if he was the man everybody thought he was... Never mind. I hadn't meant to ramble."

"Are you alright?"

"Yeah. Yeah. I'm fine. I got the message, 'don't trust Yhwh.' I'm going to bed." I pushed myself off the counter, giving him the best smile I could manage right now. Once he nodded, I darted up the stairs. I can't handle anymore socializing right now.

His voice bounced around in my head, giving me a migraine. I slipped out of my clothes, fully enjoying having free range of movement now that Roman fixed my arm. Talk about another man I want to destroy. I wonder if Roman can get my magic strong enough to punch that asshole in the face. Just once, a second chance would never happen. How amazing that would be, though. Karma punches an Archangel in the face. I want to put it on my headstone after Michael turns me to dust. Roi curled up on my chest as soon as I laid down, purring loudly. I fell asleep almost instantly.

火

I stood in the middle of an endless field. Tall green grass that has never been cut seemed to go on forever in every direction. There wasn't a cloud in the sky, and a cool breeze blew through the air, ruffling the grass. It's oddly peaceful.

…And it's ruined. Yhwh stood opposite of me with his hands folding in front of himself, "Hello, child."

"I'm not your child."

He smiled softly, his golden eyes remaining hard, "Of course you are. Even demons are my creation after all, and I love you just as I love all the rest."

I snorted, "Sure. I believe you." What a wonderful conversation filled with lies, and an utter waste of my time. If he wanted me to believe his bullshit about 'loving me' he should have started a bit earlier. Even when Mom was alive, my childhood wasn't great. *He* never hid his hatred of me. No matter how much love my mother had, living your entire life knowing your father hated you was hard, to say the least, and after Mom died… Yhwh doesn't love any of us. We're just little simulations for him to abuse at will, and when we break, he just makes a few more to play with. He's like a psychopath playing The Sims Game. "What do you want with me?"

"Your help." Like hell, I'd help him. I'd rather jump from the Brooklyn bridge. "The world needs you, Karma. Together, we can save it."

What bullshit. I rolled my eyes, "In case you forgot, I'm a Sin, Yhwh. I'm not one of your puritans. Not to mention, I'm still atheist."

Anger burned behind his eyes. It looks like the real Yhwh is finally coming out to play. "I am God. How can you claim non-belief when I am standing before you?"

Looks like I found what makes him tick. God is a damned narcissist. I knew it. "All I see before me is an asshole with a superiority complex. You are not the God they worship. That God is a lie, and he is still much better than you. You don't love your creations, you love to play with them until they break. I've seen terrible things. Hell, I've experienced some of the worst things humanity has to offer, and *every night* do you know what I did? I prayed. Over and over. I prayed to *you*, and every angel I knew the name of, and you left me to *suffer*. Get the fuck out of here."

He sighed, as if I was a petulant child refusing to go to bed on time, "I looked through your past, Karma. Though your recent past and present are hidden from me. Nothing that happened to you was all that bad." *What?* The bastard continued, "Your father was doing what he thought was best. He was trying to *help* you. I cannot condemn him for that." He smiled softly, attempting to soothe me. Looking through my past should've let him know how big of a mistake that was. "You understand? There's no reason to get so worked up. Why don't you take a breath and calm down? Then we can continue our conversation."

Calm down? He wants me to *calm down?* I'll show him how I *calm down.* Roman's voice echoed in my mind, '*Center, focus, and let it flow.*' The ground around him burst into flames, successfully ruining his crisp white slacks. Good.

"Karma," He warned from the circle of fire.

"Shut the hell up. *You* don't get to tell me what to do." The flames around that *bastard* turned a vibrant blue. "Wake me up. *Now.*"

"Karma."

"Now!" I pushed the flames closer, turning his pants into shorts. With a pissed off expression, he flicked his wrist.

火

I sat up in my bed, breathing heavily. Roi rolled off my chest, mewling loudly. I pulled him back to my lap, so I could immerse my fingers in his fur. "You're going to need a bath soon." I murmured, burying my face into his neck.

"Karma?" I jumped at the sound of Roman's tentative question. I hadn't realized he was sitting beside me on my bed. That explains why it was so hot in here. Roman is basically a space heater. "Are you alright?"

"Not really, if I'm being honest. When did you get in here?"

He gestured to the bed, "I was controlling the fire you set on your bed in your sleep." Oh. I guess that could also be to blame for the temperature rise. "Bad dream?"

"You could say that," I sagged into his side. "Yhwh was in it."

I didn't have to look up to know Roman was frowning, "What did he want?"

"For me to work with him, I guess. He's an asshole, though, and didn't know when to shut up. I kind of lost it and tried to set him on fire."

Roman shook with quiet laughter, "You are the only person who could meet Yhwh and attempt to burn him. You are a true Sin, Karma. I'd even be proud to have you as a Horse... Woman? Horsewoman."

I smiled, tucking further into his side. "Thank you, Roman. Though, he might try to smite me after that. The bastard. I knew those ten commandments were bullshit." I sighed, thinking back to that clusterfuck of a conversation. Then again, Roman made me an honorary horsewoman because of it, and that is a lot better than anything Yhwh could offer me. "Thank you for saving my bed, and Roi. Can I be alone please?"

"Of course. *Alone.*" He nabbed Roi, and darted from the room. Cat thief! I bet I could get a great blackmail picture of the two of them snuggled together, though.

Roman closed my door all of the way - like a perfect little roommate. Luckily, my phone wasn't affected by the heat. I should probably thank Roman for that too. I dialed Medusa's number, hoping she was still awake. She answered on the second ring, "Karma?" Her sleepy voice, accompanied with a yawn came over the phone in a whisper. "It's three in the morning...»

"I know. I'm sorry. I just...»

"It's okay. What's up?" She yawned again. I shouldn't have called her. I didn't even check the time.

"Michael and Yhwh are close right?"

"Yeah, I think so. Why?" She seemed a bit more awake now.

"I just spoke with him. Yhwh not Michael. Be careful around them, okay? Yhwh said somethings that make me really uncomfortable. I'm not so sure about my side of things either, but I know for sure there's something wrong with Yhwh." *Nothing that happened to you was that bad.* No one in their right mind would believe that.

"Okay, I will be careful. Karma, is everything okay? You're worrying me." She sounded fully awake now, and overwhelmingly concerned. "What's the matter? Be honest." Is this what people mean when they say 'Mom Friend?' Medusa does sort of remind me of Mom. Maybe that's why I like her so much.

I sighed, resting my head on the headboard, "He brought up the worst parts of my past, and just shrugged them off like they were nothing. There are a lot of things in my past that are living nightmares. *Nightmares.* He looked me in the eye and told me they weren't that bad. He said he couldn't condemn my... Assailant for what he did. Anyone who says that about what I went through...»

"Is heartless." She finished. I could practically see her pulling on her hair. "I don't know what you went through - which is fine, you don't have to talk about it - and I will be extra careful. Maybe add an extra extra in that. Thank you for the warning," She sighed, "I wish I could do the same. They don't tell me anything. They just boss me around."

"Just focus on being there for the other Virtues. Judging from our experiences, they're going to need it. I think if we can trust each other, it doesn't matter what Lucifer and Yhwh are doing. I'm sorry for waking you up. I'll let you go back to sleep." Now that I'd talked it out, at least a little, I was feeling ready to relax again.

"It's more than okay. You can wake me up any time." She laughed, "I agree, though. As long as we're united with each other, it doesn't matter what those trigger happy gods are up to. Goodnight, Karma. Try to get some sleep."

"I'll do my best. Goodnight, and *be safe.*" Now to go rescue my cat, and get that picture.

Chapter Ten

"All you have to do is focus your energy. You have made excellent progress over the past few weeks." Roman - despite his "confidence" in me - was hanging back. Far enough away that no explosion caused by me would touch him. I thought he had said my magic couldn't hurt him. "Remember to breathe. The magic has to flow through you. You cannot force it."

I took a deep breath, and focused on the lantern again. My goal was to light said lantern using only my magic. Roman said that limiting my magic to a single spot without burning anything else was a big step. A big, complicated step. I can feel the power in my veins, but I can't access it for some reason. Roman was silent behind me, but I could feel his impatience. I growled - a terrible habit I picked up from the resident cat thief - and dropped my hands, "Why is being a demon so *damn* difficult?"

Suddenly, the lantern in front of us exploded. Roman pulled me behind him, shielding me from the oncoming glass. Once it was all scattered around the floor, I turned Roman around to brush the glass out of his hair. Roman sighed, trying to get me to meet his eyes. "I know anger is easier, but if you want to get better..."

"I have to focus." I redid my ponytail, stepping out of the training area. "Faas, can you come clean up all of this glass, please?" I'd befriended most of the staff around here already, much to Domini's fury. Faas was a sweet guy - Roman said he was a Brownie, whatever that is - and that made him a prime target for Domini. I love him though. He always seemed to be carrying some form of food. Even now he had a five pound bag of Skittles with him. He skipped to the supply closet, munching on a handful of Skittles.

"I'm going to take a break, and get a snack." Roman looked ready to drag me back to the training area, but I was gone before he could grab me again.

I collapsed onto the couch beside Roi with an apple and the entire jar of peanut butter. Roman said that I was improving, but I don't see it. Every time I take a step forward, I take three backwards. The only thing that has stopped me from trying to blow a hole in a mountain is Medusa. We didn't text constantly, but tried to check in at least once a day. It's nice knowing I have someone to talk to besides Roman that understands all this Heaven and Hell shit. I just hope she's handling everything okay.

Roman came through the door with his head low. He's been looking more tired lately, but - in true Roman fashion - he wasn't sharing the reason. He sat beside me on the couch, putting Roi in his lap, and stole one of my peanut butter covered apple slices. "This is not bad." He commented, taking another.

"Thanks. Can you grab another apple now that we're suddenly sharing?" He nodded, munching on his third, and went to fetch it. We ate in silence, both lost in thought. Angel had face-timed us the other day. It had given us both a big boost in morale for a few days that helped us get a lot more done. Cooper had called as well, but he was much less fun to talk to. Apparently, he's still pissed about me leaving. I can't believe I broke another one of Roman's lanterns. That's the fifth one this week, and it's only Wednesday.

After a few moments of silence, Roman spoke up, "What do you call it when you do not wish to be where you are, and instead wish to be home?"

Trying to hide my complete and utter surprise at this conversation, I focused on my apple slice. "Homesick. It's called being homesick." Roman nodded, taking another slice. Is he not going to say anything? He doesn't really expect me to just be quiet after that, right? "Are… Are you homesick for Hell or Greece?" That earned me a flat look.

"Greece has not been my home in centuries." Well *excuse me*. I haven't lived in Michigan in almost ten years, but I still know where I'm from. I guess we're eating in silence again. "I am going to return to Hell for a brief time. I assume you want to stay here?"

I choked, on absolutely nothing. Roman - being the overly helpful bastard he is - merely sat there watching me. By the time I got ahold of myself, Roman had finished all remaining apple slices. Now he just sat there, staring impassively at me while I tried not to cough up my insides. "Water." I finally managed to wheeze. Roman looked surprised, and went to grab a bottle of water. He even opened it for me. How sweet. I want to strangle him.

"Is that normal? The endless coughing, I mean."

"Not really," I was still coughing slightly, but I could breathe a little bit now. "Anyway, I'd like to go with you. Can I meet Lucifer in person while we're there?" The best way to get to know a place is with a local, right? Roman is as local as they come. Plus, I'm not missing out on Hell. So many people said they'd see me there.

"Yes. You are his favorite person right now. Try to bring a single small bag, we're traveling with atheric."

"Fine, but I'm bringing Roi. You can't stop me."

"I have learned that lesson. Plus," Roman scratched behind the traitor's ears. "Eirian is going to love him."

"Eirian?" Who is he trying to introduce my baby to? He never spoke about Hell except about Lucifer, and occasionally his brothers. He was always vague about them though. "Is she a demon?" I guess she lives in Hell, so that's a dumb question.

"Sort of. She is ranked among the demons, but I believe she would be called a sub-species. Eirian is a Sprite."

"Like a fairy?" Sprites are basically pixies, right?

"That is not wise. I do not recommend calling her a fairy to her face. Fairy is a human term. They prefer Sprite." Well shit. I'm glad I didn't offend her. Offending one of Roman's friends is not something I want to do.

"So, when do we leave?" I'm actually excited about this.

"Tomorrow morning?"

What? Roman is notoriously impatient. Why would he give me so much time? Roman caught my confused glare, and returned it with his most innocent look. Too innocent for him. I peered at him, trying to find his motive. Wait a minute... "You want me to cook something." It wasn't a question. Roman had developed a secret love of human food, and - thanks to Angel and FaceTime - my cooking skill had greatly improved. My cooking was basically Roman's version of a sweet tooth. "What do you want?"

"The best thing you can think of?"

"Challenge accepted. I'll only take an hour or two to pack, and then I'll start cooking." He waved me away, too focused on cuddling my cat.

火

It was well after dark when I sought Roman out again. I found him in the backyard with my camera, and my cat. Thank not-god I saved the photo of him and Roi I took in several places. He definitely deleted it. "What are you doing?"

Roman looked up from his crouched position in the snow, "I saw you doing this the other day. Thought I'd try it."

I laughed. The mighty Horseman of War was taking cat photos in the snow. It sounds like a Tumblr post. I helped him adjust to a better, more comfortable position, and let him snap away. I have plenty of extra memory cards already packed anyway. Ooh I wonder if I could get Lucifer to take a selfie. I bet he would.

"Miss Karma?" Socrates popped his head out the door with a nervous smile, "We have set the table as you have asked."

"Sweet! Come on boys, it's dinner time." At the 'D' word, Roi darted into the house through Socrates's legs, leaving Roman and I in the snow. Roman waved for me to go in first. He wasn't being a gentleman, he was just distracted by the pictures he took. Inside we found Giacinta, Faas, Socrates, and Domini all standing around the large wooden table. On the table were two massive lasagnas, a tower of garlic bread, and a bowl of Italian roasted potatoes. Roman was practically drooling.

"Why is Domini here?" He asked, pulling out my favorite chair for me.

"Because, this is our 'Farewell for Now' dinner, and we should have a proper goodbye." I answered, taking my seat. "Plus, he's been refusing to eat my cooking since we got here."

Roman scoffed, taking his own seat, "*That* is not something you can blame him for. If Angel had not been walking you through the steps, I too would have been apprehensive."

"Fuck off. I did fantastic." That earned me a glare, but he didn't reply.

Socrates, who had a knack for perfection, took over the serving. Each serving turned out to be perfectly proportioned, and placed the exact same way on every plate. Angel would love him. I sent her a picture of the table, being sure to get everything. Roman even smiled for it. No one else at the table seemed to see it, but Angel would appreciate it.

"I am an immortal demon! Why did you insist on my presence?" Domini bitched, scowling down at his plate.

"Because I enjoy making you do things you don't like, and I really want you to try my cooking. I'll be really offended if you don't try it when I worked so hard. I'd hate to tell Lucifer that you hurt my feelings right before I left." Domini paled at that. It was almost comical. I beamed as he picked up his fork. He didn't take a bite though. In fact, no one had. They were all looking at Roman - who was looking at me.

"The head of the table takes the first bite," Roman explained, "Go ahead."

"Um, excuse me?" Faas cut in with a shaky voice, "Sir Roman, you outrank Miss Karma."

"I am aware, Faas." Roman had started using more of their names thanks to my urging. Domini only got varying versions of 'asshole' but I already know there's no point in trying to change that. "Karma."

I don't really understand the point of this, but they all seemed serious and the food is getting cold, so I did as I was told - that's definitely a first - and took the first bite. Everyone began eating after that, pausing every now and then to express their compliments. Even Domini - albeit begrudgingly - complimented my cooking. Roman ended up eating three servings, and backed out halfway through his fourth. Angel would be so proud of me. Once everyone had their fill, Giacinta stayed behind to help me pack up the food.

"Are you taking some of these to the King?" She asked. I paused, looking over the table. We did have a lot of leftovers some of which were headed downstairs, but I hadn't considered bringing some to Lucifer.

Roman - who was helping Socrates wash dishes - spoke up before I could reply, "He would probably love that."

"Okay," I shrugged. As long as they get eaten, I don't care. "I'll bring half of them with us, then." I moved some of the sealed containers to my bag. "I'll see you in the morning, Roman. Goodnight, guys!" Everyone called their 'goodnights' as I made my way up the stairs with Roi on my heels.

火

Once I was in my pajamas, I dialed a number that had been deleted over a month ago, and would be deleted from my call log after I hung up. She answered on the third ring, "Karma?"

"Hey, kiddo. How's everything back home?"

She sighed, "I'm not a kid anymore. Everything is fine. You

know how Dad can be." Nyssa sounded down. That could only mean one thing, *he* was drinking again. Dammit.

I pinched the bridge of my nose, trying to stop the anger from seeping into my voice. She didn't need me angry right now. I don't want to scare her. "I'm sorry, Nys. I thought with me gone...»

"I know, and you weren't wrong. He's been a lot better." She hesitated. I could practically picture her sitting in the middle of her bed, gnawing on her bottom lip. It's always been a bad habit of hers. "It's almost the twenty-first." Right. I hadn't forgotten, no matter how hard I tried. The anniversary of Mom's death is in a few days. I hadn't thought about how it would affect Nyssa though. I should've known *he'd* turn back to the bottle. God forbid he actually try to console his daughter.

"Angel is watching the house. If you need to get far away from him for a few days, she'll let you in. She knows the basics. I'd tell you to go to Gram's but she's in the Bahamas."

She scoffed, "He'd call the cops. He doesn't want me here, but he also doesn't want me to leave. I wish I could be you. Your life is so much cooler than mine."

Oh if only she knew. "You don't want to be me, kid. My life is no picnic. It never has been."

"That's not what I meant," She sighed again. I wish I could do something to cheer her up. "Just forget it. I've just been missing you and Mom a lot. Do you ever miss the days when we were a family?"

"Of course I do. I miss you and Mom every day, and I know she misses us too." Nyssa snorted, clearly not believing me. After Mom's death and *his* spiral, Nyssa swore off religion. She claimed that a real God wouldn't have let this happen. I could only imagine how pissed she would be if she knew the true "God" behind the curtain. *What happened to you wasn't that bad.* That bastard.

"Maybe you can come up for a visit on winter break?" For the first time since answering the phone, my sister sounded cheery. It was faint, but I could hear it.

I smiled at the foreign sound. I wish I could make her the

carefree kid she used to be. "That sounds like a blast. I'll figure out a way to get up there. Hot chocolate and Disney movies?"

"And blanket forts!" Right. I can't forget her favorite part. "Maybe Roi can come too? I wanna meet that little tyrant. Your pictures are amazing, but I want to see if he's as soft as he looks." I laughed thinking of my little furball that was probably curled up with Roman somewhere.

Roman. Shit. I'll have to find a way to ditch him for a few days while I go see her. That's going to be a pain in the ass. Maybe he'll get homesick again...

"Oh!" Nyssa exclaimed, killing my train of thought. "Guess who's coming home for Christmas!»

"Who?" I groaned. If she's this excited, I was going to hate the answer.

"Rob Summer!!" She cackled. I groaned, again. I'd be happy if I never saw him again. Nyssa continued her witch impression, "This is going to be the best Christmas ever." In the background, I heard a door slam followed by crashes and curses. *He* must've just gotten home and from the sound of it, he'd drank his weight at the bar. "I have to go. I love you, sis."

"I love you, too. Call me if you need anything. I'll send it by mail or something." I gnawed on my bottom lip. Hopefully he'll leave her alone and just be drunk and sad.

Nyssa promised me she would call if she needed me, and ended the call. Knowing she was okay - in the sense of Yhwh, at least - made me feel infinitely better. I don't know why she's hidden from Yhwh, but I'm going to do my best to make sure she stays that way. I wonder if she's hidden from Lucifer as well...

火

"Karma," Roman entered my room - without knocking - to find me shimming into a pair of black skinny jeans. "Are you ready to go?"

"I'm shirtless." I deadpanned, not looking at him. He didn't leave. He just stood there while I slipped on my tank top, and leather jacket.

As soon as my jacket was on, he spoke, "Now are you ready?"

I'm going to kill him. "No," I growled back, planting myself on the bed, "Let me get my shoes on, impatient ass." He waited silently with his eyes burning into my side as I laced up my boots as slowly as possible. Once I was done, he basically dragged me downstairs to our bags. Roman ended up carrying most of them, because I was taking *too long* picking them up. Apparently. I could barely get out the first half of 'goodbye' to Giacinta, Faas, and Socrates before the black smoke fully engulfed us.

Chapter Eleven

When the smoke cleared, Roman and I were standing in some kind of strange waiting room. Black stone chairs lined the walls with matching stone coffee tables; they even had magazines on them! I guess Hell being one giant waiting room makes sense, kinda like the DMV. I thought there'd be more wandering souls though. It was just Roman and I in here.

"Ah, Ashera," I turned to see Roman addressing a child's worst nightmare. The thing - woman? - nodded to Roman before facing me. It didn't have any eyes, but seemed to be glaring into my soul. I resisted the urge to cower behind Roman. I'm the Sin of Wrath dammit. I'm not afraid of some lower level demon.

Suddenly, it hissed at me, "I was hoping for a snack, but this," She gestured at me with a contorted sneer. "There hasn't been anything child-like about her in years. *Tsk tsk.* They're ending much too soon. *Starvation* will be my downfall." Rude.

"My job is not to feed you, Ashera. Karma is a guest. We are here to see the King." Roman demanded, stepping slightly in front of me.

She straightened her back, finally turning her head the fuck away from me. "Yes. Master will see you now."

The large shiny black double doors beside her opened with a whisper. Inside Lucifer sat in a badass snake throne made from the same black stone. He smiled when he saw us, raising both hands in the air. He clapped, bouncing up from his seat, "War and Wrath! Such a power couple! I love it!" Lucifer embraced us with the same cheerful energy. I braced for the contact, knowing that refusing would most likely be taken as an insult. Luckily, Lucifer kept the hug short. He pulled back to look at us with a wide smile, "It is so wonderful to have you both home."

I doubt I'll be calling this place home anytime soon, but I won't tell him that. Roman sat the food bag down on a nearby stool, "Karma brought you a gift. Human food. Lasagna, potatoes, and bread."

"Really? I cannot wait to try it!" Lucifer turned to face someone hiding in the shadows of the room. That's creepy as shit. How many of them were in here? "You there. Go fetch a table."

A few more shadows bled out of their hiding places, and scurried out of the room. They came back moments later with a large table, before disappearing back into the walls. Yeah, I don't like that at all. While Roman busied himself with setting up the food, I sat Roi's carrier down and let him out.

"So," Lucifer began after we'd taken our seats. "How is training going?"

"Excellent." Roman answered. He served the food on the paper plates we brought. I waved away everything except the bread. Cooper would kill me, but I can't stomach anything else right now. This place was unsettling to say the least. "Karma's control over her magic has made great progress. I believe she could stand a chance against Julius."

Lucifer looked shocked at this revelation, and I'm sure my face matched. It wasn't the first time Roman said something similar - which I chalked up to him disliking his brother - but this time he said it to Lucifer. That means he's been serious this whole time. I couldn't help the swell of pride at the praise.

Roi hopped into my lap, curling into a ball. Roman smiled at the cat, and reached over to scratch behind his ears."

"What is this? How did you come across the Beast of Bodmin?" Lucifer asked, peering at Roi.

"This is Roi. He's my cat." Though, this is the second time he's been compared to that beast. At this rate, I'm going to have to look it up.

"Ah, a human pet." He nodded, polishing off the rest of his plate. I guess that's the end of that? "I have always found human food to be interesting. There are so many flavors." He pushed his plate away, and peered at me. As if I wasn't uncomfortable enough. "Roman is correct. Your magic energy has grown quite a bit since our first chat. It looks like you'll live up to the legend."

"Legend?" From the way Roman explained it, I thought the Seven Sins were a long forgotten story to most demons.

Lucifer laughed, "Oh yes. The Seven Indomitable Sins are a great legend of our kind, and *you*, my dear Karma, are the greatest out of all of them. Wrath is the leader of the Sins, and the strongest." Sorry, what? I'm supposed the leader now? Fantastic. Can life get any better? That would have been a good thing for my *mentor* to warn me about!

"Have any of the other branches found any anything?" Roman asked, slyly taking Roi from my lap. I glared at him as Roi curled up happily in his lap. Damn traitor.

"Nothing for sure. Vaughn is looking into a possible lead. He is supposed to update me within three nights from now."

Roman nodded, "Be sure he is wise enough to not approach. Karma almost killed Domini the first time they met." Just the first time? I mumbled a half-assed apology to Lucifer. I don't feel bad about trying to kill Domini, but I should at least try. Lucifer favored the brat, for whatever reason.

Lucifer chuckled, "No need for an apology, dear. Roman has tried a few times, as well."

"The king interfered before I could finish him off." Roman grumbled, making Lucifer laugh again. So, if we work together, he might forgive us? Hmm…

"So, this Vaughn guy," I interjected, refocusing the conversation. Lucifer turned his attention to me, actually managing to look interested in what I had to say. "Does he know which Sin it might be?"

Lucifer nodded, intertwining his fingers, "There's always a small bit of confusion before we know for sure. He *thinks* it could be Gluttony."

I could feel Roman's urge to roll his eyes. Instead he snorted, "Take that guess lightly. Domini believed you were Pride before he'd taken a closer look."

"A closer look?" I scowled at him, "You mean when he tried to attack me on my front porch?"

Roman chuckled, "Yes, that." I'm almost positive he has a video of that encounter that he hasn't told me about.

"Pride isn't that far off from Wrath," Lucifer shrugged, waving his hand for people to come take the table away. "There was also a possibility that you could have been Envy as well. Every being has an aura of their strongest traits that surround them at all times. You had signature traces of Wrath, Envy, Pride, and some other things that we can't quite identify." His soulless eyes peered into me, "Wrath, of course, is your strongest, but Envy is pretty strong as well. Is there someone you are horribly envious of? Is it me?"

"No," I snorted, "Your job, and image suck. Plus, this castle is stupid dark." Like hell I'd be envious of Hell. "So, this aura thing… How exactly does that work? I thought having too much Wrath in me was what gave me the fire powers?"

Lucifer made a noise, beginning to pace in a circle. "That is true. However, you are still a demon. Every living thing, including humans, has small traces of magic in their veins. With most humans it shows itself in a small way - the ability to dance, sing, or make art. Photographic memory, incredible balance, and never being late are all forms of this small magic." He paused his pacing, yet seemed to grow even more excited. Lucifer is a nerd for demon magic, who knew? "There *are* some humans that have more magic in their veins. These humans try to subdue the formation of their magic with various ways. I have heard cocaine and alcohol are fantastic. Have you tried them?"

"No I haven't tried cocaine, and alcohol isn't that great. Back to the subject, why do they need to subdue the magic? Wouldn't they just make cool art or whatever?" That sounds much better than cocaine, and I'm never binge drinking again. I learned that lesson.

"Oh, I'll have to try it on my own then." He pursed his lips, keeping silent. After a few minutes, I debated snapping my fingers at him to get him back on the subject. "Oh! Yes! You asked a question. Human bodies are not equipped to handle too much magic, so when these humans have so much that they cannot channel it or subdue it fast enough it has the ability to drive them mad. Vincent Van Gogh, Michelangelo, Nikola Tesla, even your dear Britney Spears had an influx of magic which led to her breakdown. Edgar Allen Poe and Willian Shakespeare are other prime examples. Humans are so fragile."

He chuckled to himself, "So, when we started the search for the Sins, we began scanning the levels of magic power. The auras were an added bonus we were not expecting, but it makes it a bit easier to identify which human has the most magic power and which Sin it's tied with. In fact, the first person we found had outrageous amounts of magical power, and the accompanying insanity. He turned out to be connected to Wrath, Greed, Pride, and Gluttony. We have a whole separate department focused on discovering exactly what he is…"

I must've looked confused, because Roman cut in to explain, "The one that always make you turn off the electric box."

I rolled my eyes. How many times do I have to tell him that it's called a damn television. I knew who he was talking about though. Honestly, that's not that surprising. He's so crazy that Lucifer thinks he's bad. Maybe the world ending isn't all that terrible.

Anyway, back to the magic signature thing, "I show signs of Envy?" Hopefully Lucifer hasn't distracted himself too much already.

"Not quite." Oh good. "Your magic power is Wrath. You're the personification of Wrath. The angrier you get, the stronger you get." So I *am* a prettier version of The Hulk. That's not so bad. "You cannot draw magic from any other Sin. Despite what's in your aura.

However," Lucifer stepped into my personal space, staring into my eyes. He smells like peppermint. That's amazing. How did he get scented body wash in Hell? "Roman's aura has blended into yours as yours has blended into his. This is similar to the way Envy rests on you. Odd. Roman, did any of the humans around her reek of Envy?"

"No. However, she has given off the essence of Envy since I met her. Angel and Cooper are actually lacking in magic - I checked - so it can't be them." That's a little hurtful. Then again, magic fucking sucks. "I even checked the people she knew in passing. No traces of Envy or any significant magic signatures at all." He magic checked my students? He could've at least asked! They're just kids dammit.

"So, Karma," Lucifer turned to me, "The question is, who have you been around - for an extended time - that has immense magical power. Someone known for being envious?"

'I wish I could be you…'

'I'll never be as smart as Karma…'

'He gives you so much attention…'

'You get to go to college? I knew you were the favorite…'

"Karma?" I jumped, refocusing on the two men in front of me. "Are you alright?"

"Yeah," I shook my head, trying to get rid of the memories. Now isn't the time for those. "Yeah. I'm fine, but no. I don't know any envious people." Not any that you'll know about.

I could tell they didn't fully believe me, but Roman stepped in before Lucifer could inquire deeper. "Perhaps Vaughn will give an update soon." Roman stood up with Roi on his shoulders. "I want to pay a visit to Eirian while we are here. Is that alright?"

Lucifer finally stopped peering at me to smile at Roman. Thank god… "I am sure she is eagerly awaiting your visit. Andromeda, as well."

Who's Andromeda? He'd mentioned Eirian before, but that was it. Judging from Roman's scowl, he wasn't too big of a fan. Eirian is supposed to love Roi, so I guess I'm not getting him back any time soon. Hopefully he's nice to the Sprite. Roi has a history of being a bastard to new people. Maybe I should go with them.

Lucifer sent us away with a wave, turning to go to the balcony behind his chair. Roman gestured for me to follow him out a door on the side of the room. I followed him down a candlelit hallway without uttering a word on how overly gothic this whole castle was. Seriously. Lightbulbs exist Lucifer, go buy some.

Roman led me through a maze of candlelit hallways until we reached the last door at a dead end. He knocked twice a lot softer than he ever knocked on my door. When he knocked at all.

A light, airy voice came from inside, "Come in!"

He opened the door to reveal two drastically different looking women sitting cross-legged on a bed. The woman at the head of the bed was the definition of the word petite. Her almost platinum blonde hair was so long it piled on the bed behind her. Her neon pink eyes lit up with excitement when she saw Roman, and a wide smile overtook her face.

The other woman gave a sultry smile to Roman as she adjusted her position to make her chest more pronounced. Her crimson red hair curled on her shoulders in a retro style. Her bright green eyes slid to focus on me. Our eyes locked, and her expression turned sinister. I could practically smell the anger coming from her.

"Roman! You're here!" The blonde cheered. Her eyes moved to Roi and she tilted her head, "What is on your shoulders?"

"Eirian," Roman smiled warmly at her. I don't think I've ever seen him so friendly looking. Then again, she did seem like the heart of his homesickness. He walked over to sit on her bed, leaving me awkwardly standing by the door. He pulled Roi from his shoulder, "This is Roi. He is Karma's cat - a human pet. What kind of cat is he, Karma?"

"Norwegian Forest." I supplied, still leaning on the door.

"Karma? *That's* your *name*?" The redhead sneered, still scowling at me. Unfortunately for her, I went to middle school so making fun of my name isn't going to get under my skin as much as she wants.

"Andromeda, I would think you are too old for petty insults." Roman taunted. His eyes never left Eirian though. He just watched her pet Roi. Roi who seemed to like her, and even let her play with his tail.

"Be nice, Andromeda. She's a guest. You can come in, Karma. I'm Eirian, and that's Andromeda." The sprite smiled at me as I joined them on the pink comforter.

I would've preferred to stay by the door, but that would be rude. I can't be rude to someone Roman likes so much. Due to the space, I found myself sitting beside Andromeda. Yay. "Hi." I greeted the two.

"So, why are you with Roman?" I sighed. First Domini and now her. Was being a rude and annoying a Nascent trait?

"Karma is working a job with me," Roman answered before I could open my mouth. He gave me a look, clearly saying 'don't mention the Sins' to them. I'll have to ask him about that later.

Eirian visibly deflated, "So you're going to leave again?"

Roman smiled softly at her. I didn't think he could be so soft. "Yes, although I do not know when yet. I will try to spend as much time with you as I can while I am here."

It's so strange to see this 'Big Brother' mode in Roman. He was so soft with Eirian as he told her facts about cats, and showed her how to properly pet Roi. She was fascinated with the cat as he walked around on her bed. Roi sniffed Andromeda before hissing at her and racing to my lap.

"What was that?" Eirian asked with wide eyes. I imagined my expression was similar. It's rare for Roi to hiss at anybody. He hasn't even hissed at Domini and he's actually bit him.

I shrugged, "I guess he doesn't like her?" Andromeda glared at me, but that isn't really surprising at this point. "What are you? Maybe that has something to do with it."

"I'm a fury." She puffed out her chest with pride.

I gave Roman a flat look. This sounds like the world's dumbest joke. Wrath, War, and a Fury walk into a bar... I bet a bad argument between the three of us could level a small country. "Maybe that's why, then."

"That cannot be the reason." Oh I offended her. I wasn't even trying. "It likes Roman. Is War not similar to fury?"

I scoffed, "You're *a fury,* not the emotion. I highly doubt it's the same." Roman cocked a brow at me. I don't know what that smug look was for, but I don't appreciate it. "Okay, Roi is done. Are you going to tell me where my room is, or do I just wander until I find it?"

"Good plan. You should do that." I growled at the red haired *bitch,* but otherwise ignored her.

"No," Roman denied. A vibrant red bled into her irises as she glared at me. I smiled at her. *Bitch.* "I will take you." After assuring Eirian he'd come back, Roman led me down another series of hallways. I thought we'd made it when Roman opened a door, but we ended up in another *goddamn* hallway.

"How many hallways until one of these doors is mine?" I'm getting sick of walking. All these hallways look the same.

"A few. Eirian's room is in the slave quarters while your's and mine are near the King's. The slave quarters, kitchen, and storage are in the East Wing. Due to our rank, we are in the West Wing - there are rooms prepared for the rest of the Sins, as well. Lucifer put a lot of effort into these rooms." In other words, if I don't like the room, don't mention it to Lucifer.

Roman *finally* stopped at the end of a rounded hallway with only two doors. Behind us, on the opposite side of the hallway was a single set of double doors. Judging by the ostentatious built of the doors, it belonged to Lucifer. I turned back to Roman when he opened the door on the right. There's no way he's leaving me alone here.

Inside was *another hallway!* This was was much shorter than the others, thankfully. There were only seven doors on this hallway. Each door had a different symbol on it. Weird.

"Wait," I paused, pulling Roman to a stop. "What's in the other door?"

"My room…" I could tell that wasn't the whole truth, but Roman pulled from my hold and kept walking.

Well if he's not paying attention… I turned right back around, and went to look in "Roman's Room." Inside I found a round room with only four doors. These doors had symbols as well; a red axe, a green biohazard symbol, a white scythe, and a yellow weighing scale. Roman grabbed me from behind, and carried me back to the other hallway.

"Roman! Put me the fuck down!"

"Your curiosity is annoying." He grumbled, dropping me back in the hallway with the seven rooms, closing the door behind us.

"What are you hiding?" I gasped, "Are your brothers here? Is that why? Can I meet them?"

"No." No *what*? He stopped at the door with a red symbol. No wait. This is a human language…

"Is this Chinese?" Roman actually looked mildly impressed. I rolled my eyes, "I study languages, remember? Though, I don't actually speak it, so I don't know what it says." Japanese is close, but not close enough.

"It says Wrath. Each door has the name of the Sin they belong to on the door in Chinese. They are also color coded for convenience. Yours is red, Lust is pink, Pride is orange, Greed is blue, Envy is green, Gluttony is yellow, and Sloth is grey. There is a list in English by the door."

Oh, he was serious. I nodded, thankful for the thought. I took a deep breath, bracing for whatever is behind that door.

Oh god. I have never seen so much red. The walls, the bedspread, and all decorations were blood red while the dresser, bed frame, and carpet were all black. Roi didn't seem to mind. He jumped from my arms and went straight to the bed. Holy shit…

"What do you think?" Roman asked, amusement clear in his voice. Damn him.

"I think it's… Red." So much red. "Are the fires on the wall a light source or just for decoration?" They were all over the wall.

"Decoration, definitely. Are you alright?" Little less amusement, but it was still there.

"Yeah," I nodded, knowing he wanted to leave. Roman left. I'm sure he headed straight back to Eirian's room. Honestly, I wouldn't mind seeing her again, she was so sweet. The grumpy bitch doesn't need to be there, though. What was her problem anyway?

Someone had brought my bags up from the throne room, and neatly set them along the wall. I carefully set out Roi's things around the room, making sure he could find everything easily. I tossed my jacket onto the bed by Roi's sleeping figure, and patted his head, "I'll be right back."

I grabbed my camera on the way out, and slung it around my neck. It's time for a self guided tour.

Chapter Twelve

"The stables are that way, ma'am." The maid - or slave? - pointed me in the right direction with a kind smile. She had looked shocked when I'd first spoken to her, and informed me that I had to give her permission to speak. What a bullshit rule. Oh and apparently, everyone in the castle, except Roman and Lucifer, believed I was here as some special guest to the king.

"Thank you, Masamune." She beamed at the use of her name, and told me to find her if I needed anymore help. I wasn't honestly looking for the stables, but I was sick of being lost in these endless identical hallways. However, I know Roman has a horse here, so there has to be a stable here too.

Aha! I exited another set of massive double doors, and finally made it out of that damn maze. Hell is so weird. The sky out here is a strange dark red with light grey clouds, casting a red glow over the palace grounds. I could see a gothic style barn in the distance that I'm assuming is the stables. I took some shots of the amazingly beautiful grounds before making my way over to the stables. For Hell, it really is beautiful.

I took as many photos as I could of the barn, but without a drone or a better lens I was a bit limited. The doors to the barn were unlocked, and slightly open, allowing me to slip in. A bright red glowing light behind one of stalls drew my attention, like a flare. A black skeleton horse with a bright red mane and matching tail greeted me at the door. The horse snorted at me, blowing black smoke at me.

"Well aren't you beautiful," I cooed at the beautiful animal. The horse snorted again, pressing its nose into my palm. The bone - I think? - was warm to the touch. It was oddly comforting.

"He does not take to people easily. I am impressed." I jumped, turning to face the newcomer.

This man was taller than Roman, though a lot less broad shouldered. This man was wiry and thin, though I had a feeling he was much stronger than he looks. His black hair was neatly styled, and his deep grey eyes seemed to study everything around us. Without his vintage Ray-Ban glasses, he'd probably be incredibly frightening, but they softened his overall look. He reminded me of one of my professors. What was that guy's name from freshman year? I feel like it's something similar to bastard, maybe something with a B?

Anyway, back to the, probably, dangerous demon in front of me, "Hi, I'm Karma." He nodded at me, keeping that blank expression on his face. "Do you know his name? He's beautiful."

"This is Ruin." *This* is Roman's horse? Still not better than my cat, but he is pretty. "He is my brother's horse - who does not take to people easily either - so it might be in your best interest to avoid both."

I scoffed, "Believe me, I know, but I think I'm growing on both of them. Whoa, wait. You're Roman's brother?! Which one?"

Oh, so he does have more than one expression. Surprise was all over his face, "You know my brother?"

"Mhmm," I ran my hand through Ruin's beautiful mane distractedly. "We're friends, kinda. If he denies it, he's lying."

The man chuckled, "My name is Ace."

"Ace?" Roman spoke of him the most, "Horseman of Death, right?" He nodded. That means this is the man in charge of every grim reaper. He's the super reaper. That explains the dad look, he's the parental figure for millions or creatures. "Your job sucks."

He smiled - albeit it was minuscule and easy to miss, but it was there. "It can be difficult. Though, successfully befriending my elder brother is much more complicated." I laughed with him at that. If anyone knows how annoyingly stubborn Roman can be, it's us. "Come, I will show you a true steed."

Ace led me over to another stall. Inside stood a white skeletal horse with an intricately braided white mane and tail. Though it lacked eyes - like a lot of things here apparently - it seemed to focus on me instead of Ace.

"This is Morana." The pride in his voice was clear. How sweet. He softly ran a hand over the horse's snout. "Morana is from Slavic mythology. She was the goddess of winter and death. My Morana is no different. That puny Ruin does not compare."

I laughed, "What about your other brother's horses? Are they here too?" There didn't seem to be anything else in here. Maybe their horses just didn't glow.

Ace scoffed, rolling his eyes. "Julius and Maxon do not have horses. Due to their camouflage abilities, they can change into anything regardless of species, Maxon and Julius keep theirs in different forms."

"Ah, so you're like Roman. *Anything other than a horse isn't a real pet*," I mocked that bullshit Roman said when he first met Roi. God, that felt like such a long time ago. Now, Roman cuddles with Roi almost as much as I do. Almost.

"All other pets do not have the power or integrity that horses have." I rolled my eyes. Maybe being an obnoxious ass is a family trait.

"Can I take a picture of her?"

"A what?"

I held up my camera, "It's a human thing. It takes photographs."

"Ah," He nodded, "Last time I was in the human world, I saw photographs. They looked much different then..." He frowned at my camera.

"I guess it's been a minute since you've visited."

"Oh no, much longer than that."

My smirk fell at his reply. He gave me permission to take photos - letting me know that Morana will look much better than Ruin - and left me alone in the stables.

Ruin and Morana posed perfectly for the pictures. Moana's white bones glowed, and black shadows wiped around her hooves in the middle of the shoot. I cooed at her as she stood proudly in her stall. Ruin snorted loudly from across the hall, kicking his stall door. I laughed and gave Morana one last pat before heading over to him. Ruin stomped his hooves as I came to his stall.

"Oh, I'm sorry, did I ignore you?" He huffed at me before turning to his side. He flipped his bright red mane, and held his head high. I snapped several pictures before a few neighs came from Morana's stall. Ruin growled before his mane caught fire and red orbs appeared where his eyes should be. Black flames swirled around his hooves reaching up his legs.

"Oh wow," I marveled at the show of his power - which I'm assuming he wanted. I snapped as many photos as I could while he stood tall and proud. "Okay, I'll let you two rest. Goodnight." The horses huffed at me as I left. I took a few more close ups of the garden and castle before going back to my room.

I found Roi curled up on one of the pillows when I got back. Trying to be quiet, I changed into my pajamas and slipped into the opposite side. I could see why Roi was so comfortable, this bed is *amazing*.

火

"What do you think?" Lucifer stood at the head of the table with his arms spread wide. "Please sit."

Roman and I took our seats on either sides of Lucifer. "It looks delicious. Is it just the three of us?" There were several other chairs at the table, but they remained empty. I wonder if any of Roman's brothers would be joining us...

"Yes," Roman watched me curiously from across the table, "Who else would you be expecting?"

"Hopefully, me," Ace strolled into the dining room, casting me a small smile. "Is anyone sitting here?" He gracefully gestured to the seat beside me.

"Nope."

Ace took his seat, nodding at his brother, "Hello, Roman. How is my least annoying brother?"

Roman smirked, "I am well. Though, I am sorry that you had to meet Karma."

"Fuck off, Roman. I'm a goddamn delight." Asshole. Roman gave me a flat look. "Ruin seems to think so."

His eyes narrowed, "When did you go to the stables?"

"Last night." Yes, I was smiling. Yes, it was making his attitude worse. No, I don't care.

"You told me..."

"That I was going to bed. Yeah, I know. I wanted to get photos of the palace grounds though, so I asked someone for directions. They are beautiful, Lucifer."

Lucifer beamed at me as he took his seat, "I am glad you think so! You are allowed to live here, if you wish. Do you like your room?"

"Yeah... It's something, but I'm still in school so I can't. Plus, I have friends that will miss me, and I don't think I can get used to Hell." It's way too weird. The sun alone made me nervous. It's much more red than the sun I'm used to. What kind of tan would that give?

"Ah," Lucifer shrugged, "It's an acquired taste." Sure...

"So Ace," Roman turned to his brother as our breakfast was set down in front of us. What is this? "Why are you here? I thought you preferred to stay in the temple."

Ace sighed, leaning back in his seat. "The temple can be... tiresome. Our King summoned me, actually, although he did not tell me why."

Lucifer was too distracted with his food to notice the men

staring at him. At least, I think this is food. It definitely wasn't human food. It lacked the color that normal food had, and was shaped weirdly. I don't even know what shapes they are. Hesitantly, I took a bite of the food Lucifer seemed to be enjoying. Oh that wasn't bad. The black-ish grey color was misleading. It was actually pretty sweet. Angel would be so fascinated with this.

"Hm?" Lucifer looked up to see Roman and Ace looking at him expectantly.

"I was asking why you summoned me, sir." Ace answered calmly. I don't think he could get past a four on the emotional scale, honestly.

"Ah, yes." He wiped his mouth with his white napkin. The only white thing I've seen in this entire castle. "You've heard of The Seven Indomitable Sins, correct?"

"Of course. Every demon knows of that legend." Does Hell have mosquitoes? I rubbed my arms, trying to get the itching to go away.

"Yes. That tale is true. The Sins are reawakening. Karma here, is one of them." Ace looked at me with a mixture of surprise and something I couldn't quite place. I'd say amazement, but that couldn't be it. I'm still just me. "She is the Sin of Wrath."

If Ace raised his eyebrows anymore, they were going to completely disappear into his hairline. "The Sin of Wrath, and you paired her with the Horseman of War? Are you sure that is wise?" He gets it.

Lucifer shrugged, not seeming bothered. Not that he ever seems bothered. "They seem to get along well enough. Perhaps a little too well…" Lucifer glanced between us with an odd expression. I don't know what *that* look was, but I don't appreciate it. Judging from his frown, Roman didn't either.

"She understands the frustration that accompanies social interaction." Roman defended, "Our magic is similar as well, which makes teaching her easier." Is is? I thought he hated teaching me… Maybe I'm allergic to something. Roman glanced curiously at me, noticing my fidgeting. I softly shook my head so he wouldn't ask. "Well, it would be if she was better at control." Does he *have* to finish every compliment with an insult?

My palms heated, "*What?* I can't count how many times you've gotten on to me for focusing too much. If anything, I have too much control!"

Roman scowled as his silverware began to bend in his hand, "I was not talking simply about your control over you magic. Until a moment ago, I had thought you had come far in that aspect."

"Until a moment ago?" What the fuck does that mean?

"You have completely melted your utensils!"

"So have you!" Melted silver dripped from our fists onto the table. Roman and I were out of our seats in seconds.

"This is what I am talking about. You are still as childish as you were when we first met! You lack control over your actions and your *pathetic* human emotions!"

I could feel the table growing hot under my hands, but what the fuck do I care? It's not like I can get burned. Though, Roman's *master* might be mad about his table. Roman was still glaring at me over the table. He's so fucking condescending, "How are you going to criticize me when you're doing the *exact same thing?!* And there's nothing pathetic about human emotions. Maybe if you didn't purge yours a million years ago you wouldn't be such an *asshole!*" I threw the glass plate in front of me at him, followed by the glass cup.

He caught them, shattering them instantly. Bastard. Before I could grab something - anything - else, two firm hands pinned my arms to my sides. I turned, ready to take my anger out on Ace, but paused when I saw his eyes. The impassive grey eyes entrapped me, draining my strength. What the fuck? I sagged into his chest, allowing him to effortlessly lift me off my feet. I knew he was stronger than he looked.

"I will deal with her, Sire."

"I suppose I get Roman, then." I could hear Lucifer sigh, "Come with me, Roman. *Now.* If you take one step in Karma's direction…" His voice faded as Ace carried me away.

Soon all I could hear was Ace's peaceful humming as he walked. It didn't take long to reach my room… At least I don't think it did.

I can't really remember the journey. Whatever bullshit Ace pulled drained all of the energy from me. I haven't felt so empty in years, and it's not a feeling I enjoy. The anger was still there, though. It's always there. Is this what death feels like? Will my final moments be filled with emptiness and anger?

He laid me down on the bed gently, before moving away. After a few minutes of staring at the ceiling, my strength slowly returned. The anger stayed in the back where it normally is, and didn't make its way to the forefront like it did in the dining hall. That's good. I sat up, using the headboard as a crutch. Ace stood in front of the closed bedroom door with his arms crossed. He's expecting me to go after Roman after that? I still can't feel my legs.

"You don't have to do that. I'm fine now. I think…"

"It has been centuries since my brother has had an emotional reaction of that caliber." He stayed at the door with his eyes narrowed at me. Great. Now he's pissed at me. Welcome to level five Karma, you only have yourself to blame. "He learned that his power fed off his emotions, and to keep them under control he needed to subdue them. It took centuries to master it. Your power is similar in that respect, yes? Are those types of outbursts common for you, Karma?"

"No." Not anymore, at least. I pressed my palms into my eyes, reliving the argument. "I haven't felt that worked up in years." Not even Domini caused that kind of reaction. I consider Roman a friend. Maybe even a partner in crime. Yet, all I wanted to do back there was hurt him. He's not anywhere near Isaac, so why would I have that reaction to him? I avoided Ace's eyes, "I'm not going to see him again, am I?" There's no way they'd trust us together again. I don't even think I do.

"It is not common for him either. What could have sparked such a reaction from the two of you?" Ace was lost in thought, and didn't answer the question. Maybe it was so obvious he thought it didn't need confirmation.

I sighed, sagging into the headboard, "Honestly, I don't know. He calls me a terrible student all the time. Which isn't true." That got me a small smile. Ace came to sit on the foot of the bed. He was still in between me and the door, though. "One moment I was fine, and the next I wanted to remove his jugular."

It was like a switch had been flipped. I thought I had a hold on my anger issues, but maybe I had unintentionally been bottling them up. If that's the case, I'm glad it was Roman on the other side. If it had been someone like Angel or Nyssa, I would've never forgiven myself. Roman will understand... Right? He has a knack for understanding my magic and how it affects me. Then again, I may never see him again so what does it matter?

"Karma?" I looked up from my hands to see Ace watching me with some form of concern. "Are you alright?"

"Yeah. Yeah, I'm good. Sorry you didn't get a chance to find out why Lucifer summoned you." My childish fight with Roman completely ruined dinner. Feeling ashamed, I sank further down into the bed, "You can go seek him out if you want. I'm going to stay here. I promise."

"Actually, I did learn the reason behind my summoning. He informed me during the beginning of your argument with Roman." Cringing inwardly, I gestured for him to continue, "I will be joining you to get the next Sin. If it is Gluttony as Vaughn believes, I will be of use. I can dull the effect of their Sin - same with Greed and Envy, if we're lucky." So he has no idea what is going to happen with the other Sins. However, we both saw what he did to me, so there's that.

I pulled Roi into my lap, and managed to smile slightly. With Ace's help we had a pretty good chance of handling whatever Sin it turns out to be. Well, if Roman will be there... My smile fell. When I looked up again, Ace had a wary expression, "What is it?"

"Hmm?" He looked up with surprise. "Oh, I was just thinking. The only Sin that I do not wish to encounter is *Lust*," He shuddered as if the simple word disgusted him. "Even in my brief 'human' life, I never understood the flesh desires."

I nodded, buying time to think of answer that wasn't a joke. Dammit. Roman was right when he said I joke too much. Lucky for me, a knock came at the door before I could shove my foot in my mouth, "Come in!"

Roman entered, looking annoyed. At least he wasn't angry. I did say some shitty things, but he doesn't seem apologetic about the shit he said either though. It was like he put on some kind of cheap party mask.

"You can go, Ace. I need to speak with Karma alone." Ace rose from the bed, but hesitated looking between us. "We are *fine*. We are just going to talk. No fighting, I give you my word."

"Or destroying the castle?" Ace raised his "dad-brow" at his older brother.

"We'll be on our best behavior, Dad." Ace rolled his eyes at my comment, but left the room. Roman moved closer, but didn't sit on the bed. Now that Ace was gone, the mask was too. He looked unsure, and - dare I say it - sad. "Please sit."

He sank into the bed, looking relieved. I guess he doesn't like fighting either. "I did not mean what I said. Your control has developed exponentially and I have never considered you childish. With your magic, I mean. Domini is a completely different story." I laughed, completely agreeing with him. There's just something about that little bastard that makes me want to rile him up as much as I can. "After that display, I have no right to lecture on control."

"I didn't mean it either. You can be an ass, but you haven't loss touch with your humanity. Hell, you're more human than some other people I've met. One second I was fine - happy, even - and the next I was pissed off. *Everything* you did pissed me off."

"Yes, I felt the same. Then you threw that plate…" He looked at me with shame filled eyes. What does he have to be shameful about? "I was going to kill you, Karma. That is not an exaggeration. If my brother had not stepped in…" He let out a short sad laugh, "I cannot imagine my life without you at this point."

I pursed my lips, "Not to ruin the moment, but can I get that in writing?"

He scoffed, rolling his eyes, "You did more than ruin it."

The tension dissolved as we laughed. We're going to be okay. Whatever happened tonight was just a fluke. Hopefully Lucifer agrees. Hopefully Lucifer understands the uncontrollable rage that comes with these powers as much as Roman does. "So," I sat up, and crossed my legs. "Is that normal? For the power to bubble up and explode like that?"

Roman sighed, allowing Roi to crawl into his lap. "No. Not for me, at least. I will admit that I had outbursts in the beginning, but that was centuries ago, and they never felt like that. Despite our powers being fundamentally similar, they will become increasingly different as your power begins to mature. This was the *first* thing we worked on, though! It should not have happened. You mastered those lessons. Even in the beginning when Domini confronted you - *without my permission* - your reaction was not that severe. He'd be dead. Again. This does not make sense..."

"Well getting upset again isn't going to help us. Let's just be careful for now, yeah? We'll watch each other's backs." Together. As a team. The way we should be.

Roman was still agitated - an expected reaction from a control freak when something is going on and they have no knowledge on the subject - but it wasn't directed at me this time, so I'm taking it as a good sign. "Before I go, did you get any photos of Ruin last night?"

"Yes...?" I'm not deleting them. Yeah I was worried about losing him a minute ago, but those pictures were fantastic.

"May I see them?" He must've seen my apprehension, I haven't saved the pictures yet, because he chuckled, "I am unable to work your device other than the button on top. I will not touch it. I just want to see the pictures of the greatest being in all of creation."

"Oh!" Well I can do that. I moved to sit next to him, bringing my camera with me, and pulled up the pictures of the greatest being in all of creation.

"These are pictures of Roi. *That I took.*" I laughed, clicking to another picture of Roi. "Karma. That is another picture of your moving pillow."

"He's a cat!" Using a cat as a pillow sounds like one of the most traumatizing things ever, and I know traumatizing.

"Go to a different one. How do I do that?" He reached for the camera he said he wouldn't touch. I screamed, pulling the camera away before he could delete anything. Roman tackled me, making Roi hiss angrily and hop off the bed. That loser has been sleeping *all day* and can't help me protect his pictures?

"Roman! This is expensive! *Roman!*"

"Karma!" We froze, tangled together, with curses on the tips of our tongues, and looked at Ace - who had just barged into my room in panic. He stopped short, trying to take in the scene in front of him. I can't imagine how strange this looked to him. His alarmingly large and *heavy* brother was practically laying on top of me with his knee in a place I did not want it, my arm was stretched as far away from us as possible with my camera firmly clasped in my hand, and Roi was still hissing at us from across the room. "I recognized Karma as attractive, but I did not know you two were… Ahem. I am happy for you brother."

"*Óchi, vlasfimía!* That is not what is happening! She is refusing to show me the photos she took of Ruin!"

"Oh my god!" I laughed, well wheezed, "Are you complaining about me to your big brother? You baby!"

"I am the *eldest.*" Oops. I snorted. Roman glared at me, but it held a new playfulness I hope stuck around for a little while.

"You took photos of Morana as well, correct?" I nodded to Ace, dodging Roman's grab from the camera. I stuck my tongue out at him making him murmur something about 'childish.' "May I see them?"

I pretended to think for a moment, "Only if I can show you Roi, too."

He chuckled, "That sounds fair."

Roman sighed, and got off of me. Clutching my camera to my chest, I moved to sit in between the brothers. Thanks to Roman's random button pressing a completely different photo was on the screen.

Shit! "Who is that?" Ace asked, before I could switch it.

It was Medusa. She must've taken it when I went to talk to Roman. She was sitting on the bench with both hands holding the camera. Her blonde hair was blowing in the wind as she smiled brightly. She even managed to get one of those birds in the picture, too. It's a beautiful picture. It almost looked like a stock photo.

"That... That's my friend. On to the horse pictures!" I quickly favorited the photo and clicked away before he could inquire further. The guys complimented each photo, though I only received enthusiasm when it was their respective horse and not their brother's. Men. When I got to the pictures of the horses showing their magic, the guys lost it.

"Is there any way you can turn that into a large canvas?" Roman asked, nudging me. It was a great shot. Ruin looked like a badass.

"Well... I could if we were back in Monterey. There's a shop there that prints them for cheap, but we're in Hell. Maybe I can send it to Medusa? I think the place she works might be able to get it done." Angel is back in Monterey, but I don't need her seeing magical photos. Especially considering she knows I can't draw and will know I had to have taken actual photos of these creatures.

"I do not know who this Medusa is, but these have a clear display of magic in them. Humans react to magic poorly." Ace interjected, looking at Roman for back up.

"Actually-"

"*Roman.*" We had agreed to keep Medusa a secret!

He sighed, "We can trust my brother. Ace, you cannot share this information. Not even with the King." Ace looked cautious - as any person on that side of Roman's serious face would be - but agreed. "Medusa is the Virtue of Patience."

"Virtues? Those are real, too? I suppose it makes sense, but... Wow. Does she have a mentor as well?" Roman grimaced, "So Michael, then?"

I snorted, and when Roman turned to glare at me it turned into a full laugh. "So this *is* a childhood grudge. Did he push you on the playground, Roman?" I cooed, soothing over Roman's hair. I still can't believe his hair is so soft. It's not fair. He barely even brushes it.

Roman batted away my hand, "No! It is a feud at the very least." I'm sure it's a very grown up "feud" too.

Ace shook his head. I think he's amused, but he's still at level two emotions wise. How does he *do* that? "Basically, yes, Karma. It has been going on for centuries. However, I am more curious about Medusa. You are friends? With your Sin and her Virtue, the two of you should oppose as much as Michael and Roman."

"Maybe that's why we don't." I shrugged, "Michael and Roman seem pretty damn similar. Maybe opposites attract." Or women have less ego, but who am I to say? Ace thought over my answer while Roman grumbled about how different him and Michael are. *Big baby.*

Chapter Thirteen

Medusa: 'Got them! These are incredible! They should arrive at the cabin by the end of the week.'

Medusa: 'Apparently Yhwh wants to meet with me????? I'm so nervous!!!!!!!'

Medusa: 'Sorry that was a lot of punctuation.'

Karma: 'Thank you for doing this. I hope everything goes well with that bastard, just remember to stay as calm as you can. Oh and pretend to buy into his bullshit. He's got an ego, so as long as you stay on the right side of it you should be fine. I gotta go. Mentor gets pissy when I'm late.'

God, I hope everything goes well for her. Yhwh doesn't seem like the forgive and forget type. Ace had mentioned wanting to see my magic, so Roman had the servants set up a training area by the stables. I'm fifteen minutes early, but I'd bet my box set of *Batman: The Animated Series* that Roman was already there. Masamune waved to me as I darted down the millionth staircase, and out the - stupidly large - black doors.

Yup. Roman and Ace were already here. Must be in the genes. At my approach, Roman placed his hands on his hips and geared up for his 'you're late' speech. I beat him to the punch, "I'm fifteen minutes *early*. Check." He glanced at the clock tower with a scowl, "Now kiss my ass."

While Roman, who was used to human phrases at this point simply rolled his eyes, Ace looked horrified, "*Do what?*"

"It is a human saying. You get used to it, but you don't actually do it." Roman explained, dragging me across the area.

"Why did you reposition her?" That was a genius question, and Ace asked it so there might actually be an answer.

"She was too close to the castle. Karma has tendency to get competitive and over-zealous." And ruin parties, apparently.

I snorted, "Whatever. It's more like Roman throws a fit when I kick his ass."

The more we spoke, the more concerned Ace looked. Like he's just waiting for a repeat of yesterday. Considering how random that was, his reaction is probably correct. Roman guffawed, "You have come far, but not far enough to beat me. See, brother? Over competitive. Are you ready to begin, Karma, or would you prefer to continue spouting lies?"

"Of course I am. Am I training with you or Ace?" Both men were close to me, but Ace was the one standing opposite of me.

"Me," Ace answered. "However, we are not training. We are sparring with magic." Oh. *Oh.* Sweet! I'd only sparred with Roman before, so this should be interesting. Roman patted my shoulder, and moved a safe distance away. I guess he's really not helping.

Okay. Okay. I can spar with Death. That's fine. I can do that. Great. Yeah. Okay. Taking a deep breath, I let the magic flow to my finger tips. Flames engulfed my hands, calming my racing pulse with their warmth. Ace doesn't seem like the 'take it easy' type, so I'm giving this my all.

Ace looked impressed, watching the fire consume my hands. Black wisps swirled around his feet, turning the grass around him pitch black. Well that's... not terrifying. Ace shook out his muscles, but still didn't look ready for an actual fight. An oddly familiar tingle shot up my spine as I looked at my mentor. Roman simply nodded at me. At least one of us has confidence in my abilities.

The fight started slow with the two of us going in a tight circle. Ace's black smoke charred the ground underneath him, adding to my apprehension. This grass is never going to grow back. If it is grass. Is grass typically orange? Not the time. Now isn't the time for a nervous tick, Karma. I swallowed my nerves, and threw the first punch. He didn't dodge. It actually looked like he enjoyed the flames. *Shit.*

Ace nodded thoughtfully, "Incredibly powerful. It won't be long before she can give you a proper challenge, brother." He shifted, the black wisps formed around his hands. I gotta learn the foot thing. That's badass.

Roman hadn't spent too much time on defense training, but he did teach me how to make a shield of magic. I moved my magic energy to the edge of my skin, creating a thin layer of fire to cover me. It was one of my favorite things he'd taught me. Ace grew outwardly excited at this development. He swung at my face and stomach in quick succession. I managed to dodge both, his smoke barely scraping my arm. Holy shit. I had to move back to process what just happened. I didn't expect him to be that fast. He's in a suit for god's sake!

Roman shifted on the sidelines, I could feel his amusement from here. He was fast, but *weak.* The Horseman of Death, brother to the biggest motherfucker I've ever met, and his arm strength is worse than Angel's. All of his strength has to be magic oriented. I'm buying Cooper dinner when I get home.

Ace and I sparred for a good hour, exchanging punches, kicks, and different forms of magic and defenses. As long as I dodged the spells from Ace - which I'm almost positive we're lethal - I was fine. I'm sure I have a weird bruise on my side from one that landed. As time went on, we settled into a comfortable rhythm, but a strange itch settled at the base of my spine. It might be a side effect of that one hit from Ace.

My magic grew hotter on my hands, along with a vague burning up my spine. We danced over the ground that was now charred by whatever Ace is using and fire. My vision grew fuzzy, but I pressed on. Is this his actual power? Slowly killing you from the inside? He better have an antidote. After I win this, that is. I can't beat War, but I can sure as hell beat Death. I tried to shake away the fog that was consuming my mind. Ace stumbled after a swift kick to the stomach. Focusing my magic to my right hand, I prepared a sizable fireball. My fire didn't seem to *harm* him, but it was wearing him down.

Actually... *Let's take him out.*

I hurdled the fireball at Roman - who was busy talking to that bitch from the other day. It knocked him off his feet, and sent him flying several feet back. Perfect.

"Karma!" The haze seemed to recede at the sound of Ace's voice, but the throbbing in my back only grew worse.

"Oh god, Roman!" I moved to go check on him, but screamed when the pain grew worse. This couldn't be Ace's doing. It had to be Roman. This is his fault.

Roman was engulfed in black flamed before he reached his full height. He was pissed, despite having no right to be. I'm the one in pain. Copying his dramatics, I let the red flames fully engulf me as well. Time for a real fight. We charged toward each other...

And ran straight into a giant wall of black smoke. I landed right on the center of the pain, completely making it disperse. The red and black flames disappeared as well, after ruining more of the grounds. I groaned, rolling onto my knees. My whole body hurt. Ace was standing over the two of us with his arms crossed.

"What has gotten into you two?"

Roman was standing, but looked as worse for wear. I'm sure I looked worse, considering I couldn't even stand. Roman came to me, holding out a hand to help me up.

"Well?"

"I don't know. I was just..." I groaned as Roman pulled me up. I leaned heavily into his side.

"Angry," Roman finished, "Furiously angry."

"Karma, can we continue the sparring, or do you need a break?" I don't have the most experience with father-figures, but Ace definitely resembled a sitcom Dad right now. Even with his burned suit.

"A break sounds great." Though I hate admitting it. Roman nodded in agreement, still supporting me.

"I want you to stay by me for now," Seriously? This is the second time we've fought randomly, and they're getting worse. If Roman and I had actually hit each other there's no telling how bad we could've hurt each other. "I do not want you out of my sight until I figure out this... Odd fury that keeps affecting us."

"Roman! Are you alright?" The bitch from Eirian's room ran over. Wasn't she talking to Roman during my sparring match with Ace? How did I not hit her?

"Of course I am." I rolled my eyes not only at Roman's response - he looks like shit - but also because of her fretting over his 'wounds' like some kind of mother hen. To stop myself from gagging, I moved to lean on Ace. He kept his arms crossed as he watched the two, but didn't stop me from leaning so that's nice.

"So, you have met Andromeda?" Ace hummed, "What did you think?"

I gave him the flattest look I could manage in my current condition, "She's something, that's for sure. Eirian is nice though."

That got a small smile, "Eirian is one of the purest beings I have ever come into contact with." Huh, I guess both Horsemen have a soft spot for the Sprite. Not that I blame them. She's like some kind of tall child.

"Hey, Roman!" He looked up from the red head with a strange expression. Though, it turned into a cautious smile when I smiled at him, "I'm going to see Ruin, okay?"

"No. Stop brainwashing him. Karma. *Karma!*" I laughed mockingly as I ran toward the stables. Well, power walked to the stables.

Roman was still yelling at me when I made it to Ruin's stall. Ace, who was so quiet I didn't know he was beside me, laughed scaring the hell out of me. He wasn't even out of breath, and had somehow put on a new suit. What the hell? "Okay, how did you do that? I would love a new shirt right now."

"Magic." Why does everyone get more useful magic than me? How 'advanced' do I have to be to get cool and useful magic? For someone who hates my morning routine, Roman sure isn't rushing to help me out.

"I wish Roman would teach me non-fighting spells." I ran my hand over Ruin's warm snout, loving how shiny he looked today.

"I have had millennia to learn these spells and many others." Ace handed me a red tank top not unlike the one I was wearing this morning. I gratefully slipped out of the one I was wearing, and into the new one. My guess had been right. I now had a large black bruise on my right side from that one hit he landed. "For instance, that mark on your side. My powers can do a lot of things, that is one of them. It greatly impacts your stamina, making you weaker over time. Which is why you are so much weaker than Roman at the moment. If I had known how the fight would end, I would have used a different spell. My apologies."

"I'll be fine. I've had much worse."

"That does not make me feel better. It was not Roman that hurt you, was it?" I shook my head, but didn't elaborate. Roman wouldn't actually hurt me. Not when he's in his right mind at least. "Good. With you being the leader of The Seven Indomitable Sins, it makes sense that Roman would focus on the fighting spells that will aid you in protecting the rest. Those are the most important right now."

"Boo." Ruin snorted, seemingly agreeing with me. I knew I liked him. "Maybe you can teach me some of your spells while we're waiting for the next Sin to pop up? Even if it is a fighting spell." Roman's spells were powerful, but also destructive. From what I saw of Ace's magic and what he just told me, his worked a lot differently. "It would be nice to not destroy everything."

"I can certainly try. Some spells might not work with your type magic, though. Fire is destructive in nature." Translation: Karma is destructive in nature. Great. "That is, if I get any time to teach you anything. This next Sin could keep all three of our hands full for some time." I sighed, resting my head against Ruin's snout. There's no telling what we're going to find with this new Sin. "Nervous?"

"A little." Understatement of the year. I'm super nervous. As soon as we find them, I have to step up and be the leader. *Me!* I'm not a leader. I'm a bruised and broken replica of a person. How am I supposed to be someone who others can look up to? Despite spending the past couple days in Hell - like actual Hell - this other Sin is what is going to make all of this real, and I don't think I can handle it.

"I know how you feel." I scoffed. How could he possibly know how I feel? Unless that was part of his magic, I'm going to say that was just some bullshit to make me feel better. "When the King found me, he brought Roman. Soon after that, Roman was given another task and had to leave. The King told me what I was, and thrust me into caring for the Reapers with no preparation. In human years, I was twenty-seven. Not much older than you are now. The Reapers were a disaster, but accepted me as their leader immediately.

"They looked at me for direction in a field I knew nothing about, but I did it. You will too, and you have the help I never did. I did not see Roman again until after I had established some order with the Reapers. It was just me in the temple trying to figure everything out. It is different for you, though. Roman and I are here to help and support you through all of this. Unconditionally."

I chewed on my lip, processing everything he just said. It sounds great in theory, but I saw Roman's face. I've never seen him so out of control. "I don't think Roman and I are ever going to be the same..."

"My brother does not make friends easily, nor will he let them go without fighting for them. Even if he refuses to use the word, you are his friend. I would even say his best friend. You are not going anywhere. Although," He pulled my hair out of my face, proceeding to braid it. Why does he know how to braid? Does he actually know how or is he just knotting my hair? Either way it was soothing, and I'm too tired to fight right now. "We do need to determine why the two of you are reacting this way to each other. Does your magic feel strange when you are in his presence?"

"No." I answered without hesitation. The only thing I felt was that itching yesterday, and the pain in my spine durning our match. It had disappeared once Ace had interrupted. I wonder if Roman had felt a similar pain... Even so, it wasn't a magic feeling. It was similar to the feeling a hot whip left behind after a lashing. My magic never felt like that, and the few times I felt Roman's neither did his. Ace watched me quietly as I sorted through my thoughts, and didn't offer his input.

We jumped at a loud bang from the opposite stall. Black smoke unfurled from Morana's stall as she neighed and kicked her door again. "I think she's jealous." Ace mused with amusement clear in his tone.

I sighed over dramatically, and gave Ruin's snout a quick kiss before going to Morana's stall. The white skeletal horse immediately rushed to the door when Ace and I appeared. Luckily Ace was there to pull me back before her head could connect with mine. I can't handle a concussion on top of everything else today.

"Hello, beautiful." I cooed, petting the beautiful mare. She huffed a cloud of black smoke at me.

Ace ran a hand through her mane, a tender love shining through his eyes, "Hello, *amica mea.*"

My eyebrows rose so high they almost came off my face. I bit my lip hard enough to draw blood in an effort to hide my excitement. Ace just spoke Latin like it was the most natural thing in the world. *Latin.* The original language. The mother of all languages!

"Karma? What did you do?" Roman stood in front of me with a look of mild concern.

"What?" Why does he automatically think I did something?

"You look deranged." His chocolate brown eyes sparkled with amusement. Loser.

"Good one." I rolled my eyes. Maybe for a seventh grader. "I got a little excited. Move." I pushed Roman away so I could see his brother again, "Ace? Are you fluent in Latin?"

"As a matter of fact, I am. It was my first language."

Holy shit.

"I think you broke her." Roman chuckled. He might actually be right. Five languages and none of them were making it to my mouth right now. When Ace voiced his confusion, Roman explained my studies and love of languages. He also conveniently left out how he refuses to teach me Greek.

"Ah, well I can teach that to you as well, if you would like."

"As well?"

"Yes! Yes!" I gushed, completely ignoring Roman. Did he honestly think I would say no? Learning a dead language from an original speaker was any linguists dream! I don't think I've ever been this excited. Not even when I got accepted into MIIS.

"If you had been this excited about Greek I might have actually taught you." No he wouldn't have. "I guess that isn't as exciting."

"Are you offended, Roman?" I teased, patting his shoulder. I couldn't reach the top of his head from here. "You're still my best friend, Batman, don't worry."

Roman growled at the nickname, and batted away my hand, "We are not friends."

I smirked at Ace and winked, making him laugh. His big brother was not happy. Roman grumbled something about bathing before storming off. Ace - once we were done laughing - offered to walk me back to my room. "I'd love that. I still get lost in there."

We walked arm-in-arm out of the stables after saying goodbye to Morana and Ruin and giving each of them an odd shaped fruit - I think - as a treat. Once we were on our way to my room, Ace spoke, "Why did you call my brother a Man-bat?"

"Batman." I corrected, "Man-bat is a completely different guy. He's a vigilante superhero from a comic book. I think Roman acts like him." Roman disagrees but what does he know? He's never watched any superhero movies.

"Truly? Perhaps you can show me this Batman when we get to Earth."

"Definitely. We'll make Roman watch it, too." With Ace's help, I bet I can tie him down or something. "He's going to get so pissed." Ace laughed like a true little sibling. Now he's definitely never meeting Nyssa. I don't need him corrupting her.

Not much later, we arrived at my door. This hallway was ominously quiet. Maybe filling it with more people isn't such a bad idea. Ace bowed gracefully, "I bid you goodnight, m'lady."

"Thank you for escorting me, *monsieur.*"

"I look forward to spending more time with you, Karma. You are a true delight." He kissed the top of my head. "Get some rest. We should hear from he King and be sent out soon. The spell I cast on your stamina will be gone in the morning."

Thank god. "Thank you, Ace. For what you said in the barn. It meant a lot. Goodnight."

He smiled softly, nodding once. "Goodnight, Karma."

Chapter Fourteen

It didn't take long to realize I wasn't alone in my room. My magic surged through me as I turned to face the intruder. I'm way too tired for this shit. That damned red head that's obsessed with Roman leaned against the far wall with an ugly sneer on her face. I guess with Roman not here, her fake pleasantries were gone. "I'm surprised. When I heard his voice, I'd for sure thought you'd brought Ace back to your room for some *fun*. Roman's brother. How classy."

Classy has never been my goal, honestly. I sighed, "Why are you here, Androgynous?"

"My name is Andromeda."

"I *really* don't care." I just want to go to bed. How did she find my room anyway?

"*And* I am here to get rid of a repulsive obstacle that has gotten in my way." She pushed herself off the wall. Red seeped into her sclera as her pupils swallowed her irises. I almost laughed. She came all the way up here to fight me? With those noodle arms? "All you've done since you arrived is get in my way. Since my magic couldn't break the two of you apart, I'll just do it myself."

Her magic? "*You're* the reason Roman and I keep attacking each other!" What kind of a crazy bitch does something like that?

She smiled deviously as she stalked toward me, "I'm a Fury. *That's what we do.* I will say, I have never felt anything like you. I knew Roman would have a reservoir of aggression bottled up, but *you.* It's endless, and *addicting.* I could feed off of you for centuries and never get bored." She laughed like some deranged cartoon.

This *dumb bitch.* Roman and I didn't have "pent up aggression," those are our souls! She's not playing with fire, she's fucking around with active volcanos! Roman and I completely unhinged and pissed off was basically two atomic bombs with limited timers. She's fucking insane!

"But," She pouted, "The spell stops the minute you're not in the room with me. With *anyone* else, it would last for hours! Roman wasn't supposed to stop until he killed you!"

I snorted, "Roman isn't some basic Nascent like you, dumbass." Neither am I for that matter, but I'm not dumb enough to ruin the whole secret just because of her ego. "Did you seriously think your pathetic powers would work on the Horseman of War? Anger, fury, aggression that's what he is at his very core."

Her red hair caught fire - which I have to admit is pretty cool. I hope Hell doesn't have smoke alarms. She growled calling my attention back to her, "I know! I know everything about Roman! I don't need you to tell me anything about him!"

I laughed which only seemed to piss her off more, but can you blame me? She can't be serious. Andromeda screamed while charging at me. I laughed, again, and dodged the "attack" with ease even in my weakened state. This has to be a joke right? Like Punk'd for demons?

Apparently not. She lunged at me again, but this time had the brains to throw punches too. They weren't correct, but I got the gist. Just like Ace, this girl had zero physical strength. It's almost sad. Maybe I should talk to Lucifer about some training classes or something.

My head snapped to the side when she landed a hit. God, Cooper would die if he saw that. *'Don't get cocky and let yourself be distracted!'* He'd yell that several times a day and I still did it. I know better.

My blood boiled as I locked eyes with the Fury. She went for another right hook with crazed eyes. There's no method; it's just madness with her. I used her arm to pull her to me, so I could knee her in the stomach. She stumbled backwards, her hair burning hotter. Her read and black eyes focused on me, brimming with hatred, "You whore!" Impossibly, the red in her eyes grew brighter as she growled at me.

Suddenly, the pain in the center of my spine was back with a vengeance. I should've known that was her too. It burned its way through my body. I groaned, hitting the ground. Magic is such a bitch. I haven't felt pain this bad since...

"If we can't pry the demon out of you, we'll burn it." He stood in front of me with that now familiar sneer planted on his face. It was the only expression I saw those days.

I was only fifteen as I kneeled at his feet, the only sounds in the darkened basement being my quiet sobs and his labored breathing. He only paused his assault to re-soak the whip. My back burned from the concoction he'd started soaking it in. I'd already counted my twenty lashes, but if he wasn't pleased, we wouldn't stop until he was tired.

"Daddy, please." I begged, hoping the title would grant me a little sympathy. Not that it ever worked, but what else do I have to lose now?

"Silence!" I cowered at his booming voice; too beaten to fight back anymore. "You are not my child. You're a demon!" He grabbed the rope with his gloved hand, and moved to stand behind me once more. "Count your punishment, demon."

"One," I was always meant to start over once he took a break. "Two."
It was hours before he stopped again, "Sixty."

He only seemed angrier. What could I be doing wrong? This is all my fault. "This isn't working! There are other ways to exorcise a demon. Stop crying! You brought this on yourself! Now go!"

I stumbled to the old plastic mattress best I could. My legs barely supported me after hours on the concrete. It's not as bad as it could be though. Nyssa is at the slumber party tonight, so she can't hear. She always cries the hardest after nights like this. My back burned, bringing tears to my eyes, but I fought them back. Tears only made him angrier.

"Stop crying! You're a demon! Demons deserve pain!"

"You are a demon, Karma. The fire is yours to control. It does not control you. I believe in you."

Roman.

My eyes snapped open to find two black stilettos directly in front of me. The Fury stood with her hands on her hips and a smug smirk on her face. She thought she won. How cute.

'I believe in you.'

I'm not letting that belief be misplaced. I let go of the hold over my magic, allowing the magic to fully surge through me. White flames exploded from every pore until I was covered in them. The pain making its way through my body disappeared completely, the offending magic had been forcibly removed. Even the remnants of Ace's spell were gone. I felt more alive than I had in years.

The Fury gasped, taking a step back, "How?"

I shot to my feet, wrapping my hand around her throat. Power seeped from every inch of me as I seethed at the smaller woman. Her eyes went back to normal - albeit filled with fear this time - as she clawed at my hand. "I tried to avoid this, but I am no one's toy." I'm the Sin of Wrath, I'm the leader of The Seven Indomitable Sins, I'm a demon, and I *will not* crumble in front of her or anyone else ever again. The skin beneath my hands and along her arms charred as it came into contact with my new white flames. It was fascinating. I've never seen anything burn so easily. If only she wasn't making such loud *pathetic* noises, and ruining the moment. I growled throwing her into the wall. She hit the stone with a dull thud and crumpled to the ground, unmoving.

I straightened, catching my breath. The white flames dispersed, leaving sweat in their wake. Now I definitely need a nap, but I have to move her first... If she's alive. Fuck. I hope I didn't kill her. I don't think I threw her that hard, but she is pretty weak. What if...

"Karma." I jumped at the sound of Roman's voice. He was using his magic FaceTime thing - that I'm not allowed to learn - so hopefully he can't see his friend crumbled in the corner. "We just got word from Vaughn. Bring you bags. We leave when you get to the Throne Room." Then he was gone. He didn't even give me time to reply.

Actually, that might be for the best. I don't even know what I'd say. It sounded like he was in a hurry though. I guess I'll have to sleep after we meet this Vaughn guy. Packing my bags didn't take long - I wasn't comfortable enough to use the closet or the dresser here. Finding Roi on the other hand… That catastrophe a minute ago must've scared the hell out of him. My room was filled with all the smoke from way too much fire for a room with un-openable windows. Hopefully Lucifer won't be too offended when he sees it. We completely destroyed everything in here. Even the stuff that didn't catch on fire was broken somehow. When that bitch wakes up she can walk herself to the infirmary - assuming Hell has healthcare. I paused by her body. Maybe I should check for a pulse… Do Furies have a pulse?

Whatever. She's someone else's problem now. With Roi in my arm - he was huddled up under the top half of the bed, the bottom was gone - and our bags trailing behind us, we left to go meet the boys. New Sin, here I come. Hell was getting a little stuffy anyway.

Epilogue

"Welcome to Falkirk. Apologies for not greeting you last night." Vaughn was waiting for us when the three of us came into the room they were using as an office. He was a brawny demon with a kind smile. He actually reminded me of Socrates in a way. I already like Falkirk better than Telluride. Domini would've kept us up just to be an ass.

Roman and Ace formally shook his hand with curt nods. I rolled my eyes at their 'all business' attitudes, "Thank you. I'm Karma."

"The Indomitable Sin of Wrath. I've heard. It's an honor to be in your presence." Roman scoffed behind us. Bastard. Vaughn turned to address the group, "Would you like to see our files? I believe we have found Gluttony."

"Sure!" Roi scampered through the room before darting out some other hallway. I guess he likes it here too.

Vaughn led us to the far side of the room where one of the biggest televisions I have ever seen was mounted on the wall. Most of the room looked the same as the Telluride HQ, just more updated and a lot more windows. Oh, and air conditioning. It's already my favorite. Vaughn directed us to the massive screen as he pulled up the file on the new Sin.

A full file popped up on the screen complete with a picture, name, and several personal details. Salem Welling, twenty three year old female. She had beautiful lilac hair, and bright green eyes that sparkled with mischief even in the photo. She stood at a whopping five feet tall, and weighed one hundred and twelve pounds. She's the size of a garden gnome!

"We have not yet approached, Sir, as per your orders."

"Good." Roman replied, still reading over the file. He's never going to get over Domini's dumbassness the day we met. "Even if she is just Gluttony - and the size of an infant - she is still powerful."

No. That felt wrong. Not the height thing, that was accurate, but she isn't Gluttony. I know what Sin she is. I don't know how, but there's no doubt in my mind. "Hey, Ace?"

"Yes?" All eyes turned to me, as Ace stepped closer.

"You *might* want to go home."

"I am here on orders from the King. Going home is not an option. Why do you want to send me away? Is something wrong?" He pushed up his glasses, frowning down at me. He actually looked hurt at the thought of me sending him away.

I pursed my lips, "That isn't Gluttony. I know what Sin she is, one hundred percent. She's Lust."

Roman turned me to face him, "How can you be sure?"

I shrugged best I could in his strong grip. I have no idea how I know, I just do. "I don't know, but I am. She's the Sin of Lust, Roman. Trust me."

Ace cursed in Latin behind me. Roman ignored him, searching my eyes for any sign of doubt - or proof I was just doing this to fuck with Ace. When he found nothing but sincerity, he sighed, "The *one time* you are not playing a joke." I laughed as he let me go. He turned to Vaughn, "Change the file to Lust, and be prepared for anything. This just got a lot more complicated. Karma, with me. We have things to discuss before we go get her."

I followed Roman out of the room to a much quieter area of the house we were in. Roi jumped into my lap the second I sat down on one of the plush victorian-style couches. He stretched his furry body across my lap to Roman's once the horseman took his seat beside me. He was being oddly cuddly right now. He didn't want anything to do with me this morning.

"Tonight, we will approach Lust." Roman began, looking over at me. Those endless brown eyes bored into mine. I leaned my head on his shoulder, allowing myself to finally breathe. "Are you ready to become the leader of The Seven Indomitable Sins?"

"No. You know I'm not, but I'll do my best." I'll make him proud. "From now on, it's serious Karma all the time. I'll be the leader they need me to be."

Roman leaned his head on mine, laughing softly, "Serious Karma, huh? That will be a sight." One that will probably never happen, but E for effort, right? "You are not alone, Karma. I am here, and will help you through all of this."

"I know." *'You are a demon, Karma. The fire is yours to control. It does not control you. I believe in you.'* "You've already helped me in more ways you know. Thank you."

"If you were truly grateful, you could always make me some of the spaghetti."

He laughed as I pushed him away, "Way to ruin the moment, jackass."

Author's Note

Thank you for reading Wrath, the first book in The Event Horizon: Sins Series. I hope you enjoyed getting to know these characters as much as I enjoy writing them. Karma is dear to my heart, and I am so excited to finally share her with the world.

If you wish to see more of these characters, or see some sneak peeks of things to come, you can find me at

jasminejohnsonbooks.com

@sins-virtues on Tumblr

@Jasmine_Johnson_Books on Instagram.

About the Author

Jasmine Johnson is a self published fantasy author. She published her first book, Nyx's Chosen in 2019 and is currently working on the sequel. Jasmine has been a lifelong lover of sci-fi and mythology, and lives for a good story. She aims to write the type of story everyone can find themselves in, despite their race, sexual orientation, or gender.

Jasmine spends her time in her home in Fort Worth, Texas, researching for her novels, spending time with her two Newfoundland Dogs, and taking over various walls in her house with her storyboards.

About the Author

Jasmine Johnson is a self published fantasy author. She published her first book, Nyx's Chosen in 2019 and is currently working on the sequel. Jasmine has been a lifelong lover of sci-fi and mythology, and lives for a good story. She aims to write the type of story everyone can find themselves in, despite their race, sexual orientation, or gender.

Jasmine spends her time in her home in Fort Worth, Texas, researching for her novels, spending time with her two Newfoundland Dogs, and taking over various walls in her house with her storyboards.

Author's Note

Thank you for reading Patience, the first book in The Event Horizon: Virtues Series. I hope you enjoyed getting to know these characters as much as I enjoy writing them. Medusa is dear to my heart, and I am so excited to finally share her with the world.

If you wish to see more of these characters, or see some sneak peeks of things to come, you can find me at

jasminejohnsonbooks.com

@sins-virtues on Tumblr

@Jasmine_Johnson_Books on Instagram.

@jasminejohnsonbooks on Facebook

Patience

Book One of The Event Horizon: Virtues

Jasmine Johnson

Acknowledgments

Thank you to everyone who supported me while I wrote this book. Especially my Mom who never got mad at me storyboarding over her all of her whiteboards. And a special thanks to Kiona and Lili for teaching me the *value* of patience.

Prologue - Michael

I crossed over the flawless white marble to kneel before his throne, "You summoned me, Father?"

His white aura reached me even at this distance. The mere pressure from it made my white wings curl into my back. He is upset. "Yes, Michael. I have received some… *Unfortunate* news."

Unfortunate news? From the reports I had received, Zion was thriving. It cannot be the humans that have upset him, since Zadkiel is tasked with the care of Earth. The only thing left was Lucifer, but he has been mostly silent since the last battle. After a loss that tremendous, he shouldn't have any courage to confront our Father.

I could feel Father's agitation growing, "The Old magics are awakening." I kept my head bent. Looking up would come off as disrespectful. Disrespect would be a grave mistake, even if Father wasn't as agitated as he is right now. But, surely he wasn't talking about The High Virtues. They'd been asleep so long, my brethren had begun to believe they were never real. "I believe your fallen brother has begun searching for the Sins, but hasn't had any success." That is good news. "As for the Virtues, I sent out scouts some time ago, and they believe that the first has been found. I need you to collect it."

"What would you like me to do with it once I have it?" Legends say that the Virtues hold unimaginable power. The kind that could destroy Zion in a single blow. Perhaps killing it early is our only option.

"To be decided. If it doesn't come willingly, you are allowed to use force. However, I hope the Virtues come to us willingly."

I nodded, completely understanding. *Something* is causing them to awaken. If we want to still be standing when it comes to pass, we will need them on our side by choice. I rose from my kneeling position, "Location?"

"A place called Telluride, Colorado. Zadkiel is ready to direct you. Oh, and Michael," I tuned back to my Father to see a small smile on his face, "The Virtue seems to believe that it is human."

Wonderful.

Chapter One

I'm late. Too late for it to be okay. Maybe Brian will go easy on me if I tell him what happened.

"What the fuck?" I cringed at the anger in my father's voice. There's no way I'm going to be able to make it out the door without being seen. I stepped out of the hall, hurrying to the front door, "Hey!" He slurred, "Why the fuck is my beer warm?"

"The electricity is off," I replied, tying my shoes now that I'm not running out of the house. "I'll call the company today, and see if we can work something out until payday. Water is good warm."

I slipped out the door before he could yell that 'real men don't drink water' or something similar. Seems we both found out about the electricity in unfortunate ways this morning. For me, it was when my phone was dead this morning, and the battery powered wall clock in the hall let me know that I was three hours late for my shift.

I peddled as fast as I could to work. Luckily, there weren't very many cars on the road - everyone else in Telluride must've made it to work on time. I chained my bike to a stand by the front of the store, and darted inside.

Brian - my manager - was waiting near the door when I came in. He was frowning with his arms crossed behind the check out counter. Oh no. "Afternoon, Medusa."

I winced, "I'm so sorry, Brian."

"The store is empty. Wanna tell me what happened?" Okay, so maybe he isn't that upset.

"My electricity got turned off. It was on when I went to bed, but off this morning. So my phone didn't charge and my alarm didn't go off because my phone was dead. I'm so sorry." I'm so fired. I don't know anywhere else that's hiring. How am I supposed to pay the bills?

"You're not fired." My head snapped up in surprise. I was three hours late! He wouldn't be wrong to fire me. "You've been here a long time, Medusa. You're a great employee, and this is the first time you've done anything wrong. We'll call it a warning. Go clock in." He waved me away.

"Thank you! I won't hug you - because I know you don't like them - but just so you know, *I really really want to!*" I darted toward the back room to clock in before he could change his mind. I could hear his quiet laugh as I left.

忍

Four hours later, I was at the counter helping some tourists. Brian ghosted when we'd gotten a sudden rush of them. I didn't mind though. Tourists are one of my favorite parts of the job. I love new people.

"Have a great day!" The happy family of four waved cheerfully as they left.

The customer behind them was an older woman that seemed a bit flustered. I helped her unload the abundance of items in her ams. She should've grabbed a basket. She smiled at me while she struggled with her large floral purse, "Thank you, erm…" She squinted at my name tag. I scanned her items quietly, not offering my name. "Does that say *Medusa?*"

"Yes, it does." I chirped, trying to keep a light tone.

"That is awful! Why would your parents choose an awful name

like that?" The smile remained firmly on my face. People often asked that when they learned my name.

"My mother didn't see it that way. She studied Greek Mythology in college, and - personally - didn't view Medusa as a monster. To her she named me after a strong and resilient woman."

The woman scowled, "Well I think it's terrible. Didn't she think the other kids would bully you?"

I hummed, still scanning her items, "Perhaps the problem is with the children that bullied me, and not with my mother. Your total is thirty-three, fifty six."

She begrudgingly handed me two twenties, "You cannot blame kids for that. Kids bully other kids, it's a part of growing up."

My smile dimmed at the ignorance of that comment, but I kept it on my face. Hospitality is the most important part of my job. I handed her the change, "Have a wonderful day!"

She grabbed her bag, but paused before leaving, "You know, it's really a shame." I stayed quiet, waiting to see what was next. Normally, the word 'bullying' was the end of the conversation. "You are such a beautiful girl, but no man is going to marry a monster." She shook her head, leaving the store.

Brian approached me cautiously. I hadn't noticed him come back to the front, but here he was. She must've been the last of the rush. I smiled widely at him, trying to blink back the moisture pooling in my eyes.

"Welcome back." I smiled at him best I could.

"For the record, I would marry you in a heartbeat, but you're a little too patient for me. *That* was bullshit." I nodded in agreement. That woman was more upset with my name than most. "I think it's time for your break. In fact, I think you should take your favorite candy bar as well. No charge." He looked horrified at me almost crying.

I choked out a laugh, but did grab a Hershey's bar as I went. I collapsed into a chair in the break room, and let the tears fall. Today has been a little worse than most. I still hadn't called the electric company; I need to do that before Dad comes up here. I don't think I can handle anything else right now. Deciding to get it over with, I made the call.

Twenty minutes later, I left the break room and went back to the counter. Brian smiled cautiously at me as I came back, as if I was some frightened rabbit.

"I'm okay now. Thank you."

That seemed to relax him a little. He left me at the register, disappearing into the aisles again. The store was quiet for the next few hours; something I'm eternally grateful for. Sometimes I just need a break, and in a tourist town like ours that's almost impossible. Brian left me alone with my thoughts as I worked until about thirty minutes before my shift was about to end.

"Are you alright?" He looked annoyed. He never looks annoyed when I'm working.

He crossed to where I was straightening the candy display and sighed, "As a matter of fact, I am not. Amita just called. She's 'sick' so she won't be here today."

"You don't think she's sick?" Amita had a tendency to catch any illness that came through town, and called in sick a lot, but it doesn't seem like she'd lie about it. Why would anyone lie about being sick when they could tell the truth?

Brian gave me a flat look, "On a Friday? Doubtful. She's probably going out with some of her friends, and decided work wasn't important. I'm sure there will be a bunch of pictures all over all *eight* social media pages she has."

"I can cover her shift." Unlike most people it seems, I actually enjoy my job. Home is stressful and unpredictable whereas work is calm, quiet, and I get to meet new people every day. Who wouldn't want to be here?

"Really?" I nodded, possibly a bit too eager, but Brian didn't notice. Well, he probably didn't care. "Thank you! Thank you! I swear, Medusa, you're an angel or a saint or something equally as pure."

I laughed, "Hardly." I'm certainly no angel or saint. "I'm just a girl who loves my job. When do you head home?"

"One hour." He cheered flatly, waving his hands in the air. I laughed. He's so interesting. "Mac should be here around that time to take over for me."

Oh. That's... Good? It isn't that I don't *like* Mac. He's just, difficult to be around. I could handle a few hours. It's better than being at home.

Brian hung around the front with me for the rest of his shift, and helped me with the few customers that came through. It was oddly peaceful. Brian is great at being company, but not constantly in search of conversation. When Mac got here, Brian all but skipped out the door. He wished me 'good luck!' and left to enjoy the rest of his day.

I worked quietly, hoping to avoid Mac's attention, "Hey, Gorgon." I sighed quietly, but didn't look up. Here we go. Mac was the perfect all American guy with blonde hair and blue eyes that spends too much time in the gym. It's a shame that he has less personality than an insect.

"Hello, Mac. Do you need something?" Probably not. He just likes to use the only word from Greek Mythology he knows. Like when a toddler learns their first word and says it a million times a day.

"Just making sure you're doing your job." So I was right.

Instead of a reply, I ran through my mental list of things that I've done so far. Mac looked annoyed at my neutral tone, but didn't get the chance to further attempt to agitate me as the door chimed, signaling a new customer. Mac grew pale as he looked past me to the newcomer. Odd.

Oh, that's why. The man was beautiful. He was well over six feet tall with golden blonde hair that fell over his broad shoulders. He must be a model that came for his vacation or something. Poor Mac probably felt threatened as 'The Hottest Man in Telluride' - his words not mine - with this man here. Is this what you'd call karma?

5

"Welcome! How can I help you today?" I chirped, going to meet him at the edge of the counter.

His blue eyes focused on me, momentarily unnerving me. There was no light in his eyes. They were a shocking shade of blue, but they held no humanity or compassion. It... It was terrifying.

"Medusa Sinclair?" His voice was so melodic. It was almost soothing, but with those eyes... How could eyes be so dead?

"That's my name! How can I help?" Eyes or not, I can still be nice.

He nodded, "My name is Michael. I need to speak with you." His eyes flicked to Mac - who was shamelessly eavesdropping beside one of the shelves. He glared at Mac, *"Alone."*

That... Didn't sound safe. Before I could ask Mac to stay, he shrugged and wandered to the back. Michael seemed pleased. I resisted the urge to shrink behind the counter. Instead, I pressed my palms into the countertop, and faced him with a smile.

"I have placed a barrier around us, so he cannot listen from the second aisle that he is currently hiding in." Honestly, I wouldn't be surprised to find Mac actually hiding behind the second aisle, but how would he know if he is? What 'barrier' is he talking about? We're just in the store. "Now that he cannot hear, I am the Archangel Michael, and have been sent by my father Yhwh - human's commonly address him as God. I have been sent to begin your training."

Training? God? I don't know if we have an asylum nearby, but someone is definitely looking for this guy. Maybe he's done some type of substance? I think rich people do that when they're bored, right? I smiled, trying to appear as harmless as possible, "Okay. Do you need me to call someone for you?"

He scowled at me. Oh no. "Do not patronize me. You know you are not human, Medusa. Not fully, at least. We are not quite sure what you are, yet." His head cocked to the side as his scowl deepened. "The human is coming back. We will have to finish this later. What time do you leave here?" Before I could answer, he continued speaking, "I am bringing down the barrier now. *Speak wisely.* I am not here for execution, but I will if I have to." *What?* He can't seriously be talking about killing people!

Mac came around the end of the front aisle, and Michael's eyes seemed to lose all traces of the slight warmth they held. I turned my focus back to Michael, "I leave at eight."

He nodded with a small smile that seemed a little too forced. As if he was just pretending to be an easygoing person, "I will see you tonight then. Eight is late in the day, I will bring food." Then he was gone.

Once he was gone, Mac marched up to me with a deep scowl, "We have strict rules with personal affairs while on the clock, Gorgon. If you want to flirt with your boyfriend, do it on your own time." He barked.

"He isn't my boyfriend." I denied, keeping my voice calm. There's no point in getting upset about his antics. He could turn me in for an 'outburst' and get me in trouble with Brian or the owners.

"I find that hard to believe," He scoffed, "I saw the way he smiled at you. If he isn't buying anything, keep him out of here."

"Okay." He was taken aback by my complacent reply. It was like *not* arguing with him made him angrier. Boys are so strange. Mac stomped away from me, fuming silently.

With Mac angry at whatever I did, I was left alone with my thoughts, and they centered solely on Michael. Who was he? Maybe it was some odd church recruitment thing? He was talking about God - no wait, he called him something else. Yhwh? I think. What a strange spiel. Maybe it was just a joke being played on me by someone… Maybe it was Emilie? She spends time with the models and celebrities, perhaps she talked one of them into it. It's been years since they played a prank on me. Maybe reliving their high school days? Then again, I don't even know if Emilie or the rest of that group are even in town right now…

With that strange man keeping my mind occupied, my shift was over in the blink of an eye. I helped Mac close up the shop, before hopping on my bike and heading for home. The lights were on when

I got home, running up the electricity bill I just handled. I rolled my shoulders, trying to loosen the stress knots that were forming. The front door opened as I walked up, revealing Michael.

"Welcome home, Medusa." He stepped back, letting me in my own home. My father sat on the couch with a beer in his hand, and several more scattered around his recliner. He didn't seem bothered with the stranger in our home. "I brought you your usual from *Steamie's*." How does he know I love *Steamie's*? "They even gave you extra fries. It is all very... Unhealthy."

What? *Steamie's* is one of the healthiest places to get a burger and fries in town... I guess they do know my order by now so maybe he didn't have to read the menu. "Th... Thank you." I chewed on my bottom lip, looking through the paper sack. I led the way to the dining room.

Michael joined me at the table with his hands folded in front of himself. "I brought your father some of the '*Steamie Dogs*' as well, but he has already finished them." He pronounced '*Steamie Dogs*' slowly as if they were unfamiliar. That does explain why dad was so complacent. Still, he should know to not answer the door to any random person that appears. Michael shifted, "I have reinstated the barrier. Your father cannot hear us." I bit into my burger, waving for him to continue. "I am going to explain while you eat. You may ask any questions as I explain.

"As I said before, I am the Archangel Michael, and I have been sent here by Yhwh to begin your training. You are one of Heaven's Seven Almighty Virtues." Virtues?

"Virtues? What are those?" He said there's seven as well. He didn't seem bothered about me interrupting him - that's good.

"Virtues are the best traits a person can have, and the actual Virtues are the perfect examples of their respective Virtue. The Seven Almighty Virtues are Patience, Chastity, Kindness, Diligence, Humility, Temperance, and Generosity. You are the first Virtue we have located, but do not focus on that. We have my brethren working on finding the others. For now, you and I are going to work on your magic, and preparing you for what is ahead." Well that sounds ominous. Michael didn't stop to elaborate though. "So, what magic do you have?"

"Hmm?" He expected me to know? "I have no idea. I don't even know what Virtue I am. Am I supposed to have some type of magic?" I cleaned up my mess, before sitting back at the table.

Michael stayed quiet while I wiped the small mess off the table, but continued to think quietly well after I sat down. I waited for him to finish. The only other sound in the house was the game on the television. It was oddly peaceful. It's a beautiful evening today. Maybe Michael and I can talk outside for a while.

"You truly do not know which Virtue you are?" I turned back to Michael, shrugging at him. I had no idea which one I could be. Honestly, I don't think I could qualify as the perfect example of anything. "Medusa," Michael smirked at me. His blue eyes seemed to take on some warmth, too. He almost looked normal... Well, normal for an outrageously beautiful person at least. "You don't know which Virtue you are?"

"Nope," I shrugged, "Sorry, but I truly have no idea. Is there a test I should do? Are you sure it's me?"

He laughed a short quiet laugh, "Medusa Sinclair, we have been sitting at this table in *silence* for forty-five minutes. You are the Virtue of Patience. You did not speak up once."

"It looked like you were thinking. I didn't want to disturb you." I was just being polite. What if he was thinking of something important?

Michael shook his head, "Do you want to know what I was thinking of?" I shrugged. It was his business really. He doesn't have to tell me. "I was counting. Two thousand, seven hundred and thirty seconds of silence. Silence that you didn't interrupt. *I* had to break it."

Oh. "Well, I guess you're the angel, so you'd know." He was the most experienced, right? "So, what's next?"

Chapter Two

"Are you not cold?" Michael asked standing beside me. It wasn't that chilly yet. Over the next couple weeks the temperature would go down significantly, but tonight wasn't so bad. "I was under the impression that humans struggle under sixty degrees. It is around forty-five now."

"Nope! I think it feels great." There was a breeze tonight. I could almost taste the crisp bite in the wind. I led him over to the babbling brook that ran through our yard. It was still water this early in the year. I took a seat beside the rocks, patting the grass for Michael to sit beside me.

He reluctantly sat down, sighing quietly. "As far as Earth goes, Telluride is not so bad."

"It really is beautiful. I'm so grateful to live here." I dipped my hand in the cool water. I could feel Michael's eyes on me, but he didn't speak. Is he waiting for me again? "When you said training, what did you mean?"

"One thousand, two hundred and thirty seconds." He *was* counting! Who can count that high without losing their place? "When I say training, I mean your magic. We need to figure out what your magic is, then begin to develop it." Well, he makes it sound easy. Maybe he has a plan. "So, have you ever... Frozen anything?"

"Not that I've noticed." I do live in a ski town that snows a lot.

"Is that what your magic does? Do you have ice powers?" That could be cool.

"Yes." He held out his hand. Little flurries swirled in his hand, taking an odd shape. A moment later the flurries spun away, leaving a pristine ice sculpture of a pegasus behind. It was stunning. "Here." He handed it to me.

"Th-Thank you." There were so many details. I could see each individual feather on its wings. It's beautiful. Moments later, the entire thing was a puddle in my hand.

Michael sighed, "You're too warm for ice." Oh, I've disappointed him. I apologized, folding my hands in my lap. "Do not apologize." He snapped. Now I've made him angry? Well this isn't going well. "You are a legendary Virtue of Heaven. We will discover what your magic is. It will just take time."

"I'm sorry that I'm not much help with this, Michael." I shifted. "Is there anything I can do to help?"

"Yes. Stand up." I followed Michael off the ground. What ever we need to do, I'm ready. "Are you familiar with Krav Maga?"

"Nope! What is it?"

"Then let us begin."

忍

I whimpered, wrapping my arms around myself. The hot water prickled on my skin. Maybe if I got it hot enough, I wouldn't be able to feel how badly my body hurt anymore. Michael and I tried Krav Maga, but there was no sign of my powers, so he insisted on trying something else called Northan Shaolin. I'm not a fan of either to be honest. None of my magic appeared either. I was still just a regular human. Well, a regular human in a lot of pain.

I don't know where Michael is now. Last I saw, he was talking with my father about whatever was on the television. I can't stay in the shower too long though. Water bills aren't cheap, after all. I shut off the water, and dreaded picking up the towel that was waiting for me. Another whimper escaped as I wrapped the towel around me. I can't believe I have to work tomorrow. Maybe I have some pain pills laying around… Probably not. Dad eats them like they're Skittles, so I typically don't buy them.

With the towel wrapped loosely around me, I made my way out of the bathroom to my bedroom. "Welcome back." I jumped at the sound of Michael's voice. Why is he in my bed?! I didn't think a queen bed could look so small. Michael seemed to dwarf it with minimal effort.

"What are you doing in here?" I clutched the towel tighter against my body.

"Your father instructed me to wait in here for you." Michael sat up, patting the small spot on the bedside him. "Come sit. There are things we need to discuss."

"I'm not dressed! There's nothing under this towel, Michael. Can you step out so I can get dressed, please?" It seemed to dawn on him, and he moved from the room. I moved as fast as I could - which wasn't as fast as I normally could because I kept having to pause. I braced myself on the closet door, sliding to the ground. I'll get dressed in a few minutes. Maybe I can… Maybe I can just close my eyes for a minute.

"Medusa." I blinked up at Michael. His figure wavered in front of me. Was he holding something? "Stand up. Come on." He pulled me to my feet. When did I sit down? I don't know if my groans of pain made it out of my mouth, but if they did, they didn't deter Michael at all. I could feel my legs trembling underneath me, threatening to make me collapse again. "Stand. Just for a moment. Put your arms out." I listened to him, I think. I can't tell if I'm still moving. I feel like I'm wobbling.

Michael slipped something over my arms, before moving in front of me to do something else. "Alright. You don't have to stand up anymore. I will catch you." I sagged, falling into Michael's arms. He carried me to my bed, and tucked me in. "We will talk in the morning. Sleep."

Chapter Three

"How are you so weak?" Michael watched me move around the room at a snail's pace. He didn't sleep in here, but came in at the sound of my alarm this morning. Apparently, he had dressed me in a night shirt last night, and put me to bed - at least that's what he told me. Considering all he's been doing this morning is taunting me, I'm almost positive he made it up. "We didn't do that much training last night. It is barely a scratch on the surface on the training we need to accomplish."

Oh *fun*. That sounds enticing.

"I have to go to work before we do anything else. Ah!" I froze with my shirt still on my head. Anytime I stretched my arms too far, my muscles seemed to seize for a moment. I'll be okay in a second. I think.

Suddenly, my shirt was pulled down. Michael glared at me, "Arms, or I will do it myself." That sounds painful. With Michael's help, we got my shirt on.

"Thank you, Michael." I glanced into the mirror. My hair was in an anti-gravity mood today it seemed. "Is there any chance you know how to fix hair?"

Michael pursed his lips, "It looks fine." So, no then. I'll just have to brush it myself then. "Give me that. You look ridiculous." Michael took the brush from me. A little too forcefully if you ask me, but it felt nice to have someone brush my hair. Honestly, I can't remember the last time someone else brushed my hair. It must've been Mom. "There."

"Thank you, Michael." I laughed, "I sound like a broken record, don't I?" Ooh, laughing was a bad idea. I'll have to remember that. Michael didn't laugh or comment, he simply opened my bedroom door waving for me to go out first. Maybe one day I'll get him to laugh, or smile. Smile seems a bit easier to accomplish.

"Hey, would you smile if we learned what my magic was?" I smiled up at him.

He scowled back, "Unlikely. *However,* your magic appearing would make my life easier." Close enough.

"Medusa Sigyn Sinclair!" I flinched at the sound of my full name. Dad was angry, but why? I checked the fridge last night. We have plenty of beer, and food he doesn't have to cook. He was standing in the living room with his arms crossed when we made it to him. "What is this?!" He gestured to the neatly folded blankets on the couch. How did those get there?

"That was me, Elias." Michael spoke up, "When I found them, they were crumpled on the couch, so I was not sure of where to put them when I got up. Where do I move them to?"

"No no, Michael." Dad smiled warmly at him. I guess *Steamie Dogs* make friendships. "This is not your doing. You're a guest here! You don't have to sleep on this frumpy old couch! From now on, you take Medusa's bed, and Medusa will sleep on the couch." What? "Because that is *how you treat a guest.*"

"Oh. Right." I nodded, "You take my bed from now on, Michael, and feel free to use my room while I'm gone." Dad was right. I should've made Michael take my bed last night instead of making him sleep on the couch. I grabbed my bike, feeling my back already aching in thought of this ride. At least Whittle Corner isn't that far.

"Medusa." Michael followed me out, holding something in his hands. "This way. You are in no condition to ride that today." He waved for me to follow him to the car parked in front of the house.

When did that get here? I know it wasn't parked there yesterday. I would've noticed.

"Michael it's okay. I'll take myself. You can work on whatever it is that you work on." I don't need to be any more of a bother to him.

Michael turned, blue eyes blazing, "*You* are what I work on. Get in." I set my bike back where it goes, and moved as quickly as I could to the car. "Here." He dropped a banana in my lap. We don't have bananas in the house. Where did he get this? "Eat that. I will get you something more suitable when we get into town."

"That isn't necessary! I'll be okay. Thank you for the banana." Michael didn't reply. Once I was done with the - extremely delicious - banana, I glanced over at him again. Maybe I should say something. Is he counting again? What if he's just thinking about the day ahead? Then interrupting him would be rude. So I should stay quiet... Right? I'll just stay quiet. Just in case.

"Welcome to Whittle Corner, we have just what you- Medusa!" Brian just about vaulted over the counter. "Just for that, I'm buying lunch!"

"Just for what?" All I had done was walk in the front door, with someone extra no less.

"You're twenty minutes early! Have I ever told you how much I love you?" I am? I guess that makes sense. Cars are a lot faster than bikes. "What do you want for lunch? *Steamie's?*"

"No!" Michael snapped, startling both of us. "No more burgers. I am going to get you breakfast - a *real nutritious breakfast* - that she will eat whether she is working or not. *You* will find something for lunch that is not a greasy burger or fried anything. Do I make myself clear?"

"Umm, *Steamie's* isn't fried or greasy... That's the poi-" I caught his eye, shaking my head. Michael is determined to believe that all burgers are greasy it seems. Brian nodded back at me, avoiding Michael's glare. "Yes, sir!" Brian nodded rapidly. He looked like one of those sport bobble heads my dad collects. "I'll find something healthy. Do you want anything... Um?"

"My name is Michael. All I want is for you to assist me in keeping Medusa alive, by not feeding her *garbage*." Then he was gone.

I threw away my banana peel, and went to clock in. Brian was shaking his head as I passed, "Your boyfriend is intense. He's also obviously never had *Steamie's*. Hey, are you okay? You're walking weird. Actually, don't answer that. Never mind."

"He's not my boyfriend, and I'm okay. Thank you for asking." I moved to the back with measured steps. In case any customers came in - and partially out of fear of Michael - Brian stayed in the storefront. Luckily since it was a cold day I got away with a long sleeved shirt, so there wouldn't be even more questions.

Michael hadn't meant to hurt me. He just severely overestimated how much strength and fighting knowledge I had. Honestly, I think Michael was under the impression that - what did he call him? - Yhwh, I think, had sent him to recruit a warrior. Too bad all he found was me. I'll just have to try harder.

"Medusa, there you are." Michael was holding a brown paper sack and a foam to-go cup. "I have gotten you a green tea smoothie, and a salmon and sweet potato breakfast burrito with spinach, eggs, and cottage cheese as well." Oh.

"What an… Intriguing combination." I took the bag from him, trying to hide my grimace. Maybe it doesn't taste as bad as it sounds. "Thank you, Michael."

Brian scowled, "That sounds awful, but you do you. Michael, are you going to stay here during her shift?" When Michael turned back to him, he raised his hands as if Michael was a police officer. "Not that I mind! Go ahead and hang out. Just, ah, try not to scare the customers. Please." Brian moved to the opposite end of the store. We probably won't see him again for a while.

I pulled the burrito out of the bag, feeling the dread growing in a pit on my stomach. This was the biggest burrito I've ever seen. "Um, Michael, I won't be able finish this. It's too big." I don't think I've ever had this much food as one meal before.

"Do your best. You need the strength."

"If you say so." Oh. *Oh. That's so bad.* I blinked away the moisture in my eyes. Does he really expect me to eat this? I actually like all of these separately, but *together?* There's so much cottage cheese. Green tea doesn't help! It makes it worse! I made it halfway through the burrito and tea before giving up. "I'm so sorry, Michael. I can't. Please don't ever give me another."

Michael made a noise, "Is it not pleasant? I believe they are all edible."

"Edible doesn't really mean they taste that good together." I gave the bag with the burrito back to the angel. "Thank you, though. I appreciate the effort, and I am no longer hungry." I don't think I'll ever be hungry again. Just the thought of food is making me nauseous. I don't know if I'll be able to hold it down at all.

"I see." He glared at the bag, "I will return later. If that man brings back one of those *godforsaken grease carriers* you are to not eat any of them." I shivered. The temperature seemed to drop to freezing in mere seconds.

I gulped, "Okay!" He left, taking the chill with him. I don't think I'll be able to eat another burger again. Well... That's not true. I just won't eat them around him.

I grabbed the to-do list Brian left behind. Since he's disappeared, I'll go ahead and finish them. His parent's always give him an incredibly long list for the mornings and it makes his anxiety act up. He doesn't need that stress on top of everything he actually does.

I grabbed the cart of things that needed to be re-shelved, and began putting them away. The higher shelves hurt more to stretch to, but I managed. It was quite some time before the bell on the front door chimed, signaling Michael's return.

I moved to the end of the aisle to greet him, "Did you finish your... Oh." It wasn't Michael. It was actually a group of people I had gone to school with.

"What? You aren't going to greet us?" Yvonne taunted, smirking at me. Yvonne was someone I had grown up with. She was raised in

Telluride along with her brother Lysander, and their friends Emilie, Gideon, and Fenix. They're also the sole reason I didn't enjoy high school as much as I thought I would. Well, that isn't completely true. Lysander didn't bother me much. He didn't seem to be in the group either… He must be overseas for a modeling gig.

Still, I straightened my shoulders and smiled, "Hello! Welcome to Whittle Corner - we have just what you need, *whittle* or big! How may I assist you today?"

Yvonne pouted, "What? That's all we get?" She laughed. She seems to be in a good mood today. I wonder what has her in such high spirits.

"You seem to be in a good mood today, Yvonne. Enjoying this weather?" It did seem to be turning into a beautiful day. I haven't actually seen this entire group together in quite some time. There seems to be someone else with them now though. Surely, they didn't just replace Lysander.

"Of course I am. After all, it's a beautiful day to show Mr. Blue our magnificent little town." She gestured to the new member of her group. Mr. Blue? That sounds familiar…

"It is a cute town, Yvonne." Mr. Blue smiled at her. He seems kind. "However, you can call me Allan. You know that." Yvonne blushed. Maybe it's the accent? A lot of people go nuts over the British accents.

I guess that means they don't need help then. I moved back to the cart full of miscellaneous things I need to put back. Why did so many people put candy back? I've never seen this much in the basket before. "Medusa! Where did you go?" I jumped, moving back to where Yvonne can see me. "Don't disappear like that. I didn't bring him to see this shitty store. I brought him to see you."

"Me?" Why would she bring someone to meet me? I don't think Whittle Corner is bad. Sure, it's nothing like the big grocery stores, but it's cute and homey. It has character.

"Mhmm! Allan, this is Medusa Sinclair resident outcast of

Telluride. You see, Allan needs to do research for his new roll coming up. Who better teach him how to be a reject from society than you?"

Oh. I kept my smile up, "That is very nice of you to do for him. What is the role for?" That explains why the name sounds familiar. He's an actor. I don't know what he's been in, but I don't really watch movies… Or tv… Or anything really.

"It's a secret." Emilie snapped, "He can't tell you that!"

"She wouldn't know that, Emilie." Yvonne rolled her eyes. "Her world doesn't pass the town line." I wish that was still true. Heaven seems to come with a lot of stress. "It's simple, Medusa. All you need to do is talk to Allan for a minute. Allan, trust me. She is the best person for this. Her mother died when she was little, her father has been a miserable drunk for as long as we can remember, he doesn't work so she's forced to work countless hours here to support them in a house they can hardly afford anymore. School was miserable for her. Her clothes were always too small or from decades before. Kids bullied her mercilessly," Kids specifically being everyone standing in front of me right now, but I suppose that isn't worth mentioning. "Not even her father feels love for her. She's a true outcast of society. It's perfect!"

Allan looked taken aback, "Oh. You've had a terrible life." It isn't that bad, but Yvonne wouldn't know what my life has been like. Sympathy and pity swarmed in Allan's eyes as he took a step toward me. "I'm sure it can't be easy having it thrown in your face like that. Yvonne she's not a character in some movie. She's a person." Allan moved to me after giving Yvonne a sharp look. "I'm sorry about he-" As he reached out to me, a large hand grabbed his wrist.

Michael towered over him, glaring fiercely, "Who are *you* and what makes you believe you are allowed to touch *my Medusa?*" His Medusa? Since when do I belong to him? I suppose he sees me as his, because he's my mentor, but does he realize how that sounds to other people?

"Wait, who are you?" Emilie moved to look up at Michael. How odd. I haven't seen her look at anyone like that since she had that crush on Mac in middle school. "And why on Earth is a guy like you, with someone like Medusa?"

Michael's glare focused on the woman in front of him. He should like Emilie and Yvonne. They're both gorgeous tall women with wafer thin figures. I believe both have been recruited for modeling. They're much more angelic looking than I am. "Are you the ones responsible for the tears gathering in Medusa's eyes?"

Was it that obvious? I can't cry at work two days in a row. That's horribly unprofessional. Maybe I can force them back by blinking? Nope. I wiped my cheeks. All I had done was make them more obvious, because now they're running down my face. Man, this has been a week.

Michael grew angrier, making me shiver. The temperature beside us seemed to be dropping again. Is this because of his ice magic? I hope that isn't my magic. I don't think I can handle being that cold all the time. I'd have to wear my coat everywhere, or move to Texas. He released Allan's wrist, "Medusa, are you alright?"

What? "Oh, I'm alright! Everything she said was true. Slightly painful, but true. It's alright. I'm alright. You can calm down. It's okay."

Michael turned his frown on me, "Do not lie to me, Medusa Sigyn Sinclair." My eyes darted to the ground. I'd rather him be mad at anyone else that isn't me. He seems to be much more grumpy than he was when he left this morning.

"*Sigyn?*" Emilie grimaced, "I didn't think your name could get worse. What does that even mean?"

"She's another woman from mythology that my mother thought was a symbol of strength." I explained. My names don't make me uncomfortable or ashamed. Sigyn and Medusa have incredibly interesting stories, and my mother had a few journals where she spoke about how much she admired the two.

Emilie didn't seem to agree. She scoffed, "Your mother named you after fairytale villains."

"I don't remember her asking for your opinion." Michael snapped. "Do the five of you plan on buying anything?"

"No," Yvonne crossed her arms, glaring up at Michael. It's much easier for her to accomplish considering she's several inches taller than me and much closer to Michael's face. "You are being extremely rude! Do you know who we are?"

"Insolent little brats with too much pride is what you are." That... Seems harsh. This is just who Yvonne is. She doesn't really think about people like me. "If you are not here to shop, I suggest you leave."

"Or what?" Fenix - speaking up for the first time - stepped forward, "You do realize you're threatening two girls right?"

"I am not threatening two girls. I am offering the five of you a chance to leave before I forcefully remove you." Michael didn't seem bothered at all. Personally, I think Felix can be a little intimidating. He's tall and muscular, and seems *very* angry. He's still shorter than Michael, which probably explains why Michael isn't fazed. Well, that and the whole celestial being thing. "And I can guarantee that you will not win this, *boy.*"

Wait. He's not planning to hurt them in the store, is he? *'I am not here for an execution, but I will if I have to.'* That's what he said yesterday.

"Michael." His blue eyes had an odd golden sheen to them. I don't think that's a good sign. I moved to stand beside him, placing an arm on his - alarmingly thick - bicep. He was freezing. "Please don't."

Michael sighed angrily, stepping back. My sigh of relief didn't go unnoticed by him, though. His eyes snapped back to the group, *"Get out."*

Four of them scurried out, but Allan remained. He ignored Michael, and focused on me. "I apologize for her words, Medusa. I was under the impression that we were going on a tour of Telluride, not coming to patronize you. I sincerely apologize." With a final nod to Michael, he followed the rest of the group out of the store.

21

"Thank you for shopping with us!" Brian greeted as he came back in. When did he leave? I didn't hear him leave. He was carrying bags of food though. "Was that Allan Blue?"

"Yes. When did…"

"What did you bring? It doesn't say *Steamie's*, but that doesn't mean there aren't burgers in there."

"No, but the utter fear you put in me earlier made sure of that. I got food from *Sérénite*." Oh, wow. *Sérénite* was a nicer French restaurant in town. I've never actually been, honestly. "I got you a lemon peppered salmon salad with green artichokes. I don't know if you like those, but it sounds healthy."

"Thank you." I took the salad from him, and the offered plasticware. Oh, he got a honey mustard dressing too. How… Appetizing.

Michael peered over my shoulder at the salad, "It has many healthy elements. Eat all of it."

"Well, don't eat more than you can handle," Brian interjected, "It is a big salad." I smiled at him. I didn't think he'd care about my eating habits.

Michael rolled his eyes, "It is not that big." It was one of the biggest salad's I have ever seen. Maybe it doesn't look big, because he's some type of frost giant. I wonder what he'd think of something really tiny. Like a kitten.

Ignoring Michael completely, I turned back to my outrageously kind boss, "I'll eat as much as I can before I get back to work. Thank you, again."

"No problem. Anything for my best employee." As long as it doesn't upset Michael. He didn't say it, but with the way his eyes kept nervously shifting to the ice giant, it's a little obvious. Maybe I should talk to Michael about not purposefully scaring Brian. Not that he'd actually listen to me.

忍

"Alright," Michael turned to face me. He had patiently waited while I changed out of my work uniform into what could be considered training clothes. They were just sweats, but I think they'll work. Maybe I should've picked up some type of elbow pads on the way home. "Are you ready to begin?"

"Yup!" I had taken some pain medicine before we left the store, and couldn't really feel the bruises from last night, so I should be ready for whatever he's planned. "What are we trying today?"

"We are trying Aikido and - if that doesn't work - we will try Muay Thai." I don't know what either of those are, but Michael seemed optimistic about them. Maybe they'll work. Then I'll have real life magic like *Matilda*!

忍

"Oomph!" I landed on my back, again. I find it very hard to believe that people do this is for fun. "I don't think I like Muay Thai. Are you sure it isn't a torture method?"

"I am positive." Michael stood over me, he looked perfectly fine. We've been out here for two hours. He looks like he's just been standing here this whole time. I wish that is what he'd been doing. I'd be in a lot less pain that way. "Get up. I want to teach you the Tae Chiang. Surely one of these will get your magic energy flowing."

"Can I please go shower and lay down?" I don't know how often he does full contact sports - is martial arts a sport? - but I never do them, and I'm exhausted. I don't think I can feel my legs.

Michael sighed, pulling me to my feet, "Yes. I will be in shortly." Sounds good to me. Maybe he'll stay out until I'm actually dressed this time.

My father didn't say anything as I made my way through the living room. He was too invested in some football rerun. I wonder if he knows we have more channels.

"Medusa!" I jumped, nearly falling back down the stairs. "Grab me a beer while you're in there." Sighing internally, I moved back down the stairs to the fridge. He glanced up at me to take his drink. "Dear god," He did a double take. I don't think I've ever seen him actually focus on me like this. "You look awful. Go shower before Michael sees you like that!"

Why does it matter if Michael sees me like this? He's the one that kept knocking me over. I'm off tomorrow. We should spend the day looking for a training area inside. The ground is just going to get colder as we get deeper into winter. At this rate, I'll end up with frostbite before November.

I stopped by my room to grab clothes before heading to the bathroom. Just in case Michael comes inside before I'm out. I'm already a bother to him, the least I can do is actually get myself ready for bed. He wasn't too happy when he told me about last night.

I kept the shower temperature lower than I would normally have it. My skin is already so cold, too much heat seems like a terrible idea. At least I'm not in too much pain. Maybe the pain medicine helped past and future pains. That's nice.

Michael wasn't in my room when I came back. Odd. I wonder if he's still outside. Maybe he enjoys sitting outside in the cold, or he's too angry to look at me right now. It's probably the latter. I don't know why his methods aren't working, but my magic is staying dormant. If I even have any. I don't think I'm the type to have magic, honestly. Michael won't hear it though. He's convinced I have some somewhere in my subconscious.

Wait. What if I dive into my subconscious? Oh, where's that book? I moved to the bookshelf that was embedded into the wall. Once I was old enough to read, I had gone to the basement to see if she had any books I could read. It was where I had found her journals, and massive books on mythologies from around the world. I had also found several books on meditation and the human subconscious. Here it is!

I settled in the middle of my bed, folding my legs underneath me. Okay, I'm in a quiet place - well the quietest place I have access to. Now I just need to take deep breaths, and… Imagine myself sinking deeper into the bed. I can do that.

I closed my eyes - the book said I could choose something in the room to focus on, but that will just make me think. I need to not think. Just breathe, and sink. In and out. Deeper into the bed. In and out. Deeper into wool comforter. Now picture my perfect day…

I'm in a nice sundress with little plus and multiplication signs all over it. A room full of third graders sits in front of me, eyes bright with fascination at what they could learn today. It would have exercise balls instead of those awful plastic chairs.

"Medusa!" I jumped, completely losing focus. Michael stood in my doorway with a large smile on his face. I made him smile! "Do that again!"

"What? I was just meditating. I thought it would help with my magic, but I don't think it did anything." I certainly didn't feel any different.

"Is there a window open in here?"

"No?" All of my windows are closed. It's thirty degrees outside.

"Then why is there a breeze?" What? Wind blew through my hair, sending it flying. How is he doing that? I thought he just made ice? It wasn't a cool breeze though. It was pretty warm, and - oddly enough - quite comforting. "Medusa, you're the one doing that." He bent over to grab something from the floor. It was the book that was sitting in front of me five seconds ago. Did I blow it off the bed? "Is this what you were using? Show me where you were."

He climbed onto the bed, mimicking my position across from me. I took the book from him and went back to the chapter I was reading. Michael read it over a few times, before reading through the rest of the chapter. I sat quietly, letting him read through it. He better not be counting. Letting someone read in silence is a courtesy thing, not a patience thing.

"I never considered meditation. Do you have enough energy to try this tonight, or would you rather wait till morning?"

I felt much better, actually. It was like I'd drank one of those

Monster drinks everyone had in high school. "I'm good to go for now!"

"Excellent. How do we do this?" He left the book open in front of us, so he could peer at the directions without having to change his position. "Meditation is not something I do often, or ever, actually. This will be a first."

"Well, I've got some great news! Unlike your teachings, I don't plan on causing you any physical or mental pain." I straightened my posture, but relaxed the rest of my body. Michael followed my movements. "You're supposed to be relaxed, Michael. Just let go."

"Relaxation leaves you weak. I need to be prepared for any and all attacks."

I tilted my head at him, "Attacks? Are you expecting someone to try and hurt us?"

"There is always an opportunity for someone to hurt others. Humans hurt each other all the time without reason. Even your father could randomly decide to come in here and attempt to end your life. All it would take is a slight shift in the way his brain functions."

I laughed. Michael's frown got impossibly deeper, but I couldn't help it. It would take more than a *slight* shift for my father to deem me more important than the television. "Can you just relax for a moment with me please? I want to see if I can actually *do* something with these powers you insist I have."

"I insist, because I knew they were there, and guess what; I was correct. If we get attacked durning this 'relaxation' of yours, I will never let you forget it." I believe that. Michael shifted uneasily, glancing at the windows on either side of my bed. The angel took a deep breath, and released it letting it take all of the taught tension in his body with it. "What next?"

"Close your eyes-"

"The book says that I can focus on an object in the room."

"Well, I know you and you can't. If your eyes are open, you will be focused on what could happen or what is happening. Wether it's a bird or an assassin. Close your eyes." Looking like an angry grizzly - growl included -, Michael complied. "Release the tension. Stop growling, that's how I know you aren't relaxed."

"Stop *giggling* and I will be more relaxed."

I bit my lip, and actually listened to my own directions. How am I supposed to teach Michael how to do this, if I can't even show him I can do it? "Okay, now focus on your breathing. After every measured breath, I want you to picture yourself sinking deeper into the bed."

"Alright." He breathed.

We sat there quietly. I could hear every breath he took. He wasn't breathing loudly though. In fact, it was almost soothing. "Okay, now picture your perfect day."

"No. I want you to picture this room." My room? I could just open my eyes for that. "Trust me. Picture the room, feel the air currents. There are at least two, as we are both breathing. Focus on those."

"Umm, okay." I kept my eyes closed and pictured my room. In my head I could see Michael sitting across from me with both of us breathing with our eyes closed. This is weird.

"Now I want you to move the air that you are focusing on. Just try to move it slightly."

I don't really know *how* to move air, but I told him I'd try my best. Maybe I can just grab it and pull? I don't think it's working. Okay, so what if I inhale, and imagine breathing in all of the air. A hand landed on my calf, nearly sending me off the bed. Michael inhaled deeply, trying to catch his breath. What happened?

"Are you okay?"

"Yes," He coughed, "You did fantastic. You took the air right out of my lungs. Literally." Oh!

"I did it?" Is he serious? He wouldn't really play a joke on me, would he?

"You did it."

"Yay! Oomph," I rolled off the bed. Maybe throwing my arms

up without actually sitting in a stable position wasn't the best idea. Michael looked over the edge of the bed, raising a brow at me. "My bad."

He shook his head, "You are such a human."

"But I did it!" I held up a hand for a high five. Michael simply grabbed my hand and pulled me back up to the bed. "I wanted a high five, but thank you."

"I don't know what that is, but I will pass." Of course he would. That will be my next goal. I got him to smile when I made my powers work. Now all I need is a laugh and a high five. Shouldn't be too hard, right?

"Well, we should probably go to bed now. I'll move to the couch, so you can rest." Michael caught my hand before I could get off the bed.

"That is unnecessary. You can stay here." I shook my head. He heard my father this morning. "I will stay in here as well, so your father does not get upset. Don't worry. Just go to sleep."

Michael moved to lay in the bed, patting the space beside him. I guess he's serious. I shifted, looking down at the bed. "I usually sleep on that side…"

"Oh." He shuffled to the other side, and pat my usual spot. "Now get in, and sleep."

"Is this a normal thing in Heaven?" I asked, climbing into the bed once I'd turned out the lights. Michael wasn't under the covers, but seemed comfortable enough. "Sharing a bed with someone else, I mean."

"We don't have beds in Zion - which is the correct name of Heaven. I only experience exhaustion in the human realm." Really? What is it like to never need or want sleep? I can't imagine that. I think everything should take the time to recharge. "So, I don't actually sleep, but I have been needing to take some time to recharge."

"Oh. Well, goodnight Michael."

"Goodnight, Medusa."

Chapter Four

I flipped the pancake, humming quietly. Honestly, I don't know why I'm in such high spirits this morning. The air just felt... More crisp this morning. We must have a cold front coming in.

Speaking of cold fronts, Michael smoothly came into the kitchen. "Your father is not in his normal spot. Did he leave the house?"

"It's eight in the morning," I laughed, "He's still asleep, I'm sure. Do you like pancakes?"

"I don't eat." He peered over my shoulder anyway, to get a look at the pancake in the pan. "This does not look healthy, Medusa. I will go get you something else."

"No! No, thank you." I don't ever want a repeat of breakfast yesterday. "I've already made these. I don't want to waste food." He frowned down at me, then at the plate stacked with pancakes. "I'll eat some fruit on the side, okay?"

"That sounds a little better. I recommend avocado."

"That's not happening. I'll have an apple." I turned back to the - now burnt - pancake on the stove, and moved it to a different plate. Michael seemed appeased enough to move to the barstool, and stayed silent.

It's so strange. Normally I don't like days off. They make me stay home and be bored, but today was so peaceful. I wish I could stay in this moment forever. I wasn't alone, so I'm not lonely, but Michael didn't need me to do anything or fill the silence. The tv is off, so I can hear the birds outside. It's just so peaceful.

I slid a plate of pancakes in front of Michael along with the butter and syrup. "Just in case you want to try them. You don't have to eat them." He nodded, going back to looking out the window. Well, they're there if he wants any. I put the rest in the microwave so dad could have some if he wanted any. He usually likes pancakes. "So," I chirped, taking a seat beside Michael. "What are we doing today? More meditating?"

"In a way, yes. There is a park nearby. We are going to go there, and see if you can connect with your element there." He looked me over, "You will need to change. I don't think penguins are appropriate."

"No," I laughed. I'd had these penguin pajamas for years. They were faded, and torn in more than one place. They were still comfortable, though. "I'll change into something more appropriate." If I was going to be playing with wind, skirts and dresses are a no. Ugh, I don't really like pants.

After washing off both of our plates - Michael had eventually ate his - I headed upstairs to change. Thankfully, Michael didn't move to follow. I slipped into a comfy sweater and some jeans as quickly as I could, and tied my hair up in a ponytail. The last thing I want is to get hair in my face. It would probably kill the 'magical' aspect of all this.

I could hear Michael and my father talking in the kitchen as I slipped my boots on. Dad seemed to be in a chipper mood this morning. Must be the pancakes. Michael looked up as I entered the kitchen, and gave me a strained smile. I think it was meant to come off as easygoing, but he just looked uncomfortable.

"Medusa!" I jumped at my father's booming voice, "Michael let it slip that you two are *closer* than I originally thought. That's wonderful news! He's a good guy this one. I can tell."

He let it slip? Michael didn't seem like he'd accidentally do anything, let alone tell a secret that didn't exist. Michael moved to me, pressing a kiss into my temple. Has he been possessed? Can angels get possessed? "I may have let it slip that we shared the bed last night. Sorry, love, I know you wanted to tell him in your own way."

Oh.

He must've mentioned it casually not realizing how my father would take that. Someone should really make a human handbook for angels. At least Dad is happy about it. Most fathers wouldn't really approve of their daughter keeping a secret like that from them.

"Sorry I didn't tell you sooner, Dad. I wasn't sure how to approach the subject." I don't like lying to him, but something tells me he wouldn't react to magic as well as this. Less of two evils, right? "Are you ready to go, Michael?"

"Yes. Enjoy your breakfast, Elias." Dad smiled at us as we left before focusing back on the fridge. I'll probably need to go grocery shopping soon.

"That was an accident." Michael grumbled once we were both in the car. "I did not think he would take sharing a bed as a courtship."

I laughed, "I think everyone would take it that way. That's what it would mean if you were human, at least." I like this car. It's so cozy. The backseat was mainly for show, but could hold a handbag if needed. It's definitely a lot warmer than my bike on these Autumn mornings.

"Really?" Michael glanced over to see me nod. He shifted uncomfortably, tightening his hands on the steering wheel. I wonder when he learned how to drive. Does Heaven - sorry, Zion - have a driving school? Maybe it's a school on humanity that gets updates every two years or something. Though they seem to be lacking knowledge on common behaviors and meanings. "Well, it is a good cover for why I am in your life so much. You are not 'dating' another human are you?"

"Nope. I've never really had time." Back when I did have time, no one was ever interested in me. When there are always girls like Yvonne around, I'm the last thing anyone is ever thinking about.

"Good. We don't need any meddlesome humans butting in where they aren't wanted. They'll just hinder your process." He pulled into the park parking lot, and peered out the window. "There, by the big tree. That is where we will go."

Oh, I love that tree. It was toward the middle of the park, and easily the biggest tree around. The weekday morning saved us from having to battle a crowd to sit underneath it, too. Michael sat next to me, mimicking my crossed legs again.

"Now, don't pull the air this time. There are some humans around that we don't want to gain the attention of." Michael instructed, keeping his voice low. No one was really near us, but I guess he was just being cautious. "For now just close your eyes and try to feel the air around you and me."

Okay. I can do that. A true meditative state might not be possible for me right now with all of the sounds around us, but I can do what I did yesterday... Right? I pictured Michael and I sitting side by side in the cool shade with the wind rustling the leaves above us. I wonder if I could make a leaf fall... Maybe if I push it a little. Michael told me not to *pull* the air; he said nothing about *pushing* it.

"Medusa?" I jumped, completely losing focus. May stood in front of me, with her uniform in her hand. Her rose gold bob was tousled, but still pretty. She tried to get me to dye my hair with her, but I didn't have the funds to do something that unnecessary. Plus, I don't mind my blonde. "How long have you two been sitting here?" She laughed, bending down to brush a pile of leaves from the top of my head. "You're both covered in leaves! Who's the man? I didn't know you had a brother."

"Oh, I don't have a brother. This is Michael." She was right about one thing though. We were completely covered in leaves. I stood up to shake mine off before brushing them out of Michael's hair.

Michael frowned at me after finally opening his eyes, "You are pulling my hair out of it's coil."

"You're covered in leaves!" I continued brushing the leaves from his hair. He looked like some kind of forest nymph. Maybe a forest giant? Do they have those?

"Well aren't you two adorable." May cooed, "I can't believe you didn't tell me you were seeing someone."

"What?" I snatched my hand away from Michael's hair. I could already feel the blood rushing to my cheeks. "We... We're not... Michael isn't..."

"Well, of course I am. Are you suddenly ashamed of me, love?" I turned to him, feeling my cheeks turning pink. I didn't realize we were telling *everyone* that we were together. News travels fast in a small town, though, so everyone would know pretty soon anyway, I suppose.

"Well," May laughed, "You two are cute. I'll leave you to get back to your couples mediating." She gave me a hug before continuing on her way.

Michael huffed, placing his hands on his hips, "This is turning out to be much more useful than I had originally thought. Humans are so gullible." Coming from an angel that's a little concerning... He turned to me. I shrunk under his glare. What did I do to make him so mad all of the sudden? "I told you to *feel* the air. I specifically told you not to push the air since there are humans - your friend May, for example - around. Humans do not need to witness actual magic; they're greedy enough."

Oh. Yeah, I should've known he'd be mad about that. "I'm sorry, Michael. I just got excited."

His scowl deepened, "Well don't. There is nothing exciting about war."

War? When did war come into this? He doesn't really expect me to *fight* someone, does he? He's mentioned fighting and danger a couple times before, but I thought that was his paranoia. "Michael!" I called, chasing him. I don't know when he started walking away, but he had gotten pretty far. He paused when he realized I wasn't catching up very fast. "What did you mean? Is there a war coming?"

"That doesn't matter right now. What matters is you getting control of your powers. You don't need to concern yourself with the details, I am handling them." I pursed my lips, but didn't reply.

It's not like I'm in any immediate danger, right? Michael is here to protect me. If he doesn't think I need to know the details just yet then I should trust his judgement. He is much older than me, and has seen more than I could possibly imagine.

"Medusa?" I looked up to see the guy from the other day jogging toward us. What was his name again? Ellen? No, Allan? I think. I won't say his name out loud just in case. Michael said something under his breath that I'm almost positive was a very bad word in a different language. Can angels curse? I smiled as Allan reached us, "It is so good to see you again. I wanted to apologize once more for the actions of Yvonne the other day. It was horribly unacceptable, and I feel so terrible that anyone would talk to another person in that manner."

"Oh it's alright. I've known that group since kindergarten. They've always thought it was crazy that I didn't have as much as they did. The whole school did, really." Yvonne isn't in the minority here. I am. Always have been.

Allan didn't look convinced, "That doesn't make it okay. Maybe I can buy you dinner or something? Are you free tonight?"

"*No,* she is not." Michael responded for me. I couldn't see him since he was standing behind me, but his shadow stretched in front of us, making his presence even more pronounced.

Allan seemed to shrink into himself as he looked up at Michael, "I didn't mean it like that. I was just trying to be nice. You made it very clear that you two are together the other day." The other day? That was before Michael had mentioned anything about this lie. Allan focused back on me, "I don't mean any harm to your relationship. I just hoped there was a way I could apologize for that ordeal."

"Don't worry about it." I shook my head. I don't think I've ever met a stranger that was so kind before. "Just the fact that you cared enough to apologize makes me really happy. I hope you enjoy your stay in Telluride."

He beamed at me, "Thank you! I already think I love it here. If

I didn't love living in New York so much I would definitely move here." He waved goodbye, and continued on his way through the park.

I've never been to New York, but I don't think it could beat Telluride. I've never traveled though, so there's that. Maybe if I ever travel I'll lose some of my bias.

"Medusa." I snapped back into focus. Michael was standing several feet in front me, looking back at me with his arms crossed. Oh. I guess it's time to go. "I figured you'd be hungry. Would you like to continue working instead?"

"Nope! Food sounds great. Do I get to pick what I eat?"

He shrugged, "Not really. We are not going to one of the eating establishments that are filled with grease. We are going to the base of operations in this district." There's a base of operations for angels in Telluride?

"Oh that sounds fun!" I jogged to keep up with him as he crossed the park. How does he get so far so fast? "How close is it?"

He made a noise, but didn't answer. What does that mean? We made it back to the car without Michael giving me any further information. That's okay though. It's all part of the journey. Right? We got into the car…

And drove right back to my house. This is the base of operations?

"This is my house."

"Very good. We have to leave the vehicle here. Follow me, we want to stay away from your father's eyes as well." I followed him out of the car, and jogged to reach him again. I'm going to need stilts to keep up with him.

We made our way toward the side of the house where there weren't any windows from the living room. Michael turned to me, fixing me with a glare, "Do *not* scream." Why would I…

I slapped my hands over my mouth to stop any of the noises that were on their way out. Gigantic snow white wings unfurled from his back. They were almost as wide as the side of the house.

Michael rolled his eyes at me, "Come here. Still no screaming, and *do not* pet me."

I stepped into his open arms, and shivered. He's like a block of ice. "Medusa, wrap your arms around me, and hold on tight." I really should've worn a jacket. I did as instructed, and wrapped my arms tightly around the glacier. Michael's wings wrapped around us casting a blinding light. I buried my face into his chest to try and block most of it out. I think I finally understand the term 'blinding white light' I thought it was an exaggeration.

By the time Michael let me go, I was a shivering mess. I *really* should've grabbed a jacket. Michael frowned down at me, "Why are you so pale?"

"I…I'm…F-f-fre-eezing." Does he not realize how cold he is? Are all angels cold or is it just because of his ice magic?

"Really? I thought it was much warmer here than Telluride."

"I wasn't talking about the weather. Oh, never mind." I turned away from him to get a grasp on our surroundings. There were pine trees *everywhere,* and nothing else. Just trees, and grass everywhere. Surely he didn't bring me to the middle of the woods. How would that be any different than just walking half a mile from where I live?

"Michael… Where are we?" What if he leaves me here? He wouldn't do that… Right? What have I gotten myself into? This doesn't seem like a base of operations to me.

"I believe this is called Sapphire Falls in North Carolina. The waterfall is that way, but it's a tourist attraction. The base is further that way, but not close enough to be in danger from you. I want you to get into touch with your magic here." He pointed to a nearby tree that couldn't be anywhere less than twenty feet tall. "Blow that tree over."

"Um…"

"Do it, Medusa." He stepped away, and crossed his arms.

I guess I don't have much of a choice. I'll just have to try my best.

I focused on the tree in front of me, and took a deep breath. All I have to do is meditate and push the wind, right? I can do that. I faced the tree, and closed my eyes. Even breaths, picture the scene around me, and feel the wind move with me. I could see everything - all the way to Michael's folded arms. The breeze ruffling the leaves on the trees became a mere extension of me, allowing me to curb it any way I want.

Okay. I can do this. I pushed the breeze toward the tree Michael pointed out to me, and heard the wind smash into the tree trunk.

"Did I do it?!" Oh. The tree stood tall, and completely untouched. Not even a branch had fallen.

Michael growled behind me, "Nothing happened! I said knock it over!"

"I tried!" Michael's glare got worse at my reply.

"*Try harder.* We don't have time for these ridiculous baby steps! Do it again, and do it right." I don't know what happened between here and the park, but I don't like it. He's scary when he's angry.

"Okay." I moved closer to the tree, and closed my eyes again. Okay. This is simple. All I have to do is push harder. I can do that. I can do anything I set my mind to! At least I hope so.

The breeze came back to me, along with a few other scattered winds from nearby. Maybe with their help I'll be able to knock the tree over. Then Michael won't be so mad at me. I gathered all of the wind I could muster, and directed it at the tree. By the time I released it, I was short of breath. I tried to focus on the tree to see if it had fallen, but it swayed in front of my vision. Is it falling?

"Medusa!"

Chapter Five

I groaned, rubbing my eyes. How did I get to my bed? I thought we were in the woods. Had he tricked me with some kind of illusion? I didn't think angels could do that.

"Oh good. You're awake." Michael sat beside me on the bed. He didn't seem very happy with me.

"I take it I didn't knock the tree down?"

"No. You fainted and slowed your heartbeat down so much I thought it was going to stop completely." He sighed, pinching the bridge of his nose. "You're too weak."

"I'm-"

"I will return later. There are things I need to discuss with my father. It seems we need to rethink our plan of action. You are not a defender." I sagged into myself as he made his way out of the room. I'd failed him. Michael paused in the doorway, "You have work in an hour. Take your bike."

忍

"Medusa! So glad you're here." Brian greeted with a wide smile. He peered around me, "Are you alone today?"

"Yup! I don't know if we'll see Michael for a while, if I'm honest." He was really disappointed in me this morning. I wouldn't be surprised if he decided to abandon me completely and just go find the next Virtue. Maybe they'll be better than me.

"Oh," Brian awkwardly hesitated, "I'm sorry. Not that he isn't here because that dude is scary as shit, but you seem upset so I'm sorry about that." I laughed. Michael can be pretty terrifying. "Tell you what, I have to go help my Mom with something at home, but when I get back I'll bring you lunch. Sound good?"

"That sounds great actually. I got so busy disappointing Michael that I forgot to pack mine."

"I've got it covered!" He grabbed his phone off the counter, and made his way to the door. He paused when he reached me, putting a hand on my shoulder, "You're an amazing person, Medusa. I've known you for years and have never been disappointed in you. Sure that Michael guy is big and muscly, but that doesn't mean he's a good guy. You could do much better, in my opinion. Please don't start crying."

"Sorry." I blubbered, trying to blink the tears away. That was really nice of him to say. He patted my shoulder once more, promised to have lunch, and disappeared out the door. I think I scared him. He isn't a big fan of emotions.

It wasn't long before the door chimed, signaling a new customer. I straightened to see an older couple waling into the store. The greying woman turned to the man with a wide smile, "Look at this little store! It's so cozy, and adorable!"

"Welcome to Whittle Corner! We have just what you need, *whittle* or big! Is there anything I can assist you with today?"

The couple came over to me with the woman still smiling away. What a happy person. "Oh what a cute little pun! We're just passing through on our way to Albuquerque. I saw pictures of Telluride on that picture app on my phone and have been dreaming of coming here ever since."

"Oh! Well I'm glad you finally made it! I've never been anywhere but Telluride, but why go anywhere when I already live in one of the most beautiful cities in the world?" I wish all my customers were like her. I would love to have such happy people in here all the time.

"Oh you are just so cute! What is your name so I can let your boss know how wonderful you are?"

I smiled, showing her my name tag, "Thank you! My name is Medusa."

Her smile slipped from her face, as her husband frowned, "Medusa? Like the monster?"

"That is one take on it, yes."

"One take?" Her husband interjected, "Is there another take? She turns men into stone."

Some women don't like men, so they would think it's a good story. I can't say that though. Instead I just smiled, "Well now it can be like the nice woman at Whittle Corner."

"We're just going to look around." Off they went. I returned back to restocking the toiletry aisle while they moved around the store. Less than ten minutes later they left the store without buying anything. I guess my name upset them.

A few more guests made their way through the store, but only talked to me when they had to. Which is fine, and normal. I'd rather them ignore me than be mean to me. Sometime later, a girl around my age rushed into the store. I couldn't get the welcome phrase out before she was several aisles deep into the store. I refocused on the destroyed candy shelf until she made her way to the counter.

She carefully sat all of her items on the counter. Yvonne would hate this girl. She seems so effortlessly gorgeous. Her long black hair was falling over her shoulders. She ran her hand through her hair, making it look like an official hairstylist fixed it. Her grey eyes focused on mine, prompting me to actually speak.

"Hi! Did you find everything okay?" I smiled at her, trying to cover up how long I was staring at her.

"Yeah, thank you." Was her husky reply. I didn't realize a husky voice was an actual thing, but she definitely has one. Her head tilted, "Is your name really Medusa?" *Oh.* "I don't mean any offense. I'm just curious."

I tried to bring my smile back up, and laugh it off, "Yeah. I like my name though. It's unique."

The woman actually scoffed at me, "My name is Karma, so I feel your pain."

Karma? That's such a pretty name! I told her so, too. She basically rolled her eyes at me. Is she always this positive? "I'm being serious! I like it!"

She blinked at me. I don't think she was expecting me to be serious. "Oh. Well thank you. Sorry, I'm a little too used to people immediately mocking it." I know how that feels. Customers do that everyday I'm at work. She ruffled her hair again, showing off her massive biceps. Does she benchpress trucks? "For the record, I think Medusa is pretty badass."

A surprised laugh escaped my lips. That's... A strong word. It's nice though! "Thank you! I'm not feeling much like one lately." Michael's disappointed face flashed in front of my face. Maybe I can try knocking down a tree again after work... My life has gotten so weird lately.

"Yeah, me either. Maybe I just need a different teacher." A different teacher? That's an idea... Who would even teach me? Another angel doesn't seem like they would be much better.

I patted her hand that was resting on the counter. It had a grandma feel to it, but it's all I could think to do. She looked really down. "I don't know what kind of teacher you have, but trust me, he can't be worse than mine." I froze, remembering how I let Michael down. "I don't mean to be rude. He's helping me a lot, but he's so mean some times. I don't understand how he can be so grumpy all of the time. It's crazy. I don't think I've ever been angry for more than an hour at most." How can you hang on to anger for so long? Michael seems to always be some form of angry when I'm around. Maybe it's just me...

"So I'm not the only one with a stoic, infuriating man that I have to spend time with?"

"Absolutely not! Do you want your receipt?" She declined, smiling at me. She has a really pretty smile. Is it weird that I want to tell her everything like we've been friends for years? "I'm actually known for being patient, really *really patient,* but it's like God put him on this Earth just to get rid of all my patience. He's like a general. All. The. Time." I groaned, handing her bag over the counter. Maybe I'll get a short break from him and recharge. "Hey, how long are you in town?" I like having her around.

She gnawed on her bottom lip as she thought. Maybe I shouldn't have asked and just let her go. I didn't mean to make her uncomfortable. "I actually don't know. We're staying in a cabin a few miles outside of town, so about an hour, I guess?"

"Well do you want to meet up sometime next week? I'm off Tuesday. We can do lunch and get away from our overbearing men?" Oh god, Medusa. Stop talking. "Sorry if I seem a little over excite-"

Karma laughed, cutting me off, "That sounds great. How about one o'clock on Tuesday?" I couldn't help the excited smile that crossed my face. I think I just made a really good friend.

"That sounds great! We can go to *Steamie's.* It's the best place in town. They serve burgers, by the way. Are you a vegetarian? They have a veggie burger too." She doesn't really look like one. I think you need a lot of protein to keep up with a physique like that, but what do I know? I can barely lift a bag of marshmallows. "Sorry, I keep forgetting you're new in town. I feel like I've known you forever."

The door chimed getting our attention. Michael! He actually came back! Oh. I just made plans for *Steamie's…*

"Medusa!" I jumped at his gruff tone. I guess he's still angry. "There you are." He stalked over, but stopped to scowl down at Karma. "Who are you?"

Oh no. He probably thought she was like Yvonne. "Michael, stop. Karma, you should probably leave before he starts talking." I joked, hoping she'd take the advice seriously. I don't want Michael to end up ruining my new friendship.

Karma took my advice and grabbed her bag. As she went to pass Michael, he grabbed her forearm. What is he doing?! The look Karma gave him was deadly, "Can I *help* you?" I could feel the venom in her words as she glared back at Michael without flinching.

He was several inches taller than her, how is she not frightened? She must be a superhero.

I could feel the temperature dropping around us, signaling Michael getting upset. This is going downhill fast. I moved around the counter to get to Michael. "Ow!" Karma yelled, "Get your hand off of me!"

"Michael!" Taking a breath, I gathered some of the air around me and pushed the full weight of my body at his arm with a small wind boost. Not enough for Karma to notice, hopefully, but enough to successfully get his hand to let her go. Once she was free I turned to glare at him. She didn't flinch in front of him so maybe I don't have to either. "What is the *matter* with you?"

"Medusa move." Michael commanded, expecting me to listen. Maybe I would've yesterday, but not today.

"No! You can't do that!" I turned to Karma, "Go, it's okay. I've got him." She didn't seem sure, but listened anyway. Once she was gone, I turned back to Michael. "You *can't* harass the customers! This is my job!"

Michael rolled his eyes at me, "Medusa, there is something wrong with that girl. I'm going after her."

"Too late. Her car just left the parking lot. See?" I pointed to a random car that drove past the window. I don't know if that's really her car, but Michael seemed to buy the lie.

He cursed in that language of his again, watching the car drive off. Hopefully he can't remember license plates. "What did she say to you?"

"Nothing. It was just small talk. It's part of the job." I moved back around the counter. I hope she's okay. "You didn't *hurt* her, did you?"

Michael's frown deepened, "You are not asking the questions here. What did that girl say to you? Did she mention the Virtues?"

"What? No! She's just a nice person who was being nice to me! Do you know the last time someone was nice to me?"

He scoffed, "Yesterday. That boy in the park."

"*No.*" Moisture was gathering in my eyes, adding to my frustration. I don't think I've ever been this worked up. "Not nice to me because they feel bad. Even May is nice to me because she pities me in some way. Not Karma, though. She was just genuinely having a pleasant conversation with me, and you ruined it! She'll probably never talk to me again."

"*Good.* I'm serious, Medusa. That girl was not of this world. Her magic aura was outrageous. I've only seen so much fury in one other being..."

"Maybe she wouldn't have been so mad if you hadn't grabbed her."

Michael's blue eyes flashed a bright gold, "You aren't listening! Stop being so human! That girl has a magic signature that I have only seen in my greatest enemy. That is *not* a good thing. Stay away from her. I'll need to let my father know about her existence." What would Yhwh do to her?

"Wait, Michael..."

"Lunch has arrived!" Brian announced coming through the door with *Steamie's* bags and milkshakes. He deflated exponentially at the sight of Michael. "Hey... Man... What's up?"

"Are those burgers?"

"Get out." Michael turned to me in shock. I straightened my spine. "I'm going to eat that burger, and you can't stop me."

His eyes narrowed, "I can stop him from giving you them."

"Hurt my friends again, and I'm done. I don't care what happens. I won't work with you any longer if I can't trust you. I mean it, Michael. You went too far." Michael stared at me in silence for an eternity, before leaving the store.

I released the breath I was holding, sagging into the counter. "Holy moly... I didn't think I was going to win that."

"Holy moly?!" Brian sat the bags on the counter. "You won't get fired for saying holy shit. That was a holy shit moment! Oh, you don't curse. Well I do! *Holy shit!*" I laughed, "You did so good! Look at you being a strong and confident woman! Thank you, for not letting him murder me. Here, you can have both fries." He handed me the bags after taking his burger out, "Go take your lunch. I got things up here, you *badass.*" That's twice now. I think I like being a badass.

I settled into the break room with my lunch. My hands were still shaking from standing up to Michael. I didn't think I'd be able to do that. Next time I decide to be like Karma I should remember that she's a lot stronger than me, and could probably handle much more than I could even hope to. Yeah, I need to find a different way to be strong. Karma's way is a little too aggressive for me.

This burger is amazing. I love *Steamie's.*

"Hey, badass." Brian poked his head in the room. Is it time to go back already? "Where do we keep the powder-less gloves?"

"In pharmacy by the ankle braces. Bottom shelf."

"Thank you. Here." He tossed a chocolate bar at me. I should probably tell him that not all women will be happy to have candy thrown at them when they're upset, but then he'd stop giving me free candy. Plus what kind of girl doesn't like free candy? "Oh," He poked his head back into the room, "That's because you were shaking and I was concerned, not because I think throwing chocolate at women makes them happy."

"It *does* make us happy. Just for the record."

He laughed, giving me a thumbs up before going back to whatever he was doing. I finished my food and my free candy bar, and checked the time. I still had a few minutes. I should probably learn to eat a little slower. Ha! That'll never happen. I love food too much.

When my break was over, I met Brian back at the front. He smiled when I walked in, "Feeling better. Thank you for everything." He waved me off. I forgot he doesn't like sappy moments. "Sorry."

"You're alright. I'll be restocking the shelves and pretending I don't understand any of the customers. Those people that were looking for gloves?" I nodded, "They needed powder-less gloves to go *skiing!*"

I frowned, tilting my head. "If they're going skiing... They would need wool or the leather gloves on aisle four."

"I know! That woman yelled at me, and told me to get you. She thought you were my manager! All because I didn't know she meant skiing gloves instead of the blue ones in pharmacy! You are *not* my manager." He pointed at me. "I'm the manager. Dammit."

I laughed, "I know, and you're a great manager."

"Damn right I am. Here." He handed me another random candy bar from the candy shelf. "And just so you know, I'm keeping track of how many candy bars I give you. That way I don't confuse myself with paperwork, so don't lecture me." I wasn't going to lecture. Maybe. Possibly. Okay, I was, but I'm not the manager.

"Oh look! A car pulled into the parking lot." He disappeared like a cartoon character. There was even a cloud of smoke in his body shape. "Hello! Welcome to Whittle Corner - we have everything you need, *whittle* or big! Is there anything I can help you with?"

The new customers ignored me, and continued past me. Brian would like those people. The next group of people were a family with a little four year old dressed in the cutest ice princess costume I have ever seen. She was carrying a little snowman in her arms, too. How adorable! I bowed to her as she moved passed.

"Mommy! She thinks I'm a real princess!" She cheered, skipping behind her parents. "You can be a royal knight in my kingdom, lady!"

"Thank you, your majesty." She scream-shrieked in excitement, jumping in place. Her parents just laughed, and went back to looking for whatever they came for. I moved back to the counter, but couldn't get the smile to go away. I love kids.

Oh. There goes the smile. Michael was back. He came to rest his arms on the counter, "I have spoken to my father about that woman." I pointedly ignored him. Why would I want an update on how he's ruining an innocent person's life? "Are you ignoring me? How old are you?" I glared. Well, I think I did. I don't glare very often nor do I like to. "*Medusa.*"

"Michael," I snarked back, "Please continue telling me about how you ruined my new friend's life for absolutely no reason other than some hunch you had." Ugh. I turned back to him, laying my hands flat on the counter. "I meant what I said, Michael. If she gets hurt because of you or Yhwh, I will not help you any more. I mean it." I'll just forget I have magic and go back to being boring and not stressed.

He rolled his eyes, "She won't be hurt. Just investigated until we figure out what exactly she is and why she shares the same signature of my worst enemy."

"That's twice you've said that. Aren't you an angel? Can angels have enemies? I feel like that's against the Ten Commandments."

"It's not." He frowned at me. Not a mad frown, just a sort of confused one. "You should learn those, as an agent of Heaven."

I squinted, scratching my head. Oh I was probably ruining my ponytail. "I don't really *want* to learn the Ten Commandments. I'm not all that into religion, honestly."

"You're... Yo- Just forget it. I'm allowed to have enemies, and he is worthy of being called my enemy. Believe me. He's a terrible creature. A terrible horrible *obnoxious* vile-"

"I get it, but I don't forgive you. There's something I want you to do in order for me to want to help you." Michael sighed, ruffling his hair. He waved in a 'Let's get this over with' way. "Do you see that little girl in the blue dress?"

"Yes?" He frowned, staring at the child.

"No no. Don't stare so obviously. That's creepy. Every time she walks past that display fountain, she tries to freeze it with her ice powers. I-"

"That child has ice magic?"

"No. Stop interrupting, and whisper." He leaned forward, mocking my whisper pose. Wasn't appreciated, but at least he was being quiet. "Next time she goes to freeze the fountain, I want you to freeze it."

"Why?" The exasperation was clear in his voice.

"Because it'll make her day. Prove to me you can make someone *happy* for no other reason than for them to be happy." I sat up to smile at the girl's parents, "Did you find everything okay?"

"Yes, thank you!" The mother smiled at me. I checked them out while keeping an eye on Michael from the corner of my eye.

While I was helping her parents, the little princess went back to the fountain. Her face when it froze was a priceless show of pure enjoyment. "Mommy! Daddy! Look! Look!" When her parents looked over, the fountain was water once more. They just smiled and told her that it was pretty. When they looked away and she turned back to it, it was perfectly frozen again. On their way back out, she waved to me, "Goodbye, Lady Knight!"

"Goodbye, Ice Princess." I beamed, waving her out. When they were gone, I turned my smile to Michael. "Did you see how happy she was? You did that."

"I risked her parents seeing that, but whatever. Are you done being mad at me?"

"A little, *but* no more hurting my friends. What did you tell your dad about Karma?" Why does he think she's abnormal in some way, anyway? She seemed perfectly normal to me. Then again, he did say something about her having a magic signature, so maybe it's some form of magic I don't have.

"That is none of your business. She won't be harmed." That... Didn't sound like the whole sentence, but I'll let it go for now. He did make that kid happy today. That's good enough for now. "When do you leave here?"

"Four hours. Are you staying the whole time? You make Brian nervous." Hopefully he didn't hear me. I was right, but he wouldn't like that. Something about masculinity, I suppose.

Michael rolled his eyes, "I ha-"

"Sir Michael." A tall golden haired boy, probably only a few years younger than me, walked in coming straight to Michael. He actually looked a lot like the angel, other than being much shorter.

Michael nodded at him, "Adakiel, what brings you here?"

"Father sent me. He needs to speak with you urgently. He sent me to watch over the girl." Do I really need someone to watch over me? I'm just going to be working.

Michael glanced at me, then frowned at his... Brother? He called Yhwh father, so surely they're related. "I will return as soon as I can. Do not let her out of your sight." Where would I go? Does he really think I'd just run off somewhere during my shift?

"Yes, sir." Adakiel nodded, moving to stand behind the counter.

"Oh no." I stopped him at the little swinging door, "You aren't allowed back here. You don't work here." Michael rolled his eyes, but I held up a hand. "I could get *fired*."

"Fine." He huffed. He grabbed a stool from behind the counter - without actually getting behind the counter. Being tall must be so nice. He sat the stool toward the back of the counter where his new friend could watch me without freaking out my customers. Adakiel took the seat with his eyes firmly focused on me. This should be fun...

"So, how are you liking Telluride, Adakiel?" The angel just sat there silently. I guess he isn't much of a talker. That's okay I'm good at being silent. Really good at it. Michael gets annoyed with how silent I am. So I can tota- Oh good. Brian is here. "Brian! How're you?"

"Fine?" He frowned, looking at Adakiel in the corner. "Who's the kid? Do I need to kick him out?"

Adakiel scowled, rising to his feet. "No no. We're good." I cut in before he could speak. There's no telling what he was going to say. I've only met one angel before and he's a little... Aggressive. "This is Michael's," Think Medusa! "Little brother! Yeah this is Aidan. He's just visiting. Said he really wanted to meet me."

"Oh," Brian blinked, "I didn't realize you and Michael were at the meet the family stage already. Well as long as he's not some creep he can stay. Just don't mess with the customers, kid."

Adakiel nodded, slowly sitting back down. "I assure you the only thing I am here to observe is Medusa. I am very curious about the woman my *brother* is spending time with." Oh good. I was worried he would call me out.

49

"There are more of them? *Jesus.*" Poor Brian. He looked so troubled at the mere thought. "Well I'm glad you're alright. We're in the homestretch now."

Four hours later, and I think I have officially lost my title as the Virtue of Patience. Adakiel had stared at me the whole time without saying a single word. He restocked the shelves with me. He waited silently while I went to the back to get more inventory, and followed me when I stocked those items as well. I offered to let him stay at the front while I went through and straightened some miscellaneous items, but he declined. Apparently when he told Michael he'd watch me, he meant like a hawk. I've had to pee for an hour! Adakiel wouldn't let me go by myself because, and I quote, "Women climb out of bathroom windows every day." This bathroom doesn't even have a window!

"Michael!" Before I could even comprehend what I was doing, I was throwing my arms around his neck. Michael caught me effortlessly, albeit more than a little confused.

"Medusa. Are you ill?" Michael asked holding me.

"Nope! Just happy to see you." I don't think I could ever handle Adakiel for as long as I handle Michael. At least Michael talks to me. "Please don't leave me with him again."

Michael laughed, "You are free to go, brother." He bent over to set me back on my feet. "I thought you would like Adakiel. He is one of the more quiet of my brethren."

"He's *very* quiet. So quiet that he was driving me crazy. I don't think I can be called patient anymore. He just followed me around silently the *whole time.*" It was maddening. Michael just raised a brow at me. "I'm just glad you're back, okay? Is it wrong to say that I missed you?"

"Oh, ew." I jumped, turning to face Brian. He held his hands over his eyes, "Are you two being a couple?"

"No." Michael answered, "I thought you said being - *ahem* - romantic at your job would get you fired?" Where did he- Why would he *say* something like that?! I never said that! We never even talked about anything like that! Michael stepped toward me with a playful look in his eyes. I don't like that at all.

"Yes! Yes! That is now true! No couple stuff." Brian quickly cut in before Michael could reach me. Thank goodness.

Michael just sighed, letting me go, "Rules are rules, I suppose. I'll be good." I frowned, watching him go back to being the stoic man he always was. What just happened?

"Thank you. You about ready to close up, Medusa?" Brian asked, looking over the register.

"I'm never ready to leave this place, Brian. I love it here." My boss just snorted. Even Michael rolled his eyes. They must think I'm joking. I'm really not. This place is much better than home most of the time.

"Right. Well you go clock out, I'll take care of everything up here. Ah, Michael you can't go in the back…" Michael nodded, moving to stand by the doors. Brian shot me a wide eyed glance making me laugh. I guess he just realized he left himself with Michael. I'll have to hurry before Brian has a full scale panic attack from standing by Michael for too long.

When I came back, Brian looked significantly paler, and Michael seemed as bored as always. Brian basically shoved me out the door, so he could lock up the store. Michael must really make him uncomfortable. Brian used to hate closing up alone.

"I make that human uncomfortable, don't I?" Michael mused, easily walking ahead of me. He almost seemed proud.

I jogged, trying to keep pace with him. He didn't slow even a little bit. Chivalry really is dead. "Immensely." Michael waited impatiently on the driver's side of the car while my horribly short legs made up the distance. I climbed into the car with a quiet huff.

Michael scowled at me as he took his seat, "Must you walk so slow? You already get off work so late, then you take hours to make it to the car. It's like you don't want to train at all today."

I don't. I really *really* don't. Every time we 'train' I end up bruised and exhausted. "You know," I pointedly looked out the window, avoiding his gaze. "I think there's some things you could learn from me."

The giant scoffed obnoxiously, "What in the world could you possibly teach me?"

"How do be more *patient* seems like a good place to start." I didn't have to look to know he was rolling his eyes at me.

"I am the Chief of Heaven's Angels. I commanded my father's forces, and personally made sure my fallen brother's *lapdog* was sent back to the depths of Hell where he belongs. Believe me, Medusa, there is nothing I need to learn from *you*." Well there goes my joke. I sighed, resting my forehead on the cool window.

Chapter Six

I sighed, taking a seat by the quiet brook. Michael was inside somewhere. I don't know what he was doing, and at this point I don't really care. I'm not angry with him. I'm just tired. He's been in a mood for the past couple days. I have that lunch with Karma in a couple days, so that's something to look forward to.

"Medusa!" I definitely flinched at the sound of his voice. Darn it. Michael's shadow loomed over me, ruining the peaceful slightly warm atmosphere that Telluride had gifted me with today. I huddled into myself, not looking at him. He could have at least brought me a jacket if he was going to make it snow. "*What* are you doing?"

"Enjoying the peacefulness of my home." I replied, still not looking away from the water. I dipped my fingers in the brook, letting the water run over my finger tips.

Michael growled behind me. I guess he doesn't like me being indifferent to him. He sat down beside me with an incredibly loud huff. "We are supposed to be training today. You still haven't got a tree to lose a branch. You *have* to get stronger."

"Why?" It was a simple question. One that Michael didn't seem to have the answer to. Maybe I should start counting how long it takes him to speak again. He'd probably yell at me. I don't want that. He can be very loud when he wants to be.

"You don't need to know why. What matters is that it needs to happen. You have to get stronger before the other Virtues are found." That didn't last as long as I thought it would.

But since he seems a little more open to talk about everything, "So," I shifted toward him, finally looking at him. He looks as grumpy as usual. "What is the plan when we find the other Virtues?"

"To gather and train them. The same as I am doing with you." He gave me a blank look. "I thought that would be obvious."

"It was." Is he sure his goal isn't to *break* us? I can't be the Virtue of Patience if he kills all of my patience, and he is doing a *spectacular* job. I tugged on my ponytail, and pressed on. "I mean what is the plan after that. What do you plan on us *doing*?"

"That is not something you need to know at the moment." Just because I don't *need* to know doesn't mean I wouldn't like to know. It is my future, after all. I doubt that would change Michael's mind though. Suddenly, Michael straightened, his brows furrowing. "My father has requested me. I will return shortly."

Before I could reply, the little bursts of light appeared over his body. It was as if his body was being swallowed by little stars. I had to block the radiance with both hands before he accidentally blinded me. Well, I hope it was accidentally. No more than twenty seconds later, the light was gone taking Michael with it. Well, that was interesting. Will I be able to do something like that?

If I do make it there, it'll be much later. Wind needs to be my main focus. Michael said I need to be stronger before we meet the other Virtues. Maybe I should practice my magic while he's not here to yell at me. I pushed myself up from the ground, and made my way to my room. Dad was asleep on the couch when I came through. An old football game was still playing on the tv, but I left it on. Hopefully it will keep him asleep while I practice my magic.

I shut my bedroom door, and settled into the middle of my bed. Okay, small steps first. There's no need to push myself too fast without a certain someone breathing down my neck. Lucky for me, I had left a book on my dresser some time ago. It wasn't by anything breakable either, so I could just get started. Thank you, past me.

"Okay," I sighed, letting the breath take my tension away. I can do this. Keeping my eyes open this time, I focused on the book.

Every other time I've used my magic, I've had my eyes closed. Maybe if I keep my eyes open, I will have a better chance of succeeding. I centered my focus on my breathing. I could feel the crisp air as it entered my lungs, and the warmth of the air as it left me.

I could feel the air in the room as if it was breathing with me. There wasn't any form of negative energy disrupting my focus, or anyone to make me feel stressed. It was actually *really* nice. I miss how much alone time I used to have. No, Medusa. That is not what we're focusing on right now.

Right. I gathered some of the air around me, and focused it on the book. If I could just get it to move *a lit-* "Oh no!" Oh no. No no no no no.

"*What was that noise?*" My father roared from the living room.

I cringed, "I fell!" *Please* believe me. I've never been very good at lying. My father didn't reply, though, so I guess I was believable enough. Now, what to do about that...

忍

It's been two hours, and I've come up with *nothing.* Not a single plausible solution. "Where's Michael when I need him?" I'm not usually a whiner. At least, I try not to be. There's always a positive side. That's what my mom believed, and I try to stay true to that. But, I can't find any positive side of this.

"Why is there a hole in your closet door?" I squeaked, whipping around to face the frost giant that *definitely* wasn't in my room a few minutes ago. "Medusa, stop gaping at me. What happened to the door?"

"Well," I twisted my hands in front of me, looking away from him. He didn't seem particularly mad at me, but that could change. He was going to be furious when he found out I was practicing magic without his supervision. "I was practicing my magic while I didn't have any distractions. I was going to see if I could push the book that was on the side of my dresser, and make it fall on the floor.

55

I must've pushed too hard though, because it went through my closet door, and a replacement door is really expensive, and I can't afford it, and I definitely can't tell my dad that I broke it, so now-"

"Stop talking." Michael grumbled, effectively shutting me up. He's definitely mad. The angel moved toward the closet door to peer through the giant hole. After a few moments of deafening silence, he hummed, straightening back to his full height. "I didn't think you were capable of that much force. I will fix the door. Your father will never know it was broken."

"Really?" He'd do something like that for me?

"Yes. I have to return to my own father. Practice your magic while I am gone. Find out why you were so much stronger here. I will return."

"Wait, Micha-" Too late. Well, at least the door was getting fixed, I suppose.

忍

"Medusa." I jumped, turning to face Michael. He'd been gone for about day now. He'd fixed my door while I was sleeping, but didn't wake me up. I should probably tell him what creepy means. "Get dressed. My father wants to speak with you." God?! Wait, what's wrong with what I'm wearing? Michael scowled at me, "You cannot wear those unreasonably short shorts to meet with the AllFather."

They're not that short, but I got up to change anyway. I slipped on a floral accordion skirt and a light pink shirt with some flats. That should be nice enough. I'd wear it to church, if I ever went to church. I came out of the closet to show Michael. The frosty giant gave me a once over before nodding, "Good enough." He held out an arm for me to loop mine through, "Do not scream. Do not let go. Do *not* pet me."

White fog completely overtook us, making me clutch him tighter. Why would he think I would let go? I can't see my own feet! Maybe I should just keep my eyes closed. That's a good plan.

I went ahead and buried my face into Michael's arm too, just to be sure. I'm not sure what this magic is called, but it's nauseating.

"You can open your eyes now, Medusa." He growled, gently prying me from him.

I blinked, using my hand to shield away most of the light. Why is it so bright in here? Michael was blocking out some of the light, but it seemed to radiate from every surface. "Oh my god…" Michael's wings were back. They looked so soft.

"Yes?" I turned to see a man with long white blonde hair, and cold golden eyes that chilled me to the bone. I thought Michael was the most apathetic person I've ever met. This guy is something else entirely. He was wearing a crisp white three piece suit that was almost as bright as the rest of the room, and kept his hands folded in front of him. *This* is Yhwh? "Medusa, correct?"

"Y-Yes, sir." He nodded, coming closer. Michael was silent beside me with his arms folded. He seemed more tense than usual.

"You're smaller than I imagined. Much more… *Fragile.* Like a porcelain doll." Maybe creepy is just the theme for today. My eyes darted to Michael, but he wasn't looking at me. He was in full statue mode. I would've felt less alone if he wasn't here. Yhwh was standing in front of me now, the white reflecting so much, I had to turn away. His hand grasped my chin, facing me to look at him, "Let's stick to Yhwh when you speak to me, child. God is a term humans came up with."

"Okay." I hadn't been talking about him when I said it, I was talking about Michael's wings, but I don't think he cared.

"Now, I heard you've been struggling with developing your magic. Why is that?"

I frowned. How am I supposed to know? "I don't know. I'm trying, though."

Yhwh scowled at me, gripping my chin even tighter, "That isn't good enough. We are strengthening your training. You need to be stronger." He snapped his hand away from me, taking a step back. "Michael, this way."

Michael followed him toward the far end of the room, his unreasonably soft wings brushing me as he passed. I was left to stand there alone while Yhwh spoke to him, "You have failed me with this Michael. She's *weak*. I could snap her in half with minimal effort. I told you to make her stronger. Her magic signature is that of a basic human! Perhaps I should've chosen one of your brothers to train her instead. You obviously cannot handle training her." I wonder if he knows sound carries in an empty stone room, and I can hear everything he's saying about me. What was the point of walking away from me at all?

"No, Father. I can do this. Medusa is improving every day. She just needs time." He thinks I'm improving? That made me smile. I fiddled with my skirt, slowly walking in a circle. Heaven certainly seems boring. Shouldn't there be other angels here?

"Time?" Yhwh scoffed, "I am running out of patience, Michael. Fix her or I will find someone who can."

"Yes, Father."

"Medusa," Yhwh called. He was scowling at me, "I expect better." He waved his hand in my direction, making the white fog come back to cover me completely.

"Father! She can't-"

Then he was gone. Or rather, I was. I landed back in my room on my feet, but fell almost immediately as my legs gave out. I hit my bedroom floor with a thud, whacking my head on my bed frame on the way down. This has been an exhausting day. Oh no. I slapped my hand over my mouth and darted to the bathroom. Hopefully my own father can't hear me throwing up. I don't think I can handle anything else right now.

Once I was done and could stand without falling back over, I brushed my teeth and washed my face, and went to lay in my bed. I don't have any plans today. What's a nap going to hurt? I do know one thing. I am so sick of magic. Literally.

忍

58

'Hey girlie! Are you busy tonight? I was thinking a mini girl's night at Serenity. I'm buying.'

It was May. I thought she'd given up inviting me to her girl's nights after I said no half a million times. Normally, I'd say no because I was broke or had work the following day or just tired, but after my little meeting today I could really use a fun night. Plus, I'm off tomorrow so I can stay up a little later tonight.

'Don't panic, but I would love to. What's Serenity?'

'Yessssss it's about damn time. Nightclub. I'll swing by and grab you around 8?'

'I'll be ready!'

I'll need to be ready at seven, just in case she arrives early. Oh my God. What am I supposed to wear to a nightclub? Why did I toss my phone away? Don't let me down internet. Okay, well I don't have a skirt that tight. Ooh! I have jeans kind of like that, and I *think* I own a crop top. I have to have at least one. Found it! Yeah, I bought this without unfolding it so I didn't know it was a crop top and was too embarrassed to return it. Being socially awkward had to work out for me sometime, right?

Now, what to do with this blonde mop? Maybe a messy updo. Those are in style... I think. Why did I agree to this? I don't know how to go to a nightclub. Too late now, Medusa. You already committed. Now, go find your heels, and pray they still fit.

'Here. I'm a little early, so don't worry about rushing.'

Already? Oh god! It's fifteen till eight! I'm never this bad with time. I grabbed my bag, and rushed out the door.

"Where the hell are you going?" For the first time in possibly forever, I ignored him.

May beamed at me as I climbed into the car, "Wooo! Well don't you look like sin." I laughed. She looked much better than me. In fact, she was dressed almost identical to the photos I looked at for reference before I got dressed. "Ready for your first girl's night, Medusa?"

"Ready as I'll ever be. Do I look okay?" I fiddled with the hem of my shirt. May certainly looked much more sexy than I did.

"You look great! I didn't know you owned crop tops. Oh, look in the grocery bag in the floorboard. I got you something. Now," She held a hand up, pausing my movement. Her blue eyes were shining with sincerity, "You don't have to use them, but if you want them they're brand new and all yours."

I peered at her, reaching for the bag. It wasn't from Whittle Corner. It was from an actual beauty supply store that I know we don't have in town. Where did she get this? Inside the bag was mascara, eyeliner, a beautiful lipstick, and a pallet of eye shadow.

"Oh wow, May. I can't accept this." I put them back in the bag as softly as I could. They looked expensive, I'd hate to mess them up "I wouldn't even know how to use them."

"You've never done your makeup?" She asked, incredulous. She couldn't look at me since she was driving, but it was clear she wanted to. "Do you want me to do yours? I'm pretty good. I mean, I'm not a professional or anything, but I get by."

I could tell that much the first time I met her. It never looked like too much when she did it. Last time I attempted makeup, I looked like I let a four year old do it. "Would you?"

"Hell yeah!" She didn't mind me laughing at her enthusiasm. In fact, she even laughed with me. Michael would never do that. Maybe she's right. I do need a girl's night.

We pulled up outside a cool looking restaurant called Embers a few minutes later. I thought we were going to a place called Serenity? "Alright, hand over the baggie, and face me." I did as I was told and May got to work.

"Hey, May?" She hummed, tilting my face up a little. An intense look of concentration had settled on her face as she applied the makeup. I felt a little bad for disturbing her train of thought. "I thought we were going to a place called Serenity?"

"Hmm?" Her eyes refocused on mine, losing some of the intensity. "Oh! We're meeting Kat and Zelda here before we head over. It's right next door. That's why I parked a little over instead of right by the door or Ember. It's always good to eat something before a night out. Close your eyes for this next part."

I closed my eyes, trying not to react to how weird the little brush felt. I'm not used to this at all. "Kat and Zelda are your friends, I take it?"

"Yup!" She chirped, popping the 'p' in time with the brush stroke off my eye lid. What is she doing? "Keep them closed. Time for liner. You'll love the girls though. Pretty sure they think I made you up." She laughed, "All done. You can open your eyes. Do you want to do the lipstick?"

"Yes, please." I took the offered tube, and turned to my visor. Oh wow. I looked... Really pretty. May must be some sort of wizard to pull this off. My eyes looked a lot more green than usual, too. I applied the red lipstick as well as I could, and smiled at May.

"Beautiful! Ready?" She shimmed at me before turning the car off, and hopping out.

"As ready as I'll ever be..." I murmured, getting out myself. It was a warm night for Fall in Colorado, and we weren't the only people out enjoying it. This place is packed! All of the rounded furniture were shades of black and grey, while the lighting that was hidden somewhere in the walls cast a red glow over the place. "I can see why it's called Embers."

May nodded, "Pretty cool, huh? They have some of the best food. Oh, hey," She paused, turning to face me. Her blue eyes were intimidatingly serious - I didn't realize she could look so serious. She almost resembled Michael. "I meant it when I said that I'm buying, so no unreasonably small meal because you feel bad. Actually order some food or I'm getting you a sixteen ounce steak."

"They make sixteen ounce steaks?" That seemed way too big to be real.

May pursed her lips. I think she was trying not to laugh at me, but she held firm. "I'll make them put two on the plate. Just don't worry about the money, okay. I know how you are."

Well, she did have a point. I sighed, "I will do my best." Especially since she said the two steak thing. Steaks are crazy expensive! No way can I let her spend that much on me. I don't even think I can eat that much either, so I'd feel twice as bad.

"That is all I ask. Remember, tonight is a fun night. Oh look!" She pointed a little past the hostess stand. The hostess seemed startled at my friend's outburst, instantly making May put her hand down. "Sorry! Our friends are a few tables behind you."

"Oh! You can head on back. Enjoy your meal!" The sweet girl motioned us past the stand. She couldn't have been older than eighteen. I think I was a hostess when I was sixteen, if I remember correctly. That is definitely a job I don't miss.

"Hey! You ready to relax?" A girl about my height with shoulder length curled blonde hair wiggled her eyebrows at May. "Oh! You must be Medusa! It's so nice to meet you!"

She pulled me into a hug, swaying us in space for a moment. "Well aren't you sweet! It's so nice to meet you… Kat?" Kat is an upbeat name, right?

"Oh, no." She laughed, "I'm Zelda. This is Kat."

She waved her hand to the other person at the table. A girl with a black faux hawk hairstyle with the top combed forward, and fierce honey brown eyes wearing a blue tailored pantsuit and stilettos raised her whiskey glass at me, "Are you going to make them stand all day, Z?"

Zelda moved back to her seat, gesturing for us to take the remaining two. I settled into the seat beside Kat while May took the seat beside Zelda. "It's nice to meet you, too, Kat. You know, I think I know someone you'd like a lot." She looked like the kind of person Karma would like.

She quirked a brow at me, taking another sip of her drink. "Not a big fan of people." Yup. Karma would like her. I just know it. "So, Medusa, what made you finally join us for girls' night?"

How do I word this without magic, or God, or archangels? "Men are exhausting." It came out more like a question, but all three girls nodded along with me.

"The guy at the park? He does seem a little stoic to be with you. You need someone happy. Not always smiling, but certainly not so grumpy. Sorry," She waved her hand, "I don't want to butt in."

"Wait, wait." Zelda cut in, pushing two plates to the center of the table, "Crab Cakes and Beef Wellington, help yourself. Do you have a picture of this boyfriend? Just so we can all weigh in."

Oh. Oh dear. I don't have a picture of him. He's supposed to be my boyfriend and I don't have a picture of him? "Let me see if I can find a good one. He doesn't really like them." I pulled my phone out of my pocket to see a message from a number I didn't know I had.

'**I saved my number in your ridiculous mini box since you always have it on you so you can't pretend to ignore me.**'

Oh please, please reply quickly. '**Send me a picture of you that looks like I took a cute picture of my boyfriend. Please!**'

'**Why aren't you training!**' Well, I gave myself away, but he sent a picture! It even looked like I took it at the park. He wasn't smiling, but that would be expecting a lot. I enlarged it, and showed the girls.

"Goddamn," Kat hummed, "I don't even like men."

"I do! He is very fun to look at. Why no smile, though?" Zelda asked, tilting her head slightly.

"Michael doesn't really like to smile. Or laugh." Or have any sort of fun really.

"He did seem to like Medusa when I met him. They do couples meditating in the park. He even calls her 'love' as a pet name."

Zelda cooed at that, "That is so sweet. I like the long blond hair. Does he wear it down a lot?"

"Why does that matter?" Kat cut in, "What did he do to make you so exhausted?"

I sighed, taking one of the Beef Wellington from the plate, "He's helping me get healthier." That's believable, right? It's mostly true. "And he's just pushing me a little too hard. Have you ever tried Krav

Maga or Northarn Shaolin? They're awful. Truly the worst thing I have ever done."

Kat frowned, finally setting her drink down. She actually turned to face me. Does this count as progress? "He looked at you - little, fragile Medusa - and thought you should try *martial arts*? That's so dumb. You look like you can barely handle a bag of jumbo marshmallows."

"Mildly offensive, Kat. Tone it down." May warned, "Do we have a waitress?"

Kat groaned, rolling her eyes, "Yes. One second." Her eyes scanned the restaurant floor for a moment before nodding. "She's on the way, and definitely into me."

Zelda and May just rolled their eyes. I guess they're used to her antics. It was an odd change of pace, but I don't mind it. I actually like Kat's confidence and air of superiority. Michael would hate her. *A lot.*

"Hello! So sorry for the wait!" A perky waitress who had to be a few years younger than all four women at the table. Kat was correct, though. She was certainly the waitress' main focus. "Can I get you something to drink?"

May and I gave our drink orders. All three girls ordered food as well. I quickly chose a burger that looked delicious with some sweet potato casserole and broccoli. May smiled at me when I was done. I guess I passed.

"Be honest," May rested her head on her hand, "Do you eat anything that's not burgers?"

I laughed, "Not usually. I do love burgers. Michael hates that I eat so many." That's a little bit of an understatement. Michael *loathes* hamburgers. I think Brian is afraid of death if he brings me a burger again.

'Where are you? Are you training?'

"*Good lord*. Is that the boyfriend?" Kat asked, waving her crab cake at me. "Fuck him. For one night, turn off the phone, ignore your boyfriend that seems *way* to fucking overbearing, and have fun."

"*Kat,*" Zelda snapped, "Too harsh. Seriously, we talked about how to talk to people." She flicked Kat's hand, still glaring at her. Is this a mom friend? I think I'm finally understanding that phrase.

Kat rolled her eyes, taking a long sip of her drink. The waitress came back with a tray of shots. Who ordered shots? Judging from the expressions on the girls' faces, they were also confused. Kat pursed her lips, "We didn't order jäger shots, because we're not in college."

"Oh," The waitress blinked, clearly not expecting Kat's tone. "That table over there sent them."

We turned to see a table of men in pastel collared shirts smiling widely at us. Kat made a disgusted noise, "I'm way too gay for this." I laughed despite myself. Kat just winked back at me. How have we never met? Well, I know how, but I'm definitely regretting being such a hermit.

"Don't encourage her." May sighed. She turned to the waitress, smiling sweetly, "Can you throw those in the trash? Or give them to the table that ordered them? We won't drink them, and *someone* has a *very* protective boyfriend who *really* won't like her accepting these." Was she talking about me?

The waitress' eyes widened and she nodded rapidly, "I completely understand. Your food should be out shortly." She took the tray of shots and darted over to the men's table.

Kat nodded, leaning back in her chair again, "The one good thing about you having an ape of a boyfriend, Medusa. Gets rid of guys like that."

"Do you deal with guys like that a lot?" I'd never experienced anything like that. Then again, I don't really go out all that much.

"Yes." Kat rolled her eyes.

Zelda gave her a flat look, "They're not all bad. Kat just doesn't like men." Kat rolled her eyes again. She unbuttoned one of the top buttons on her blouse, and pulled it to the side to reveal a pink, white, and red flag. It looked like a pride flag of some sort. "We *get* it." *Oh.* It must be her pride flag. That makes sense.

"But," May cut in, holding up a hand. "Tonight is a Girl's Night. No boyfriends, and no boys."

Zelda sighed, *"Fine."*

"If you're interested in them, they were probably no good anyway, Z." That got a crab cake thrown at Kat. Zelda just scowled as her friend adeptly caught the small cake in her mouth.

"Alright," A cheerful waiter appeared at the table, "We have a barbecue burger with sweet potato casserole and broccoli." This looked *amazing*. I was practically drooling. Now *this* is one of those greasy monstrosities Michael would hate. I should send him a picture. No, I shouldn't. He could probably track me down with minimal effort. Kat got a steak with a lobster tail while May and Zelda got some sort of fish that I couldn't identify. "Anything else?"

We declined. Well, May, Zelda, and I declined. Kat was already eating her lobster tail. I really hope she gets to meet Karma some day. They'd get on like a house fire. At least, I think they would. Who knows, Karma liked me, so maybe they wouldn't get along since they seem pretty similar.

"You okay, Medusa? You zoned out for a moment." May called me back into focus.

"Oh!" I blinked at her, trying to get out of my thoughts. I have to remember to not go quiet when I'm around people. This isn't work, they actually want me to talk to them. I just worry about saying something stupid. "Sorry I get a little lost in thought sometimes. This is delicious!"

"You're okay." She laughed. She'd made significant progress with her fish plate, and her mashed potatoes were completely gone. I should hurry. "You're resting face is sad looking. It's like the opposite of RBF."

"What's RBF?"

That got me a shocked look from everyone else at the table. Kat even paused eating, "Resting Bitch Face." She explained, laughing a little. "You don't get out much, do you?"

"Not really." I shrugged, "I work a lot. That's why I'm usually

too tired to come to these. I'm glad I'm here though. I like you two."
Zelda beamed back at me, but didn't reply since her mouth was full.

Kat smiled, "I kinda like you too. You're like some sort of kitten."

"*Kat.*" Zelda scolded, holding a hand over her mouth.

"It's not an insult! Kittens are cute!" I laughed. She wasn't bothering me, honestly. There are worst things to be compared to than a kitten. Kat waved at me, "See? Medusa doesn't mind!"

"You could steal food off her plate, and she'd apologize that her plate wasn't closer to you." May replied, rolling her eyes. "She's extremely nice and compassionate. Don't be an ass." May pushed her chair back, and stood up. "I'll be right back. *Behave.*"

Kat scoffed, crossing her arms. Her eyes darted to my sweet potatoes one more time. I pushed the small ceramic dish over to her. I couldn't eat anymore anyway. There's no way I can handle a sixteen ounce steak.

"Seriously?" She quirked a brow at me.

"Yes," I laughed, "I can't eat any more."

"*Yesssss.*"

"Goddamn it, Kat. I was gone for five minutes." May scowled down at Kat. That was fast.

"She gave it to me!"

"I did give it to her." I backed her up. Kat waved at me like 'See? I'm telling the truth.' May just scowled harder.

"Fine. Does that mean you're ready to go?" May let it go. "I already paid the check." Oh. Dang it. I was going to insist on paying for my meal or at least covering the tip. I thought she was going to the bathroom not paying the bill. Judging from her smirk, she was well aware.

"*May!*" Zelda and Kat scolded at the same time. Huh, I didn't think they agreed on anything.

"That means drinks are on me. Yours too, Medusa." Kat smoothly got up from the table, setting the napkin over her plate. She held a hand out to help me get up. I didn't need it, but took it

67

anyway. Once I was standing, Kat swung her arm over my shoulders. "Cute outfit. How gay are you?"

"Seriously?" Zelda gave her a flat look, pushing past her.

"*What?*" Kat tried to make an innocent face, but failed when a wide smile spread over her face. Now I have to wonder if she's like this when Zelda isn't here to agitate.

"See?" May pointed to an orange sign once we made it outside. "It's right there."

"Oh." How did I miss that? That sign is huge. Plenty of people were already parked, and heading inside the nightclub.

Music greeted us immediately. There were people *everywhere.* Holy cow. Kat, who's arm was still slung over my shoulders, seemed perfectly at ease in this loud atmosphere. Then again, with her confidence, wardrobe, and general attitude that shouldn't be such a surprise.

"Oh my god. Kat, is that you?" Kat froze, her arm slipping off my shoulders. She also looked significantly paler.

"Hey, *you.*" Uh oh. That can't be good.

The girl's sultry smile morphed into a much more angry expression, "You don't know my name, do you? I guess that's not surprising for someone who ghosted me."

"I didn't ghost you. People don't talk after one night stands. That's how it goes." Sounds normal to me, but what do I know? I've never done anything like that. This girl didn't seem to agree, though. "Why are you mad?"

"I thought we had something special!"

"You didn't." Zelda deadpanned, pushing herself in between Kat and the girl. "There's nothing special. She's just a pro at impressing coeds. You promised me a drink, Kat."

"I promised you several, actually." That got a smile out of Zelda. May appeared beside me, nodding me along. I followed perhaps a little too eagerly. If I was with the group maybe that girl wouldn't yell at me next. I haven't done anything to her, but I am here with

Kat. We got to the bar, where there were two barstools available. "Medusa, you're on a stool."

I hopped on the stool Kat pulled out, turning so I could still see the girls. Zelda got on the other stool, with Kat and May standing behind us. I'm assuming they were the ones standing due to their much taller stature than ours. Zelda waved the bartender down with a bright smile. The man smiled back, and motioned he'd be right over.

"Oh, but I flirt with the waitress and get in trouble." Kat snorted, "What're you drinking, Kitten?"

"Oh, I don't drink."

"Really?" Zelda looked completely taken aback. She frowned slightly, "What if it is a really weak drink? I know a good one. Not very much alcohol, just enough to make you feel a little lighter."

I shook my head, "No, thank you. It's not really my thing." I already know there's at least a slight addictive gene in my DNA. I don't need to play with fire.

"Ooh," May tapped her chin, "Have you ever had a Shirley Temple?" I shook my head. I've heard of them, but I'm pretty sure they have alcohol in them. "Do you like ginger ale?"

"Not particularly..."

"What about coke?" Kat asked. May looked at her, the confusion clear on her face. "It's a drink similar to the Shirley Temple with zero alcohol, but instead of ginger ale, it has coke." That sounds interesting. Kat fist pumped at my agreement. "It's called a Roy Rogers. I assume you're ordering?"

Zelda smiled sweetly at Kat, snatching the taller woman's card. They have such an odd relationship. May just rolled her eyes at them. I suppose she's use to all this. The Dj said something over the speaker system before shifting to a much louder song. The crowd on the dance floor cheered, easily dancing to the new beat. May and Zelda were nodding along to the music, with May even dancing in place.

May leaned in so I could hear her, "I'm going to dance. I love this song! Do you wanna come?"

"Oh! Um, maybe later?" I'm going to need some time before I'm brave enough to wade into that monstrosity.

"Okay. Be back later!" She was dancing long before she reached the dance floor.

Zelda shook her head, "That girl and her music." Then the bartender was here, and Zelda became a whole different person. She sat up straighter, she was smiling brightly, and blinking much more than she should be. I suppose it worked though, because when the bartender finally left to fill our order he looked a little dazed.

Kat just rolled her eyes, "This is the only reason you come out. Oh, I see a table. I'm going to sit down. I'm going to sit down. You coming?"

I hesitated, looking at Zelda. I shouldn't leave her alone over here with this many people… "You're okay, Medusa. I work best alone anyway." Whatever that means. I did get the message that she wanted me gone though, driven home by the raised blonde eyebrows.

Kat walked confidently through the club, seeming to know exactly where she was going. I don't know how she saw any tables over all these bodies, but then again, she has to be six feet tall. She slapped the table when we reached it. It was a tall table with tall barstools that Kat slid on with ease. She laughed watching me struggle onto the stool that came up to my chest even in heels.

"Glad you enjoyed yourself." I huffed, finally on my stool. Kat continued to laugh into her hand. "What are you, seven feet tall?"

"I'm six, one if you must know. Are you tall enough to ride any adult rides at Six Flags?" She jested back, pulling my stool closer to her. "I can barely hear you from how far down you are from me."

"Alright, alright. I give. You are a superior tall person."

"Damn right." She winked, "So, how do you feel being away from the boyfriend?"

How *do* I feel? Michael had become such a large part of my life so quickly, and he *did* end up fixing my door. He can also be horribly mean and impatient at times. I sighed, resting my head in my palms.

How do I answer that? *Do* I miss him? "I guess I miss him a little, but he would hate this entire environment."

"You sure about that, dear? Your eyes scan the club every five minutes. Looking for some light blue eyes?" She waggled her eyebrows at me. "It's okay to admit it. You get no judgement with me. I get it."

"You get it? Aren't you the gayest gay to ever gay?"

She guffawed, "Hell yeah I am!" She shook her head at me, still smiling. "But that isn't what I meant. May doesn't talk about it, because it isn't her story to tell, but she alluded to you being a bit of a loner. Couple that knowledge with the name Medusa, I have a general gist of what your life has been so far. If you ever need anyone to talk about anything, don't be afraid to give me a call. There are some things people like May and Zelda can't understand."

Deep emotion reflected in her light brown eyes. Kat's eyes grew hazy as she stared down at the table. It was a look I recognized well. "Hey, Kat?" She hummed, blinking at me. She was still slightly lost in thought, but seemed to be coming back. "Kat is short for something, isn't it?"

She laughed once, ruffling her hair. "Hecate, actually." Oh. *Oh.* Now I understand. "Don't tell the girls, though. They think my name is Katherine. Once I suffered through middle school, and got to high school I figured Katherine would be easiest. The teachers and staff agreed that it would help ease my issues with my classmates."

"Hecate was a witch, right?"

She shook her head, "That's what everyone thinks. She's a goddess in Greek Mythology. She's the goddess of magic, witchcraft, the night, moon, ghosts, and necromancy. *But* because of the magic, and the witchcraft, and necromancy people tend to associate her with a bunch of negative stuff." She coughed, "I'm sure that sounds familiar."

"Yeah," I scoffed, "I'm glad you had a nickname, though. Medusa doesn't really have any nicknames." Besides 'Gorgon' which Mac loves so much.

"For real." She sighed, looking past me. "Here comes Zelda. Let's table this, yeah?" I nodded, watching a smile appear on her face. Gone was any trace of the sadness that she showed me a moment ago. In fact, it was like she completely closed up. Became a different person. "That is *much* more than you ordered!" She teased.

Zelda slid the tray on the table before hopping up on the stool with practiced grace. Benefits of coming to bars more frequently, I guess. She handed out drinks with a smug smile, "Here is your purely non-alcoholic drink, Medusa. I double checked. Kat, double whiskey, and a Carthusian Sazerac which Lucas was very proud that he knew how to make."

"Lucas, huh?" Kat raised a brow, tasting the strange looking drink. "That's not bad. Very lemony. Want a taste, kitten? You can't taste the alcohol."

I thought it over, looking at the drink. Kat lifted it for me to sniff. It did smell a lot like lemon. "Hey you!" Another girl slipped onto the stool beside me. She had curled black hair, and wide dark brown eyes. She scooted close to me, leaning into me while laughing. Once she was close enough to whisper to me, the fear became prominent in her eyes, "Please pretend you know me. This guy won't leave me alone." My eyes flicked to the girls, both seeming to get the message. The girl leaned back and smiled widely again, "I couldn't see you for the life of me! Glad I finally found you!"

"Bout time too!" Kat laughed, "Though you should know better than to look for these shorties."

"Yeah," The girl laughed, "I should've kn-"

"So these are your friends, baby?" Some guy slung his arm around her shoulders, leaning in way too close for anyone to be comfortable. He seemed to be acting loopy, but... Wasn't.

"Yeah," This laugh was much more strained than before. Our new friend was radiating discomfort. "Thanks for helping me, but I'm with them now."

"Well, they know you're here, so let's go grab a drink." Does he not *see* how uncomfortable she is?

"The point was that she is with us - her friends that she came to hang out with - and that you were no longer needed. You can leave now." I interjected, tilting my head slightly. I studied him. Every few moments he'd wobble slightly, his voice would slur purposefully, and he'd sway closer to the girl's face. The rest of the table seemed to blink at me in shock.

Not unwanted guest though. His face transformed from his slimy smile to a sinister glare in my direction. Oh, there he is. I was right. "I am just trying to give Kali here a good time. Why are you trying to stop that? Don't you want your friend to have a good time?"

I scowled back at him. It was glaringly obvious that she *didn't* want to have a "good time" with him. Whatever that meant. "I don't know what makes you think spending time with a sleazy man who *pretends* to be drunk at a bar in an attempt to excuse his behavior is a good time. Which is still unacceptable even if you were inebriated - which you are *not*." I've seen drunk, and this man - if you can call him that - definitely was sober.

"Listen, bitch." Well he finally got off of Kali, but now had his hand wrapped firmly around my wrist.

"Hey, jackass." Kat's hand was on his wrist immediately, "I suggest you back the fuck off."

"I don't need some butch bitch and her bratty little whore telling me what to do." He snapped back. His other arm reared back, his hand already formed into a fist.

He was really planning on hitting us! When he was the one harassing someone! Suddenly, his grip was removed from my wrist as his hand shot to his own throat. The man gasped for air, dropping to the ground. Was this another poor acting job? What was the story this time? He wasn't eating or drinking anything, so it couldn't be choking. Why can't he just stand up and apologize? He could-

"Medusa." I blinked, looking up at the last person I wanted to see. Michael rubbed his hand over my back. Concern was so apparent in his eyes even I almost bought the boyfriend act. "Are you alright?"

"I'm fine. Why?"

"What the hell did you do to me, bitch?!" The man from before was back up and breathing… What did I do? Oh my god. My eyes shot to Michael. Surely that wasn't me. I wasn't even thinking about my powers! We both know that I can't use them without severe concentration… Unless I can, and just didn't know it. Oh no. "What are you? Some kind of *freak*?" His next attempt at a sentence was garbled as Michael grabbed him by the throat, lifting him off the ground with ease.

"If you must know, *pathetic insect,* she is an angel." He growled at the man. The air in the club dropped below freezing instantly, but that didn't stop the wet spot from spreading over the man's expensive looking slacks. Not that I could blame him for that. I can easily see how Michael became the general he's known to be. He wasn't yelling or cursing, but he didn't have to. His eyes said it all. They were several shades lighter than normal with a gold sheen, and held no warmth or humanity. They were the eyes of a man that had reaped more souls than I had ever met, and if this man didn't comply to whatever order he was about to be given he was going to be the next one. "I suggest you get as far away from me as possible within the next two minutes." He dropped him as quick as he grabbed him, and stayed standing in between him and me. To his credit, the shaking man with soiled pants landed on his feet and ran out of the club like his butt was on fire. Once he was out of sight, Michael turned back to me. He looked like the Michael I had come to know, and even smiled, "I leave you for five minutes and you start a fight at a nightclub?"

"Medusa!" May darted around the ice giant, and wrapped her arms around me. "Are you okay? What the hell happened? Who is this?" I choked out a laugh, and hugged her back. I caught Michael's eye over her shoulder, and gave him a weak smile. He just nodded. We'll definitely be having a conversation about this later. Though I should probably have him take me home now. Just in case I get emotional and my powers act up again…

May kept her arms wrapped around me as Kat and Zelda launched into the story, and introduced Kali who admitted that she told the not-drunk the wrong name and her real name is Amber. "Thank you, Medusa - right?" I pulled away from May, and nodded to her. She just smiled, not seeming put off in the slightest about my name. "Thank you so much. I'm sorry I got you into that situation. He wouldn't leave me alone, and I was getting nervous."

"As you should've been," Kat scoffed, "That guy was a grade A jackass. Hey, M, how did you know he was pretending to be drunk? I certainly thought he was." And here I thought she was determined to stick to 'kitten' as my nickname.

I shook my head, "It wasn't right. All of his moves seemed too calculated. Like he was planning them beforehand. It was very strange." I still don't get it.

Zelda coughed, "I actually heard about that, and now I'm mad I didn't catch it. Apparently it's a way to get girls to lower their guards because 'Duh the drunk guy wants to get more drinks' then he waits for you to drink with him and slips something in your drink. Good catch, Medusa." Where was she that she heard about something that awful? Goodness.

"So," Kat cut in, looking past May and me, "How about I buy you a drink for going all Superman for Medusa and me?"

Michael wasn't listening, though. He was scanning the area while scowling at every person he saw. I pulled away from May completely, and crossed to tap his arm. His eyes shot to mine, softening slightly, "Kat asked if she could get you a 'thank you' drink."

And he's scowling again. That was fast. "I don't drink, and you shouldn't be putting that poison in your body either."

"I haven't had any alcohol, if you must know." I stuck my tongue out at him.

He blinked back at me in shock, before his face relaxed back into a frown. That has to be its relaxed position by now. "*You* are a child. Do you need me to take you home?"

"No." I straightened. He was being nice because we're in public, but I just know he's furious with me for not training. "I'm having a good night with my friends - including Amber - but I'll see you tomorrow morning? I'm off tomorrow." He nodded, "Tomorrow then. Have a good night with your friends." He pressed a soft kiss to my temple and disappeared into the crowd.

Kat hummed, tapping her fingers on her chin. She was peering at me, "I think I approve of the boyfriend. That was pretty badass, showing up in the nick of time like that." I laughed. I'm glad he came, though I have no idea what he was doing here. Maybe he does have some kind of tracker on me. Oh, I don't like that. Regardless, I'm glad he showed up when he did. If he hadn't showed up that guy could've... He could've... I could have...

"Medusa! Come on." I looked back up to see four wide smiles. May rolled her eyes at me, "Stop daydreaming about the boyfriend. Girl's Night, remember?"

"I remember. Do you need a dance partner?"

"Hell yeah!"

Chapter Seven

Is it possible to have a hangover if you didn't drink? Like a people hangover, from being around too many people. If so, I definitely have one. My bed dipped, making me roll over till I hit the glacier that was sitting on my bed. I guess when Michael says morning, he means the early morning.

I opened my eyes only to immediately regret it. Evil man. Who opens every single curtains in a sleeping person's room? Evil people, that's who. "Are you going to pretend to be asleep forever?"

"I'm not pretending, I just can't open my eyes because my room is so bright. Can you close the curtains back, please?" I burrowed further into my blanket and his back to drive home my point. Maybe he'll show mercy.

Probably not, if his scoff was anything to go by. "Absolutely not. I need you awake for this conversation. We don't have a lot of time."

Now I'm awake. Darn him. "Why don't we have time? What's going on?"

Michael smirked at the sight of me fully sitting up, "I have to get back to my father, remember?" Oh. I should've thought of that. Michael moved back on my bed, pushing my pillows out of his way. Jokes on him. I'm willing to sleep on his shoulder too. With my blanket bunched around me, I scooted over the mattress to curl up against his side. He huffed, but didn't make me move, "We need to talk about what you did last night, Medusa." What are the chances that he just wants to hear about the good time I had after he left?

"Specifically, when you used your powers to attempt murder." So zero, then.

I swallowed, curling tightly into myself. That's the *last* thing I wanted to talk about. "I didn't mean to."

"You were angry. That man made you so angry, your powers came out full force. If I hadn't shown up, you would have ki-"

"Please don't say that out loud." I really try to not cut him off, but I think I can make an exception today. "I had a good time with the girls, but once I got home and tried to go to sleep... I kept seeing him there." My dreams would flash between him gasping for air on the ground, his face when he was going to hit Kat because of me, the fear when he was being held by the throat, and, of course, Michael's eyes. A shudder racked down my spine.

"Are you cold? Do I need to grab you another blanket?" How can he be so different now?

"No, I'm alright. I don't know what happened last night. Honestly, I didn't even know that I was the one *doing* that until you showed up. How did you know where I was, anyway?" I still hadn't figured that out. It had nagged me most of the night.

"I felt your power surge, and came immediately in case you needed assistance. Which you did." That last bit wasn't really needed, but I doubt he could help himself. He shifted, drawing in a breath. "Medusa, I have concerns. Your powers surged with your anger, but anger is not meant to be your strength. If anything, Wrath is meant to be your weakness."

Wrath? That seems like a specific word choice... Michael didn't explain though. I pushed off of him, still keeping in my blanket cocoon, but now I could see his face. He did look concerned as he studied me, but that didn't make the staring any less unnerving. Finally, after what seemed like forever, he shrugged and got off the bed, "I need to return to Zion. Be careful, and actually *practice* your magic."

"Aye aye, captain!" I saluted. He gave me the best disgusted look

I had ever seen, before sparkling away. Ooh he'd get so mad if he ever heard me call it that.

My phone chimed with a reminder, making me wobble to the other side of the bed to see it.

'Lunch with Karma'

Oh yeah! Good thing Michael left before my reminder. He'd blow a gasket if he knew who I was going to lunch with *and* where we were going. That being said, I don't have much time if I want to get there on time, but a quick shower is definitely needed.

I scanned *Steamie's* as I came through the door looking for any sight of Karma, but didn't find any. Good. I would hate to make her wait on me.

"Look what the cat dragged in. I thought you were banned from burgers." May laughed, leaning on the bar by the front door. "I'm surprised you're up. You looked exhausted last night."

"I was, and didn't really sleep so I still sort of am." I shrugged, "But I had already made plans today with a friend."

"A friend, huh? Did Kat bribe you with burgers? She seemed pretty taken with you last night." May didn't say it in a teasing way, but I could see a glint in her eyes that said she really wanted to.

"How would you know how Kat felt about me when you were distracted all night by a v-neck?"

She guffawed at me, "It was a very nice v-neck with even nicer abs, can you really blame me? Not that you'd care. Michael is built like a damn beast." She straightened moving to the hostess stand, "So, is it just the two of you or boyfriend, as well?"

"Just two, and if you could not mention this to Michael - like ever - that would be fantastic. Oh, and it's not Kat, though we did exchange numbers."

She raised a brow at me, but didn't say anything as she led me to a table toward the back, "Want anything to get you started? Chili, Mac and cheese, a drink?"

"I think I'll wait for her, actually. She should be here soon." May shrugged, and patted the table before wandering to her other tables. She had barely walked away when I saw a familiar ponytail walk through the front door. I stood up when she got close to me, and motioned for a hug. She laughed, wrapping her arms around me. "Hey! How's your arm? I know Michael grabbed you a little hard. I'm so sorry about him." When we pulled away I could fully see that both of her arms looked pretty normal, but that also begs the question of who wears a tank top in Colorado during Autumn? She didn't have a jacket on when she came through the door either. "I haven't ordered anything, yet. I wasn't sure what you'd want."

She waved off my question, her eyes scanning the menu, "My arm is much better, thank you. Any ideas on what I should order?" She seemed slightly bothered by the question, but maybe that's just the hunger. I know I can get cranky when I'm hungry.

Leaning forward, I pointed on her menu, "I prefer the steamie, but if you like barbecue sauce, I suggest the yeti." She nodded, making a deep humming sound. "However, I will cut you a part of mine to try for next time. They make their own sauce and it's *amazing*. Best burgers in town, hands down. Oh, and you have to get a milkshake. It'll change your life." Am I a little biased? Yes. But that doesn't make me wrong.

Karma smirked at me, finally lifted her head up, "You might be my new favorite person. Don't tell my best friend that's taking care of my house." I laughed, drawing an X over my heart. If someone is having to take care of her house, how long is she planning on being in town? "So, how's Michael and his sunshiny optimism?"

I was rolling my eyes before I could stop myself. I would approve of an optimistic Michael, but if this morning is anything to go off of, I'm not going to be seeing him until I'm dead. "I don't know." That's honest. Well... "Well, I do know he's never happy. He's been having some...Ah," How do you say this without saying he's arguing with God himself?! That's a crazy person thing to say. "Issues. With his dad." Good save. I hope.

Karma sighed, "Medusa, I need to be honest with you..."

"Hi! Welcome to *Steamie's*! Are you ready to order?" I could already tell May was having a field day now that she's seen my fitness model lunch buddy. We gave our orders. Mine coming with a warning look for her to not embarrass me. May promised to be back soon, giving Karma one more once over before going. Once she was out of Karma's sight, she turned back to mouth at me, *'Holy shit!'* While making a fanning motion.

I rolled my eyes at her, and refocused on Karma. A dark look had taken over her face, and she was clenching her silverware in her fist. "Um, Karma?" I asked, reaching out to place my hand on hers. "Are you okay?"

She blinked, "What?" Her eyes darted down, and she released them as if they burned her. The previously normal silverware was now partially liquid on the table. She tossed a napkin over them, pulling on her ponytail.

I should've known this was too good to be true. *I need to be honest with you.* I should've expected him to send someone else to watch after me. Michael didn't react too kindly to her, he must not like other angels stepping in his space. "You're one of them, aren't you? Look, I'm cooperating with Michael, do I really need two angels hanging around?" I don't think I can handle that right now. Even if she is more tolerable than Adakiel.

"Oh no, I'm not an angel." She reached out to me, but didn't actually touch me. Her grey eyes seemed to plead with me, "Honestly."

"You're not?"

"Well, no. I am a demon, though." She laughed sheepishly, rubbing the back of her neck.

I'm sure me completely freezing up totally helped her awkwardness. Good job, Medusa. Maybe I just heard her wrong, "A what?" Oh my god. "Do demons eat people? I thought this was a soon-to-be-friendship..." I'm definitely taking a nap when I get home. If I get home...

Karma seemed to think for a minute. Apparently 'do you eat people' is a hard question to answer. Who knew? "It is. At least, I would like it to be. I'm not evil. I'm a normal person. I was raised by humans - like you - but when an asshole showed up at *my* front door, he told me I was a demon instead of an angel."

Michael technically didn't call me an angel until last night, but I don't think that matters right now. "So, yours is a jerk too?"

"Oh definitely." She laughed. Then, she leaned forward on the table so she could speak at a lower volume. That's probably a good idea. They're not overly busy right now, but they're busy enough for us to be cautious. "Are you really a Virtue? That's our theory, at least."

I tilted my head, "*Our*? Does your mentor actually talk to you about all this Heaven and Hell stuff? Michael doesn't think my *tiny human mind* could handle it." Not that he said those exact words, but he has no problem implying it. "All he told me was that there's an apocalypse coming, and that I have a roll to play in stopping it." I would *like* for him to tell me more, even if it's scary, but I can't even ask him since he hasn't been *home* in a week.

"Really? Roman is pretty open with this stuff." She paused, cursed, and ran her hand over her face. "Don't mention his name to Michael, please. Apparently they know each other."

"They do? Are they friends?" Can angels and demons be friends? Can Michael actually *make* friends? I pursed my lips, "Do archangels and whatever yours is have friends?"

Karma smirked, her eyes darting to the windows again, "According to Roman, they aren't friends. Imagine a fourteen year old boy talking about the kid that stole his first girlfriend."

I laughed at that. So Michael has a frenemy then. That's adorable. This must be the 'arch enemy' Michael was talking about. "I won't mention his name." Just then, May came back out with a tray. "I can see our food coming, but after we eat can we go somewhere without human ears and you can get me a little more up to speed? Would that be okay?"

Karma nodded, "Yeah! I'll do my best. Being in the dark about all this can't be fun." Understatement of the century. All I've learned is that there's much more to this than I've been told.

忍

"That was one of the best burgers I've ever had." Karma declared, rubbing her flat stomach.

I laughed at her antics, "I could tell. You ate all of yours *and* half of mine."

"You gave me permission." She reminded, bumping shoulders with me. I stumbled a bit, but I don't think she noticed. She's much stronger than she looks. "If you're ever in Monterey, I'll take you to *The Monument*. It's my favorite burger place back home. Though, warning, they're not steamed. I'd never had a steamed burger before." Ever? How crazy. Monterey must be where her house is. I wonder if it's anything like here.

Karma let me lead the way when we left the restaurant - and luckily was too focused on looking around to notice May teasing me on the way out. We were headed to the park Michael and I practiced magic in that first time. That seems like light years away now. Karma was still in a tank top, but didn't seem bothered by the fifty degree weather in the slightest. When we got to the park, Karma produced a camera with an expensive looking lens she screwed on after wiping off with a cloth.

"Wait," She grabbed my arm, effectively stopping me from moving. She approached the bench we were headed to with practiced stealth, and snapped some photos of one of the many little birds that lives here perched happily on the back of the bench. She was still snapping pictures as it flew away. "Beautiful." She murmured so quietly, I'm not sure she even heard it.

"You're a photographer?" I asked. A gust of wind blew past us, bringing a harsh chill with it. Karma didn't even notice. How strange.

She just shrugged, "Not a professional. It's just a hobby. This park is every photographer's dream. This whole place actually."

I shrugged, Telluride is a beautiful place, but I'm sure it pales in comparison to some other places. I sat of the bench, crossing my legs underneath me, "I grew up here, so it's hard to appreciate it the same way a tourist would. I've never been anywhere else. What about you? Did you grow up in Monterey?"

Karma sat beside me, dropping her arm over the back of the bench, ever so gracefully. For someone who looks so muscular and stocky, she was always so effortlessly graceful. I don't understand it. She sighed, "No. I moved to California when I was seventeen to finish high school at my grandmother's house. Then when I graduated, my grandmother signed over my mom's old house in Monterey to me so I could go to college there. I don't know where I was born exactly, but I was raised in Michigan." She tilted her head, frowning at whatever was in front of her, but I have a feeling it was an internal issue. "I guess I'm technically from Hell? I don't know if I was born there, though."

I shifted, turning my whole body to face her. She doesn't seem like someone who opens up easily, that deserves my full attention, "Do you miss it? Michigan?"

She let out a single dry laugh, like the mere thought was outrageous. Her eyes darkened as she glared off into space. I wouldn't be surprised if she forgot I was here.

"Karma?" She jumped, turning to face me with glossy eyes. I shouldn't of stayed silent so long, and I shouldn't have asked. That was a rabbit hole she was avoiding, and my nosiness threw her in. "Hey," I gently covered her hand with mine. Her skin was on fire, but I kept my hand there. "It's okay. I'm glad you got away from whatever was in Michigan." She still seemed lost. Her eyes wouldn't focus. "So," I pushed forward, "I have a few questions. If that's alright."

There we go. Her eyes finally refocused on mine, and she straightened. "Of course. I'll do my best to answer them."

I wrung my hands out, taking a steadying breath. I don't know if I'll get to see her again any time soon, so I should start with the important ones. "You're a demon, but you didn't know before you met your mentor?"

She nodded, "Yeah. I'm one of the Seven Sins, but I thought I was human - and was raised as one - until Roman showed up."

"One of the Seven Sins..." Seven Sins and Seven Virtues. That can't be a coincidence. "I'm one of the Seven Virtues. Do the Sins have specific qualities, too? For instance, I'm the Virtue of Patience."

She blinked, "Are you fucking serious?" What did I say wrong? "Sorry. I'm the Sin of Wrath." *Wrath is meant to be your weakness.* "I'm almost positive we're each other's opposite. We're probably not meant to be friends." Then she laughed, shaking her head.

"We seem to be okay," I giggled, gesturing to our hands in between us. "Is it just us? I haven't been told if there's any other Virtues, but I don't think Michael would tell me." He'd probably say it was just a distraction. "We're on a pretty need to know basis. Not by my choice."

She scoffed, "Doesn't the lack of answers drive you crazy?"

I shrugged, "Not really. I'm sure to a great celestial being, I do seem too small to understand things like this. He doesn't seem to spend much time around humans in general." Sometimes it's hard to remember that he's actually this powerful being that's literally the stuff of legends when he's yelling at me about grease, but that doesn't change what he is.

"You are patient," Karma snorted. She seemed almost amused by me. At least she's not counting. "We haven't found any other Sins. Yet. We're looking, though."

"Do you know what the other... Ah... Sins are?" What has happened to my life? "Michael said the other Virtues are Chastity, Temperance, Generosity, Diligence, Kindness, and Humility." I laughed, shaking my head at how ridiculous I sounded. "We sound like a church group. The kind that goes caroling on Christmas morning." I wonder if people actually do that.

"They do sound like a... Fun bunch." I gave her a flat look. That was the most blatant lie. You'd think demons could lie better. "According to Roman, the other Sins are Lust, Gluttony, Greed, Sloth, Envy, and Pride."

"So... A bar fight?" She smiled at me. "Are you sure you want to find the rest? One bad argument could get bad alarmingly fast." If it does happen, I hope it's not an argument that takes place around me.

Karma sighed, running a hand through her hair, pulling the ponytail out with it. "I think so. I mean, yours sound like an absolute bore, and mine sounds like tequila personified." I snorted, that's an insanely accurate description. "At the same time, they are the few people who will understand what it's like to be us. Plus, we can't save the world without them."

"Right." My shoulders sagged as I rested my head in my palms. "I don't know how I forgot about all that. It's all Michael and Yhwh seem to talk about."

"So you've met him, too? I've recently met Yhwh. He's... Not what I expected." She met Yhwh? Michael actually told him about her. So much for him not hurting my friends anymore. I guess he must really be like his father.

"You mean terrifying?" I shuddered, thinking back to Yhwh's eyes. "He's so *cold*. I never thought God would be so scary. When Michael said I was going to meet him, I was so excited. I'd thought Michael was just stressed - being in charge of God's army can't be easy, right?" Not to mention he's also training me. Hopefully God can't hear me calling him God after he told me not to.

"In reality, he's just like his father?" A part of me really hopes not.

"Yeah," I sighed, "Though, I don't suppose I can complain..." Michael could just stop teaching me and leave me to someone else. From the way Yhwh talked, the next person would definitely try to break me.

"Why not?" Karma's grip tightened on the bench, "Some *jackass* shows up on your front door, drops a crazy amount of responsibility on your shoulders, won't tell you a damn thing, introduces you to one of the scariest beings in the universe, and a truck load of other shit. You have every right to complain." I couldn't help laughing. Michael would absolutely hate Karma. She's so outspoken. It would drive him crazy.

"Well, yes, but you have Lucifer. Surely he's worse, and a lot scarier." He *is* Satan, after all. He's like the supreme evil.

Karma shrugged, watching a squirrel dart way too close to the bench, "I've only spoke to him once, but he wasn't like Yhwh. Yeah sure, he was scary and I couldn't really see any compassion in his eyes, but he was honest. With Yhwh, he looked at me like a pawn. Like some*thing* he could maneuver the way he wants and dispose of after." Yeah, I can definitely see how she got that impression. He even treats Michael that way. "Lucifer didn't want to play games, though. He doesn't want the world to end. He doesn't seem to care if I'm on his side or not as long as everyone survives. I don't really know *why* he wants the world to survive, but obviously he does."

"Lucifer is better than God? That's fantastic." Maybe I'm on the wrong side. "This whole thing is crazy."

"Definitely, and I don't think our "mentors" understand how much of a shock this can be for a person." Now, *that* is something I can fully agree with.

I stiffened, seeing an incredibly *large* man approaching us. He looked like seven bodybuilders smooshed into one person. "Um, is that Roman? He doesn't look like an actual human male." I'd never seen anyone so *big*. No wonder Michael hates him. He's several inches taller Michael and much wider... Maybe not with Michael's wings, but he doesn't have those when he's here.

Karma groaned, "Hang back. *Damn him.*" Roman stopped when he saw Karma jogging to him angrily. In her haste, she forgot her camera, leaving it beside me. I picked it up carefully, and snapped a couple photos of myself with plenty of goofy faces. If I know anything about her, it's that she'd laugh when she saw them.

Across the park, Karma and Roman were arguing, standing closely together - I'm assuming to avoid anyone overhearing - or they just don't realize they're that close. Karma stuffed her hands into her back pockets. It wasn't a show of her being relaxed, though. It was definitely a way to hold herself back. Maybe I should go help.

"Karma?" I asked, coming up behind her. Karma pulled her hands out of her pockets to take her camera back, and put it in her own bag. "I should go. Michael gets angry if I disappear for too long." Michael isn't home so he probably wouldn't *know,* but I seem to be causing some issues with the two of them. That's the opposite of what I want to do. I'd hate for Karma to have problems because of me. Friends don't do that to each other.

Roman scoffed, crossing his arms across his chest. I thought Karma's arms were muscular… Jeez. Roman's arm was bigger than my head. "That is because he is a… What do humans say? Control freak." He nodded at the phrase, "And an *asshole.*"

I snickered into my hand, "So you were right about that, huh?" Karma smirked, holding in her own laugh. She avoided Roman's eyes, still smiling.

"So when you said 'discussing sensitive information' you meant talking ill about me? How *mature* of you, Karma." Now Karma was full on laughing, which only made him glare harder. It wasn't even focused on me, and it made me nervous. Karma cared less about his glare than she cared about the cold weather. He rolled his eyes at her, and focused on me, "Hello. Medusa, correct?"

"Yeah," I laughed, "Hello. Is there a formal introduction I'm supposed to do? Medusa Sinclair, Virtue of Patience. It's nice to meet you." I smiled. Should I bow, or curtsey, or something?

Roman stopped glaring, and smiled softly at me, "That was exemplary. Karma could never be that polite." Karma flipped him off. He smirked at Karma, "How are you getting along with the Virtue of Patience? I would have thought simply being around her would put you on edge. Is that not the case?"

"*No, actually.*" Karma snarked back, "She's pretty calming. Oddly enough, we get along great. Maybe it's a yin and yang thing."

I think that's the nicest thing I've ever heard someone call me.

I like the thought of being calming. "Opposites attract," I supplied, "Not all of the time though. Michael doesn't seem to like me all that much. The two of you get along much better than we ever could." They bicker a lot, but even I can tell they get along really well. The pair exchanged a glance before frowning at me. Perfectly in sync. I laughed again, "You have no idea how the two of you look right now. Arms all crossed, standing with your feet equally apart, frowning down at me." Karma shifted, dropping her arms. She looked over her male counterpart before rolling her eyes. She really didn't know how similar they looked. How funny. "You're adorable. Do you have something I can write my number on? So we don't lose contact."

"Yeah." Karma produced a receipt from her bag along with a pen, and handed them over. "Good luck with Michael." I beamed at her, and kissed Roman's cheek before heading back to my bike. He reminds me of a bulldog. All grumpy looking but really just wants a hug.

May was waiting outside *Steamie's* when I got back. A smile overtook her face when she saw me approaching, "Hey, gorgeous. Who was your friend?"

I gave her a flat look, unlocking my bike. "I don't like your tone. She's just a friend."

"A very attractive friend. What is it about you that attracts tall lesbians?"

I'm so happy she's having such a field day with this. Even if she's completely wrong. "I don't attract lesbians. I met my first lesbian *last night* with you. I don't even know if Karma likes women."

She huffed, "She should. With an ass and legs like that, I'd switch teams."

"You're terrible." I laughed, shaking my head at her, "Don't you have customers waiting on you?" She *is* still in her uniform.

"I'm on break, but I should head back. I'll text you later, yeah?" I nodded at her. It should be a quiet day when I get back home. At least, I hope so. May paused at the door, "Oh and if we're placing bets, my bet is totally on you and Karma. You vibe better. Michael is still sexy, though, so it's not like there's a losing option."

Chapter Eight

I leaned my bike against the house, and headed inside. Dad was on the couch, drinking a beer, watching whatever is playing on the sports channel. He didn't even glance at me when I passed him, but what's new?

I felt much better after talking to Karma. Minus the fact that she's spoken to Yhwh, which is *completely* my fault. If I hadn't held her back at the store, Michael would've never met her. I do wish I could apologize for that. She probably wouldn't let me, and it might make her more inclined to hit Michael, so it's probably best to leave it alone.

Oh, darn! I meant to ask if she was struggling with her magic. She definitely has some form of it, if the silverware is anything to go by. Hopefully I'll get the chance to see her again before she goes back home.

"There you are." I screamed, not expecting him to be there. Michael, now scowling, crossed his arms, "*Why* are you screaming?"

"Why are you suddenly in my room?! You scared me half to death!" I slipped off my shoes, and climbed onto my bed. Michael stayed standing so he could have an optimal glaring angle. "You've been gone for days. Some warning would be nice."

"How was I supposed to warn you? You're never *home*. You heard what my Father said, you need to be improving. Not going out with the mortals, or that ridiculous boy that keeps seeking you out." What is he even talking about? The only male I see on a regular basis is Brian, and he does not seek me out. "Get changed out of that pink monstrosity. We're going to train."

I moved to get up, but paused. Maybe Michael does need someone like Karma. I moved back to a sitting position, square in the middle of my bed. *You have every right to complain.* And dang it, I have some things I really want to get off my chest. "No."

"*What* did you say?"

"I said, no. I don't want to train; I want to talk. So sit." I pointed to the opposite side of the bed.

"Medusa-"

"*No.* I'm sick of this, and I'm sick of being in the dark about everything. So sit down. We are going to talk like normal people. I *deserve* that." My hands shook as I glared back at Michael. He hadn't moved, but neither had I. I need to stand up for myself or I'm going to get stomped on. Maybe not by Michael himself, but I'm sure Yhwh can find someone to do it for him. "Be honest with me," I pleaded, "*Please.*"

He growled, but took a seat on my bed. Michael sat fully facing me with his arms crossed, "I don't know what the hell has gotten into you, and I *do not* approve."

"Well, I'm sick of caring." Maybe not completely, but enough. I straightened my spine, refusing to acknowledge the chills running down it. Michael was making the room much colder than it was supposed to be, and my thin sweater wasn't doing much to protect me. But if I get up now, I lose this chance. "I have questions, and you need to answer them. You can't expect me to just keep following you blindly. Have you found any other Virtues? Does anyone have an idea where they might be? What's the plan when we find them?"

Michael relaxed slightly, but was still scowling at me. Baby steps, I suppose. I was right, though. He'd really hate Karma. "No, no other Virtues have been located. I believe my father has some scouts in several places, but I do not know where. When they are found, they will be sent an Angel guardian to train them, as I am training you. Is that all?"

"Nope. Settle in, I'm just getting started. I want to be there. When the next Virtue is training, I want to be there with them. Going through this alone isn't something I would wish on anyone. I can help them."

Michael scoffed, "Help them? You can't even master your own magic. What help are you going to be to them?"

I will not cry. I balled up my fists to stop the tremors, "Stop it. Don't belittle me." That's all everyone has done my whole life. I don't need it from him too. Or Yhwh for that matter. "I want to be there to help the people going through what I'm going through." If they have a mentor like Michael, they're going to need me. It's impossible to succeed with people constantly knocking you back down. "The last thing Humility or Kindness needs is for someone like *you* to burst into their life and make them miserable."

"Someone like me?" He huffed, "Do you not realize how lucky you are to have me here? You are being trained by the greatest general of all time. I have trained many great soldiers-"

"But I'm *not* a soldier!" Why can't he *get* that?

"You need to be!" Great now we're both yelling. A vein was bulging in Michael's forehead as he yelled back at me, "This isn't some ridiculous game, Medusa! The world is coming to an end and you are in charge of stopping it. Do you think the apocalypse is going to cease because you bat your big green eyes and *ask* it to? Are you going to tear up like you're doing now and pray it works?"

I wasn't... Okay I was, but it was out of anger. I didn't know anger could make you cry, but I've learned a lot today. Michael watched me get up from my bed looking stupidly smug. He probably thought I had given in and was going to change. Well screw him. I slipped on my flats, and marched out the door.

"What the hell was all the yelling about?" I ignored my father on the way out the back door. What does he care? It's four o'clock in the afternoon, he's already too drunk to remember any of this anyway.

"Medusa, where are you going?" Michael ignored him as well,

following me. "If you were going to leave, you went out the wrong door."

"Oh wow, Michael, thanks for telling me how to operate the house I've lived in for twenty three years. I still get lost in there sometimes. Thank God I have someone like you constantly telling me how stupid I am." Anger is exhausting, but that didn't make me any less angry.

"You are being irrational. What happened to the Medusa that was here when I left?"

I spun around, facing his scowl head on, "That's what happened! You left! You only came back to gripe at me, and then to whisk me away to meet the most terrifying being I have ever met, and then you left me alone to deal with that. God himself basically called me useless. Do you know what that does to a person?" I let out a dry laugh, "Actually, I'm sure you do know. You just don't care." That's the base of it, really. Karma and Roman showed me that, most likely without either of them realizing. Roman cared about Karma. He cared about where she was, they joke together and bicker one second later, they know each other so well that most of their conversations were spoken through glances and eye rolls. *That's* a good partnership. I'm just...

I'm just a pawn.

"Medu-"

"Brother, there you are." I turned to see some other tall man in my backyard. Well, angel, I suppose. This is the longest Tuesday ever. "Father said you might need my assistance with the Virtue. Is this her?"

"I do not need your assistance." Michael grumbled, moving himself in between his brother and me.

The new angel huffed, "Yes, I can see that by the way she is yelling at you. You made the Virtue of Patience yell at you."

What? I moved around Michael, forcing the air around us forward. Newcomer flew backwards, only stopping when he slammed into a tree. Michael raised a brow at me, "You've been practicing."

"As a matter of fact, no I have not." I turned my back to him, and sat by the brook. What kind of world is this where the *demons* are nicer than the angels? I should've asked Karma to kidnap me.

"*Have you lost your mind?*" New guy was back up, and angry. Michael can handle him.

"Jophiel, that is a mistake." Michael warned. Hopefully Jophiel listens to his much bigger brother. A giant wall of ice appeared next to me, pulling another scream from me. I turned to glare at him, but he wasn't looking at me. He was scowling at his brother, "I told you that it would be a mistake."

"Wait, did he *attack* me?" I guess that's fair. I did throw him into a tree.

"*Yes.*" Michael still didn't look at me. He kept his eyes trained on his brother.

"Why would you do that? Have you forgotten that she is a soldier? She needs to be able to take an attack!"

"No, I am not!" Michael grabbed my outstretched hand, and pulled me to my feet. The angel scowled at me - unfortunately it didn't have the desired effect since I've spent the last few months with the champion of glaring. "I am *not* a soldier."

His golden eyes focused firmly on me, "Then you are useless."

I am so sick of men telling me how useless I am. "Did it ever occur to you that you can stop someone from being the Virtue of Patience by driving her insane? You're all really good at it."

"Translation; you are making it worse." Michael gave him a cold smile, "Time for you to go."

Jophiel shook his head, "Father will not approve of you sending me away."

"He wouldn't approve of me killing you either." Michael shot back. Why is he so okay with murder? "Now, Medusa has done enough for today. How about a nap, Medusa?"

"That sounds fantastic." I nodded, heading back into the house. So much for calming down outside. Stupid angels.

"Oh, and brother," Michael called, walking beside me, "You

attack Medusa and you attack me. Whether the two of us were arguing or not. I suggest you remember that."

We made it back to my room in silence. Dad was asleep when we went though the living room. How did he fall asleep so fast? I paused to turn off the television before continuing to my room. Electric is expensive enough. Michael leaned on my closed door, watching me move around my room.

"Have you ever heard the word creepy, Michael?" I asked, moving into my closet.

"Once or twice I suppose. I know what it means, if that is what you are asking. Are you done being angry at me already?" He didn't follow me into the closet - thankfully. I guess he finally learned *that* lesson.

"I don't know." I shrugged, "I was mad and I'm still angry about things, but I'm tired. I'm just *so* tired. Anger is exhausting."

"Especially for you, I'd imagine. As I've previously stated, Wrath is your weakness. Being too angry could have a series of negative effects on you. How are you feeling?"

"Fine. I feel fine." Just tired. It's been a long day. I came out of the closet fully dressed in pajamas.

Michael frowned at me, "I have seen you wear the same t-shirt no less than thirteen times, but have never seen you wear the same set of pajamas twice. Why do you have so many?"

"I like pajamas." I shrugged, settling into my bed with my smaller pillow in my lap. "Why do you always wear really tight shirts?"

He pulled his shirt away from his chest, "Is this not normal?"

"Not really, but it looks nice on you. Are you going to sit down?" I tilted my head at him. Michael sighed, moving to sit on the bed beside me. "I'm sorry I yelled at you."

"It was well deserved on my part. I do believe in you, Medusa. You've gotten so much stronger since we started training. I apologize for what my father and my brothers have said about you. I do not believe that you are useless. However," He held up a finger, "I do agree that you are not a soldier. Not in the slightest." He chuckled.

"Okay, okay." I laughed, leaning my head on his shoulder. "I could still be of use to the other Virtues, though." If Karma is correct, maybe I can help them feel a little less stressed with my 'calming' affect.

"I do believe that. I will tell my Father that we need to be the ones to train the next Virtue, and I vow to not make you angry this time. How was the transport for you? I was careful to hold onto you when I took you to Zion. Did you handle the trip back alright?"

"No," I scoffed, "I threw up for about two hours, and I might have a minor concussion from hitting the frame of my bed."

"What? Why didn't you say something? What spot?" He bumped me off his arm, making me sit up. I showed him the spot that I hit. "I can fix this." That makes me nervous. Michael rubbed the spot on my head leaving a cool sensation in his wake. I couldn't help leaning into his touch. My head did feel much better. "You did have a concussion. I apologize for not checking on you sooner." I didn't think he would ever apologize this much.

"Thank you, Michael. Do you think, that maybe, we can try to be honest with each other from here forward? I'd like to be friends."

"I don't really have friends, Medusa, so I cannot promise that I will be any good at it, but I will try to be easier to work with. Now, you get some rest." He rubbed my back, "I will come and get you in a few hours."

忍

My eyes fluttered open, immediately shutting once more. Did Michael open my curtains again? I thought we'd come so far. I pulled my blanket over my head, well, I tried to anyway. I ended up just dumping grass all over my face. Now I'm awake.

"Michael!" I groaned, wiping the dirt off my face. Why would he do this? "Michael?" I blinked. I was alone in a massive field. I clambered to my feet, brushing the grass off of me. There wasn't anything for miles. Just grass and wild flowers. So many flowers, holy crap. It definitely isn't Telluride, that's for sure.

"*Ciao c'è qualcuno?*"

He left me with people? What kind of training exercise is this? And why is it *so hot* here?

"*Ti sei perso?*" A woman slightly taller than me with her hands clasped in front of her approached me. Her light brown eyes were filled with concern, "*Parli Italiano?*"

"Um," I glanced around. Where had she come from? "English? Sorry I don't speak… Italian?" I think that's what she's speaking.

"*Oh! Americano?*"

"Yes!" Now if I can figure out where we *are*. I guess Michael couldn't drop me off with my phone. That would be too easy. I turned back to the woman, "Do you know where we are?" She gave me a pained smile. She can't understand me. Dang it, I should've taken Italian in high school instead of French.

"*Da dove vieni?*" I guess she understands my frustration with this. Though, judging by her lack of pockets, I'm assuming she doesn't have a phone either. "*Ah, no Italiano.*" She wrung her hands out, "*Mi chiamo* Jez. *Vieni con me?*"

She held her hand out to me, trying to wave me along. "Oh, no, I should stay here." Hopefully Michael will come and grab me soon. What did he expect to happen when he left me out here?

The woman frowned, "*No no, vein con me.*" Well at least I think I learned a little Italian from this. She's definitely trying to get me to go with her somewhere. Is there a better patch of flowers than this one?

"Medusa."

I whipped around, "Michael! Michael?" There was no one there. It was still just me and this woman.

"*Con chi stai parlando? Siamo solo noi qui fuori.*"

I ignored her, looking around for him. "Medusa, come on." Come on where? "Medusa!"

I gasped feeling a hard tug on my chest. I was pulled from the field... And sat up in my bed. Michael was sitting next to me, violently shaking me awake. "Okay okay. I'm awake. Please stop doing that." That was a dream? It felt so real.

"What happened? Your magic aura was more active than I had seen... Well, ever. Are you alright?" What is a magic aura?

"I'm okay. Can magic give weird dreams?"

"I don't dream, and as far as I know, they can not trigger dreams. What kind of dream was it? My father can travel through dreams, but he has other ways to reach you." That's creepy, but what else is new when it comes to Yhwh?

"I was in a beautiful field surrounded by wildflowers... There was a girl there. She kept talking me, but not in a language I know. I only know English and *very* basic French, so that doesn't leave much room, but still."

Michael nodded, staying quiet. He thought for a moment. Well, I think he's thinking. Hopefully he's not counting. I pulled my hair back into a bun while I waited. Michael refocused on me, "Can you attempt to repeat something she said to you?" Oh dear. I tried to repeat her 'come with me' sentence she kept saying. Michael flinched at my butchering of the language, but nodded nonetheless. "I believe the original language is meant to be Italian. Any other details about this woman?"

"She's very conservative? Lots of hair?" I shrugged.

Michael frowned at me, "That isn't helpful. Anything near by?"

"Lots of flowers, and a giant hill that looked to have a little church. Maybe a town?"

He nodded, seeming to think it over. "A church? That could be helpful. Did it look like she was part of the church? A nun, perhaps?"

"A nun? Why would you *want* me to dream about a nun?"

He gave me a flat look, "Nuns devote their lives to my father. Do you know who else is most likely to devote themselves to Yhwh?" People that haven't met him? "*Virtues.*" Oh. "Exactly. There's a chance you're connected with this person because she's another Virtue. Your magic could be on the same... Um..."

"Wavelength." I finished. I hadn't even considered that. Could I really be connected to the other Virtues? "I don't think you're going to have a strong team, Michael. I didn't learn much about her though the large language barrier, but she seemed to be similar to me in terms of physical strength. She's a little taller, but she was out there with a basket of flowers."

Michael just sighed, "Your magic can be your strength once we figure out how to truly harness it. As for the girl... Well, let's wait and see if she comes up as a Virtue at all before we do that." Yeah, best not to stress about a possibility. For all we know, it could've been some magic induced dream with no base in reality. "I will need to update my father, though. He can have some of his scouts focus on Italy."

"Wait," Michael got up to leave, but paused, "I still want to be the ones to mentor her."

He gave me a single nod, "I will make sure we are the ones to go meet her. I give you my word." The word of an angel? Hopefully it means something.

Once he was gone, I climbed out of bed, and made my way downstairs. Dad was no where to be seen. He must have relocated to his room before crashing again. I made my way to the fridge to see if we had anything. I should've really gone grocery shopping after lunch.

"Oh," Did I forget that I went grocery shopping? Surely, I wouldn't forget something like that. At least I hope I wouldn't. Dad doesn't leave the house, and I seriously doubt he knows about grocery delivery. Even if he did, he would never buy this much fruit. Or kale. *Oh my god.* Michael got groceries. He even bought a stand with little baskets to hold the apples, oranges, avocados, lemons, sweet potatoes, mushrooms, garlic, ginger, and more things that I've never even seen before. I do know one thing, he certainly didn't buy any bacon, beer, or red meat. He really is sticking to this no hamburger rule. "I guess it's a good thing I actually like fruits." We're going to have to talk about the lack of bread though. That's too far.

When Michael got back, he found me at the table eating a plate full of sliced fruits. He actually smiled at me. That's all it took? "Look at you." He took the seat beside me, still smiling. Then, he frowned. That didn't take long, "Why are there no vegetables on your plate? You need to have balance."

"It's a snack. Not a meal." I resisted sticking my tongue out at him. "You know what I do need?"

"If you say burgers, I'm making you try Muai Thai again." He threatened.

"*Bread.*" I'm never trying martial arts ever again, either. That was brutal. "You didn't buy any bread. Do you know who doesn't have bread in their house?"

"People who care about their health."

"Serial killers. They might be healthy, but they're definitely crazy. Plus, you got that turkey breast, and the lettuce. I could make such a good *healthy* sandwich." Healthy enough anyway. He doesn't have to know I'm going to put chipotle mayonnaise on it. Oh my god, did he throw out my chipotle mayonnaise?

He rolled his eyes at me, "You know, I have seen that people make these things called 'lettuce wraps' it's like a sandwich, but instead of bread they use lettuce. You should try that."

"*Or* I buy bread and don't get hamburger meat or sodas. Oh, and you have to deal with my dad when he finds out you didn't get any of the foods he actually likes." That is definitely not something I want to deal with.

"The only person more unhealthy than you, is Elias. Some healthy eating could do him some good, and *sunlight*." He sneered at the television in the next room. I wish him luck with that. That tv has been his constant companion since Mom died. He watched me for a moment before pushing his chair away from the table, "I'm going to make you something with more nutrients."

"No! That is not necessary. This is enough for me." He scowled at me, eyes flicking between my plate and my face. He obviously didn't believe me, but I'd rather starve that have to suffer through that burrito again. My stomach churred just thinking about it.

"You need *sustenance*, Medusa. I am making you an actual breakfast. What do you want in your omelet?" Omelet? That doesn't sound bad. Plus, he's actually asking me.

"Eggs, cheese, onion, and the red bell peppers. No avocados. Absolutely zero." I can't. Michael rolled his eyes at me, but I didn't see him grab any when he gathered his ingredients. Though, I'm sure that it's possible he snuck some.

Michael was still cooking when my father hobbled into the kitchen some minutes later. Here we go. He made his way to the fridge and peered in. Glasses clinked as he shoved things around the items in the fridge. Michael spoke up when he started moving the plastic bags, "Those are delicate. Don't break or bruise them, Elias."

My father ignored him, "Where the hell is the beer?" He straightened to glare at me over the fridge door, "Did you forget to buy beer?"

"No," Michael answered, transferring the omelet to a plate. It actually looked pretty good. "I purposefully didn't grab the beer. Alcoholism can cause memory loss, affect your coordination negatively, weaken your heart, break down your liver, lead to fat gather in your liver, cause liver failure, cause pancreatitis, and several other complications. You need to stop drinking it."

My father whipped around, his face already turning red. He got in Michael's face - to the best of his ability. Michael has nearly a foot on him in height, pointing a finger at him, "Listen, *boy,* you don't tell me what to do. Now go get me some *damn beer!*"

Michael scowled, slowly moving my father's hand away from his face. Frost gathered on the stainless steel of the refrigerator as Michael glared back, "No." My father turned to me, "Don't yell at her either. She isn't bringing any alcohol in this house, just as I am not." I shrugged at my father. There's nothing I could do. Michael is much more terrifying than my father could ever be.

Michael crossed to the table, setting the omelet down in front of me, "Elias, there is food in the kitchen that will not kill you. If you are thirsty, there is water and natural fruit juices."

My father glared at him. He moved around the kitchen while I ate my omelet. Michael ignored him in favor of watching me eat. Maybe I should go help him. I was on my last bite of the omelet - which was much more delicious than I dared to hope it would be - my father had another outburst, "Where is the bacon?"

"In Hell where it belongs." Michael deadpanned, still not turning around. I coughed to cover up my laugh. My father didn't appreciate either of our responses.

"Do you want me to make you something, Dad?"

Before he could answer, Michael cut in, "No time. Your father is a grown man. We have things to do." We have more things to do? He got up, waving me along. I pulled myself from my chair, opting to follow Michael then suffer through another explosion from my father.

I jogged to catch up to Michael as he made his way out back. How does he walk *so* fast? I was slightly out of breath when I caught him, but I did catch up. "So," I stopped, putting my hands on my knees. Okay, maybe more than a little out of breath…

"You're horribly out of shape." He commented, stopping a few feet in front of me.

"Thanks. I have a question." I dropped onto the soft grass, crossing my legs. Michael scowled, but waved me to go on. I guess he isn't sitting with me. Not that I can be all that surprised. "What is a magic aura? It's been bugging me since you said it." And if there's one thing I've learned from him, it's that if I don't ask he'll never tell me.

"Do you know what an aura is?" I nodded. Michael moved closer to me, but remained standing. "Humans came close to understanding what an aura actually is, of course they never *fully* understood it as they refuse to believe in magic. However, the belief that your aura is an essential part of who you are and reflecting your spirit are actually correct. All humans have magic inside them, some just have less than others. You can tell how much magic someone has by seeing how vibrant their aura is, or the color of it." That's... interesting. "For example, your aura closely resembles that of an angel. If another angel were to see your aura, they would assume you are one of us without question. Until you spoke, that is." He shrugged, "When I woke you up, your body was covered in your aura, and was so bright I could barely see your body *or* your bed. I've never seen anything like it." I don't think he meant for that to be as scary as it sounded. Surely, it was just because that girl is a Virtue. If the scouts come back and say that she isn't, then I can have a minor nervous breakdown at being turned into a star. Simple.

"So if my aura looks like an angel, what do normal people's look like? Like my father."

His face twisted. Michael looked toward the house as if he could scowl at my father through a wall and a wooden door, "Your father does not have a normal aura either, Medusa." That doesn't sound good. Is it because he lives with me? Or because I'm his daughter? "Elias' aura is filled with browns, blacks, and purples. His soul is filled with sin and sadness." Michael settled into the ground in front of me, clasping his hands in front of himself. "If you were to see your father's aura, your female friend from the park's aura, and your boss' aura side by side you would see a distinct difference in colors." I guess that makes sense. They're all very different people. "Starting with your boss..."

"Brian." I filled in.

He nodded, "Brian's aura is a mixture of light grey, vibrant pinks, and royal blues - all of which are positive things. Mainly meaning that he's content with his current situation in life and is a generous person. However, he also has a silvery blue mixed in with his aura which is a side effect of spending time with you. Your father who lives with you and has for your entire life, *should* have that on his aura as well."

I shifted. A chill made its way up my spine as he stared impassively at me. Something tells me I'm not going to like the answer to this question. I drew in a deep breath, "What does it mean if he doesn't have any traces of me?"

Michael sighed, "It means that his soul is overpowering any affect yours could have on him." My soul can have an effect on someone else's? If I can make other people more patient, Brian is going to strangle me. "Stop making that face. It really isn't that surprising considering how long his addiction has run rampant."

I pursed my lips, looking away from him. Michael didn't seem to notice, not that I really expected him to. He's becoming less like a living Brillo pad, but not that much. "Are you crying?" I shook my head. Michael scoffed, "Well, at least you're a terrible liar."

"Is it time for me to go to work yet?"

"It's still Tuesday." I groaned, flopping on my back. This day is the longest day in history.

Michael leaned over me with a brow raised, "Do you want dinner?"

I laughed, "I just ate." I don't really eat that much. Michael just shrugged. "I want to go to bed and not have a confusing dream." Oh, and for my magic aura to not go crazy. I didn't feel it, but I definitely don't like it.

"Then stretch and we'll go to bed." Stretch? I glanced at him, not moving. He gave me a flat look, "It will relax you, so hopefully you'll go into a deep sleep easier. Unless you want to try an actual work out to tire you out?"

"Stop threatening me." I grumbled halfheartedly. Michael smirked, rising to his feet as well. "Know any good stretches that won't put me in pain?"

"I guess we'll find out."

忍

My phone rang, startling me awake. I snatched it off my bedside table, glancing at the clock. Who in their right mind is calling me at three in the morning? Oh, it's Karma.

"Karma?" I paused to yawn, "It's three in morning…"

"I know. I'm sorry. I just…" She sounds so defeated. I didn't think she could be defeated.

Feeling more awake, I sat up in my bed. I have no idea where Michael wondered off to, but I'm glad he did. He'd give me the lecture of a lifetime if he found out I was talking to her after deeming her 'suspicious' or whatever word he used. "It's okay. What's up?" I couldn't hold back the second yawn.

Karma sighed, "Michael and Yhwh are close, right?"

"Yeah." Weird direction of conversation. Then again, nothing is really normal at three in the morning anyway. "He's the golden boy. Why?"

"I just spoke to him." *What?* "Yhwh, not Michael. Be careful around them, okay? Yhwh said some things that make me really uncomfortable. I'm not so sure about my side of things either, but I know for sure there is something wrong with Yhwh."

That doesn't sound good at all. "Okay, I will be careful." I promised, "Karma, is everything okay? You're worrying me." Chills made their way down my spine in a never ending loop. Something was *seriously* wrong. I don't know how I know, but there's not a doubt in my mind that she isn't okay. "What's the matter? Be honest."

Karma let out a frustrated sigh, growling slightly, "He brought up the worst parts of my past, and shrugged them off like they were nothing. There are a lot of things in my past that are living nightmares. *Nightmares.* He looked me in the eye and told me they weren't that bad. He said he couldn't condemn my…" She paused, almost choking on her next words. If it was anyone else, I'd think she was feeling depressed with the whole situation, but this is Karma, the Sin of *Wrath.* She's *angry,* and Yhwh is making it worse. "Assailant for what he did," She finished, "*Anyone* who says that about what I went through…"

"Is heartless." I finished for her. I ran my hands through my hair, wishing I had something, anything, to say that could make her feel better. "I don't know what you went through - which is fine; you don't have to talk about it - and I will be extra careful. Maybe add an extra extra in that. Thank you for the warning." I sighed, "I wish I could do the same. They don't tell me anything. They just boss me around." I would love to give her some form of advice or information that could be a leg up, but I just didn't have any to give.

"Just focus on being there for the other Virtues. Judging from our experiences, they're going to need it. I think if we can trust each other, it doesn't matter what Lucifer and Yhwh are doing. I'm sorry for waking you up. I'll let you go back to sleep."

I smiled, despite her not being able to see me, "It's *more* than okay. You can wake me up at anytime." I laughed, "I agree, though. As long as we're united with each other, it doesn't matter what those trigger happy gods are up to. Goodnight, Karma. Try to get some actual rest, okay?"

She laughed, "I'll do my best. Goodnight, and *be safe.*"

Aye, aye Captain. I settled back into my bed. I hope Karma is alright. Wherever she is.

Chapter Nine

"Honey, I'm home!" Where is he? I didn't see Brian when I crossed through the store, the entire front was a ghost town. That's strange. I made it into the break room and found him sitting at the table with his arms folded. "Brian? Are you okay?"

"Hmm?" He blinked, turning his head slightly, but not enough to look at me. "Hey, Medusa. You're early again."

"Benefits of Michael being so on top of things," I shrugged, "You okay? I didn't see anyone at the front." I clocked in, keeping him in my peripheral vision. He seemed so down. It was bizarre.

"Oh they're up there. Nitpicking everything, I'm sure." He sighed, deflating into his chair.

"Who?"

"The shelving could be straighter, and we saw an entire basket of un-shelved items by the front counter." An older couple burst into the room, frowns firmly etched in their faces. The woman had designer glasses perched on the top of her blonde hair, and one of the tightest pencil dresses I have ever seen paired with sky high pointed toe heels. The man was dressed in a crisp button up and black slacks. All in all not unusual for visitors in Telluride, but it *is* unusual for the break room. The woman gave me a once over, "Who is this?"

Brian sighed again, rising to his feet. He stood next to me with his hands in his pockets, "Mother, Father, this is Medusa. She is our best employee and has been for the past six years." *Oh.* These are his parents? They don't look anything like him. Maybe the eye shape is the same? I guess. "Medusa, you can go ahead and man the store."

"Empty the cart by the front." Mrs. Whittle snapped as I passed her.

"*No,*" Brian all but growled, "Medusa stick to the normal way we do things. Mom, you can't do that. You'll mess up-" I was gone before he finished.

He doesn't need me butting in on his family drama. Brian has always respected my personal space when it comes to personal issues. It's only human to give him the same curtesy. Plus, I've never minded working the store alone. Now that the holiday season is picking up, we'll have to have more people working at a time to handle the influx of people. Right now, though, it was nice and cal-

"There you are, Patience." The angel I threw into the tree yesterday waltzed into the store, and up to the counter. "We have things we need to discuss without my brother hovering."

"My name is Medusa. Just like yours is Jophiel, correct?"

He nodded, once. His eyes scanned the empty store, "Patience is your Heavenly name. You should want it to be spoken."

"I do not, and I would like for you to respect that." I replied, folding my hands together on the counter. This one talks more than Adakiel did, and now I'm not sure if that's a good thing.

The angel scoffed, "There is a *point* to this conversation, Patience." So there goes that, I guess. "Now to discuss my assisting you. I know my brother has been teaching you fighting styles and *trying* to hone your magical abilities." He straightened his shoulders, "I am here to teach you how to present yourself as the Heavenly being you are."

"Presenting myself to *whom* exactly?" I whispered, pausing to welcome the people coming into the store. "And do we have to do this here?" There are people here.

"Yes." He sneered at the family walking past. The father of the group scowled back at the angel. Jophiel rolled his eyes, refocusing on me. "Ignore the humans. They're irrelevant. You have plenty of people you need to worry about. Starting with my father, my brothers, and the remaining Virtues. The way they see you is imperative to how they view you as a leader."

"A leader?" Is that what I'm supposed to be to them? I was thinking more of a guide, and a friend. Maybe a mentor if they're up for that, but I don't want to be a *boss* to them.

Jophiel scowled at me, "Of course. Who else is meant to lead them? *Michael?*" He laughed dryly. "My brother cannot do that. Just as he showed he cannot even mentor you properly."

"Michael is doing a fantastic job as my mentor. Move please, I have actual customers." He scowled at the people as they passed him. I focused all of my attention on the customers as I checked them out, and sent them on their merry way. Such a happy group of people. They must be thrilled they beat the holiday rush for their vacation.

Before Jophiel had the chance to move back to lecture me or whatever he was here to do, Brian and his parents were moving to the front. His mother scowled, "The basket is still full. Do you *do* anything besides standing there like some kind of Barbie robot?"

"Do you know who you are *speaking to?*"

"Jophiel, these are my bosses." I interrupted, "Sorry about him. He's a little protective." I beamed, twisting my hands in front of me.

The only one not agitated was Brian, well I'm assuming he's not agitated with me. "Another brother, I presume?"

I giggled, biting into my lip. Brian's father glanced between the two of us, "Brian you are not fraternizing with one of our employees, are you?"

His mother hummed, "Well, I don't know if that's such a bad thing. She's cute. In a mousy way. Brian's honey brown hair, this girl's big green eyes that would be a perfect looking grandbaby to show off. I approve." Then she was gone with her husband trailing behind.

Brian rolled his eyes, "Ignore her, Medusa, and Michael's brother. I have no problem with the M and M wedding."

"Michael and I are not getting married any time soon." Let's not start *that* rumor. Michael didn't like the boyfriend thing starting, now we're talking about a *wedding*. Oh lord.

"Ah," Brian nodded, "Haven't asked your dad yet? What does he think of your Yeti, anyway?"

I glanced at Jophiel under the guise of not saying something in front of Michael's brother. Jophiel took it as an invitation, though, "Does your father disapprove of the work you and Michael are doing?"

"*Work.*" Brian scoffed, taking the basket his mother was so worried about. He got to work in the farthest aisle possible. So subtle that guy.

"So," Jophiel made his way back to me. He crossed his arms tightly across his chest as he glared at me in a poor attempt to mimic his older brother. He probably didn't see it that way, but that's how it looked to me. And unless he can read minds, he'll never know... Can angels read minds?! "Your father disapproves of our work?"

"No. He also doesn't *know* what Michael and I are doing. He thinks we're dating. It's a whole thing. Just don't interfere, okay?" This is exactly what I was afraid of. Angels invading my quiet hometown, and messing with the humans that live here. Michael is easy to nod at and ignore, because he's likely already ignoring them. But this guy? He tried to talk about who I was - *what* I am - to my bosses!

He made a noise, and nodded, "Patience." Then he was gone, leaving a single white feather in his place.

"Oh god." I darted around the counter to get the feather. The entire front of our store is windows! Someone could've seen him do that! "I definitely prefer Michael."

"That is good news." A laughing reply came from behind me. I dropped my head onto the counter top, ignoring the thud it made. I could feel the chill spread over the counter as Michael came to stand in front of me. "What is the matter? You seem worn out."

"A little." I finally picked my head up to look at the giant.

Michael glanced around, "Brian is in the back of the store, if that's who you're looking for."

He scoffed, "I have never looked for Brian. No customers today?"

"Calm before the storm. People are going to start flocking to Telluride soon for their winter vacations. This is a ski town, you know?" He pinched the bridge of his nose, releasing possibly the longest sigh I have ever heard.

Brian actually made it back to the front before Michael was done sighing. He glanced at Michael before gesturing to him. I just shrugged. A good five minutes later, Michael's sigh tapered off, "I hate this town."

Brian laughed, "I hear that...Ahem." He coughed when he caught Michael's eye, "Sir. I met your brother, Michael. Lot more talkative than the last one."

"That isn't always a good thing." He is definitely correct about that. I never thought I'd agree with him so much. The last thing I need is Jophiel coming back here and telling Brian everything about me. "Did he irritate you, Medusa? I wasn't aware he was coming to see you today."

Oh no. That's bad. Michael seemed to have it controlled, but his eyes had frozen over, and his hands were balled into fists. He's going to *lose* it. Probably not near me, but it'll happen. At least, I hope it isn't near me.

"I'm fine, Michael. Why did you stop by?" He wasn't supposed to be here either.

"I wanted to check on you, and make sure you're doing alright. I know your health was called into question after your nap."

"I'm alright. Thank you for checking on me."

"That's my job." He tilted my chin up to kiss my cheek. "I'll see you when you get off."

When he was out of the store, and out of sight from all of the windows, Brian shook his head. He's going to get whiplash. "You two are the strangest couple."

忍

Michael waltzed into the store hours later, two minutes before I was set to clock out. "Your timing is amazing." He smirked at me, taking up his spot leaning on the counter. "You know, it's rare for me to leave work on time, right?"

"I know it's more likely you'll leave on time if I am here." That fair, I suppose. Though, I don't think scaring my boss is a good way to go about it.

"Hey, Misery." Amita bounded into the store, loudly smacking her gum. She did a double take when she spotted Michael leaning on the counter, "Oooh, and *who* are you, Adonis?"

Michael frowned, "My name is Michael. Do not compare me to the *Greeks.*" He spat the word. He hates the Greeks? Surely he knows where my name comes from, right?

"Uh huh," She continued smacking, still looking him over. I doubt she heard anything he said, honestly. "Surely you don't want to be in this dump. Did'ya come to see me, *Michael*?"

"Go clock out so we can go home."

"Yes, sir." I saluted him as I passed. He didn't appreciate my 'good luck' as I went, though. Amita continued to loudly chew her gum while she attempted to flirt with the angel. Hopefully he isn't too mean to her.

Brian was in the break room when I entered. His head shot up, "No! No. Don't leave me with her."

I laughed, clocking out as dramatically as possible. "I think it's only fair since you abandon me with Mac constantly."

He scoffed, pushing himself up from the table. Brian met me at the door, "I always try to schedule us on the same days, because you're my favorite person to work with. You're my prized employee. And, like, my best friend."

"Fine," I gnawed on my bottom lip, trying to hide my smirk. "But Michael is waiting for me at the front, so if you want me to stay *you* have to tell him."

"Dammit. Damn boyfriend that benchpresses fucking trucks. Go have fun cuddling on the couch with Michael and a kale salad or whatever it is that you two do when you're alone. Don't tell me. That isn't information I need."

"I didn't *plan* on telling you what we do when we're alone, but I can tell you that if we're doing any cuddling and he grabs *kale;* that will be the ending to the cuddling." I'd also never cuddle with a glacier when stuffed animals exist, but Brian didn't know that. I bounded back to the front to find Michael glaring at the much smaller girl who was still popping her gum at him.

"Medusa! Are you ready to go?" I nodded at him, not caring to hide my smile. He nodded, gruffly pushing past Amita, "Goodbye, person I didn't care to learn the name of. Learn how to chew with your mouth closed. You are not *an infant.*" Amita gasped dramatically. Michael didn't slow his exit from the store.

"Amita! What did I say about gum?" *Uh oh.* Judging from that tone, she was definitely getting written up again. What does that put her at now? Surely, it's getting close to double digits.

"Brian can get angry?" Michael asked, leading me to the car.

"Oh, very." I'm not the one that normally sees it, since I prefer not to irritate the person who decides how many bills I can pay. From what I've heard, though, he can be pretty scary when he wants to be. "So, where are we going?"

"Your house," He scoffed, "We cannot train in that horribly colored shirt." What's wrong with orange? I thought it was a nice color. "After that, I have some ideas for how to further your magical abilities." Hopefully it's nicer than our other attempts at Michael's ideas.

We pulled up to the house moments later. The street was silent, almost eerily so, and a slight chill had settled over the silent town. It looks like we'll be getting snow soon. That should be fun. I wonder if

I can get Michael to build a snowman with me. I bet with ice magic, we could build something amazing.

"Hey, Michael?" He hummed behind me, seemingly scanning the front yard. Is he ever relaxed? "How do you feel about snowmen?"

"I don't know what that is, so I don't have any particular feelings about them." He was still scanning when we entered the living room. "Where's Elias? This house is suspiciously quiet, don't you think?"

"I dunno," I shrugged, "Maybe he's showering?"

"Do you hear your loud water system? I don't." Okay, that was a fair point.

I pursed my lips, "Okay. Now you freaked me out. I'll go check his room. He's probably napping or something." I'm sure it's nothing. Who knows, maybe he actually wanted to get out of the house. That would be nice. Maybe he's taking the first step to fixing his aura.

Michael followed me to my father's room. This is where him constantly being on edge is a bad thing. I'm sure there's nothing to worry about, but the super general is on red alert. Surely that has to be exhausting. I pushed open my father's door with practiced silence - he can be extremely angry when he's woken up randomly. His bed was empty - a mess, but empty. "Dad?"

Michael pushed in the door further. He scanned the room before pointing, "His blanket is falling on that side. Perhaps he has started to fall off his bed in a similar manner that you do."

"I've only done that twice." But he did have a point. I moved to my dad's bed, stepping over all the random trash he had on the floor. How did he get this much stuff in here? I guess it *has* been a minute since I've cleaned it.

"You have done it several times. I found you on the floor just the other morning."

That isn't even slightly- "Oh my god! Dad?!" He was laying face down on the floor in a giant red circle. A dark red circle that had seeped so far into the carpet it wasn't even wet anymore.

"Medusa, get back." How can he say that? I can't just leave him here. I can't. I just… "Medusa. I need to analyze his wound so that we can find out what happened."

"What wound? I don't see an- Oh." What is with me? How could I miss the gaping hole in his back? Why is everything so blurry all of the sudden?

"Medusa. You are seconds away from hyperventilating. You need to step back, leave the room, and *breathe*." He hauled me to my feet, and away from my father. I protested as he dragged me to the door. He completely ignored me, though, and slammed the door in my face.

"Michael! Michael, please! Let me back in!" I hit the obnoxious door, not caring about the paint I was chipping or the red streaks that were appearing. I just… I need to be in there. "*Michael!*"

"Yelling does not equal breathing." Michael sighed, opening the door. I darted forward, rushing past him. My father wasn't on the floor anymore. He was on his freshly made bed with his hands folded on his stomach. "The stain in the carpet is gone as well. I thought this would make it easier for you to say goodbye."

I coughed, feeling my throat burn. Michael didn't speak as I sat beside my father on the bed. He didn't speak when my vision blurred so much I couldn't see the difference between my father's bo-body and his bed. Oh god. He's so cold. I can't remember ever being this close to him. After mom, he never wanted to be too close to me. I forgot about his laugh lines around his mouth, and that scar he has by his right eye. He always said it was from a fist fight, but Mom had written about him running into a wall the day he met her. She had to take him to the hospital. He said he was so distracted by her radiance that he stopped watching where he was going. He always called her his Angel for saving him that day. I thought it was a sweet story. I just wish they would've been able to tell it to me, instead of leaving it in a journal in the basement.

"You know, I don't remember my mom that well. I was so little when she died that it's hard to even picture her face some days." I cleared my throat. I don't even know if Michael is even in the room anymore. "But I remember when I was little, I would watch my parents cook together. They made a night of it, twice a week. They'd clear their schedules every Tuesday and Friday, and they'd spend hours cooking and playing around in the kitchen. They were *so* happy. And weekends they'd find some new recipe from the library or something and they'd perfect their method of making it. I'd just sit at the dining room table and watch them chop vegetables with giant smiles on their faces. I never understood it, but what all does a four year old understand? They acted like a night shut in the house chopping vegetables, making a roux, or having pots boil over on the stove was the perfect day.

"Then she was gone, and so were those days. I remember bringing him all her cookbooks every Tuesday and Friday after she died. He always ignored me. Until one day I came home, and he was standing over the grill. I thought he was *finally* cooking again. That I was finally waking him up. But when I went out there, I found ashes. He'd burned all of the cookbooks. Even Mom's favorites. She had this one, it was massive. I'll never forget the look of that thing. Wide spine with a blue and white checkered pattern, and some strange little macaron cartoons and their cake house. He said he burned that one first."

I don't think I'll ever forget that day. That was the day I stopped trying. The day I gave up on him. Then it was down the beer and hotdog hole for him. Only for him to end up like this. Dead on the floor with a whole the size of a dinner plate in his abdomen. Michael found a way to cover it up when he moved him to the bed, but I doubt I'll ever forget it. I need to plan a funeral. Oh god, how do I plan a funeral? He did Mom's. They wouldn't let a seven year old plan a funeral.

A hand landed on my shoulder, before running over my back in soft soothing circles. I guess he has been here this whole time. He sighed, bracing both hands on my shoulders, "Eight thousand, eight hundred and twenty two seconds."

"Really?" I coughed out. Michael chuckled behind me, "Wow.

So you're comforting me, *and* laughing. I guess that's how I know this is bad."

"Your last parent just died. I don't think you need General Michael of the Almighty Forces of Zion right now."

"Is that your full title?" I shifted, finally looking at him. "It's a little long winded, don't you think?"

"No," He scoffed, "It commands respect. Now, what is the next step after a human dies?" My throat burned as my eyes lowered from his, "I apologize. That was insensitive."

"You're okay. The next step is a funeral. We bury him in the ground. I know where my mom is buried, maybe that funeral home will be able to let me know how exactly I'm supposed to do that." That should be a fun visit. "I have no idea what I'm supposed to do with- Um. With…"

"I understand. I will handle it." He squeezed my shoulder, "Come on. You need to sleep."

He's kidding, right? I can't sleep right now. I need… I don't know what I need. I need a walk. Outside. "Yeah. I'm going to do that." Michael let me go. At least, I think he did. I don't really know if I'm honest. It felt like someone had shoved a handbell in my skull and shook me like a crowded Etch-A-Sketch. I slipped on my tennis shoes, and made my way out front.

The neighborhood was silent except from the ringing that persisted. Mrs. Mitchell was outside of her house getting her mail when I passed. She scowled at me, but that isn't really a new thing. I crashed my bike into her flowerbed when I was ten and she has never forgotten. She's known my family since I was born. Would she come to the funeral? I can't remember if she went to Mom's.

There was no one else wondering around outside as I strolled. Strange for this neighborhood. There's almost always kids outside, or people walking their dogs. Especially that group of teenage girls that's started to hang around every time they see Michael's car in front of the house. He waved to them the other day, I think he nearly gave one of them a heart attack. They were new to the neighborhood; moved in a few years ago. So, I doubt they'll be there.

I'm going to have to make invitations. Oh god and a eulogy. I'm terrible at writing. What am I even going to write? Who am I supposed to be inviting, anyway? It's not like he has friends. And it's been so long since he's left the house. I wouldn't even know how to find out who he was friends with.

"Medusa!" I jumped as two large hands landed on my shoulders. Michael spun me around to glare at me with full force, "*What* are you doing?"

I gestured to the sidewalk, "I'm walking." Is that not obvious? I thought the running shoes, and me going around the block was a good indicator of that.

"You cannot be walking right now."

"Why not? I'm just going around the block. It's okay. The fresh air is calming." I was just clearing my head. Surely he can understand that.

"Then explain to me why you're a quarter mile from your house." What? I can't walk a quarter mile. Though, none of these houses looked familiar. It definitely wasn't the way I took to work. "Medusa, your skin is cold. Even to me. We need to get you home."

"Relax, Michael. It's not cold, that's just you." He's always cold. What does he know?

"*Medusa,*" He growled, "It is twenty degrees outside. That is the lowest it has been for the past *two weeks.* You are coming home. I am not asking." He grabbed my arm, and hauled me to his car. He drove to get me?

"I told you I was going for a walk."

Michael scowled at me, but before he spoke he leaned over to buckle my seat belt. "You still must buckle your seatbelt. You *can* die, Medusa." I sighed, loosening the belt. "And, you did *not* tell me you were leaving. I told you to go to bed, and *you* said that it was a good idea. Then you walked out the door and walked *twenty blocks!*" He glanced at me before refocusing on the road, "Your body temperature is at seventy six degrees. Why does this glass keep doing that?"

"Because when you are angry, you start huffing out frost and freeze everything near you. Glass collects frost just like anything else, Michael." He just sighed at me. Guess he's back to being a quiet brooder.

Chapter Ten

"And now, Elias James Sinclair, husband to Emilia Grace Sinclair, and father to Medusa Sigyn Sinclair, we lay you to rest beside your wife. May the two of you find peace together in our God's heavenly embrace." The preacher continued his never-ending speech over my father's closed casket. Michael stood beside me in a full suit with his hands clasped in front of him. Then there was me, sitting in a ridiculous white lawn chair *surrounded* by empty white lawn chairs.

I sent the invitations. No one came.

"Wait! Wait! Shit! Sorry. Yelling in cemeteries is bad, apparently. You should put a sign up that says that." May made her way across the grass with a few red roses grasped in her hand. "Sorry, I'm late. My manager was being a dick."

"I'm here as well. Terribly sorry about being so late. I meant to get here early, but-"

"You failed." Michael finished for Brian.

My boss slid past Michael to come sit on my other side. May took the seat closest to Michael, not seeming to care about the frost giant standing in front of that chair. Brian pulled three mini packs of tissues out of his pockets and handed them all to me. May pulled one out of the packet and cleaned my cheeks.

"There you go." She rubbed my back, "Alright priest you can continue."

"He's a preacher." Michael corrected, "Please continue."

May and Brian grabbed my hands as the preacher droned on. I

rested my head on May's shoulder, and she leaned her head on mine. Brian kept ahold of my other hand for the rest of the speech, and tightened his hand when the casket started it's decent. The preacher waved me up to drop the first flower in the grave. I dropped the red poppies, "I didn't know your favorite, so I went with Mom's."

"May I? No pun intended." I choked out a dry laugh, waving her forward. She dropped on of her flowers in the grave, "I didn't know you, and truthfully, I'm not here for you. I'm here because your daughter is my best friend. I hope, for her sake, that you found Emilia and the biggest bag of *Steamie Dogs* God has ever seen." Then her arms were around me, not caring about the massive wet spot I was making on her shoulder.

"Well, I did meet you, and I don't truly have anything even remotely nice to say about you. That being said, you raised one of the greatest human beings I have ever met, and I thank you for that." He dropped one of the flowers May had brought with her. Apparently she'd brought one for everyone. Even Michael was holding one.

"I do not understand this talking thing you are all doing." He dropped the flower, though. I guess that's something. Plus, he saw a lot of sides of my father, and none of them were decent. Since Michael is so good at curbing his tongue, I doubt he would have anything positive to say. Not that Brian or May did, either, but the thought was there.

"Medusa, is there anything else you want to say?"

"No. Hand me the shovel, please." This was much heavier than I was expecting. Shouldn't shovels be lighter?

"Do you need help lifting that?" Michael came to help even without my reply. "This isn't that heavy."

"So you act the same no matter what's going on then?" Brian interjected. He moved away when we finally got the shovel off the ground, probably for the best. The person most likely to hit him with a shovel *is* Michael.

"He likes to stay consistent." I quipped, finally tipping the dirt

Jasmine Johnson

out of the shovel. Michael handed it off to the men waiting on the sidelines.

"Want to get a burger?" May asked, tentatively.

"Yes." Michael answered for me. When three pairs of eyes turned to stare at him in shock, he sighed. Did he get replaced with a different angel, and forget to update this angel on his stance against burgers?

"Are you sick? Am I being Punk'd?" I laughed at Brian's comment. It was hoarse and weak, but it was the first real laugh from me since... I can't even remember when.

"I am not sick. Medusa just lost her remaining parent. It is only right she gets her favorite food; even if it is a greasy mess of carbs. I'll even pay for it."

"For the record," May turned to Michael, "As an employee I am obligated to tell you that *Steamie's* steams their burgers so that theirs is actually healthier than the traditional greasy burgers. So technically, it's the healthiest burger Medusa could eat." Michael hummed, not replying, but also not disagreeing with her.

I shook my head, turning to Brian, "Definitely some kind of shapeshifter. Michael is somewhere being held captive, screaming about his hatred of burgers." They laughed. May looped an arm over my shoulders, promising me a super sized basket of fries.

"I'm so glad you think you're funny." Michael snarked, staying behind my small group of friends.

We got to the small parking lot, and May pulled away, "I'll see you at *Steamie's*, okay? Do you want to ride with me?"

"No I'm alright. I'm going to stay with Michael. I'll see you at *Steamie's*. You're meeting us, right Brian?"

"Hell yeah! Love me some *Steamie's*. Meet you there." He waved, heading toward his car.

"Yeah, I parked that way too. See you in a sec."

Michael stayed beside me on the way to his car, ever so silent. I paused when we got to his car, and turned to face him, "Wait. For just a second, I promise." Michael crossed his arms, looking down at me. He didn't seem angry, just as impassive as usual. "Thank you for everything. You've been by my side for the past week and a half, no matter how many times I randomly burst into tears, or stopped moving. You made sure I was eating, and didn't make me any monster foods. And, most importantly, you *came.* No one else was there for the planning, or the eulogy, or the first three hours of that preachers speech about how wonderful of a man my father was. I know May and Brian were there toward the end, and tried to make it, and I appreciate them for that, but I cannot express just how much I truly and honestly have appreciated you during all of this. *Thank you.*" Without Michael, there wouldn't have been a funeral. Every time I spoke to the funeral director, my throat malfunctioned and I couldn't speak. Michael could though. He even helped me with the invitations. "You could've left. I know Yhwh didn't order you to do all of this for me."

"No, he didn't." Michael answered. He had a vein that was becoming more and more prominent each day. I thought it was in reaction to my almost constant crying, but now I'm not so sure. When I said his father's name, his eyes turned to that icy light blue color that screamed murder. "However, my father does not control every aspect of my life, and I wouldn't abandon you during a time like this. I consider myself honorable. Leaving you right now, after the way your father was murdered would make me the exact opposite of an honorable being."

"So you do think he was murdered? Do you know by who, or who would even want to? It's not like he had any enemies. Except for maybe the lady at the cable company when the snow storm stopped him from watching the game."

Michael gave me a scathing look, "You ramble eighty five percent more when you're upset, are you aware of that?" Well I'm getting in the car now. Michael climbed into the drivers seat, reaching over to buckle me in. He keeps doing that. I was going to get it. Once I remembered. "Do I think he was murdered." Michael scoffed under his breath, "Of course I do. He had an enormous hole in his chest."

"Too far." He could kill a moment better than anyone I've ever met.

"I apologize. Would it make you feel better if I promised you *two* burgers?"

I rolled my eyes at him, "That isn't how you apologize. The actual apology was enough."

"That's what Brian does, and you stop being angry with him!"

"No he doesn't. He does that when I'm upset for a reason that doesn't include him. Crying freaks him out. That is completely different from you being callous." I huffed. Exhaustion had settled in days ago. I've been walking through sludge ever since.

Michael just huffed, pulling into a parking spot. May waved us over to the table her and Brian were sat at, "Got you some fries, *and* another surprise is on the way. Probably breaking a speed limit or five."

Brian frowned at her, raising his hands in surrender, "I have no idea what she's talking about."

"That isn't surprising." Michael snarked, taking the seat beside my boss.

I slid into the seat beside May, laying my head back on her shoulder. When the waitress stopped by the table, May rattled off my order along with hers. Michael went ahead and ordered me a second burger along with two for himself. Brian almost had a meltdown at that. Not that I could blame him. Michael was the king of 'I don't eat human food' and then listing the reasons it was a terrible creation. The only person that knows that better than me is Brian. I lost count of how many lectures he's had to endure.

"So are we going to ignore Michael liking burgers now?" Brian asked, once he was sure to scoot his chair away to the giant that was glaring at him. "For the record, he *is* still scary. Just in case you thought that changed."

May laughed at him. Judging from his expression she also called him a bad name when she mouthed something. I couldn't see her mouth from her shoulder, though I wouldn't put it past her. "Medusa, are you going to eat your fries? No one likes cold fries."

"I'm not really hungry." I probably should be. I can't remember the last time I ate. Michael probably has it logged somewhere. He's the one that keeps threatening to force feed me. Honestly I'm surprised he isn't threatening me right now. Being in public shouldn't stop him. I pulled away from May to look at him. He was just staring off into space. "Michael? Are you alright?"

He didn't respond. He just sat there. Motionless. May and I looked behind us, but the wall didn't seem to be doing anything. Even Brian was frowning at him. When he didn't respond to any of us, Brian poked him in the shoulder. Finally, Michael blinked, "I have to go. Medusa, eat something."

"Wait. Wait." I tripped over the leg of my chair, hitting the corner of the table with my hip. Michael caught me, keeping ahold of my arms until I was steady again. "You're leaving me? For how long? Where are you going? What's the matter? What am I supposed to do?"

"Breathe, for starters." Yeah, that's probably good advice. I have no idea what just happened. He got up, and I… Panicked. Maybe that's why he's leaving. I've become too dependent on him. "I need to speak to my father." He pressed his forehead to mine, burying his hand in my hair, "I will be back before you go to bed. I promise."

"Okay." I nodded, going back to my seat, "Okay. Don't tell your dad I said hello, okay? I'd hate to give him the wrong impression."

Michael nodded, "I understand. Take care of Medusa, you two. I am *not* kidding. Even if she's crying, *Brian.*"

"Yes, sir." Once Michael was out the door, Brian turned to us, "Why am I in trouble?"

"To be fair," May laughed, "Are you ever not in trouble with him?"

Not usually. Brian scoffed, crossing his arms. They didn't stay crossed for long though. He wouldn't be able to shovel fries in his mouth if his hands were crossed. "I hope you never change Brian." I don't know how I'd react if I lost him too.

"You're about to start crying again. Your eyes are going all red."
The fear was palpable in his eyes. It almost made me laugh. May
definitely laughed.

"Well that's ridiculous. Medusa would never cry while I'm here."
A haughty voice paired with the longest pair of leather pants, leaned
on the table. Honey brown eyes met mine, the smuggest smirk I have
ever seen with them, "Hey, kitten. Life sucks, wanna talk about it?"

I laughed, pursing my lips at her, "What are you doing here?"

"I came to see one of my favorite girls. May told me about your
dad. I'm sorry I couldn't be here in time for the funeral. Z sends her
love, she couldn't get away." She grabbed a chair from a nearby table.
Kat sat on the chair backwards, with her back facing Brian. The man
looked a little perturbed at that, but not more than when she moved
the basket of fries away from him. "God, I love *Steamie's* fries."

"Yeah so do the rest of us. That's…" He grabbed the basket of
fries from her, putting it back in the middle of the table. "Why it's
in the *middle*. It's for sharing. Who are you?"

"I'm that bitch. I assumed that was obvious with the demeanor,
and the outfit, and the shoes."

"All I got from that is that you're into women. Not that you're
a fry hog."

She gave him a scathing look, "Is he always like this?"

May scoffed, "You're one to talk. You can be the hardest person
to get along with. You know that, right?"

Kat gasped dramatically, placing a hand on her heart, "Medusa
doesn't think so. Right?"

I just shook my head at her, still smiling. I don't know what
it is about her, but for the first time since I walked into my dad's
bedroom I could finally feel the fog clearing. May ran her hand over
my back soothingly, "You don't have to lie to her. It's okay. Medusa's
been through a lot, Kat, don't pester her."

"Here you go!" The waitress unloaded the food onto the table,
looking around in confusion at Michael's empty seat. "Did you get
a replacement?" She laughed, gesturing to Kat.

"Who was there? Oh, the boyfriend?"

"Michael, yeah. He had to run." I explained, though I'm not sure anyone heard it. I hope he's alright. Speaking to his father isn't exactly the most positive sounding thing in the universe.

"His loss is my gain, right?" Kat winked, skimming her fingers over my hand.

"Are you capable of saying anything that isn't flirting?"

May scoffed at that, "Not when Medusa is involved, apparently." She rolled her eyes at her - our? - friend; not that Kat seemed bothered in the slightest. "She's some kind of lesbian magnet. Same with that *outrageously beautiful* woman that was here the other day. What was her name, anyway?"

"Karma," I supplied, "And we *don't* mention her to 'the boyfriend' deal?" Kat raised her brows at me, "Not like that. He just doesn't like her. It's easier to avoid conflict that way."

"We won't tell him." May promised with the other two nodding in agreement. "That being said, he will find out if you don't eat this food. I don't know how he would know, but I don't doubt that he would."

That's a fair point. I can eat a burger. I love burgers. I swallowed, staring at the burger in my hands. Everyone else dug into their own burger - Kat took one of Michael's. No one seemed to notice my staring contest with my burger... Or the way my hands were shaking. It's just a burger. I can take a bite out of a burger. I just have to move my hands, and my face.

Kat patted my knee when I took my first bite. I guess someone was paying attention. She flashed me an encouraging smile when I caught her eye. I huffed, refocusing. I can do this.

I can't do this. I dropped the half eaten burger back onto the plate. That's just going to have to be enough. My stomach churned as I settled back into my seat. "You did great." Kat soothed, polishing off her own burger. "God I love this place."

"Me too." I just wish I could enjoy it. It's almost like I couldn't *taste* anything I've eaten in the past two weeks.

May rubbed my back, "I'll go pay, and we'll take you home, okay?"

"No need!" The waitress chirped, startling the four of us. "Supermodel man paid before he left."

"How did he…" Brian huffed, "That man isn't human, I swear." Oh, how close he was.

I pushed myself up from the table, twisting my hands in my skirt. Kat slung her arm around my shoulders, "I'd offer you a ride, but something tells me you aren't a fan of motorcycles."

I laughed, resting my head on her shoulder, "I've never been on one, but I'm already queasy so now probably isn't the time to test it." She made a face, squeezing my shoulder. It's going to be a long time before she offers me a ride on that bike again. Michael would probably throw a fit if I got on a motorcycle. He already thinks I'm made out of glass.

"Come on. Michael took your car, so you're with me. Are you coming Brian?"

"Of course. I gotta run by the store, first." So he's never coming. He can't stand having someone else running his store. He complains about the work, but it's all a cover. He loves our little corner of the world.

May turned on the car, but didn't shift gears. I frowned at her, silently asking why she was staring at me like that. Her eyebrows nearly disappeared into her bangs, "Seatbelt?"

"Oh." I shifted, buckling my seat belt.

"You're normally more on top of that." May hummed. She turned like it wasn't a big deal, but I could see the worry in her eyes.

"Sorry. Michael has been doing that so much that I guess it slipped my mind." May smirked at that, but stayed quiet.

Michael's car wasn't in the driveway when we pulled in, but Kat was there; leaning on her bike with her ankles crossed looking like a cover model for some magazine. She smirked, running a hand through her hair before opening my door.

"Nice place you got, but I would love to see a *specific* room." She winked.

I climbed out of the car, smiling at her, "My bed smells like Michael, are you sure that's something you want to endure?" She gagged, pulling away from me. May just looked at us in shock. It was strange to me too, but at least he kept the nightmares away.

The girls followed me into the house. Kat walked over to the oversized recliner, running her hand over the back. Her eyes grew cloudy as she stared at the old fabric. Before I could say anything, she was straightening her spine and settling back into her flirtatious persona. Whatever was going on with her, was gone as quick as it came.

"You alright, Kat?"

"Yup. All good. Got any games? Game nights always cheer people up."

"Ooh! That's a great idea." May cheered, settling onto the floor. "You know, Medusa's never been to a sleep over?"

"I did not." Kat looked downright predatory as she settled onto the floor. I took a seat in between the two, leaning against the couch. "I had my first kiss at a sleepover."

"It took you five minutes." May rolled her eyes.

"*What?*" Kat's attempt at an innocent face was pitiful at best. May didn't fall for it for even a fraction of a second. "Sleepovers are for figuring out your sexuality."

That... Doesn't sound true. "I thought sleep overs were about spending time with your friends, and playing games..."

"That's exactly what they are."

Kat rolled her eyes, "Only if you're boring."

"Or straight." May argued, "Like Medusa and I are."

She frowned, "*Bullshit* on both accounts. I saw the way you talked about the '*outrageously sexy*' friend Medusa brought to *Steamie's*."

"That's not fair." While they bickered, I pulled out the stack of dusty board games from the cabinet by the tv. I can't remember the last time I actually played one of these. "You haven't seen this Karma lady. She can make anyone have gay thoughts. It's the arms, I swear."

"They are really nice arms." I confirmed, settling back into my spot.

"God dammit. Who's this girl? Why is she moving in on my territory?"

I laughed at Kat, "I don't think that's what she's doing." May pulled out a thing of cards from the stack, shuffling them in her hands. Kat was too busy giving me a flat look to comment on the game choice. "I'm serious. She doesn't really seem the type to just jump in bed with someone. Karma can be pretty closed off."

"Good." She sulked, "She can stay that way. The last thing I need on this vacation is someone with '*those* arms' and '*those* abs' wondering around."

"We didn't say anything about abs."

"Anyone who has arms that nice, has abs. I promise."

"She does." I confirmed. Two sets of eyes whipped to my face, "Not like that! She wears a lot of tight tank tops!" All her shirts are tight. Her, Roman, and Michael have that in common. They have to know what they're doing.

Kat huffed, "No wonder you aren't affected by my charms. There's some kind of goddess wondering around."

A knock came at the door before slowly opening. Brian poked his head in the door, "Can I come in?" I waved him in. I really wasn't expecting him to make it back here. He came in holding a filled grocery bag.

Kat perked up at the sight of it, "Alcohol?"

"No. You have met Medusa, haven't you?" He sat down, completing our little circle. He sat the bag down in the center, "Candy. Chocolate bars, gummy worms - sour, because I'm not dumb - and those strawberry things you love. Why are we sitting in a circle?"

"Blackjack. Know how to play?" May asked, sliding the hands

between her cards in an awesome and smooth move. One that I could never do.

"Of course I know how to play Blackjack. My parents could've bought college scholarships for your entire graduating class with the money they've spent in Las Vegas." Kat agreed that she knew how to play as well. I suppose now would be a good time to mention that I don't know how to play this game.

"Alright, Medusa. I'm going to run over rules, then we'll play a practice round." Oh I guess she didn't need me to say that. That's good. May went through the rules, which didn't sound so difficult, and started the practice round.

忍

Four hours, and a candy coma later, I was feeling much better. Everyone hugged me on their way out. Kat squeezed me, putting her lips right at my ear, "You're going to be okay, Medusa. You're a lot stronger than you let on." Then she kissed the side of my head, and walked out the door.

Brian made me promise to take the next couple weeks off, but also to call him if I needed him. Meanwhile, he promised me that he wouldn't let Mac and Amita ruin our favorite place.

May promised to come by to spend some time with me so I don't go crazy while I'm banned from working. What kind of boss bans people from working, anyway? She also ordered me to ask her if I want something - *"Anything! I mean it!"* - to eat or snack on.

Once they were gone, I cleaned the kitchen... And the living room... *And* the rest of the house. Michael came back sometime later, pulling the duster out of my hand. "It is time to sleep, Medusa. It's eleven-thirty at night."

"What does it matter?" I sighed, leaning against him. "It's not like I have work tomorrow."

"No?" Oh I don't like that look on his face at all. "Sounds like we have some time to focus on training."

"My father's funeral was today. Can you take it a little easy on me?" He dropped me onto my bed, moving to grab pajamas from my dresser. He threw those at me too. "I guess that's a no." I slipped into my pajamas. I stopped caring about changing in the same room as him a while ago. It's not like he's going to look. "I take it the talk with Yhwh didn't go so well?"

Michael huffed, now dressed in his own pajama pants. He'd gotten them while we were funeral planning in an attempt to cheer me up. It worked a little bit. Who wouldn't laugh at a man like Michael in panda pajama pants. He slipped under the covers beside me, not objecting to me curling into his side. I suppose he's gotten used to my codependency. "It's… Complicated."

"How complicated?"

He ran his hand through my hair, "Even I don't know that yet." Well, that's horribly ominous. "I believe the second Virtue is almost pinpointed."

"Isn't that a good thing?"

"We can only hope." I hope this isn't him trying to make me feel better. He's doing a spectacularly terrible job. Michael's hand tightened on my shoulder, "Don't worry, Medusa. I will keep you safe. I promise."

"Thank you." I take it he isn't going to tell me what he's going to protect me from. Then again, I doubt that's information I want to know. If it's something I need to know, he'll tell me.

"Believe me; it's an honor."

Chapter Eleven

"Dammit!" I flinched as Michael hit the tree closest to him. The tree snapped in half, luckily toppling *away* from me.

I pulled my sleeves down over my hands, and crossed my arms. I thought I had been doing a good job. I still can't grasp the whole fist fighting thing, but I did clear that whole tree of leaves! That's progress. Not enough, apparently, since I've never heard Michael curse.

"I'm sorry, Michael. I'll try harder."

"You're doing a fantastic job, Medusa. You've come so far." He sighed, "That's not what is bothering me." I stayed quiet. Michael was basically word vomiting information. "Your powers are stronger. Which *should* be a good thing, except the only reason they got this strong is because your personal attachment that ties you to your mortal life - and makes you feel inferior - is now gone."

"I don't know what that means."

"Your father dying is what made your powers stronger. Which is *exactly* what they wanted." He cursed again, hitting another tree.

Once the tree - loudly - hit the forest floor, I put my hands on his upper back. The goal was his shoulders, but they're way too high without a stepping stool. He sighed, turning slightly, "Who are you talking about? You know who killed my dad?"

He sighed deeper, "I've had an idea since it happened. There's really only one thing that could leave a clear hole like that in a person. It was Jophiel." He arched a brow at my gasp. "Are you truly that surprised?"

"Why wouldn't I be? Your father had my father killed? For what? I thought he wanted me on his side!"

"My father doesn't think of life the same way others do. Human attachments are frowned upon in Zion. If an angel was to…" His eyes seared into mine, "If an angel was to fraternize with a human, the punishment would be unimaginable. In his mind, he's freeing you."

"Well, in my mind he's a jackass!" I gasped, slapping my hands over my mouth. Michael's brows shot to his hairline. "I know what I said, and I meant it." Michael went to wipe away the tears streaming down my face, but I slapped his hands away. "He wanted me angry. Well, I'm angry."

Wind blew through the trees around us, taking the leaves with it. Leaves of all colors and shapes whirled around the two of us. Michael held a hand over his face, still squinting at me. When I was done, the trees were bare, and we were standing in every kid's dream leaf pile.

"Medusa-"

"Just take us home, please."

Michael brought us back to my bedroom. Once he let me go, I grabbed my things for a shower. I didn't speak to him while I gathered my things, or as I left. When I was out of the shower, Michael was gone from my room. Where did he go? I found him in the kitchen, making lettuce wraps.

"I'm not hungry."

"You will eat at least two, or I will put them in your food chopper and feed them to you as if you were an *infant*."

I scowled back at him, but took a seat at the table. Michael sat down a plate in front of me, and stood over me with his arms folded. I ate while glaring at him until it was gone.

"I'm not angry with you, Michael." I huffed, putting my plate in the sink.

"I didn't think you were, but I am concerned about how this

newfound anger will affect your judgment. We can't have you doing anything irrational. We can't locate the other Virtues without my father's help."

"I'm not going to do anything dumb, Michael. I'm not abandoning the other Virtues to this... Whatever he's doing. They don't deserve this." I sat on the couch, leaning my head on Michael once he sat beside me. "I'm not really a *leader*, but I refuse to abandon them in this."

Michael chuckled at that, "I believe you will be a patient and understanding leader of this team-to-be." I was a little too stunned to thank him; not that he seemed to mind. Michael's arm stayed firmly wrapped around me, "And I will be there, so you have someone-"

"That can terrify them and make them behave?" That just got me a 'harrumph' noise, but he didn't deny it.

"I am a warlord, remember?"

"A warlord that really likes brownies." I snorted. I'd used my mom's old recipe when Michael insisted I eat, but I couldn't find anything that tasted good. I only ate two - a personal low for me -while Michael finished off the rest. Despite him claiming that he threw them away.

"You cannot prove that. And for the millionth time, you are getting off topic." He huffed, "Once we get the location of the next Virtue, we'll go retrieve them, and welcome them into this team we seem to have created." I like him calling us a team. Probably shouldn't share that, though. Michael can't handle too much sappyness at one time.

"You're getting emotional. I can *feel* it." That got me to laugh. Michael just grumbled, settling deeper into the couch. "You did a good job today. Maybe a little too much of a good job, considering that trees have leaves for a reason, but still you did well."

"Thank you, Michael. I'm sorry about my outburst."

"No need for an apology. I have had my share of outbursts."

"I would've *never* guessed that."

"Sarcasm is the product of a weak mind." He snarked back,

pulling a lock of my hair. I didn't have to look at him to know he was smiling when I yelped. God, he can be mean when he wants to be.

"So is bullying." I stuck my tongue out at him.

"You are a *child*. Do you need a nap?" I scowled back at him, slapping his arm. He guffawed at the attempt, "Magical strength is improving, but your physical strength is still non-existent. We should work on that."

"I thought that was how our team worked? I'm the caring team leader and you're the muscle who doesn't take anyone's crap."

"Oh is that what I am?" I beamed at him, nodding. He sat up, getting close to my face. I stared right back at him, not backing down from whatever kind of challenge this was, "You still need to know how throw a proper punch."

"I think I can agree to that, but no more martial arts. I wasn't made for the superhero life. I'm not a Batkid or whatever they're called."

"I haven't the slightest idea what you're talking about. Come on; break time is over." I groaned letting him pull me up from the couch. Michael took me back outside into the crisp cool air of the evening. I really need him to understand that I can actually get cold. Maybe he should've been Karma's mentor. The cold didn't seem to bother her while she was wearing a tank top at the park the other day. Oh wow, that was much longer ago than a few days now.

"Now here's what you do. Hold you hand like this, put your feet shoulder width apart, and balance your weight evenly. No like this." He moved me to where I was standing the way he wanted me to. "Holding your hand like this will break your thumb. You need to do it like this." He explained why I had to hold my hands a certain way, and how to follow through with my attack. He glared at me when I tried to oppose the thought of me attacking anyone or anything. I'll drop it for now. "Just like that. Good job. Do it again."

He made me repeat the movement several more times with both hands, giving me mini critiques with each repetition. "You can stop now. Excellent job. Next we'll work on different types of punches."

"That doesn't sound so bad. This seems much easier than your other torture methods that you try to pass off as training."

He scoffed, "I can show you torture methods."

"Hard pass." Grumpy old man.

忍

Karma: *'Hey, if I send you something would you be able to make prints of them at your store? Like big canvas prints?'*

I curled around my phone, thankful that Michael had insisted on making breakfast this morning. He gave a long speech about how if I wasn't going to eat a lot then I needed to stuff as much nutrition into what I do eat. I'd prefer to not face that music for as long as possible.

Medusa: *'Yeah! I can do that easily at Whittle Corner. Do you want me to send them to the cabin?'*

Karma: *'Yes, please. How much do I owe you?'*

Medusa: *'How does a burger sound?'*

Karma: *'It's a date.'*

The pictures came through a few moments later. The utterly breathtaking pictures. The first few were of a black skeletal horse with a bright red mane that looked to be entirely made of flames. Black smoke swirled around the horse's hooves, adding to the majestic atmosphere of the photos. The next set was of a similar horse with a white skeletal body and a braided white mane and tail. This horse's bones practically glowed in the pictures. These are *breathtaking*.

Medusa: *'Got them! These are incredible! They should arrive at the cabin by the end of the week.'*

"Medusa." I jumped, clutching my phone to my chest. Michael frowned at my actions, "My father has asked for a meeting with you. Come eat. We need to go."

"Okay. Let me put on real pants." Once he was gone, I went right back to my phone.

Medusa: *'Apparently Yhwh wants to meet with me????? I'm so nervous!!!!!!'*

Medusa: *'Sorry that was a lot of punctuation.'*

Karma: *'Thank you for doing this. I hope everything goes well with that bastard, just remember to stay as calm as you can. Oh, and pretend to buy into his bullshit. He's got an ego, so as long as you stay on the right side of it you should be fine. I gotta go. Mentor gets pissy when I'm late.'*

Yeah, I understand that. Speaking of mentors… I slipped into the first pair of leggings and shirt I found, and darted to the kitchen. Michael had a plate of bacon, eggs, and a small bowl of oatmeal waiting for me on the table.

"I thought you were putting on real pants? Here, you don't have to finish all of it. Do your best." I squinted at him, sliding into my seat. He's being oddly supportive all of the sudden. I stole glances at him as I ate the surprisingly good food. His fists had a slight tremor to them that he seemed to be hiding to the best of his ability. He's upset about this meeting. That's not comforting in the slightest.

I gave up about halfway through. It tasted better than most things I've eaten recently. Maybe my taste buds are coming back. "I'm ready to face the beast."

His lips quirked, "Lets not call him that when we're in Zion." He offered me an arm, and waited until I was tightly holding on before traveling, taking us to Zion.

Chapter Twelve

"Patience. Welcome to Zion." Jophiel greeted us with a smile. His eyes, though, were focused on mine and Michael's intertwined arms. I could see the resentment flooding them. "Since this is your first time here, I will go over the rules."

"I have already been here." I straightened my spine, pulling away from Michael. My mentor stayed by my side as I walked past his brother, "And I don't take orders *from you.*" Michael chuckled at that. Jophiel didn't seem quite as amused, though.

"Michael. Medusa. Welcome back." I stayed silent as we approached Yhwh. Karma's warning echoed in my head. Whatever he had claimed 'wasn't that bad' had a direct affect on my friend. One that still meant a lot to her, judging by her reaction. He also ordered Jophiel to kill my Dad. Jophiel wouldn't act on his own like that. He'd be too afraid to face Michael if he got in his way without the proper backup.

"Father," Michael nodded, "You said it was urgent."

"It is. Another Virtue has been located. I'm sending Gabriel to retrieve it. You asked to be made aware when we found it. I'll let you know when it's brought in."

"No." Michael raised a brow when I interrupted whatever he was going to reply with. "*I'm* going to bring in the next Virtue. Michael and whoever Gabriel is, can come with me if they'd like." I crossed my arms, glaring at the man who is credited with creating the planet.

Yhwh raised a brow at me. His golden eyes seared into me. This must be the ego Karma was talking about. It seems I have upset him. Michael placed a firm hand on the small of my back, earning a noise from Jophiel. Jophiel crossed to their father.

"Father, I have a better idea. Gabriel goes to retrieve the next Virtue, Michael returns to his normal duty, and *I* will *correct* Patience."

I scowled, focusing on the annoying angel. Just a *little bit-* Jophiel flew several feet backwards before he came to a stop. He didn't get back up either. Good. My life is much better without him talking. "*Or,*" I refocused on Yhwh, sounding much more confident than I currently felt, "We do this my way."

Yhwh drew a deep breath, his eyes flaring, "I suggest you don't forget who is in charge here." I raised a brow at him, keeping my arms crossed. He doesn't need to know my hands are shaking. "Fine. You will go with Gabriel. Michael you are allowed to return home."

"Thank you, Father, but I am going to travel with Medusa. I find that it's best to not leave her alone." Michael smirked down at me. He doesn't really think I'm some type of loose canon… I hope. But I am glad he spoke up. There's no telling what this Gabriel guy is going to be like. He could be worst than Michael was in the beginning.

"Gabriel is still going to accompany you." Yhwh was still angry, but he rolled his shoulders and moved on. "Your brother will tell you the details of your mission. Go back home and await further instructions."

Yhwh extended his hand toward me, sending the lingering clouds to bolt to us. "Father wait!" Either Michael spoke too late or Yhwh simply wasn't listening, because moments later we were in my living room. My legs immediately gave out, landing me on Michael's arm. "I've got you."

"Thank- Let me go!" Shock flittered across his face as he released me. I darted down the hall to the bathroom, not bothering to close the door. I doubt Michael would follow once he heard these noises.

When I was done heaving, I settled back against the bathtub. Michael handed me a damp washcloth, and flushed the toilet. "I didn't realize you were in here." I rasped, wiping my face. "That feels nice. I need to brush my teeth."

"I second that." I shot him a glare, and let him help me back to my feet. Michael stayed by the door while I cleaned myself up. Once I was done, he slipped his arm under my knees and swept me off my feet.

"Are you carrying me?"

"Yes. Your balance is off. You need rest."

"I'd argue, but I'm super tired."

忍

"Am I in Hell? This is my Hell. You know it's almost Christmas, right? I thought you liked me. I thought we were friends." Brian paced the floor of the break room, pulling on his beard.

I'd told him about my 'vacation' when I first came into the store. That's when the rant started. Then, I made the canvases for Karma, wrapped them securely, sent them to the address she had sent, and deleted any trace of Karma's magical pictures from the systems. After that, I went back to see if Brian had finished his rant, and found him still ranting as if I never left the room to begin with.

"Would you believe me if I said that I'm sorry?" I stepped in his path, effectively making him stop pacing.

"No." He scowled, "No, I wouldn't. You're going on a vacation with your gladiator boyfriend to god knows where, and leaving me here with the rest of my employees that can't make up a fourth of you! No, no. An eighth. They can't make an *eighth* of you! You're abandoning me!" Okay, so he's really upset.

"I'll bring you anything you want back from my trip?" I bit my lip to stop my smile.

Brian raised his brows at me, "You know what I want? My best employee back without a massive diamond on her finger that means she doesn't work anymore."

I rolled my eyes at him. Like I would ever marry Michael. "We aren't getting married. I will be back in a few weeks. I *promise.* You banned me from working for a few weeks anyway, remember?"

"So? You're Medusa! I figured you'd last a week before clocking in while you made Michael glare at me so I couldn't stop you. I didn't think you'd actually take a vacation! Argh! You're lucky I trust you." He huffed, "Have fun on your trip. Don't forget about me."

"I would never." I kissed his cheek, and squeezed him as tight as I could. "You're one of my favorite people."

"You'll have your job waiting for you when you get back. Try to see if you can tan. You're looking a little ghostly." I laughed at that. He knows just as well as I do that this skin is only capable of burning. The chances of me getting a tan without a spray is impossible.

"Thank you." Now time for the next stop.

I made my way down the street to *Steamie's*. May waved at me when I came in, and finished whatever she was talking about with her current table. "Hey! How've you been? I wasn't expecting to see you so soon."

I gave her a tight smile. This is harder than I thought it would be. "Hey, I wanted to say goodbye. Michael and I are taking a little vacation, and I won't be back for a couple of weeks."

Her brows furrowed as her eyes searched my face, "Are you sure that's a good idea?"

"Yeah," I was being totally honest, too. This didn't feel like me running away from dealing with what happened to my father. It felt like I was finally taking the first real step toward my destiny. "Trust me. This is going to be a really good thing for me, and I'll be back before you know it."

"Well," She wrapped me in a tight hug, "I'll have a table waiting for you when you get back. Bring me something cool from wherever your beau takes you."

"I can do that." I promised, giving her another hug. "Tell Kat I'll see her when I get back. Oh, and Zelda. I like her too. Maybe we can have a girl's night."

"Sounds like a plan." She beamed at me, "Maybe you can even bring the fitness model back with you."

"I'll see what I can do." I laughed. The chances of Karma ever joining in on a Girl's Night is incredibly slim, but it wouldn't hurt to ask. Though, I don't know if Telluride could handle Kat and Karma teaming up. Heck, I don't know if *I* can handle the two of them in the same room. "Take care, May. I'll see you soon. If you don't mind, can you stop in and check on Brian? He's not handling this well."

"See you soon, and yeah I can. He's a pretty cool guy. If you end up on a beach, send me a bikini picture. I'll need it if I ever need to Kat to do something." I snorted at that, and did *not* promise to send her one. I could still hear her cackling as I left *Steamie's*. For such a nice person, she can be pretty diabolical.

Now that my friends know Michael wasn't kidnapping me, it's time to head back home. Michael said his brother Gabriel should be there by the time I made it back. I can't say I'm too excited about meeting another angel. Michael was a nightmare, and gave me several bruises when we met, Adakiel was unnerving and almost got me fired, and Jophiel murdered my father *and* got me to curse. In short, angels kind of suck. Michael is better *now,* but we only got this close to a friendship after he made me contemplate throwing myself off the nearest bridge. At least bridge jumping wouldn't hurt as bad as Krav Maga did, and don't even get me started on that other one I can't remember the name of. I'm just glad he settled for basic punching. He can do the rest of the kicking and special stuff.

Epilogue

"Medusa, welcome home. This is my brother Gabriel; he is an Archangel as well." Michael was standing in the living room with a man of a similar height and build, but this man had dark brown hair and warm brown eyes. He smiled at me when I caught his eye. Like and actual *genuine* smile. Is Michael sure he's an angel?

"It is wonderful to meet you, Patience. My brother has informed me that you prefer to be called by your human name, is that correct?" I nodded silently, stuffing my hands into my pockets. Maybe I should just be nice while he is. "Medusa it is then. I am Gabriel, messenger of Yhwh, and the patron of communications."

"Which is why you're here; to help us communicate with the next Virtue. It's nice to meet you, Gabriel." Even if you are a strange angel.

"You as well!" He clapped, making Michael sigh. "Now, time to talk about the next Virtue and where to find her. It was actually your intel Michael that helped us find her. Her name is Jezebel Nacar, and she lives in *Aurora de Numismata*, Italy. We have set up a base to house the three of us while we are there retrieving Chastity."

"Chastity? Is that he Virtue we're going to get?" What is that going to be like? What would the physical embodiment of Chastity be like?

Michael did not look as excited as I felt. In fact he looked even more upset than he did before, "Stop looking so excited. You're forgetting the fact that Jezebel has seen you."

"That's only if she remembers the dream."

"You remember the dream why wouldn't she?" I settled for sticking my tongue out at him, and heading into the kitchen. "Where are you going? I already packed snacks for the trip."

"Snacks?" Gabriel asked, mimicking his brother's crossed arms.

"Yes." Michael nodded, "Medusa needs to be able to access food at all times. She hardly eats, so when she *is* hungry she needs to have access to food."

"I thought humans were on schedules."

Michael gave him a flat look before gesturing to the isolated bag in my hands, "First lesson, brother; Medusa is on her own schedule since she is team leader. Everyone else is following her schedule. Including us."

I have a feeling laughing would ruin whatever lie he's trying pull off, and it's definitely a lie. Michael has never followed me anywhere. He normally just grabs me and flies us to wherever he deems we need to be.

Gabriel didn't seem to catch on, though, "I will keep that in mind. Are you ready to go then, Medusa?"

"Sure! How are we traveling to Italy anyway?"

A set of firm hands landed on my shoulders. I turned my head, trying to see Michael's face. I shouldn't have done that. He's smiling. Michael smiling *can't* be a good thing. "Probably shouldn't have asked." What does that mean?

Oh my God. The floor disappeared from beneath us, being replaced with clouds. Clouds! "Michael!" His arm stayed firmly wrapped around my waist as his wings flapped. Gabriel was beside us with all three of my bags in his grasp. His wings were white like his brother's but with a much shorter wingspan. They have the same build shouldn't they need the same size wings?

"Stop squirming. I won't drop you."

"Why are we *doing* this? I like the other way of flying. The one where I don't have to see *the actual flying!*" Well good news, I learned something new about myself. I hate flying.

146

"Italy is too far for that method, I'm afraid. Just relax." I don't believe him. If we can make it to Heaven, we should be able to make it to Italy. He just likes seeing me panic.

Hours later, we landed in the same meadow from my dream. I planted myself on the ground as soon as he let me go. "Next time, we're taking a plane. At least those have seats. Flying is only for trips shorter than an hour."

"That was shorter than an hour. It was a thirty minute flight, Medusa. Thirty-two minutes specifically." Gabriel unhelpfully added, "Oh. Would you like a snack?"

"Sei tu! Sei tornato!" The woman from my dream knelt beside me. She placed a gentle hand on my forearm, *"Ti senti meglio?"*

"Medusa, you aren't replying to her."

I frowned at Gabriel, "And how do you expect me to do that? I took French in high school, and I don't even remember most of that."

He blinked, "Oh. Why did you not say so sooner?" He poked my forehead with two fingers.

"Miss? Did you find whatever you were looking for?" She's speaking English? No that would be ridiculous. This must be Gabriel's magic. Well, that's useful.

"I did, yes. My name is Medusa."

Surprise washed over her face, "You learned *Italiano* since our last meeting! How wonderful!"

"Yes! Yes, I have. Um…" She remembers! What am I supposed to do now?!

"Excuse me, miss, we are looking for the *Monasterium Quod Patientia*. Do you know where it is?" Gabriel butted in, smiling down at the woman.

"Of course I do." She laughed, "I will show you. Are these men companions of yours?" She glanced nervously at the two towering men behind me.

"Yes, we are." Michael stepped up, excluding a charm I didn't know he possessed. "We are here to explore the Monastery, and see this stunning town."

Jezebel smiled at him, raising to her feet. I suppose I should get up as well, now. "Oh wonderful! The nuns are so kind, and the city is beautiful this time of year!"

Alright. Step one complete, now we just have to get Chastity on our side, convince her we're not crazy, figure out what kind of magic she has, and train her to use that magic. Shouldn't be too hard.

Right?